The Rice Kings

Book One

The Beginning

David Henry Lucas

Books may be purchased in bulk or otherwise by contacting the publisher at the address below or for an autographed copy visit the author's website:davidhenrylucasbooks.com

Books may also be found at createspace.com or Amazon Online: Amazon.com

Tell Publishing,LLC
3760 Bethune Highway
Bishopville, SC 29010
thericekings@gmail.com

Publisher: Tell Publishing, LLC
Tellpublishing.com
Editor: Martha Black-Lucas
Design: Ken Maginnis
Illustrations: Nina Uccello

Library of Congress Catalog Number: 2014920620

ISBN-13: 978-0-9895730-3-0
First Edition Printed in the USA

Dedication

This book is dedicated to the seven known generations that have come before me. Many family members have tried to go further back but unsuccessfully. My grandfather, Henry Simons Lucas was the first person to begin the process of instilling a love of family history in me. My father, William Dollard Lucas and his brother, Darby Fulton Lucas, finished the job. There are also many interesting stories that emanate from the various maternal lines but I am only one person. If my remaining time will allow, perhaps I can tackle a few of those tales for those interested.

Josh,

Best of Luck,

Timothy Lucas

Table of Contents

Foreword

Jonathan Lucas I was from Beckermet Parish, Cumberland, England. He was the son of John Lucas and his wife, Ann Noble. Trained as a millwright, he was shipwrecked off the coast of South Carolina. This man was the first of this Lucas line to be introduced into South Carolina. After his unintentional arrival in America he invented the rice mill and prospered in Charleston. Joined by his son, Jonathan Lucas II, the two controlled the rice industry in the Carolina Low Country. This book is a fictionalized account of Jonathan's life from his birth, in 1754 until his arrival in America circa 1786. It is intended that other books about the descendants of John Lucas and Ann Noble will follow, spanning over a quarter of a millennium to the present day.

Introduction

The purpose of this fictionalized work, is to bring to light the lives of seven generations of my forebears. The most prominent among those are, Jonathan Lucas I and Jonathan Lucas II. Jonathan Lucas I was the inventor of the rice mill. Jonathan Lucas II improved on that invention and introduced it throughout the British Empire in the 1820s and 30s. During this time the firm of Lucas and Eubanks controlled the worldwide rice industry. Until now, only the accomplishments by my ancestors have been chronicled by historians. This book is intended to bring to life The Rice Kings.

Prologue

It was a time of beginnings. This was the inauguration of a new era for mankind, later called the Industrial Revolution by historians. Life was hard for all people, from antiquity up through the eighteenth century. The rich, the poor and everyone in between, struggled to survive. The odds were stacked in favor of the rich and powerful, as usual. They didn't have the daily drudgery of the lower classes, but they had the same susceptibility to disease, catastrophe, war and the indifferences of life. In the eighteenth century, a group of Englishmen began to lift mankind out of its long dependence on the old traditional methods of powering production; namely muscle, wind and water. These newer ways of powering industry spurred the Industrial Revolution. It was slow going at first, but gained headway before the gathering winds of advancement. This is the story of one of the families whose men added to the parade of improvements. Those innovations helped spark a rushing flood of knowledge and know-how in what continues to float the ship of mankind's progress higher and higher with ever increasing rapidity. To modern man, quick advances and innovation are now considered normal. This was not always true.

Today, change is welcomed with pleasant anticipation. Conquering a millennium of inertia, these men and women of the enlightenment championed knowledge and progress over tradition. These advances came often at great personal risk. Sometimes the resistance came from the ancient authorities who opposed progress as coming from the devil, or from the difficult natural obstacles presented by mother nature herself. The people in the forefront weren't necessarily cognizant of leading mankind to a brighter future, but usually were in competition for money, power and of course, amour. This was a time when if you could build a better mousetrap, then you built it and society rewarded you by buying your product. Follow the adventures of Jonathan Lucas as he lives, learns, and loves his way through 18th century England.

Jonathan Lucas

Chapter 1

ONATHAN LUCAS WAS BORN IN MAY OF 1754 IN Whitehaven, Cumbria, England. He was the only son of John Lucas and his wife, Ann Noble.

After giving birth to three daughters, the obviously proud parents were delighted at the arrival of their lone male child. John and Ann both were descended from families that had arrived in England with William the Conqueror 700 years before. The Noble Family hailed from Normandy and were directly attached to the Conqueror's personal retinue. The Lucas family came from a small town in Flanders as allies and vassals of the new Norman King of the English.

Three years after the Norman conquest of 1066, the north rebelled against the rule of William the Conqueror. The rebels followed Edgar the Atheling, who was the last Anglo-Saxon claimant to the throne in opposition to William's rule. Edgar was the sole male member of the royal house of Cerdic of Wessex left alive. He was proclaimed, but never crowned, King of England in 1066.

In response to this challenge to his rule, William brought an army north under his personal command. He was determined to destroy any further opposition to his three-year-old reign. His response to this serious threat from the Northerners was the same as that of the fourth century Roman writer, Vegetius, who wrote: "It is better to overcome the enemy by famine, raids, and terror tactics, than by battle, in which luck has more influence than courage."

This was the infamous "Harrowing of the North" that reduced the population of the Northumbrian area by sixty percent. The conqueror was successful in quelling the rebellion with these harsh tactics and he then proceeded to parcel out the emptied, ruined lands to people who were his loyal followers. They were the very people that had helped King William with the shattering of so many lives and properties in the north.

Thus the Lucas Family and the Noble Family came to settle on the West Coast of Cumbria. They remained loyal to the English crown throughout the intervening years and prospered. But on this day, their mission was not to reduce the population, but to celebrate another addition to it.

John was sitting on the side of a large four poster bed that was ornately covered in a green canopy, holding his new son in his arms. His wife Ann, was propped up on several goose down pillows watching the proud papa beam at his brand new son.

This birth had been one of the easiest Ann had experienced. Her labor pains had not been severe and the baby had taken only about an hour and a half to arrive. They had sent for Dr. Phillips, but by the time he had made it to the Lucas home, Miss Trinity, the head of the housemaids, had everything under control. She had delivered the baby and her assistant had bathed the newly born child while Miss Trinity had seen to the comfort and needs of the mother. The doctor had remarked what a wonderful job Miss Trinity had done in bringing this child into the world. The boy had come so quickly that John, alerted earlier in the day, had actually arrived after the doctor. Meeting the doctor on his way out the door, John anxiously inquired about his wife. It had been several years since her last child; seven years to be exact. This pregnancy was late in life and rather unexpected. Ann was no longer a girl of seventeen but a woman of thirty-six. She had always had an easy time with child birth, but delivering this late in life worried John. He was anxious at the sight of the exiting doctor and was about to ask about his wife and expected child when the physician announced, "Not to worry, John, I shan't be able to charge you very much for this one. I've been here less than an hour and all is well. Both your wife and your ...," the doctor deliberately paused, knowing how anxious John was for a male, "... new son are doing quite well. I may have to hire your Miss Trinity as an assistant for my next deliveries."

"You mean it's a boy?"

"Yes, John, you are now the proud father of a healthy baby boy!"

John took a deep breath, let out a long sigh of relief, both for his wife's health and his child's safe arrival. He flushed with guilt for not being there for the birth.

"Doctor, please excuse me, this sort of thing usually takes longer." He looked away from the doctor and up the stairs where he heard the newborn's cry. "I must go now to meet my new 'early bird' son."

He moved up the stairs quickly, taking two-to-three steps at the time. Entering the room, he saw two women standing by the bed. He paused and looked at the scene. The youngest of the two women was his sixteen year old daughter, Julia. She was holding a bundled-up infant, smiling and cooing at the small treasure in her arms. The older woman was combing his wife Ann's hair. When Ann saw her husband enter the room her eyes lit up like stars peeking out from behind the dark wintery clouds after a storm.

"Ann, how do you feel?"

"I am just fine my dear. Your new son got here in just a matter of minutes. It really was no trouble at all."

His daughter Julia walked across the room, smiled at her father and placed the blue bundled boy into his arms. "Poppa, he is a beautiful little brother. I even got to help bring him into this world! Don't you think he looks a little like me?"

"Julia, he might very well look like you, but all babies look the same to me. They look like babies."

"Oh, Poppa, look closely, I think he looks more like me than he does, either Kate or Ellen."

"Where are your two sisters?"

"They went downstairs to get something to eat. After all the excitement they were hungry."

"Well, why don't you give me some time with your mother. Go check on the girls and make sure they don't get into mischief. I'll be down after a bit."

"What are we going to name him, Poppa? I like Richard."

"Your mother and I will soon make that decision. Now go downstairs to see what your sisters are up to."

"Yes, Poppa."

Julia turned and started for the door.

John rocked the baby back and forth as he walked toward the bed. Miss Trinity gave one last stroke with her brush and said,

"I'll leave you two alone to get acquainted with this fine young man."

"Thank you, Miss Trinity, and thank you for doing such a fine job of taking care of my precious wife and this charming young fellow."

"Ah, t'wer'nt nothing. When you've brought as many young'uns into the world as I have, you find it gets easier all the time. With my pull'n and your wife doing such a great job with pushing, we got it done in no time."

"Nonetheless, I am grateful. You have always been here when we needed you the most."

John reached the bed, looked down and smiled at his wife, who was smiling back at him. He climbed the two steps and sat down on the side of the high bed.

As he looked at his new son, his smile turned into a grin that lit up his entire face. He sat silently for five minutes, looking first at his son and then at his wife. Still grinning at the child and his wife, he began trying to coax a smile from the tiny infant. Using his right forefinger, he was inexpertly attempting to tickle the child underneath its chin. It had been so long since he had held an infant that he felt a little awkward holding his new son. A slight crease crossed the mouth of the newest Lucas. Whether it was a grimace from being poked, or an attempt at his first smile wasn't clear. No matter; the reaction pleased John greatly. He was overcome by a feeling of happiness, well-being and love. Looking into the glittering eyes of his wife, it was apparent that she felt the same way. Slowly, his face took on a more serious look.

"Ann, my dear, what shall we call this handsome young lad? I'm not a fan of the name Richard. I don't believe there are any Richard's in your family and certainly none in the Lucas Family.

Since he is our first son, I believe the privilege of bestowing a name belongs to you."

"That is very thoughtful, my sweet, but you have worked so hard to bring him into this world that even though he is our first son, I will not dictate but only suggest."

"John, your family is full of names that are renowned. There is your name and William, your brother's name and of course, there's the fine name of General Charles Lucas who died so nobly for King Charles's cause. He was one of your most illustrious ancestors. George is another Lucas name that is popular with your American cousins. They seem to be doing rather well for themselves in that far off land. I believe some are even royal governors of the mysterious island, Antigua."

"Yes, . . . Yes, all that is true, but I've been thinking about naming him Jonathan."

"Jonathan, after my uncle?"

"Yes my dear, he was always one of your favorites, and I was fond of him as well. It's a shame he did not live to help greet our little fellow."

"I have always liked that name. I suspect because I always liked Uncle Jonathan. I think I was his favorite."

"Jonathan, it is then. Your uncle was a brilliant man with a lot of talent, particularly with the invention of the new weaving machines. There's a new one developed it seems, every year. It's very hard to keep up with all the changes taking place. How he kept up with all of those new inventions, I'll never know.

Without his help, our two families would certainly not have been as successful as we have been for the past few years. I miss his wisdom and intellect. We owe a lot to his thinking and to his talent, therefore, the least we could do is to honor his memory by naming our first son after him."

Ann was pleased. Jonathan Noble had always been her favorite uncle. He was an unconventional person and always liked to tinker with machinery. He had made her wonderful toys from the time she could remember. When toys no longer suited her as she grew older, he was always bringing her wooden chests with built-in mirrors or large doll houses that he had handcrafted. He even built her a pony cart that she enjoyed for years, but most cherished was the marriage bed he had built that she and John were in at the very moment. It only seemed right to remember her favorite uncle in this way.

"He would be so honored and very pleased. Oh thank you John. You are so good to me."

John glanced down at his wife and a wave of intense affection rolled over him like a warm breeze. He loved this beautiful woman and was enormously happy with his life. There had been success in business as well as in his home life. When he had married Ann she was just a girl of seventeen. John was already a prosperous owner of woolen mills that made sails for ships that were being built in Whitehaven. The Noble Family had been mill owners as well in Whitehaven, long before John or his family. The Lucas Family had been minor gentry. As landowners of some note, they had done very well in the old feudal ways of lands and lords. Land had been and remained the key to wealth in England.

This economic climate, however, had begun to change during the last few years. Cumbria had always been a land rich in minerals. There were iron and coal mines, granite, limestone and slate quarries and gypsum was mined as was graphite. Additionally, in most of England, the sheep industry was lucrative and trade in wool very important. These industries had always been a big part of accumulating wealth in Cumbria. Modern and more productive machinery was actually making each of these resources more in demand than ever before.

The coal and iron mines were deeper in this area than most places. Three of the collieries had been even dug out under the Soleway Firth. The coal seams extended under the Irish Sea, all the way out to the Isle of Man and beyond.

John and his in-laws had taken advantage of these changes in the Cumbrian economy and were so far, doing well in this ever changing, but fast growing area. Competition for business in this expanding environment was heating up and one had to stay abreast of the latest developments in commerce, mining and industry. If you fell behind, you would find yourself struggling like a fish flopping in the mud, left high and dry by the receding tide.

The Nobles had been in the mill business for many generations and knew what they were doing in that industry. John Lucas was relatively new in the weaving business, but his marriage into the Noble Family had brought with it, in addition to a lovely wife, all the knowledge of the mill industry that generations of Nobles had gleaned.

The newly named Jonathan began to cry.

"I believe our young man is calling for his supper."

"Now that's something that I cannot help you with."

"Hand Jonathan to me, my love," said Ann.

John did as he was commanded and watched as his son finally found his mark and went to work extracting his meal.

John stood up and walked over to the window. His thoughts turned to the world that his son had just entered. He looked out in the distance toward the harbor and could see the ships filling the entire port. The growth of Whitehaven had been phenomenal over the past few years. Of course, London was the most prosperous and largest city in England with a population of over half a million people. There were about fifteen other cities, mostly port cities, that were populated by ten thousand or more.

Whitehaven had grown from a sleepy fishing village owned by St. Bee's monastery with under five hundred people, to one of the largest ports in England with a population of just under ten thousand. It had been independent since Henry VIII had destroyed the monasteries of England in 1541.

Part of Whitehaven's present good fortune had been the result of the burgeoning coal trade with Ireland, which was just a short distance across the Irish Sea. Coal mines were very profitable and enterprising men from Whitehaven had built a fleet of over four hundred ships to help with that trade. John had a few ships of his own. Shipbuilding had brought further prosperity to the area. John had been a part of that industry, importing timbers from Scandinavia to build the ships and his mill had turned out woolen sails used on the trading vessels. Some of his friends had begun the importation of rum from the Americas and it had also been very profitable, but it was a three legged stool. The three legs of the stool were rum, sugar and slaves. John was not fond of the slave trade, so he had not invested but he was close to the people in the tobacco trade, which was also becoming more important to the economy of Whitehaven. Tobacco was imported from Virginia and Maryland into Whitehaven in return for manufactured goods such as clocks, furniture, weapons and farm implements. Of course, slaves were used in the tobacco industry, but this was an indirect result of someone else's actions, unlike the slave trade itself.

As he gazed out into the harbor at the four hundred ships resting on their sides at low tide, he was amazed at the changes he had seen over the past twenty years. With the birth of his new son, John was thinking of all of the opportunities that would be available by the time Jonathan was old enough to take advantage of them. As is the way with people, John recalled all of the difficulties he had encountered as a young man in his career. Hopefully, Jonathan would have an easier time than he had experienced. John had been able to marry into a family that was very helpful to his endeavors which were now flourishing. He was well aware of the contributions that the Noble Family had made to his successes.

"Ann, you know what I'm thinking about?"

"Probably your business, dear. You are always thinking about keeping up with the latest trends happening in the world."

"I was just looking out in the harbor and thinking about all of the changes that have taken place since you and I became man and wife."

"Well, there have certainly been a lot of those in the last seventeen years. But this latest change, our new son Jonathan, I suppose, is the best change of all. His arrival makes me so happy."

"I agree with you, my love. I'm just wondering with all the adjustments that have taken place in the last twenty years what the next twenty will bring and what young Jonathan will be facing when he grows into manhood."

"John, you are a good man, but you are not a prophet. If Jonathan is anything like his father, he will do just fine."

"Naming him Jonathan has reminded me of all of the things your uncle did for us. He was one smart man. He always seemed to be able to see the future. If there is such a thing as a prophet, he was certainly one. Hopefully Jonathan will inherit more than just a name from his uncle."

"Your brother William, although somewhat too serious for my taste, has also kept up with the way of industry in the world today. Is he still digging canals with that Brinkley man?"

"Yes," replied John. "William is doing well for himself. He certainly does have a mind of his own. I wish that we got along better, but unfortunately we do not. We tried it for a while, but the results were not taking us in the proper direction. On the contrary, we were headed in precisely the wrong direction."

Whitehaven Harbor

"Yes, you two are so alike in so many ways, but so different, in others. It is good that you separated when you did before irreparable harm was done to your relationship and to your business ventures," said Ann.

"So true, many families are torn apart by less than separates William and I. He is a dreamer and would spend all of his time tinkering with new things rather than concentrating on what brings in profits," replied John.

"That's true, but the last few times he has been to visit, it seems that he has settled in and found a way to make those inquiries profitable."

"His ideas have always been good, though not always practical. I think that he has realized that fact and has been able to build practicable waterwheels and windmills as good if not better than anyone else in England. His reputation has grown over the last few years, and if he will stay with the things that he does well, I believe that he will continue to prosper. Anyway, I'm sure he will be pleased when he finds out that his first nephew, Jonathan, has arrived. You know that I love my brother, but sometimes I feel like I've got to kill'm," mused John.

John and Ann laughed. William was always a man who was well-meaning, kind and generous, but there was so much frustration sparked by his ever-changing interest in anything that was new and mechanical. It seemed that there was never an end to the number of projects he tried to take on. He was always trying to improve something that he had already enhanced over and over. The undershot waterwheels never turned fast enough. The angles on the blades were never exactly right. The number of cogs in the gears always needed adjusting. The windmills he built were never quite good enough to be left to do their work. It had driven John to distraction. He could never understand why his brother could not stop trying to perfect something that was working just fine. They had been partners in business, but it soon became apparent that the arrangement was not going to work. Jonathan Noble had understood William better than his own brother. Jonathan, of course, was older and more experienced, but he had been like William as a young man. He saw the conflict between the two brothers and negotiated a buyout of William's partnership interest. It was difficult but necessary and thankfully, resulted in restored peace between the brothers. Jonathan had even provided the capital for the buyout in the form of a loan to John. In his will, he had left the note from John to his niece, Ann. There was more to naming Jonathan after his uncle Jonathan Noble than had been said that afternoon.

"John, why don't you go downstairs and take supper. After I feed Jonathan, I think that I could use a nap."

"Of course, my dear. Let me have a kiss from you, and I'll give Jonathan a small one on one of those little pink cheeks and I'll leave you two alone to rest for awhile. Shall I send Miss Trinity up with something for you?"

"Nothing right now, my dear. I could take a little tea and maybe a biscuit after some rest, but I'll ring for Trinity when I wake up."

"You have always made me a happy man. But today, I must say, I don't see how I could ever be happier. They say that becoming a grandfather rivals this experience, but that's hard to imagine," replied the proud father.

John turned and walked toward the door. Ann watched him go. She glanced at the broad shoulders of her six foot tall husband and then looked down at her son. She thought to herself, "Jonathan, if you grow up to be half the man your father is, then you will make us both very proud."

Jonathan reached up with both of his hands and pressed them against her breast as if in answer to her thoughts about his future.

Chapter 2

JOHN STOOD AT THE END OF THE SUGAR TONGUE Quay. He was speaking with Toby Graham, who was the pier master. Toby was a big man with slightly bowed legs. He wore a gray woolen cap and a three quarter length leather vest over a dull white shirt. His physical presence spoke of great strength from years of hard labor with hard men. The two of them were discussing where to dock John's new ship, *The Julia*. It's cargo was to be tobacco from Virginia. When Toby spoke, he emphasized his point with his hands.

John had only recently invested in the tobacco business. He had connected with a new partner, a prominent merchant with a solid reputation from a nearby town, Aleyn Eedes. John imported the tobacco from the colonies and Aleyn supplied the manufactured goods to send back to Virginia. This offered good profits on both ends of the transaction. It could become a very lucrative arrangement for the both of them.

Toby was complaining about how busy the port was becoming.

"Mr. Lucas, sir, we get them unloaded and reloaded as quickly as we can, but human beings can only do so much. We need more men to work the docks."

"With all the work going on and the wages going up, it looks like you would have your pick of quite a few workers."

"Well, it's like this, you see, men are leery to come into this town looking for work."

"And the reason for that?" asked John.

"It's the press gangs. If you're not careful, you may find yourself waking up on some outward bound ship heading towards God knows where," replied Toby.

"I thought the press gangs didn't work around here anymore?"

"Well, sir, they don't station themselves here, but they show up mostly at

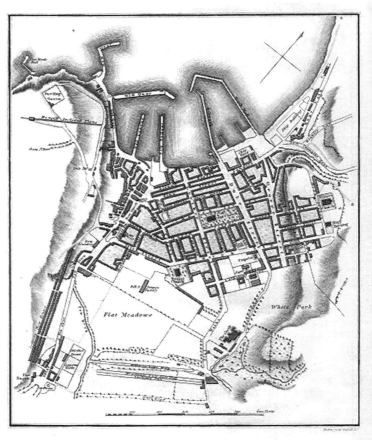

PLAN OF WHITEHAVEN.

Published Nov.ᵗʰ 1st 1804 by T. Cadell & W. Davies Strand London.

night and we never know when they're coming. When the lads leave the taverns is when they strike. Instead of waking up with a bad head at home in your own bed, you wake up in chains on a wagon or some foul boat already at sea."

"Aye, it's a sorry business and I don't like it. If others would offer fairer wages, finding good workers and able-bodied seamen wouldn't be such a hard chore. We didn't have any trouble filling up our ships with capable men."

"Well, the wages that you pay, Mr. John, are better than most and running over to Virginia doesn't take all that long. Three or four months at the most and then you're back home with some money in your pocket. But the conditions on some of the other longer runs ain't always the best. Most of these press gangs either put the men in his Majesty's Navy or you could get stuck on a slaver bound for hell. It's not the best way to spend six months to a year of your life for low pay and foul treatment."

"I understand his Majesty doesn't pay very much to his sailors, and the conditions are harsh. But the slave trade is a different story. Many men take to it because of the profit that can be made. But even at that, what they are forced to do gets to a man after a time. Most sailors that I know want nothing to do with the trade. Its a harsh way to go and sometimes turns a man into something he never expected to be."

Toby glanced up and looked toward the town over John's shoulder. He saw a woman step onto the quay, pushing a three-wheeled baby carriage.

"Aye, would you look at that? You don't see many ladies down here on these docks and with a babe at that. She could get hurt coming out here."

John turned to look in the direction Toby indicated, just as his wife Ann and son, Jonathan, came out onto the edge of the Sugar Tongue Quay. A look of alarm came over John's face as he saw all the activity swirling around the two. Ann stopped and waved, realizing that to try to navigate through all of the men, carts, swinging ropes with pulleys and wagons being loaded and unloaded would be very hazardous for her and her son.

She backed away from the crowded quay and waved again.

John held up both of his hands and waved to signal for her to back up. When he saw that she had not moved any nearer and indeed was now out of the hustle and bustle, he turned to the quay master.

"Toby, we'll finish this conversation later."

It was John's turn to take the hazardous walk from the end of the quay to his wife and child. After dodging through the mass of people and draft animals loaded with barrels, bundles, bins of coal, bolts of cloth, furniture, glassware and all sorts of farm implements, he finally reached his destination. Somewhat anxious and a little cross at her unexpected arrival on the Quay, John grabbed the handle of the carriage with one hand and the arm of his wife with the other and quickly moved them back away from the bustle that was taking place in front of them.

"Thank God you stopped. You and the baby may have been crushed by these workers on the dock. They're not used to looking out for a woman and baby out there. It's just too dangerous."

"John, I know that. Please don't be vexed with me. You don't think I would have been so foolish as to try to walk to you through all of that commotion, do you? It's such a beautiful day and Jonathan has never seen the docks before. I hope I didn't interrupt something important?"

"No, of course not, but just when you first stepped onto the dock, I didn't realize you weren't going to try to make it to me. That is what made me anxious for your safety. I was just talking to the pier master about where to dock *The Julia* when she arrives. She's due any day now."

"Let's hope all is well with our daughter's namesake and she brings back a good load of tobacco from Virginia."

"How did you find me down here?"

"Your man, Barton, back at your warehouse, told me you would likely be here. Weren't you supposed to meet Mr. Eedes sometime today?"

"Yes, I'm supposed to meet him at Nicolas Allison's Tavern on the other side of the harbor. Since this is our first venture together, he's as anxious to hear from *The Julia* as am I."

"I know he's just a year old, but the sooner we can get Jonathan started learning his father's business, the better it will be for him," she said with a giggle. She knew that her husband, John, was not pleased that she had been so reckless as to come to the waterfront, but with her coquettish smile, big brown eyes and long fluttering eyelashes, she still knew how to influence him and melt his bad moods. Just as she planned, the tension had gone out of her husband's face as he replied, "Well, he's a mite young yet, but he is growing fast."

John smiled down at his wife and gave her a quick kiss on the lips. They turned away from the harbor and John pushed the carriage back toward the center of town with one hand. He held out his right arm to his wife. Ann leaned over and wrapped both of her arms around his arm and laid her head on his shoulder as they moved off to his warehouse just half a block away from the Sugar Tongue Quay.

Aleyn Eedes was just exiting by the front door as they approached. He was about sixty years old, slight of build, but still robust in mind and movement. His hair was totally gray underneath a black top hat. His hazel eyes looked around quizzically at the surrounding clamor from beneath two very bushy eyebrows. He wore a black coat that was cut just above the waist in the front, but continued down to above his knees in the back. He was wearing a white shirt with a cravat and tan knee britches. His knee stockings were white, finding their way into a pair of black shoes with silver buckles. The heels of the black buckled shoes were built up by three to four inches to elevate his person above the muddy streets. This added elevation brought him up to eye level with the tall John Lucas. He was carrying a silver tipped black walking cane with a large silver globe as the top knob in his right hand. In his left, he carried a pair of soft tan deerskin gloves that matched his britches.

Aleyn was a native of Whitehaven, but now hailed from Carlisle, some forty miles away. He had been a friend of Ann's Uncle Jonathan. John had traveled to Carlisle and enticed Aleyn to join him in the importation of Virginia tobacco. Aleyn had put up the capital to purchase the tobacco and John had supplied the ship for transportation. They had a 50-50 partnership and this was their first venture.

Looking up, Aleyn Eedes saw his partner and his friend's niece turning the corner. At the sight of Ann, a warm smile took charge of his face. Extending both arms to her, he moved forward to greet them.

"Ann, my dear! It is so nice to see you again. You are as beautiful as ever, just like your mother."

Releasing John's arm, Ann moved quickly and embraced her uncle's friend whom she had not seen since the funeral, five years before.

"Aleyn, it has been way too long."

The two embraced with genuine affection. There was an exchange of kisses on the cheek and Aleyn got in one more on the top of Ann's head. She turned and with a gesture of her left arm extended to her husband and son, she said, "Aleyn, it is time that you met the newest member of my family, our son, Jonathan."

Aleyn stepped forward and extended his hand to John.

"I hope all is well with you today, John."

"So far, so good," replied his new partner.

Aleyn then look down into the three-legged baby carriage. He glanced back up at John and asked, "May I?"

"Of course you may."

Aleyn reached down into the buggy taking hold of Jonathan and lifted him out. He cradled the boy in his arms and said, "By God, I think he even looks like Jonathan . . . Jonathan Noble, I mean. Let's hope that he turns out to be as fine a man as his great uncle." Jonathan had a quizzical look on his face, for he had never seen this stranger. He had not decided whether he would cry, smile or remain indifferent. But Aleyn's smile was contagious and the baby now smiling, reached out and took the older man's small finger.

"Look at this! Our first handshake. I wonder if he can get as good a deal on a handshake as his father has?" he asked with a laugh.

All four were now smiling as they crowded around the child. Then, from the direction of the harbor came an undercurrent of sound indicating that a sail had been sighted heading into port. John stopped a man walking up from the harbor and asked, "Is there a ship coming in?"

"Aye Sir, she's still a ways out, but should be here in a couple of hours, depending on the tide."

Turning to his wife and business partner, John said, "Excuse me, let me see if I can get Barton to put a glass on the vessel and see if he can tell who she is."

John turned and disappeared into the warehouse. Ann and Aleyn returned their attention to Jonathan, who now had a grasp on the golden ring that was on Aleyn's finger. A few moments later Alex Barton stepped out of the doorway and said, "If you two don't mind, Mr. John asked that you follow me up to the roof platform. We have a large deck up there for just such times as these."

Ann took the baby from Aleyn and the two turned to follow Barton into the warehouse. They climbed two sets of stairs and walked to the end of the building. There was a small spiral staircase ascending up to the roof. Ann went first with Jonathan, followed by Aleyn. Barton brought up the rear. As they cleared the roof line, John reached down and helped them up onto the platform. Although two rows back from the harbor, with the rooftop perch they had a panoramic view of the harbor and its approaches. John opened his glass, and with his left hand pointed at a distant spot out on the Soleway Firth.

"She's still far away, but I think I may be able to make her out from here."

John raised his glass to his eye and peered into the distance.

"Well, she's got three masts, just like *The Julia*, but she's not quite close enough for me to make her out."

"John, this is my first venture into this American colonial business. Isn't the ship a week or so overdue?"

"Two weeks to be exact. We had word from a ship that left Jamestown the day before *The Julia* was supposed to leave. That ship has been back for seventeen days."

"Shouldn't we be somewhat anxious?"

"Sailing is not a precise occupation. There are many things that could influence the voyage. She could have been delayed in her departure from Jamestown or hit some contrary winds. It is possible that she could have lost her winds and been becalmed. There's been no mention of any storms of late. "

John raised his glass again and the ship was suddenly bathed by sunlight as the clouds at sea parted as if on cue.

"Now if I can steady my hand, that bow piece looks awfully familiar." The figurehead on the ship was a wooden sculpture of his oldest daughter, Julia. It showed her with her hair held back by a braid and clothed in a very light, loose fitting dress. The entire family was proud of this beautifully carved figure of Julia.

They stared off into the distance, straining their eyes and wishing into existence, the arrival of their ship. Suddenly, there was a shout from the street. They all looked down to see a small young boy cupping his hands and shouting at them.

"Master Toby sent me to tell you that *The Julia* is on her way in."

"Boy, wait right there," he shouted down to the lad.

"Barton, here's twelve pence. Take 'em to that lad and thank him for being the bearer of such good news."

"A whole bob for that street urchin?"

John was obviously delighted by the welcomed news.

"When he brings me that kind of news, yes! Maybe it should be a quid?"

"No, Mr. John, sir, the twelve pence should do nicely. I'll hand it to the boy myself and then we best be making preparation to store some tobacco."

Barton took the money and disappeared down the stairway. They watched as he approached. He handed the boy the twelve pence and returned to the warehouse. The young boy looked at the handful of money, counted it and broke into a huge smile. He took off his cap, and with a sweeping move that would have done credit to a Spanish Grandee, bowed low to the people up on the platform above. He stuffed his money into his pocket, put his stocking cap back on, turned and ran toward the harbor.

Finally, *The Julia* was home. She had been delayed almost a week sailing out of Jamestown and then had hit contrary winds on her crossing. She brought back a full load of some of Virginia's finest tobacco. John had hired a Captain Benson for this first trip who was experienced in the tobacco trade and had a good reputation in Whitehaven.

John and Aleyn had been very fortunate to obtain his services. They had offered him more than ten percent of the normal captain's percentage of the cargo and Benson had more than made up for it in the quality of the tobacco he had brought back from Virginia. He was also very experienced in storing his cargo for the difficult crossing of the North Atlantic. A barrel called a hogshead was used to ship tobacco to England. A hogshead was a type of container made by a Virginia cooper. By Virginia law, it had to be 48" tall and 30" across the head and held between 1,000 - 1,500 pounds of tobacco. Captain Benson made sure that his hogsheads weighed close to the high end of the 1,500 pounds. He was also very meticulous when loading his cargo onto his ship.

Many first time merchants had received their cargoes only to find that most of the shipment had been ruined because enough care had not been taken to protect it from exposure to the elements of the sea. If not stowed properly, the barrels could also be smashed in a rough storm. Captain Benson's extra ownership had been well worth the money. The price that this first cargo brought was the highest received by any importers of tobacco into Whitehaven so far that year, which was 1756.

The English use of tobacco had outstripped all of the other Europeans in the amount bought and used. It seemed that every strata of English society used tobacco in some form or another. The silver snuff box was an item that no aristocrat would be without. It had become quite a ritual among the elite. After dinner they would take out their beautifully engraved snuff boxes and take a small pinch of snuff. The resulting sneeze was done with eloquence and dash. The lower classes "chawed" tobacco and spit streams of brown tobacco juice in all directions. The middle class and gentry mostly drank tobacco (smoked from a pipe) in their homes or taverns. The demand for Virginia tobacco was great.

But that had not always been the case. Early attempts to sell Virginia tobacco had fallen short of expectations. The English smokers felt that the tobacco from the Caribbean was much less harsh than the native Virginia tobacco. The Virginians imported seeds from the West Indies and began cultivating the less harsh plant in the Jamestown Colony. The West Indian plants thrived in the fertile Virginia soil. Those transplanted tobacco seeds resulted in the huge trade that the two partners now enjoyed.

Ann Noble

Chapter 3

JOHN'S FORTUNES HAD CONTINUED TO GROW during the next five years. He and his business partner, Aleyn Eedes, had added another partner and another ship to their tobacco venture. It was a larger vessel and therefore able to haul more cargo. Captain Benson was also put in charge of this new addition with his usual eye for sound sailing and business dealings. The additional partner was a Whitehaven man named J.D. Younger.

John Lucas and J.D. Younger had known each other while growing up in Whitehaven, becoming friends at an early age. J.D. Younger had been in the tobacco business his entire adult career and his knowledge in importing tobacco for the English market had made him very successful. Younger did have some financial distress because of his taste for gambling, wine, women and song, on which he spent most of his profits. John Lucas knew his strengths and his weaknesses and his strengths were in his vast knowledge of the tobacco business. When it came to turning a profit by selling tobacco to the English, J.D. Younger had no equal. His weaknesses were, however, more than a match for his strengths and he found himself in some serious financial trouble as a result. That's when he had turned to his friend, John Lucas, for help.

The Friendship belonged to J.D. Younger's company, but it was leased to the new company of Eedes, Lucas and Younger. The new ship accommodated bigger cargoes and this was especially important as orders were growing and there was more demand for imported goods from England.

Aleyn Eedes was not keen on the idea of this new arrangement, but he had recognized the loyalty that lifelong friendships could engender between gentlemen, so he agreed to this new partnership. He had insisted, however, that the new venture be shielded from John Younger's numerous creditors. This was accomplished through their attorneys and when Aleyn was satisfied with the new agreement, he acquiesced. The new partnership leased *The Friendship*, for the new company, preferring not to become involved in Younger's other companies or past transactions.

It was a warm April morning. This far north, the month of April often brought cold and rain, but this was an exceptionally beautiful morning. *The Friendship* was due to sail for Virginia as soon as she was loaded. Her cargo for the return trip to America, was to be comprised of fine furnishings that Aleyn Eedes had been assembling in the warehouse from all over England. Captain Benson had brought back specific orders for merchandise from some of the largest and richest planters in Virginia.

Furniture from the designers of Chippendale, Inigo Jones, Johnson, Lock, and Pether were all on the list of goods. The planters and merchants of Virginia were looking for the best furnishings to enhance their magnificent plantation homes. They sought the same luxuries their English cousins had access to in England. The Virginians had ordered chairs, dining room tables, bookcases, mirrors, commodes, writing desks and beds. Most of the items were made of mahogany that had been shipped from South and Central America. In England they had developed special tools for the South American hardwood. The wood was imported in the form of broad boards or planks and the furniture that the designers turned out was as beautiful as it was useful. It had taken Aleyn several weeks longer to procure his orders than they had expected but they were certain that the result would be pleasing to their customers, as well as profitable to the partnership.

Toby Sullivan and Captain Benson had worked as a team to stow as much of the furniture as *The Friendship* could safely handle. Only about three quarters of the orders had arrived in Whitehaven by the second week of April 1760 and what had arrived had already been loaded on board for shipment. Some of the more elegant pieces could only be found in London at the factory of Thomas Chippendale and these purchases could not be rushed. The last of the items were finally en route to Whitehaven and would arrive within a few days. The trip over to Barbados and Virginia and then back to Whitehaven promised to be one of the most profitable in the history of the company of Eedes and Lucas and a big boost to the new partnership between the company of Eedes, Lucas and Younger's company. Younger was entitled to one third of the profits made on this voyage and he was anxious to get the voyage underway. His creditors were pressing him for payment and the stress was beginning to show. Waiting for the final shipment of furniture to arrive, he was passing his time at Nicolas Allison's Tavern. There he was drinking wine and spending time and money on a young, very pretty barmaid named Jaden Duff.

Jaden was barely a woman grown. She had just turned eighteen, but you wouldn't know it from the look of her. She had hair as black as the coal her father mined under the sea at Saltom Pit. Her tresses were thick and long and hung down to her waist. Her eyes were as black as her hair and the stares from them were as bold as brass. She had high cheekbones and when she smiled, her teeth glistened like pearls. There was a small gap between her two front teeth that spoke of raging passion. She was dark skinned with a figure that turned heads no matter how often she passed by. A man had to be well into his cups not to notice this sassy female, so no one could blame Younger for doing what every other male wanted to do.

"John, you know I have to work," purred Jaden.

"Yes, I know, but when are you finished?"

"I can't meet you today. I've already told you, I've got my cousin Johnny to take care of."

"You told me he was thirteen. He's old enough to take care of himself."

"I need to find him some work. The boy eats like a horse."

"You told me he was from Scotland. The Scots can take care of themselves, even at a young age."

"Aye, he's from just over the Firth, a town called Kirkbean. His father is a gardener on the estate at Arbigland, just outside of town. He's married to my father's sister, Jean."

"Thirteen you say? Do you think he'd be interested in an apprenticeship at sea? " queried John.

"Sure I do! He loves looking at ships. They say that when he was a wee lad that he would run the two miles to Carsethorn whenever his father would turn his back. He would spend the day talking to the sailors and if they let him, he would climb all over their ships. That's what's brought'im over here. He's always wanted to go to sea. He's working out back right now; that's if Nicolas ain't fired 'em for sneaking off, and watching them ships in the harbor. He says that we got much bigger ships here than back in Carsethorn and more opportunity to become a good sailor."

"You mean he's working in this tavern?"

"Sure he is. Let me go get the lad. You'll like the boy. He's named John, just like you; John Paul, but we call him Johnny Paul."

Before he could protest, she was up and in a flash turned and disappeared into the kitchen. John would have been irritated with anyone else. He had been seeing this girl for over a month and it had been some of the happiest moments he had spent during his time of financial trouble with his business. When he was

Jaden Duff

with her alone making love, he was able to forget all about his financial problems. The arrival of her cousin had put a stop to this pleasure. The boy, Johnny Paul, had been accompanying her to work and had been hired by Nicholas to wash dishes and keep the place relatively clean. Perhaps it would be smart of him to find this young man a spot on the soon to depart ship for Virginia. Captain Benson could always use another able-bodied man.

Well, at thirteen, young Johnny Paul was almost a man. He was watching the door as Jaden returned, followed by her young cousin. He was an intelligent looking young man with some of the same features as Jaden. He had dark hair and eyes that bore a striking resemblance to his cousin's. He was not tall for his age, standing at about 5'4"and had the same bold look as the vivacious barmaid. They reached his table and she stepped aside to make a path for Johnny Paul to approach.

"How do you do, sir? It's a pleasure to make your acquaintance."

"And yours as well," returned the older man. John was impressed with the look of this young boy. There was no contriteness, nor look of inferiority about Johnny Paul. That was one of the things that he liked about Jaden. It was as if her status of being a coal miner's daughter and a barmaid was only a temporary situation. It seemed as if she and her cousin both realized their futures would be brighter than their present situation.

"Jaden tells me that you might be interested in going to sea? Is that right? Do you have an interest in becoming a sailor?"

"Not just a sailor, sir. I plan to become a captain and have my own ship one day. I plan to sail all of the seven seas!"

"Well, Johnny, many men have made their fortunes in that way. I see no reason why a smart young lad like you couldn't do the same. I have a ship that is scheduled to depart in a few days for Barbados and then Virginia.

"Virginia, sir? My older brother, William, is a tailor in Fredericksburg, sir. Wouldn't he be surprised if I showed up on his doorsteps one day soon."

"*The Friendship* will be taking over a shipment of furniture and bringing back Virginia tobacco. We've got a first-rate captain. His name is Benson and he's been a seaman for many years. I'll ask him if he's interested in training a bright young lad as an apprentice. It takes quite a commitment to learn about the sea. You'll have to sign on for a period of seven years and that's a long time under the mast. What do you think of that idea, my young Scottish friend?"

"Sir, that's why I'm here in Whitehaven. If you can help me obtain a position, then I shall be eternally grateful. I've heard of Benson and would deem it an honor to serve an apprenticeship under him."

John smiled and turned to Jaden. "And how about you, my dear? Will you be grateful, as well? "

Jaden smiled back and said with a turn of the head, "I am grateful for every day that I am alive and in good health."

John turned back to the boy and said, "There's no time like the present. Jaden, do you think Nicholas will allow him to go with me to meet Captain Benson?"

"I don't think we have to ask him. He says the only thing Johnny does all day is watch the ships come and go. You two go on and do what's needed and I'll make Mr. Nicolas understand."

John turned to Johnny and said, "Follow me to the harbor and let's go see if we can find Captain Benson before the sun goes down."

The two were soon standing by *The Friendship* watching Captain Benson and John Lucas come down the gang plank.

Captain Benson said in greeting, "Aye, Mr. Younger! The rest of the cargo will be arriving tomorrow. It shouldn't take but another two days to finish the loading and we should be sailing with the tide on Monday."

"That is good news. The sooner you can get out to sea, the sooner you can return. "Luke," (his nickname for John Lucas), it looks as if this could be one of our better ventures since we were lads together. It couldn't come at a more auspicious time for me."

"John, who is this bright young fellow, you have with you?" John Lucas asked as he noticed Johnny Paul move into view from behind John David Younger.

Turning to allow the two men to get a good view of the wiry lad with the intense stare, Younger said, "Gentlemen, may I present to you, Mr. Johnny Paul. Johnny Paul is from Kirkbean over across the Firth. He's thirteen years old and a very strong and intelligent lad, and my dear Captain, he is anxious to become an apprentice of yours and learn to sail the seven seas. He even has a brother living and working as a tailor in Fredericksburg, Virginia."

"Well, he's got the forward look of a sailor. It just so happens that we could use a smart young lad on this voyage. There's no better time or place to learn the art of seamanship than aboard this vessel. You understand you'll be bound for

seven years in return for being schooled in the art of the sea? Are you prepared to come aboard now? Where are you staying, son?" asked Benson.

"Right now, I'm staying with my cousin up in Newtown. They've only got two rooms and there's eight people living there. It won't take me but a little while to grab my bag. I can be back before dark. I think I'll have more room aboard ship than I do in that coal miner's shack. I've never seen so many people crammed into such little places in all of my life."

John Lucas interrupted, "But aren't you interested in what your wages are going to be?"

"Aye sir, but seeing as how I am dealing with fine gentlemen such as you three, I'm sure I can trust you to take care of me in a fair manner. Now, if you will excuse me, I'll be back in three shakes of the cat's tail." With that young John Paul turned and disappeared rapidly around the corner of the building.

"You know I've a liking for that lad. I think he'll do well at sea. I'll have the apprenticeship papers drawn up and ready for him to sign by the time you sail," exclaimed J.D. Younger.

John Lucas said, "Captain Benson, if anyone can teach him the ways of the seven seas, I have no doubt that you are the one to do it."

J.D. Younger was no longer paying attention to the conversation. He was gazing across the harbor at Nicholas Allison's Tavern with a thoughtful look on his face. The nautical term, "clearing the deck for action" came into his mind.

Four days later, about three hours before high tide, the three partners stood beside the now fully loaded 170 ton brig, *The Friendship*. In addition to the three partners, John Lucas' wife, Ann, and his now six-year-old son Jonathan, were also there.

Jonathan was being entertained by the excited thirteen-year-old Johnny Paul. Jonathan was asking questions about the big ship and the adventure on which Johnny Paul was about to embark. Johnny Paul was just a young apprentice to everyone else there, but he was a newfound hero to the young Jonathan Lucas. Johnny Paul warmed to his role as hero to the six-year-old as he told him outlandish stories of sea monsters, pirates and mermaids. Each time the stories began to get a little too graphic or too far outside reality, Ann would make a motherly comment that would bring the story back to the appropriate realm of a six-year-old boy.

"Now Johnny Paul, you have to promise Jonathan and me that when you do return from your voyage, you will come stay a few days with us and give us some real stories of sailing to America."

Johnny Paul smiled at Ann Lucas, then looked over at her son Jonathan, and winked, "It would be a great pleasure for me, ma'am, and maybe I'll even bring you an Indian chief to play with, Jonathan."

"Will you really? I want an important chief! I want one with war paint and a real tomahawk."

"It all depends on whether or not the captain lets me bring one with me," said the smiling Johnny Paul. "I'd best be moving on board now, ma'am. You take care of my new little friend. I bet that he'll almost be a grown man by the time I return."

"Let's hope that it doesn't take you that long to come back to us, but I'm sure he will have grown quite a bit. Don't forget our invitation! As soon as you return, you're to stay with us."

"Yes ma'am and I thank you again for the invitation."

Johnny Paul saluted the mother and child and turned to board the ship. The young Jonathan already seemed like a younger brother to him.

He began walking up the gangplank, passing by Captain Benson who was saying goodbye to the three owners. The captain turned toward the ship and followed Johnny Paul onto the deck. Soon the brig was underway and each of the four adults stood watching the sails grow smaller on the horizon.

Each one had their own thoughts about what the voyage meant for their future. J.D. Younger once again turned his gaze from the sea toward Nicholas Allison's Tavern. Sure enough, standing in the doorway watching the same set of sails was the shapely silhouette of Jaden Duff, anxiously watching her cousin go to sea for the first time. She was not sure if she was happy or sad for him, for the sea could turn out to be a hard life and often, a short one. But it was adventure on the seas that the young man wanted and she was happy that she had been the one to give him the opportunity to fulfill his dreams.

William Lucas

Chapter 4

ILLIAM LUCAS WAS TWO INCHES SHORTER than his six foot tall older brother, John. He was slighter of build and not quite as intense in his nature as his sibling. John, as the oldest, was much more serious minded and he felt responsible for the fortunes of the Lucas Family.

William was more carefree in his approach to life. When he was younger, his interests were drawn to all sorts of machinery. He was fascinated by anything mechanical and was always asking how it operated. The bigger the piece of equipment, the more interested William became. John and William had started off in the milling business together and at first, it had promised to work out well, but as the years moved along, it became apparent that John was more the businessman and William was the tinkerer and dreamer.

While John was thinking about ways to increase profit and expand the business, William was trying to get another few percentage points of power out of his waterwheel. He had learned the millwright trade from Jonathan Noble and had become proficient with the axe, hammer and plane. He had built waterworks to drive their mills that were very dependable and efficient. The trouble with William was that he was always interrupting production to make adjustments to his newly installed mills. He would run across a new idea, and without regard to production, would interrupt the work flow to try out his new scheme. This, of course, resulted in frustration for John and heated arguments had become a common occurrence.

The two brothers tried to work together for several years before their differences came to a head. Much of what William had learned had come from Ann's uncle, Jonathan Noble. Jonathan Noble had been a successful millwright and was famous in the Whitehaven area for being the finest in all of Cumberland. He combined the trades of carpenter, blacksmith and stonemason to power the machinery of the mills. In those days, there were only three methods of powering equipment. You could harness water, wind, or you could use animal power. The steam engine was on the horizon, but had not been perfected for widespread use.

William also learned from Jonathan Noble how to design mills and milling machinery, which required the application of arithmetic and geometry. This knowledge was necessary for the creation and production of all the components of a working mill. A millwright was responsible for designing the equipment to power the mills, designing the equipment used in the mills and building the equipment as well. It was a huge responsibility to be placed on one man's shoulders and William had a great aptitude for that profession.

William's problem was that he loved his work too much and could not stop trying to improve what he had already completed. When he designed, built and completed a project, he'd come up with a new and better way to accomplish one of the tasks and would often implement his ideas without permission from either his partners or his clients. Fortunately, with age, came the ability to curtail these youthful impulses. He finally spent more time with the initial design and less time trying to improve what was already built.

Presently, he was returning to Whitehaven to visit his brother, John. It was late afternoon as the coach rocked and bounced from side to side, covering the last five miles between Egremont and Whitehaven. J.D. Younger had boarded the stage at Egremont. The coach was crowded and William was looking forward to the end of his journey. The conversation had died out several hours before arriving in Egremont. The discourse between the other passengers had not been very interesting to William in any event. There was a clergyman dressed in black, who was clutching a Bible and took every opportunity to bring any conversation to a religious turn. He was a round-faced fellow of the Methodist persuasion and although jovial in manner, his discourse was all intended to draw his fellow passengers to the Lord.

William had not seen J.D. Younger for several years and at first did not recognize him. J.D.'s visage looked very familiar to William, but it took several minutes for him to realize who his fellow passenger was as his old friend's face had grown much older looking and the lines were much deeper than the last time William had set eyes on him. Because of his financial problems, he wore a frown most of the time. The heavy drinking of late had brought temporary relief, but also had caused additional aging. John was still able to dress the part of the successful businessman, but the sky-blue suit that he wore showed uncharacteristic neglect. His lace cuffs were ragged and dirty and his britches were threadbare at the knees. It was obvious that he had not recognized William. The two sat facing each other, but J.D. had a blank stare and was lost in his own thoughts.

"Excuse me sir," said William, "but I do believe we know one another."

J.D. took no notice and continued to gaze straight ahead without acknowledging William. William then leaned forward and repeated in a louder voice, "Excuse me sir, but I do believe we know one another. Are you J.D. Younger?"

With the mention of his name, J.D. focused his attention back to his surroundings. He looked at William for a moment and then began to smile as he recognized his old friend.

"William, is that you, William Lucas?"

"Yes, J.D. How are you? It has been a few years since we have seen one another." William extended his hand and Younger grasped it with both of his and shook it firmly.

"My God, it's good to see you, William. I heard that you were coming for a visit, but it's still a surprise to see you here."

"Yes, I've been traveling for a length of time and I'm ready to get off of this contraption and rest from the bouncing about for awhile."

"Where are you coming from, William?"

"I've been up in Scotland, at Falkirk. I've been studying with a man named John Smeaton. They're building a big cannon mill there. They've just gotten a big contract to produce cannons for the Royal Navy and the Army."

"That sounds interesting. William, you were always one to search out fascinating projects. I've heard of this John Smeaton. I thought he was a builder of lighthouses."

"Yes, that's where I met him, down in Plymouth. He built a new type of lighthouse for the Eddystone Rocks. That man is someone to watch. Things are changing so fast. If you think about it too much, it will make your head spin."

"Yes, I know what you mean about trying to keep up," John said as he gazed wistfully out the window at the passing scenery. He seemed depressed by this statement of fact. His excitement at seeing William suddenly vanished and thoughts of his troubles welled up inside of him, forcing out any pleasure that meeting an old friend had brought. He choked back his feelings and forced a warm friendly smile.

"I hope you will have time to dine with me before you are off again. I would be delighted to hear more of your adventures."

"Yes, certainly. Thank you for the invitation, J.D. By the way, I met another man named James Watt. Smeaton and the owners of the iron works have supplied some of the parts for a new steam engine that Watts has just completed. He calls it a condensing steam engine. I think it will be able to do more than pump water from mines."

"Yes? I can't wait to hear more about it. Tell me William, have you met your nephew yet?"

"No, I've been away for too many years, but I'm anxious to finally see him. From the letters that I've gotten from my brother, John, he seems to be quite a precocious young fellow. They say he even takes after me in the way he loves to tinker with things."

"I sure didn't realize that you had been away that long."

"Yes, a good deal of time has past since I've seen John and his family. We have stayed in touch by letter, but it sure will be good to be reunited in person."

The coach had slowed to a walk as the outskirts of Whitehaven appeared. They soon reach their destination and the two old acquaintances shook hands and turned to go in different directions. William had promised J.D. that he would meet him for drinks and dinner three days hence.

William was glad to be able to stretch his legs after all of the time in the coach. He found a young boy willing to carry his two bags for the three blocks to his childhood home. The Lucas home was on the corner of Strand and Lowther Streets. A three-story dwelling, it was unpretentious, but very inviting.

William stepped up to the front door and pulled the knob to ring the bell. The door opened and there stood Miss Trinity who had not laid eyes on William since Jonathan Noble's funeral. She of course recognized him immediately, and a delighted expression passed over her face.

"Master William, what a great pleasure it is to see you! We weren't expecting you until tomorrow."

"Miss Trinity, you haven't changed a bit in all these years. You're still the same young lady all the boys chased after."

William stepped inside, grabbed Miss Trinity around the waist and lifted her up, swinging her around. They were both laughing as he put her down.

"And you, William, you're just as big a liar as you always were. We girls still like to hear it though, even if it's not true. Now let go of me so that I can go tell your brother you are here."

"You don't have to tell me, Miss Trinity. I heard the bell. I was hoping that it might be William and here he is."

John walked up to his brother and held out his hand. William took it with his right hand and placed his left hand on his elbow. They both stood for a second looking into each other's eyes, when suddenly John pulled his brother forward and gave him a warm embrace.

"Damn William, it's so good to see you again," John said with heartfelt emotion. He was truly glad to see his brother. Tears welled up in William's eyes as the two brothers clasped each other by the shoulders, taking a step backward. Ann stepped out into the wide hall, followed by her two youngest daughters and her son, Jonathan. The two girls ran up to their uncle and each got a turn to hug and kiss him. Ann also took her turn, giving her brother-in-law a warm welcome. Jonathan, who had never seen his uncle stood back a few feet, watching the enthusiastic greetings. Releasing his sister-in-law, William turned to look at the young lad.

"And you must be Jonathan."

"Yes Sir, that is my name."

"Well, I'm your Uncle William."

"Yes Sir, I've been looking forward to meeting you, sir. My father and mother have told me so much about you."

"I hope they have been kind in what they said," replied William.

"Oh yes sir, they say you're one of the smartest men in all of England. They say if I can be half as smart as my Uncle William, then I should do well for myself in the world."

"Oh, so that's what they say, is it? Well, I shouldn't think that you will have much problem being at least as intelligent. The key is the desire to be knowledgeable about many things. You need to be so curious that you're inquisitiveness can never be satisfied."

"Father says I'm as curious and nosy as a cat. I love to take things apart to see how they work. He tells me he should have named me William after you, instead of Jonathan."

"No, Jonathan is a fine name. I understand you're named after your Great Uncle, Jonathan Noble. He taught me quite a bit, you know."

"That's what my mama told me. She said that you and Uncle Jonathan were inseparable when you were my age."

"That's true, nephew. He was quite a man. It's a shame you never got to know him before he passed away."

As the other family members gathered around the two, John and his wife exchanged knowing glances. It seemed that their conversation might continue indefinitely, if they didn't intervene.

"Well William, it looks like you and my son, Jonathan, will not have much trouble getting acquainted. He certainly has your love for tinkering. You must be tired after your journey. Let's get you up to your room so you can rest before dinner."

John turned to the young man who was still standing in the doorway holding his bags and said, "Young man, would you be so kind as to carry those bags up to the third floor. Miss Trinity will you show you the way."

Turning back to his brother, John offered, "William, how would a drink of brandy be about now?"

"It would go down very well."

Chapter 5

For William, this was somewhat of a bittersweet homecoming. The long separation of the past few years had not been without its acrid moments. He knew that his brother had been disappointed in their business arrangement, but he had never expected it to come to the point of dissolution. He had been forced to admit, however, that his brother had been very generous.

The money that John had paid him for his half of the business allowed him to seek out prominent men from all over England and some were brilliant with respect to improving the way things were powered in manufacturing. William had been rewarded by the education he received in the latest and most modern methods of machination. Although they had stayed in touch by letter, William was excited about the prospect of sharing his newfound knowledge with his older brother in more detail. He was hoping that John would show interest in the areas that William had explored over the last decade. However, what William considered interesting and what John considered interesting could sometimes be very different.

He was pleasantly surprised with his nephew, Jonathan. He had shown a certain amount of curiosity and wonder and William hoped it was an enduring part of his character. Over the next two weeks, he would be able to measure the boy's true interests. The one thing that William knew for certain was that in the coming years, to be successful, Jonathan would have to hone his desire for the newest trends in production and industry, or failure would surely follow. New fortunes were being made every day, but fortunes were lost every day, as well.

Dinner had been pleasant, and the girls were growing into charming young ladies. The oldest, Julia, was married and expecting her first child. She was living with her husband in Carlisle, forty-five miles away. William could not tell whether John was more excited about the news of a grandchild or flustered by the fact that he was growing older.

He was intrigued upon the introduction to the young seaman apprentice that John's entire family seemed to like. At seventeen, Johnny Paul had a very engaging personality. Kate, the youngest daughter, certainly seemed enchanted by the tales of adventure that he spun for them at the dinner table.

William told them of his short coach ride with Johnny Paul's benefactor, J.D. Younger and had relayed his concerns about the mindset of their friend and his aging appearance. His brother brought him up to date on the deteriorating financial situation in which his partner found himself. Johnny Paul took umbrage to the suggestion that his sponsor was anything but in the best of circumstances. The young man was quite bright and likable, however he also seemed to have a very quick temper, but then most Scotsmen he knew did, as well. The young seaman quickly remembered he was a guest and had apologized quickly for his outburst. He and young Jonathan had formed a fast friendship based on the older boy's sea stories and love of adventure. He had not brought an Indian chief home for Jonathan as he had promised, but he had brought a tomahawk for his young friend. While in Virginia, Johnny Paul had spent time with his brother, William Paul. Like others before him, he was quite taken with the American colonies. His brother, the tailor, was prospering in the New World. *The Friendship* had recently completed its second voyage to the New World, but both voyages had taken much longer than anticipated. There were many reasons for the delays. Affected by storms, *The Friendship* had suffered damage that had to be repaired, negotiations on the rising price of tobacco precipitated a delay and caution had to be taken on the voyage due to the French and Indian War that was raging in America. In Europe, the French and Indian War was called the Seven Years War as it had become a conflict that raged across the globe. Commencing in 1754, the year that Jonathan was born, everyone was hoping that it would soon end.

Martin Trinity had been the family butler, employed before the two boys, William and John, had been born. He was still engaged by John and was the father of Miss Trinity, who had never married.

"Master John and Master William, I have prepared the brandy and the cigars in your drawing room. I have not sampled the cigars, but I can assure you that the brandy is first class."

"Well, brother, I see that Martin has not changed much over the years. He has a little less hair and what he has, is peppered with gray, but he behaves just the same as when we were kids."

"Yes, he is still the same grand rascal he's always been. He is, however, one of the best butlers that anyone could employ. I don't know what I would do without him. I am away so often on business nowadays. He is a great help to Ann in managing our affairs while I'm traveling."

The two brothers stood, excused themselves and followed Martin to the drawing room. Two chairs were arranged facing the fireplace with a small table between. There were two glasses, a bottle of port and a bottle of brandy, neatly arranged on the table. The fire was very welcoming as William sat down facing his brother. John asked," Port or brandy?"

"I prefer the brandy."

"I remember."

John poured a tumbler full of brandy for his brother. "I think I'll stay with the port this evening."

John filled his own glass, and with a long sigh, sat back in his chair and looked at his brother with a smile.

"Here's to your health, brother."

"And yours, as well," came the reply.

"Tell me, William, if it's true that you are very well settled in London?"

"Yes, that's where I have my shop set up. I take commissions from all over England and travel quite a bit. I have also taken my earlier experiences with you, my brother, to heart and now I design and construct my creations, usually only once." He added, "Unless, of course, the client orders it and pays me up front."

The two brothers chuckled together. John was relieved to know that William was able to laugh about their break ten years before. That had not always been so. It was said that time heals all wounds, and hopefully that was the case with his younger brother.

"From the letters that I've gotten from you, it seems that you've been quite busy over the last few years. I assume that you've been prospering."

"Yes! As you know, I have been building at least one mill each year since I departed from Whitehaven. I have installed waterworks, windmills, and even some Newcomen steam engines to drain mines down in Cornwall. I really believe that this fellow I met in Falkirk, James Watt, is on to something. He's developed a new way to use steam power. He calls it condensing power."

"Yes I've heard of him. He's a Scotsman, isn't he?"

"Indeed, yes he is. I had the chance of working with him while he was constructing his version of the steam engine. Currently, the distance that the extant Newcomen steam engine can pull water is limited to a depth of thirty feet. Watt feels that the engine design wastes a great deal of energy by having to repeatedly cool and then reheat the cylinder. Watt has designed a separate condenser, which helps avoid wasting energy and will be capable of pulling from greater depths. I think that it will greatly improve the power, efficiency, and cost of operating steam engines and could open up a whole new power source."

"He sounds like a man after your own heart."

John was becoming concerned that perhaps William was slipping back into old habits of dreaming about better ways to do things, while losing touch with the here and now. William noticed John's slight change in attitude and expression and smiled reassuringly, "No, this is no idle dream, John. I've seen this machine work. In any event, don't worry! I intend to stick with building what I know. I have learned my lessons over the past ten years, and I learned them well," stated William as he saw the look of relief on his brother's face.

"Tell me John, my nephew, Jonathan, is he really as interested in how things work as he seems?"

"If I didn't know better, I would think he's you all over again. Perhaps, in the near future, you can recommend a proper place for him to receive some training. I want him to understand his world and how it's changing."

"Well, of course. I would be happy to help with his education. When he's up around twelve or thirteen years of age, we'll seriously consider an appropriate starting place."

"That was just what I was thinking. His mother will be the problem. She doesn't see the need for shipping her son to some far away place. I'm not sure that I'll be very fond of it myself. But absence from home and hearth sometimes can be a tutor, as well. It would prepare him emotionally to withstand periods of separation from his family. It seems we must move farther afield for longer periods of time to learn all the new strides in industry."

The next morning John invited his brother William to a scheduled meeting with his two partners in the tobacco venture, J.D. Younger and Aleyn Eedes. As William had expected from the distressed look on John Younger's face during the carriage ride, Younger was facing financial issues. A man named Thomas Dacre had bought up all of Youngers' notes and immediately called them due. It was rumored that he was a rival for Jaden Duff's affections and he was intent on his competitor's ruin. It seemed that the brig, *The Friendship,* had been taken by the courts to help pay his debts and was to be sold at auction to the highest bidder. While the profits from the partnership of Lucas, Eedes and Younger were secure, obviously the lease agreement for *The Friendship* was not protected against this type of legal action. The vessel was lost to the partnership.

The Lucas Brothers walked into the warehouse and were greeted by Younger and Eedes. Aleyn and J.D. had a very strained relationship and were sitting at the table in silence. John introduced his brother, William, to Eedes and William and Younger again shook hands.

"Gentlemen, I hope that you don't mind my brother sitting in on this meeting. He has some very interesting information about what is going on in several areas that pertain to our businesses, particularly sail making production. He is recommending that we obtain some new weaving machines for our mills."

"I have no qualms about William being here," said a morose J.D. Younger. "I'm sure he's already heard the rumors of my financial demise. I'm also sure his suggestions will be valuable. However, at this point I don't believe that I will be in a position to make new purchases for quite a while."

His face flushed at the admission of defeat. He stepped away from the group and looked out the window where his pride and joy, *The Friendship,* was docked. John stepped over to his friend, and placed his hand on his back.

"My friend, you don't need to worry so deeply over your future. Once you are cleared of these bankruptcy proceedings, your friends will see that you get a fresh start. Our business community cannot lose an experienced man like you. You'll have to begin again, but you won't be starting from the bottom and you won't have to learn everything all over again. You'll just need to be re-capitalized."

"I know. I appreciate my friends for standing by me, but it is still quite a blow to one's self-esteem to be put in this situation."

"Well, the wind doesn't blow in the same direction all the time. We have to learn life's lessons when we fail, as well as when we succeed. Think of this as a play and the curtain has gone down on act two. We will simply open the third act and hopefully this one will have a happy ending."

"Gentlemen, if you will excuse me, I have an unpleasant duty to attend to, for as you know, young Johnny Paul still has three years to go on his apprenticeship under me. Since I'm no longer able to provide him with a vessel for his apprenticeship, I'll have to release him."

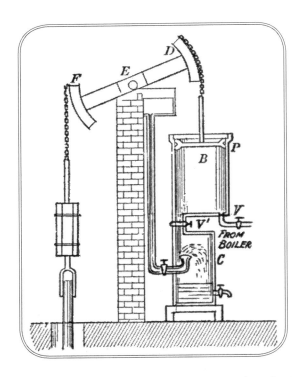

"It is unfortunate for the lad. He was learning so much under Benson."

"Well, I've found him another situation. He's young for this new assignment, but I believe it to be one that he will profit from in more ways than one."

"What do you have in mind for the little Scotsman?" inquired John.

"It's a venture that will toughen him up, but also earn him more wages, since he will not be an apprentice any longer. I have arranged for him to sail as third mate on the just commissioned *King George*."

"*The King George*! Isn't that a slave ship?"

"Aye, that it is, but it's the best position that I could find for Mr. Paul. I feel that I owe him an opportunity."

"That's a tough position to put a young man in and a hard way to make money. But as third mate, it is quite a promotion. You know I'm not keen on the slave trade. I don't condone it, and I have never participated in it in any way, shape or form. The conditions those slaves have to endure crossing the Atlantic Ocean should never be allowed. Have you told the boy about this offer yet?" asked John with worry in his voice.

"Yes, I have and he's reluctantly agreed to accept the position. I don't know if he'll have the stomach for it or not. Only time will tell."

"If he's got the stomach for that kind of sailing, it can certainly make his fortune. He has not mentioned it to Ann or me. He knows my feelings on the slave trade. A lot of people around here would like to see this trade abolished. It's an abominable thing. I find myself in agreement with Granville Sharp. Slavery should be abolished totally."

The meeting lasted for another hour and a half. The affairs of Lucas, Eedes and Younger were at an end. It had been very profitable in the four years in which it had operated. There had been profit, both in selling goods to the colonies and selling tobacco in England. In a addition to furniture, they had shipped other items such as shoes, textiles, muskets, saddles and bridles, fine china, linen, brass, copper-ware and even gunpowder to America. But the big profits came from returning to Whitehaven with the cargo of tobacco. As of late, the Scottish merchants of Glasgow had been cutting in on Whitehaven's tobacco trade with Virginia. They were bidding up the prices of tobacco and thereby driving down profits, so the last trip had not been as profitable as the first. Younger said his goodbyes and headed off toward Nicolas Allison's Tavern. The two remaining partners still owned one ship, *The Julia,* which was smaller than *The Friendship*, but could still carry on trade with Virginia. John Lucas had additional ships about the same size as *The Julia*, but they were set up for the coal trade with Ireland and were not be suitable for anything else.

The coal trade with Ireland offered a secure and steady income. It was a safe trade, but one with a lower profit margin. John realized that the greater profits he had realized from the trips to Virginia would need to be invested in something that would improve his profitability.

"Aleyn, William has been telling me about some new weaving machines that he has encountered down in the village of Stanhill, Lancashire. A man by the name of James Hargrove has come up with a new way of spinning thread. It's a spinning frame that he calls a Spinning Jenny. He tells me it has multiple spindles all working at the same time. You know, our biggest problem is keeping enough of the spindles going to keep up with the weavers. Today it takes eight people spinning to produce enough fiber to keep up with one weaver. Hargrove's machine, the Spinning Jenny, has forty or fifty spindles to make yarn."

"Yes, John, that does sound impressive. Are you thinking about equipping your sail mill with some of these new, what did you call them, Spinning Jennys?"

"Well, I want to see some of them first. William, who was the other man that you told me about from Derbyshire?"

"His name is Richard Arkwright. I think that he's onto something even better and more productive. He calls his machine the Water Frame."

"Tell Aleyn what this machine can supposedly do."

"His idea is to use a series of four pairs of rollers, each operating at a successively higher rotating speed. This will draw out the fibers, which are then twisted by the spindle. He'll have to keep the roller spacing slightly longer than the fiber length. If the rollers are too close in their spacing, it will cause the fibers to break. But if they are too distant in their spacing, it will cause the thread to be of unequal length. The top rollers that I saw were covered by leather and the loading onto the rollers will be applied by a weight. These weights keep the twist from backing up before they get to the rollers. The bottom rollers, I think, are made from wood and metal, and the bottom part contains fluting along the whole length.

This water frame machine of Arkwright's should be able to produce a hard, medium count thread suitable for warp. If you install this machine, John, no one else will be able to match the quality of the sails that you build."

"John, I'm just a simple merchant. Your brother speaks an entirely different language than the English that I know. Do you have any idea what he is talking about? I can not make heads nor tails of it."

John shook his head and with a laugh replied, "Since I'm in the sail making business, I do understand what he's saying, but for the life of me, it's hard to follow. William, can you draw it for us?"

"Yes, I think I can illustrate it for the two of you. It'll take me a couple of days, but they're really good ideas. He's installing his first machines in a factory town called Cromford. I'm sure, for a price, he would allow us to build one of his new devices here."

John and Aleyn looked at each other and nodded in agreement. All of this talk had made the two men thirsty. It was agreed that they should adjourn in the warehouse and resume the meeting at Nicolas Allison's Tavern. Perhaps a glass of port could help impart a better understanding of the particulars concerning sail making to Aleyn.

Chapter 6

THEY DID NOT SEE JOHNNY PAUL AGAIN FOR over sixteen months. When he returned he did not visit the Lucas House as he had at the end of his Virginia voyages. The return of *The King George* to Whitehaven had not gone unnoticed by young Jonathan.

He had asked his mother if something had happened to his friend, Johnny Paul, to keep him away from the house. With a woman's intuition, Ann feared that this voyage had changed the young Scotsman, and not for the better. Jonathan was persistent, however, in asking about his friend. Ann had finally asked John to see if he could locate the boy and find out why he had not visited them upon his return.

John agreed and left after lunch to go in search of seamen Paul. He walked the few short blocks down to the harbor and asked some of the crew members of the ship where he could find third mate Paul. The response was that he was staying in a room at Nicolas Allison's Tavern. This made sense, even though his cousin, Jaden Duff, was no longer a barmaid there. It seems that when J.D. Younger ran out of money she had moved on and found someone who had not run out of money. She had become the consort of none other than Thomas Dacre. He was the man who had finally been the one to force J.D. Younger into bankruptcy. It had all been perfectly legal. But the fact that John had lost Jaden as well as his money, seemed to have rubbed salt into his wounds. He was now bitter, bankrupt and depressed.

John approached Nicholas and inquired as to which room young Paul was occupying.

"He's at the top of the stairs, first room on the right, but I'm not sure you want to see him."

"Why not?"

"Well, for the last few days he's been keeping close company with several bottles of rum."

"Hmmm, I've not known him to touch that before."

"He's changed since his return. I don't think this last voyage of his has done much good for him. He seems like a much troubled young man."

John nodded and started climbing the stairs. He reached the door of the room and knocked softly. There was no answer. He tried the door and it was not locked. He stepped into the room and there, lying on the bed asleep, was his young friend. The smell of rum was strong in the room. There were several empty bottles lying by the bed and the breath emanating from Johnny was as strong as a northern gale. John approached the bed and taking hold of Johnny's shoulder, began to shake it gently.

"What the hell is it?" asked an agitated rum-head.

"Johnny, . . . Johnny, it's me, John Lucas."

The young man gazed up into his face and the light of recognition came into his eyes. Startled, he sat up quickly, turning away from the older man. He started rubbing his eyes and said, "Master John, wha. . . wha, . . . hat are you doing here?"

"Johnny, we were all worried about you, especially Jonathan. Your ship has been in for several days and we're used to seeing you after a voyage. We felt something may have happened to you."

"Something did happen to me. I've taken part in an abomination. I thought the rum could wash the horror away. But, so far, it's only made it worse."

"I was worried that something like this might happen. Ann said she had a bad feeling when you hadn't returned to us for several days."

"I'm not sure I'll ever be fit company for proper people ever again." John Paul buried his face in his hands.

"The first thing we've got to do, my young friend, is to get you cleaned up and out of here."

"I don't think I can bear to face your family after the things that I've seen and done."

"You let us decide that. Here, let's get you up and over to that pitcher of water. We've got to get you cleaned up and sobered up and from the looks of you, I think you could use a good meal."

The third mate tried to argue, but in the end, he accepted the invitation. John went downstairs and waited. After half an hour, young Johnny came down the stairs with a sea bag over his shoulder. John took him to the warehouse and they talked awhile about his trip.

"They had crammed over five hundred men, women and children into the hole of *The King George*. We crossed the middle Atlantic from Angola, destined for Barbados.

"They packed men in like animals. They were all chained together; men, women and children. It was sweltering down below, and they had no way to relieve themselves. They wallowed in their own filth. The stench was unbearable. The only place you could go to minimize the awful smell, was upwind. It took us six weeks to cross and they started to die off after only two or three days. We had to take turns going below, taking the irons off of 'em, hauling 'em up and tossing 'em overboard. If there is a hell on earth, it was there."

John let him talk and he did, for the next three hours. His moods fluctuated from melancholy and depression to extreme, violent anger. Talking seemed to help and in the end he began to sound like the young man the Lucas Family had taken in as a friend, but for Johnny, that seemed like an eternity ago.

Jonathan greeted his father and friend at the door.

"Johnny, where have you been? I felt something had happened to you ... that you had been eaten by one of the savages or something!"

"Well, it wasn't quite that bad, but it was bad enough. My goodness! You sure have grown up. I'll be having to look up to you soon. I think you've already got me by an inch or two."

"I think you're right. I'm twelve years old now and you know I'll be thirteen before you know it."

"Well, your father is a six-footer and your uncle is almost as tall, so I guess you'll be up there, as well. You'll be having 'Ole Johnny to stare up at you Lucas men. I'll get a crick in my neck."

"Let me go get Kate! She'll be glad to see you."

Jonathan turned and ran toward the staircase. "Kate, Kate, he's here, he's here," he shouted, as he disappeared up the stairs.

After the excitement in the Lucas Home, it began to quiet down at dinner. John explained to his family that the past year and a half had been hard for their guest. He asked his family to talk only about what they had been doing over the past two years and what they intended to do in the future. They were instructed not to ask questions of Johnny or what he had gone through on his last voyage. He added that if Johnny wanted to talk about his experiences, he would.

Jonathan began by relaying to John Paul that he had been helping his father install some new equipment in their sail mill. His Uncle William had gotten permission from the man who invented the weaving machine, Mr. Arkwright, to build one in Whitehaven. Of course, they had to buy the right to use the machine after it was installed, but his father and uncle thought that the cost would be well worth the improvement in production. The young sailor was impressed by the detailed explanation that young Jonathan was able to give about the intricacies of the new machine. Jonathan would stop every so often and looked at his father for either verification or correction. John would usually reply, "Son, you're doing just fine."

Kate was growing into a fine looking young lady. She was about the same age as Johnny Paul and obviously was interested.

"Kate, I suppose you've had every eligible man in Whitehaven chasing after you since I've been gone."

"Why, my dear John Paul, where in the world did you get such an idea as that?" exclaimed Kate.

"Because, if I had been here during that period of time, I would've been the first one knocking on the door."

"There have been a few young men who have come calling, but I find them boring. I think the farthest they have ever been from Whitehaven is Egremont. Oh, but Allen Jones has been as far away as Carlisle."

"And who might be this Allen Jones? Should I be jealous of this man?"

"He has been rather persistent and he is a very nice young man from a good family. He'll be rich one day."

This had the desired effect on John Paul. Jealousy! He felt the color change to red on his face. He had always had a temper, but since his African voyage, it had gotten much worse.

"Are you saying that those are the requirements for young gentlemen to pay attention to you?"

Taken aback, Kate replied, "Of course not, Johnny! You're as good as any 'old Jones'. Besides, even though he's been to Carlisle, he's just as boring as the other boys. And he hasn't been to America."

This brought Johnny Paul back to his normal charming self.

"I'm sorry, Kate. I know that you didn't mean anything by it. But if it's a Jones that you're fond of, well, maybe I'll become a Jones one day." He looked around the room, his anger evaporated. He smiled and said, "Jonathan, can you take me to the mill tomorrow and show me all of this wondrous work that you've been doing?"

Jonathan looked at his father for permission. His father nodded his head in agreement.

"Of course, Johnny we'll leave right after breakfast in the morning. The job is almost done, but we're still working on the water wheels. We are to finish up tomorrow. It's fascinating to see how it all works."

The next morning, right after their breakfast, John, Jonathan and Johnny started to walk towards John's sail mill. It was a walk of about a mile and a half. The mill was located close to the road to Egremont. When they arrived, they found that William was already there, putting the finishing touches on the Arkwright equipment. As soon as they arrived, Jonathan's interest in what William was doing took precedent over everything else. He was right beside his uncle watching everything he was doing and asking why he was doing it. The two of them were soon lost in their work.

John gave Johnny a tour of the mill and explained that the ships he had been sailing on probably had gotten their sails from this very mill. The cloth in the sailor's pants he was wearing was also most likely had been made at John's mill. Johnny was interested and asked Mr. Lucas to explain the industry to him. This was a subject that John warmed to and he went into great detail about the linen trade, of which, he had long been involved.

"Flax and hemp has been grown in Cumberland for many centuries. The growing of hemp is more common than that of flax, particularly here in Western Cumberland. There is, however, never enough to meet demand for the mill, so extra shipments of the two crops are imported. Most of it is imported from as far away as Archangel and the Baltic ports of Riga, Nava and St. Petersburg. This trade is plagued by various hazards, such as bad weather, when the ships pass to the north of Scotland. Importation is limited to late summer, after the flax harvest, but before the winter sets in, so it is necessary to purchase enough for the entire year's worth of manufacturing.

Linen has been made in mills such as this one well before the application of water power. The Lucas Mill is set up to make plain linens for export to the West Indies and for local consumption. For as you know, Whitehaven has a prospering shipbuilding industry to supply. All the flax brought in is prepared by a flax dresser employed here at our factory. It is then sent out to be spun by the surrounding workers in their cottages. Spinning wheels are given out to as many as ninety households to produce the yarn we need. When the yarn is spun, it is brought back to the factory where specialists wash and bleach it. After the yarn is completed, the weaving process begins. When the weaving is completed, the cloth is calendered."

John explained to Johnny what was meant by calendaring, "The most essential thing in calendering is having the correct amount of moisture present in the cloth at the moment of calendaring. The cloth is rolled between bowls made of metal. The metal bowls are usually made of iron with a hard, highly-polished surface. Our bowls are generally hollow, so that they can be heated. It makes the cloth dirt resistant and much stronger."

John continued, "The biggest problem we face is getting a regular yarn supply," he continued. "That is why we have decided to install machine spinning here. Several of the bigger mills, such as Jonathan and William Harris of Derwent Mills and Cockermouth to the north of here, have already done so. Joseph Waithman of Holme Mill in Milnthorpe, just to the south of us, is also installing these kinds of machines. To be competitive, we must keep up with the times."

Jonathan had begun to listen to his father speak. John turned to his son and said, "Why don't you explain for your friend what products we make in this mill?"

Young Jonathan was thrilled at the opportunity to get to show off some of his knowledge of the family business.

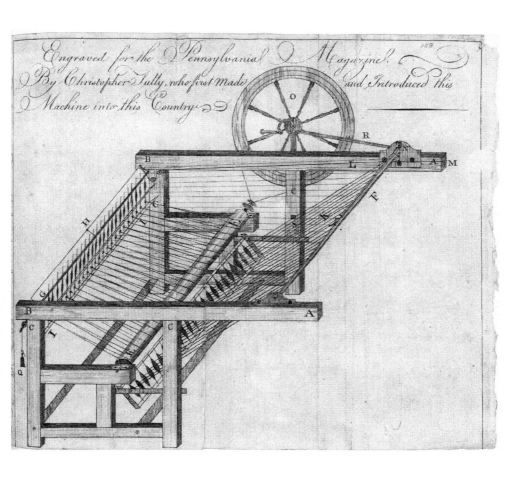

Engraved for the Pennsylvania Magazine.
By Christopher Tully, who first Made and Introduced this
Machine into this Country.

Warming to his part of the story he began, "The linen that we produce here is intended for two types of markets. Some we make for export, mostly to the colonies, but most of our product goes to our local market and other industrial users. We have to be careful because the first category is subject to changes in fashion. The other category, which is comprised of sailcloth, different kinds of packaging, ropes, twine and fishing nets, are where we concentrate most of our efforts. Here in Whitehaven, because the British government enacted policies that forced the colonies to buy only from the English market, we enjoy quite a lively colonial trade with the Americas. Here at home, we sell to several of the local merchants, as well as the shipbuilders. One of our Whitehaven customers is Mr. James Ryley. He sells our products such as checks, stripes, coarse and fine linen, huckaback and canvas for sailors' trousers, while just down the road from us, Mr. Thomas Barton, an upholsterer, requires blind canvas, fringes, lines and tassels, matting and carpeting, all made right here in our mill."

Jonathan stopped and looked at his father, who responded with, "Go ahead, son, you're doing just fine."

Reassured by his father's comment, Jonathan continued, "Our main product is sailcloth. It is used by the shipbuilders of Whitehaven, Lancaster, Ulverston and numerous other small ports as far south as Morecambe Bay and as far north as Ballantrae in Scotland. When we make sail cloth it is about two feet wide, and we have to sew it together into the size sail that is needed. We can only produce two foot wide pieces because of the size of the weaving machines. Uncle William and I are working on a way to weave both a wider and a stronger sailcloth."

Jonathan paused to catch his breath. He had noticed that John Paul's eyes were beginning to glaze over. He smiled and said, "Johnny, I'm sorry. I get carried away. This is so much fun. Have you decided what you going to do next? Are you going back to sea?"

John Paul's smile faded as he looked from one friend to the next. His brow became furrowed and he shook his head and looked down at the floor.

"I've been offered a promotion. I'll not go back to *The King George*. I'm not thrilled with that captain and the way he does things. I've been told conditions are a little better on *The Two Friends*. They say this captain feeds his captives better and fewer of them die on the trip, so I've accepted the position of first mate. I'll be under Captain Richard Millerson and we sail in two days. I hope I'm not making a mistake."

"Johnny, you know how we feel about the slave trade. Perhaps your being on board can help better the treatment that those poor wretches receive." John was hopeful, but suspected nothing would change. He also knew that keeping more slaves alive meant better profits for the voyage. It was not all out of the kindness of his heart that this Captain Millerson treated his slave passengers better than other slavers. After all, there was no market for dead men. John started to explain this to his young friend, but thought better of it.

"All I can say, sir, is that I'll try to do what I can to improve things. I have to report to the ship this afternoon. If you don't mind, sir, I would like to pay a visit to your daughter before I ship out."

"That would be fine with me, Johnny and I'm certain that Kate won't mind one bit." They all had a good chuckle.

The next day the entire Lucas Family went down to the docks to see the

departure of *The Two Friends*. They had met Captain Millerson and he seemed like a jovial sort. He was very friendly and seemed kind, but one could tell that underneath that friendly exterior, he was hard as steel. Whether it was from the years at sea, the slave trade, or a combination of the two, it was definitely there. He was polite and charming and had good things to say about Johnny. However, John was not fooled by his exterior demeanor and was concerned about the young sailor as he climbed on board. John Paul had been deeply affected by his first slave voyage and John was afraid that he would might not be the same person the next time they met.

As they got underway, Johnny turned and climbed on the rigging halfway up. With a big smile on his face, he waved goodbye to his friends on the quay. It was a good way to remember John Paul, for it would be fourteen years before Johnny and Jonathan would meet again.

Chapter 7

OHN AND HIS WIFE, ANN, WERE ENCOUNTERING something that was very rare in their marriage. They were having a heated discussion that some might even call an argument. John had produced a letter written by his brother, William, from London, offering to take on Jonathan as an apprentice, so that one day he could become a millwright. Ann was not very happy at the prospect of her son leaving home and living over three hundred miles away in London.

John was apprehensive as well, but he realized that his brother would take good care of Jonathan. William had grown very fond of the lad on his trip to install equipment in the Lucas Mill. John had seen the two of them grow close as they worked side-by-side installing Spinning Jennys and water frames. He had also become aware that Jonathans' interests were more in line with the mechanical end of their business, like his brother, than running a business and making a profit, like himself. Reluctantly, he had come to the conclusion that the best way to continue to prepare his son for the future was to put him under William's care for the next few years. Seven years was the normal time for an apprentice to learn a trade, but John felt that it would not take the boy that long to become proficient.

"I don't like the idea that Jonathan will be so far from us any better than you do. But you know, as well as I do, that if he is to continue his education, there is no one nearby that can prepare him for the future. It seems like every year, there are innovations and new advances in production and manufacturing. If it hadn't been for William's fortuitous visit, two years ago, we would likely be out of business by now."

"John, you know, I understand all of that. And I am grateful to William for what he has done for our family. But this equipment he installed is working just fine and we still have the tobacco trade with Virginia. And aren't the two coal ships doing well?"

"Yes, for now, all is well. But we have been losing tobacco business to those Scots merchants up in Glasgow. It's still profitable for us, but I don't know what the future might hold. We're still hauling coal to Dublin, but there are now over four hundred ships sailing out of Whitehaven. There's a lot of competition in shipping, even in the coal business. We're fortunately staying profitable in all three of our businesses, but I've never seen things change as rapidly as they have in the last few years. It'll do no good to educate Jonathan, if it's the wrong education. It does no good to teach him how things were done yesterday, if that's not the way things will be done tomorrow."

"But London is so far away," Ann said, making her final plea. But John could tell that her resolve was weakening. She knew as well as he did, that things were changing at an accelerated pace. Whitehaven had grown from a fair sized village of three thousand people to a town of over ten thousand in the past thirty years and was now the sixth largest town in England. There was a new business opening its doors almost every day and it wasn't just Whitehaven that was growing. Even the small nearby village of Egremont now had its own factories, as did most of the other small settlements in their area.

When Sir Christopher Lowther purchased the rights to the area back in 1630, Whitehaven had been a large village of no more than two hundred and fifty souls. He had built a pier in 1634 and started to export coal to Ireland. In just over one hundred years, Whitehaven had seen phenomenal growth. It was now one of the biggest manufacturers of all sorts of goods, from glass to grandfather clocks, as well as a large exporter of coal. These industries were the foundations of Whitehaven's present prosperity.

"Have you talked to Jonathan about how he feels on the subject?"

"Not yet. I thought that it was only proper to discuss this with you first so that when we talk to Jonathan, we can do it with one voice and one mind. Isn't that the way we've always approached things?"

Ann turned and smiled at her husband. She reached up and put her arms around his neck, pulling his face toward hers.

She held him closely for a moment, staring into his eyes.

"Yes, my darling. It's one of the things that I have always loved about you. You've treated me like an equal partner ever since the day we met. If Jonathan is for it, then off to London he goes."

Ann brought him the last few inches to her for a warm kiss. Ann's large, dark eyes, long slender neck and full mouth still had the same effect on John as it had thirty years before, when he had first met her. He was devoted to her and remained in love with his wife throughout the years and that fact had served them both well throughout their marriage.

Jonathan awoke the next morning to a loud knock on his door. The door opened and Martin stepped in. He walked over to the window and pulled the curtains back, letting the sunlight stream into the room. Jonathan sat up in bed and rubbed his eyes, blinking at the sunlight. Martin turned and looked at the young boy stretching and yawning.

"Good morning, young Master Jonathan. I trust that you slept well last night,… and had pleasant dreams."

"Yes I did, Martin, and would still be sleeping if you hadn't pulled those curtains back."

"Yes, you are the third-generation of Lucas men that I've taken care of and I do believe that you love to sleep more than the rest of them combined. It is breakfast time. This morning your mother and father have instructed me to be sure that you are down as quickly as possible to have breakfast with them." Martin walked over to the ètagere and pulled out a suitable set of clothes. He laid them out on the dressing table at the foot of Jonathan's bed. Turning to the young man he said, "They are waiting downstairs for you now!"

"This is rather unusual, is it not? I don't suppose it's Sunday, is it?"

"No, Master Jonathan, far from it. It's actually Tuesday. But all the same, your presence is requested,- downstairs- in the dining room,- for breakfast, -this morning,- presently."

"Very well, very well, and I should add very well."

Jonathan stretched a little more and climbed out of bed and walked over to the commode where a basin of water had been poured by Martin. He washed his face, turned to the dressing table and began to put on his clothes.

After checking himself in the mirror and combing his hair, Jonathan turned and followed Martin out of his room into the hallway and over to the staircase. The two of them approached the dining room. The doors were closed, so Martin slid back the double doors, bowed graciously and announced, "Master Jonathan Lucas, expert sleeper, has arrived."

Miss Trinity looked up from serving Ann's plate and said, "Father, I think we know who this young man is."

"I'm just trying to prepare the young lad for his future success," replied Martin dryly.

"Good morning, father, good morning, mother and how are you this morning, my sister Kate?"

"I'm just fine, brother."

Jonathan moved to his seat as he normally would have, but Martin stepped up behind him and with an elaborate show of formality, pulled the chair back, allowing him better access to his seat. Somewhat puzzled by Martin's behavior, Jonathan had a quizzical smile on his face as he pulled his chair under the table. Taking his napkin off the table and placing it onto his lap, he noticed that his mother and father were staring at him with very unusual expressions.

"Jonathan, I have just received a letter from your Uncle William. "

"Is anything the matter?" Jonathan suddenly looked worried.

"No son, nothing of that sort. He has made a proposal for us. It involves you and that is what we want to talk about this morning."

Jonathan looked from his father to his mother and then to his sister. Their expressions were all the same. For some reason, they were all very interested in him this morning. Miss Trinity was smiling her usual smile, but Martin had certainly been acting strangely.

"Your uncle has offered to take you to London with him to become his apprentice so you can learn to become a millwright."

"London!" Jonathan had fairly shouted his reply. His mouth was agape as he looked around the room.

"London?" He repeated more sedately.

"Yes," his father continued, "it is a good offer and your mother and I have discussed it in detail. We feel this could be the best course of action for you to continue with your education. Neither of us are thrilled that London is over three hundred miles away. That is a week's journey by coach. If it were anyone but your uncle, we would not be interested in this arrangement. But it is indeed your Uncle William and we are therefore inclined to accept his proposal. But, if you are opposed to the arrangement, then we shall look elsewhere to continue your education."

Jonathan was speechless. This offer was just the adventure he had been dreaming about for the past two years. The time with his uncle in their mill was some of the happiest moments that Jonathan had known. He and William had become fast friends and his uncle had been very patient in answering all of the questions from his young nephew about how and why things worked. He had also listened to Williams' stories about the great city of London and about his travels to other areas of England. He had been hoping for a proposal such as

this. Now here it was, at last. Not only was he going to get to see London, but he would be traveling throughout England as well.

"I can't think of anything that I'd rather do than what you have just proposed to me, today."

His mother made one last attempt, "Jonathan, my darling, are you sure about this? You would be a very long way from your family. I mean at least the rest of your family that will be here ..., that is ..., beside your Uncle William ..., Oh you know what I mean, dear."

"Yes, mother. I know what you mean. But I can't stay here forever. Even birds push their young out of the nest or so I've been told. I do believe it's time for me to learn to make my way. Besides, the only other place I want to go, is America, but that really is a long way. It's more like three thousand miles, instead of three hundred."

"Well, young man, you will not be going to America anytime soon! I can promise you that!"

"London will be just fine for now, mother."

John was satisfied. He could tell from Jonathan's reaction to the news that this was the right thing for him to do. He was thirteen, going on fourteen and it was time for him to have some different experiences in his life. He was pleased with the fact that his son and his brother had become close. If this had occurred ten years earlier, when William was unsettled, then it would have been a different story. But from what John had seen of the changes in his brother and the excellent work he had done installing the new equipment, his mind was at ease.

"I'll write to your Uncle William tonight, and we shall post the letter tomorrow morning. According to his letter, he will soon be heading to Manchester to begin construction on a new cotton mill there. The project is due to begin next month. That is where we will meet him. It may be six months to a year or longer before you are able to see the sights of London."

"That will be just fine, father. I haven't been to Manchester either. I don't think I've been out of Cumberland yet, have I?"

His father chuckled at that remark.

"No son, you have not. That is about to change, however. It is settled then. I'll make the travel arrangements. You and I will take a coach to Manchester. Once you're settled, and I'm satisfied with the arrangement, you will be under your Uncle William's care and supervision."

The realization that separation from his only son was just a matter of weeks away suddenly penetrated John's thoughts like a dagger. A large knot built up in his chest and was trying to force its way up and out through his eyes. He brought the napkin up as if to wipe his mouth, but the real target was higher. He coughed to hide the tears that had welled up. He turned and smiled at his wife, hoping no one had seen. She was not fooled and placed an understanding hand on his arm. It was time for John to grow up as well.

Kate turned to her brother with tears in her eyes and said to him, "Jonathan, I'm going to miss you so much. Johnny Paul has left me and now you're going away as well."

Miss Trinity teared up and brought her apron up to her eyes. She looked around the room at all the tears that were beginning to fall when Ann said, "Now, now, my dears, none of that. We should be happy for Jonathan. After all, as he said, even the mother birds push their young out of the nest, that is, when they're strong enough to withstand separation. I'm sure that my Jonathan IS strong enough and I'm confident that he is ready for the next step in his life."

She turned to her husband, smiled, and said in a quiet whisper, "Well, at least one of us didn't cry."

Chapter 8

THE JOURNEY TO MANCHESTER WAS ONE NOT to be taken lightly. Although travel conditions had improved throughout England, there were still many hazards that faced the traveler. Along with the coming separation from their only son, this hazardous journey was also one of the main concerns for John and Ann.

It would take five days of hard traveling to cover the distance of one hundred and forty seven miles to Manchester by coach. John had considered taking his own coach, but felt that they would be safer traveling with a group. There were still bandits around on horseback called 'highwaymen', or if they were on foot, they were called 'footpads' and these robbers continued to work the roads making travel dangerous.

The newly styled flying coaches were a significant improvement over the old style public coaches. They were advertised in the newspapers of the day thusly: *"For the better accommodation of passengers, altered to a new genteel two-end glass-coach machine that are on steel springs and exceedingly light"*.

John had gone to the booking office to secure seats for their journey. He would have to enter both of their names in the stage company's book and pay a portion of the fare to hold their inside seats. They would be traveling only during the day, because it was much too dangerous to travel at night, spending each evening of the journey, hopefully, at a 'posting house', but most likely in a 'hedge inn'. If he had been taking his own coach, there would be no question that they would be staying at a posting house, but since they had decided to take one of the flying coaches, they would spend the night in one of the English inns referred to as a hedge-inn.

The posting houses only entertained travelers of the highest class who posted in their own carriages or in post-chaises. They might accommodate gentlemen on horseback, if they were duly accompanied by their servants. Only under extraordinary circumstances, did they stoop so low as to take in the passengers that were riding on the common stage.

The hedge-inns were a good deal less expensive than the post houses, but the accommodations were still adequate. They usually charged around nine pence or one shilling for bed and supper. If you wanted a room to yourself, then you would be charged an extra six pence. The food in the hedge-inns was decent enough, but of course not of the quality of that found in the post houses.

The arrangements were made, usually to the next stop. Upon reaching the following day's destination, booking for the subsequent leg of the journey was required.

They were scheduled to be off at five o'clock the ensuing Monday morning. John returned home and began preparing for the journey. Traveling light was essential, because if their bags weighed over fourteen pounds, an extra charge was levied. Jonathan would be given extra money to purchase what was needed when he arrived in London, but until that time, they would be taking only the bare essentials. Most travelers, taking along extra money, carried two purses with them. The larger, carrying most of their funds, was hidden on their person; under a cloak, in a hat or even in the hollowed-out heel of a shoe. They would also have a much smaller purse containing a lesser amount of cash and it was usually carried in plain sight. If robbed, hopefully, the small purse was all the thief took. This conspicuous leather pouch was referred to as the 'robber's purse'.

John and Jonathan said their goodbyes to the family and arrived at the booking office at four o'clock Monday morning. At about 4:30, the coach arrived and began loading baggage.

The coach was quite elegant. The walls were lined on the inside with soft leather padding with two bench seats that were facing each other and large enough to accommodate six average sized passengers comfortably. The doors had glass windows that could be raised or lowered as the weather demanded.

The carriage was painted a glossy black, except for the doors, which were a bright red and the coach company's logo was inscribed on both the front and back. At the rear of the coach was a large open space to carry luggage or cargo. At the back of the "boot" was an elevated bench seat to carry as many as three additional passengers. Passengers were also allowed to ride on the top of the stage, but this was very uncomfortable. Brass rings were bolted onto the top, so these passengers could 'hang on' when the ride got rough. This particular coach was going to be pulled by a team of four beautiful bay horses. Each coach had its own name and this particular coach was known as *The Highflyer*. The driver of the coach, Walter Salter, was well known in the area. Walter was famous for his ability to play many different tunes on his horn as he approached villages, towns and finally, his destination. He would play 'Arthur O'Bradley' or 'Blackeyed Susan', as he came dashing into town, scattering pedestrians in all directions.

The cost of the journey to Manchester would be about two pence per mile or about fifty shillings one way. On top of these charges were tips for the coachman and the cost of lodging and meals, which usually added another fifty shillings. For John to get his son to Manchester was going to cost him at least one hundred shillings or about five pounds. Educating Jonathan was not going to be cheap.

As he and his father approached the coach, Jonathan noticed that there were two young ladies preparing to make the same journey. They were boarding the coach along with a chaperone. In the early morning light, it was difficult to make out who the three women were.

The older woman was dressed in a blue suede jacket with a tan suede skirt. Her hair was dark brown and thick. Her locks were arranged up on her head, underneath a large blue hat with a blue ribbon on the top and a blue feather about a foot in length, protruding from the side. Jonathan wondered if she was going to be able to wear that hat inside the coach.

The taller of the two girls was wearing a red cloak with a full hood that covered her entire head. She had a matching red muff and underneath her cloak, she was wearing a light green dress. Her movements were quick and deliberate, but very graceful, as she moved toward the coach.

The other young lady was about an inch shorter, with light brown hair underneath a dark brown woolen scarf. Her dress was a mustard color and was gathered tightly around her waist. As she waited her turn to board, she turned toward the two men. Jonathan suddenly recognized her and began to smile and raised his hand in greeting.

"Mary? . . . Mary Cook, is that you?"

A look of recognition came into her eyes as she broke into a smile. "Jonathan Lucas, what are you doing here? Did you come to say goodbye to us? "

"No, Mary, I'm going on this coach, as well. My father and I are off to Manchester to meet my Uncle William. I'm going to be his apprentice and live in London," he said with great satisfaction.

"Oh, how nice for you. That means that we shall have the pleasure of your company for our journey."

"Who do you have with you?" queried Jonathan.

"This is my friend I told you about, Ann Ashburn? She is with me, as well as my aunt, Felicity Cook. We are going to her home in Leeds to stay a few months and further our education. We're going to learn to speak French from a real Frenchman, who lives there and also study geography. I can already play the piano, as you know, but I'll be taking lessons from a fantastic pianist that is well known in Leeds. We shall also be practicing the latest dances from London and the Continent. We are both very excited!"

Mary's friend, Ann Ashburn, descended from the cabin of the coach and pushed back the hood on her cloak. Jonathan saw a rich, dark auburn head of hair and a set of sparkling pale blue eyes. She was also blessed with a flawless, ivory complexion. Ann extended a very elegant hand to Jonathan.

"Mary, my dear, aren't you going to introduce me to your handsome young friend here?"

"Ann, I would like for you to meet Jonathan Lucas. We attend Saint Nicholas Church together."

John walked up about that time and remarked, "Don't tell me that we have the great luck to be traveling with two such beautiful young women on this trip?"

"Mister Lucas, It is so nice to see you again, sir. Please meet my friend, Ann Ashburn. She lives in Cleator Moor, just over yonder." Mary turned and pointed eastward toward the rising sun.

"Yes, and it's a pleasure to meet you. I am familiar with your family. I believe your father was Richard Ashburn and he was married to Elizabeth Musgrove. Is that not correct, my dear?"

"Why yes sir, it is. I am flattered and honored that you know of my family," Ann said, as she executed a deep curtsy and bowed her head slightly in John's direction.

The chaperone started to exit the coach, but John stopped her, "Please, ma'am, don't go to the trouble. My name is John Lucas and this is my son, Jonathan. We shall become better acquainted over the next couple of days, I'm sure."

Mary smiled and said, "Mister Lucas, this is my aunt from Leeds, Mrs. Felicity Cook. We're going to stay with her to further our education."

John and Jonathan helped the two young ladies into the coach just as the sixth passenger with an inside ticket approached.

He said, "Good morning, ladies and gentlemen."

Jonathan and John turned to see a short, very well-dressed young man approach, wearing a top hat and carrying a cane with a large golden lion's head as a top knob. By his expression, he was obviously very pleased with himself. Jonathan recognized him immediately. His name was Hugh Dacre. He was the son of Thomas Dacre, who had figured in the financial ruin of his father's business partner, J.D. Younger. Younger had died just six months before, never recovering from the shock of losing his business and his girlfriend to Thomas Dacre.

The Dacre Family was descended from a ruthless group of individuals known as Border Reivers. The Reivers were made up of both English and Scottish clans that raided homes on both sides of a shifting border. It didn't matter on which side they fought, as long as the people they raided were weak, had no powerful protectors, or were not related by blood in any way to themselves. Their activities extended both north and south, depending on the border of which the raiders stayed, mostly within a couple of day's ride. It was reported that English raiders struck as far north as the outskirts of Edinburgh and Scottish raids were executed as far south as Yorkshire. There could be as few as two dozen men in a raiding party or as many as three thousand riders in a highly organized military campaign. Kidnapping and extortion were some of their favorite tactics. Ann Lucas' family, the Nobles, had been affected by this very same Dacre Family over one hundred years before. There had been a kidnapping for ransom of a Noble Family member by the Dacre clan and a subsequent murder had resulted. This had not been forgotten and there was still bad blood between the two families. "Reive" was an early English verb meaning "to rob".

Their two hundred year reign of terror came to an end upon the accession to the English throne of James VI of Scotland, who became James I of England. He moved hard against the Reivers, dealing out stern justice to them and their kind. The King effectively eliminated them as a band of organized mayhem, but emotions were still strong against descendants of the Reivers. People felt that old family habits often die hard and could be awakened again if the right opportunity unexpectedly presented itself.

Young Hugh Dacre seemed to be a chip off the 'old Reiver' block. He was arrogant and a bully in ways that reminded everyone that his family was once a prominent Reiver clan. Unlike his father, he was proud of his outlaw heritage. Jonathan had known Hugh while growing up. Hugh was a couple of years older and had delighted in taunting the younger boy at every opportunity and Jonathan had been intimidated by his constant bullying. Jonathan was delighted to find that the two young girls would be traveling with him, but suddenly his delight turned to dread, as he realized Hugh would be journeying as well.

The coachman, Author Salter, yelled in a loud voice, "All them that's going with me on *The Highflyer*, ye better get aboard and get settled. Them what's inside, I'm sure you're gonna have a comfortable journey. Them what's outside, pray we don't have rain. You better grab for the brass ring and hold on tight, for if you falls off, you'll have to walk and there'll be no refunds."

He walked around the rig of horses and coach looking closely for irregularities. Satisfied that everything was in readiness on the outside, he opened the door and looked into the now crowded cabin.

"Is everyone comfy?" he asked.

John looked around the cabin. It was a tight fit for everyone, but even Mrs. Felicity Cook's large blue feathered hat had managed to fit inside.

"I think we're as ready as we will ever be," John said as he smiled at the other passengers. The two younger girls sat with their backs to the driver with their chaperone in the middle. John and Jonathan had the outside seats facing the two young girls with Hugh Dacre sandwiched in between. Jonathan was sitting on the left-hand side facing Mary Cook, while John had the pleasure of facing the young Ann Ashburn. Hugh Dacre was not pleased with the fact that he was sitting in the middle, facing the older lady, Felicity Cook.

The coachman reached inside his breast pocket and pulled out a flask of brandy. Taking a long pull, he hacked and coughed. He shook his head and in a croaky voice he uttered, "By damn, that was a good breakfast to start the day. Now we'll be off."

He moved to the front of the coach and climbed up the wheels to the front box where two more passengers sat. Taking the reins in his hands, he shouted down to his post- boy, "Turn 'em loose."

Cracking his whip into the air, he yelled, "Hup-Hup, get up there, Molly."

As the coach lurched forward, Walter began to blow a song on his horn. The name of the tune he played was 'A Soldier And A Sailor'. They passed out of Whitehaven and were on the road to Egremont. Walter brought the horn down from his lips and started to hum loudly.

It was a beautiful sunrise in the month of May. The weather was as good as it got in that part of England during that time of year. The countryside began to fly by as the travelers peered out of the windows. It was a 'bluebird' kind of day and the bluebirds were chirping loudly at the flying coach as it rushed along the road to Egremont.

Not to be outdone by mother nature, Walter Salter pulled his flask out and after another long pull, began to sing the same tune he had blown on his horn earlier. In a very lusty, booming voice that was only slightly off key, he sang:

A Soldier and a Sailor,
A Tinker and a Tailor,
Had once a doubtful Strife, Sir,
To make a Maid a Wife, Sir,
Whose Name was Buxom Joan,
Whose Name was Buxom Joan.
For now the Time is ended
When she no more intended
To lick her Chops at Men, Sir,
And gnaw the Sheets in vain, Sir.
And lie o' Nights alone,
And lie o' Nights alone.

The soldier swore like Thunder,
He lov'd her more than Plunder,
And show'd her many a Scar, Sir,
That he had brought from far, Sir,
With fighting for her sake.
The Tailor thought to please her
With offering her his Measure.
The Tinker, too, with Mettle
Said he wou'd mend her Kettle
And stop up ev'ry Leak.

But while these three were prating,
The Sailor slyly waiting,
Thought if it came about, Sir,
That they shou'd all fall out, Sir,
He then might play his Part.
And just e'en as he meant, Sir,
To Loggerheads they went, Sir,
And then he let fly at her
A shot twixt Wind and Water,
That won this fair Maid's Heart.

With the jolting of the carriage and the lusty tenor of Walter's ballad, some of Jonathan's lost excitement and enthusiasm had crept back into his spirit. He was sitting across from Ann Ashburn and he found her new, fresh and exciting. She was as captivating as she was pretty. He had asked some questions about exactly where she lived in Cleator Moor. He had been to the village on numerous occasions, but they had never met. After she described her home to him, he knew exactly where it was located and told her he had passed by many times.

Ann felt giddy, as well. Although Ann wasn't considered poor, the loss of her father business three years before, under mysterious circumstances, had forced her family to live more conservatively. Her mother was a Musgrave and in years past, that family had also been linked to the Reiver lifestyle. The Musgrave's had also been in a long-running feud with the Dacre Family. Although quite young, Ann had remembered the old stories from her mother and had developed a natural aversion to the name, Dacre. She was polite to Hugh in conversation, but her smile was slight and her glances did not linger in his direction very long.

Jonathan Lucas was interesting and attractive to her. She was aware of the history of the Lucas and Noble Families from which this young man sprang. It seemed they had always been people of honor. This Jonathan was very attractive, although still quit young. Ann had a natural coquettish streak that was quite effective and she decided to try it out on the young man sitting in front of her.

When the coachman started singing, Ann suddenly joined in. Her voice was as pretty and clear as the coachman's was gruff and rugged. Hugh Dacre began trying to hum along as Ann sang harmony with the coachman. His voice was sour and off key. Jonathan glanced over at him and saw that he was just as enthralled with this young girl as he was becoming. Suddenly, there was a certain flash of jealousy in Jonathan's mind. He no longer dreaded being close to the bully. Instead, he was becoming just plain resentful of Dacre's presence in the coach. This feeling was exacerbated by Hugh's pathetic attempt to sing along. Just as he was about to express himself along those lines, Mary Cook joined in, singing a different harmony part. Jonathan was enchanted by the lilting sounds of Ann and Mary. To him, their voices sounded as if they came directly from heaven. Sitting close to these two pretty young women and listening to them sing along, coupled with the fact that he was on his first big life's adventure, was overwhelming for the young man. He was totally enamored with it all.

Jonathan looked across at his father, who was obviously enjoying himself, as well. John smiled and nodded to his son as if to say, "Enjoy this moment. This kind of bliss is very rare."

Thankfully, Hugh Dacre realized his voice was certainly not needed, so he had become silent. He was still staring intently at Ann Ashburn but she had chosen to sing directly to Jonathan. Dacre noticed the attention his bullied victim was getting and was not happy. He sat back with a glum expression on his face and folded his arms across his chest. Trying to mask his disappointment, he did manage a weak smile and a nod to Aunt Felicity.

When the song ended, John asked, "By Jove, that was splendid. Where did you girls learn that great old tune?"

"Oh sir, my mother plays the harpsichord and she has taught me to play and sing. We order sheet music from Carlisle and we have a very good library of music."

"Well, I can tell that you did not learn that particular song in church. But it was quite a contrast. Your two voices blended very well with the coachman's. I found it very pleasant. Perhaps the two of you could sing a few more for us as we continue on this journey."

Mary leaned forward, "Mister Lucas, we shall be glad to, but there is one condition."

"A condition. And what would that be?"

"I have often heard you sing in church and you have a wonderful voice. During the next tune, you must join in."

"But my dear Miss Cook, we are not in church today and I'm not sure that our coachman would appreciate our singing hymns."

"You are right about that, but I am sure that there are some songs that are of the common variety that are known to you. If we don't know them, you can teach them to us as we go along."

"My son, Jonathan, sings as well, you know. Perhaps we can all learn a new song or two. Together we'll have a regular 'Highflyer Chorus'. By the time we finish this journey we may be good enough to become professionals." With that they all had a great laugh, everyone except Hugh Dacre, that is. Hugh only managed another weak smile.

Mary glanced over at Jonathan and realized that the young boy she had known was turning into a young man. They had spent time together at church functions, and he had even tried to kiss her once on a church picnic. Actually, he had kissed her or perhaps she had kissed him. She noticed that he was watching her friend, Ann, with a look she had not seen before and Mary was not sure she liked it. Due to that circumstance, Mary considered switching seats with Ann at the next stop.

Jonathan was overcome with the moment. What a trip this was turning out to be. Enamored with Ann, the thought hit him. He was going to be leaving for several years and would not have the opportunity to see her again, anytime soon. He hoped he would be allowed to return to Whitehaven for the holidays. If he could talk his father and his uncle into allowing him to return once or twice a year, perhaps he would have the chance to see both Ann and Mary again. He had been very fond of Mary when they were children and as he looked at her sitting in the coach, he realized she had blossomed into a very attractive young woman.

Very different from Ann, she had a more demure look about her. Mary was an elegant young woman who was both poised and charming. The Ashburn girl was just as lovely, but she seemed strong and defiant. She was no shrinking violet, to be sure. Her manners were exemplary, but there seemed to be something bubbling just under the surface. In any event, this new adventure was already more exciting than Jonathan could have expected.

Chapter 9

THE COACHMAN BEGAN TO BLOW ANOTHER tune as they approached their destination late in the afternoon. The name of the tune was 'Blackbirds and Thrushes'.

It was a sad tune about a girl yearning for the return of her lover, Jimmy, who she fears will be slain in a far distant war. After a long absence, Jimmy returns safely home but finds that his love, Nancy, was lost instead and lies buried in the nearby forest. This time Mary sang the lead part as soon as she recognized the song the Coachman was playing. Jonathan and John led the girls in singing several other songs and the four voices blended fairly well together. Everyone inside and outside of the coach enjoyed it, except for Hugh Dacre. Dacre had tried to participate, but he couldn't carry a tune even if it had been loaded in the boot behind the coach.

The singing was accompanied by a beautiful sunset over the Irish Sea. Their journey had taken them along the seacoast and off in the distance, from time to time, the passengers would catch a glance of the Isle of Man. As they finished their ballads, the coach entered the last village on this leg of their journey. They were staying at an inn, called The George and Dragon, which was in the center of a small village known as Broughton in Furness. It was an ancient village mentioned in the Domesday Book, which was completed by William The Conquerer in the year 1086. Broughton in Furness was a little over thirty miles from Whitehaven.

The inn was not a difficult place to find. The George and Dragon was the most important building in the small town. It had a wide archway leading to an expansive courtyard. There were three tiers of galleries surrounding three sides of the enclosure. People were standing on the galleries as the coach entered. The inn's two signs proclaiming the entrance into The George and Dragon were enormous. One boasted a large painting of St. George on his white charger with lance lowered, ready for action. Opposite and facing St. George, was the dragon of legend, breathing fire at the oncoming knight.

The Highflyer slowed down as it passed beneath the arches and into the courtyard. They were welcomed by the landlord/proprietor, a rubicund man who had become rotund from too much drinking and feasting while entertaining his guests. He was a man of some wealth and position. Because of this, he ranked above the tradesmen and other merchants of the town. He had become the mayor of Broughton on Furness.

Followed closely by his wife, who was a tall, thin, homely woman with stringy grey hair, he reached out and opened the door of the muddy coach. Ann Ashburn was the first to emerge into the twilight.

"Oh how lucky we are today. We have a beautiful young lady to entertain," exclaimed the landlord. Hugh Dacre made a move to depart next, but was checked by Jonathan's right arm. "Ladies first, Hugh."

Dacre was taken by surprise.

"Miss Felicity, if you please," Jonathan continued.

As Miss Felicity moved to take advantage of the offer, Jonathan reached his hand over to Mary Cook. As she grasped his hand that he proffered gallantly, he commented, "And last, but certainly not least, especially in beauty." Mary smiled and then blushed, "My my Jonathan, how gallant you have become."

It was Jonathan's turn to blush as he added, "In the presence of so many beautiful ladies, how could you not be gallant."

He turned and looked Hugh Dacre square in the eyes as his smile evaporated. Dacre understood his meaning quite well and was not pleased at the sudden transformation that had just occurred in his former victim. The impertinence of his inference was obvious. But under the circumstances, without making a scene and with Jonathan's father watching, there was nothing he could do, but utter a weak, insincere agreement. After Mary stepped down, Jonathan turned and offered Hugh the opportunity to be the first man out of the coach.

Hugh sarcastically replied, "No, Master Lucas, after you."

"I was wrong," said the innkeeper, "We have three lovely ladies to attend to this evening!"

Altogether there were seventeen passengers that exited *The Highflyer* that evening. There had been six passengers riding inside of the coach, three riding on the boot bench in the rear, two tradesmen riding with the coachman and six more passengers that had been clinging precariously to the rings on the top of the coach. Without those brass rings, screwed into the top of the coach, it was almost certain that some would have been thrown from the rocking coach.

The innkeeper called out, "Thomas, where are you?"

A young man of about fifteen came running toward the coach.

"Get their luggage and bring it inside."

Hugh called out, "Miss Ashburn, . . . Miss Ashburn."

At the sound of her name, Ann turned and halted.

Hugh continued, "May I have a word with you?"

Ann, who had been walking with Jonathan, stopped and turned as Hugh called out.

"Do you mind, Jonathan?"

"Certainly not, I'll wait here."

Ann walked back to Hugh, who was standing a few yards away from the coach. As she approached him, he took off his top hat and put on his brightest, most charming smile.

"Miss Ashburn," he hesitated, "or may I call you Ann?"

"Of course, you may call me Ann," came the noncommittal reply.

"Ann, my father has rented a house not far from here, and I was wondering if you would like to have dinner with me this evening?"

"Why Hugh, what a very nice gesture. My friend Mary and her aunt will be delighted. But I'm not sure that it would be wise for us to accept, because we shall be departing very early in the morning."

"I was thinking of having only you over for dinner ... alone."

Ann's face flushed with color and her eyes flashed with anger.

"Sir, you know it would be impossible for me to accept an invitation without the presence of my chaperone. What do you take me for?"

"I am sorry, I did not mean to offend you. I would just like to have the opportunity to spend some time with . . . with just you. On our journey today I never had the opportunity to get to know you."

In a much softer, sexier voice Ann answered, "Hugh, I thank you for your compliment and also for wanting to get to know me better, but I'm afraid you'll have to wait for another opportunity."

Ann's first blush of anger at the forward invitation had passed. She was, again, in the coquettish mode that she usually possessed as she worked her feminine wiles on her young suitor. Even though she didn't care for the Dacres, in general, and this one in particular, one never knew what the future would bring. She believed in the old saying, 'Never burn your bridges'. After all, he was wealthy.

"Aren't you coming in, at least to say goodbye to Aunt Felicity and Mary?"

"No, it's too crowded in that place, but I do have a question for you."

"And what would your question be?"

"May I write to you in care of Ms. Cook's residence in Leeds?"

Ann hesitated a moment, as if thinking about the propriety of this proposal. She looked down for a full three seconds before lifting her head with a bright smile, "Of course. You may send me a letter." The relief on Hugh's face was tangible. Ann knew she had produced the desired effect, even on this boorish fellow. Her answer had been pure female instinct.

"I would be delighted to hear from you. It will be fun to correspond. I have never received a letter from a stranger before. I have only received a few from family members. Thank you for being so kind. I shall look forward to receiving your correspondence. But now, you must excuse me. I think it is time for me to join my friend and her aunt."

With that, she extended a graceful hand, which Hugh took as he bowed and kissed her offered hand. She curtsied and smiled politely, then turned and started walking to the entrance of the inn.

Hugh stood and watched as she walked away, noticing she looked as good from the back as she did from the front. Jonathan was waiting by the door and it pained Hugh as she took his arm and gave him a kiss on the cheek.

All of the passengers, but Hugh, had moved inside of the inn. The landlord was watching his young helper, who was attempting to unload the luggage from the boot of the coach. Hugh walked over to the innkeeper and proclaimed with a sideway glance, "My good man, my father is staying in a private residence nearby. If you would be so kind, I'd like to have my luggage delivered there."

"So you won't be staying with us this evening?"

"No, thank goodness for small favors!" Hugh had not been well schooled in the art of manners or gentility. A look of recognition dawned on the innkeeper.

"Oh yes, you must be the son of Thomas Dacre. I believe he's taken the House of Lord Pickford. Pardon me, sir. I should have recognized you sooner. Your father has told us to expect you. I am the mayor of this small village, and I have had some err -shall we say-business dealings with your father. He drives somewhat of a hard bargain. I shall be more than happy to have your bags delivered wherever you like, sir."

"That is more like it. I shall be sure and tell father of your kindness and cooperation," Hugh said smugly. He turned to walk away when the innkeeper added, "Of course, there will be an additional charge of a half shilling for each bag that I have delivered."

"That price seems exorbitant," retorted Hugh.

"It's the going rate sir, but if it's too much for you, then I'll ...."

"No, no, just have the bags sent over and father will be glad to pay."

Walter Salter, the horn blowing coachman, approached Hugh as he turned to leave once more.

"Laddie, you wouldn't be leaving without showing your appreciation for me getting you here safely and entertaining you along the way, would you now?"

"My God, I thought paying the exorbitant sums your company charged for a seat in that horrible coach would have been included in your pay. How much do you expect on top of the fare?"

"Gentlemans generally gives me a couple of shillings and fools with more money than brains, a full crown," was his caustic reply.

Grudgingly, he reached into his purse and pulled out two shillings. With a look of disgust on his face, he put them into Walter Salters' hands. Looking about the courtyard, he said in a rather loud voice, "Are there any other robbers around?"

With that he walked out of the grand entrance into the street and turned right toward his father's lodging.

Inside, the rest of the passengers were trying to arrange accommodations for the evening. The innkeeper's wife was aware that the passengers who traveled on the inside of the coach were charged more money than the other passengers and because John Lucas was the perfect portrait of a gentleman, she began negotiations for lodging and victuals with him.

"And what will you be looking for in the way of accommodations this evening, sir?"

"First, let's me defer to the needs of these ladies," replied John.

He turned to Felicity Cook and asked, "Would you like for me to make the night's arrangements on your behalf? I would not like to be seen as interfering with your personal plans, but if I can be of service, I would take great pleasure in assisting you and the two young ladies in any manner possible."

Felicity smiled and addressed John, "How nice of you to offer. If possible, we would require a private room with accommodations for three people."

The innkeeper's wife overheard her statement and said, "We have just the spot for the ladies. It's a corner room overlooking the street, as well as the courtyard, and the bed is large enough for all three to sleep very comfortably."

John turned to Felicity with a quizzical look and she replied, "If the room is clean and neat, it certainly sounds like it would be acceptable."

"My son and I will require accommodations that match those offered to these young ladies. I must also inquire as to your prices for these rooms "

"Normally, for sleeping quarters and the evening meal, it's one shilling. But since you're wanting private rooms, we'll have to charge an extra sixpence. Breakfast in the morning will also be an extra six pence. Now ain't that fair and reasonable for a gentleman like yourself?"

John looked once again at Felicity. She looked at each of the girls and nodded her head in approval.

"There's one other thing. If possible, we would like a private room for dining this evening, that is, if you ladies would care to join Jonathan and me for supper tonight? We would be most honored."

"We certainly would," Ann blurted out enthusiastically.

"Oh yes, auntie, may we please?" Added an excited Mary.

"Girls, girls, you mustn't show so much enthusiasm. It's not very ladylike." After chastising the girls, Felicity turned to John and said, "Of course, we accept your generous offer."

The innkeeper's wife was obviously pleased at the opportunity to earn extra income from this group of travelers.

She said to John, "Yes sir, we have a room that is perfect for dining. I'll have my girl here show you up to your rooms and your bags will be there shortly. The room for dining is right over there, just past the fireplace. Of course, there will be a slight charge for private dining. We'll have tonight's fare ready in one hour."

The innkeeper's daughter said, "Excuse me sir, if you'll follow me, I'll show you the way to your chambers."

They all turned and followed the girl up the stairs to the rooms. The bags were delivered and after freshening up, they all met at the appointed time, just outside the dining room. Inside, they were pleasantly surprised to find a large table that occupied the entire center of the room. The repast was already set out, waiting on them to arrive.

The table was covered with fowl, fish, meat pies and wild game. They all knew it was illegal to sell nature's delicacies. How the landlord was able to procure this illegal bounty no one knew, nor did they inquire. There were also slices of beef and veal that had been cut very thin and beaten until tender.

The places were set with silver dishes and wine glasses, instead of pewter mugs. They had even set out cloth napkins, which was very unusual for an English inn. Each place setting included a knife and a two-pronged fork. As they were seating themselves, the innkeeper's daughter brought in a large bowl of large boiled potatoes with salted butter. Good English beer and surprisingly, a very good Bordeaux wine was also provided.

The innkeeper had gone to great lengths to please his guests. This was not just an evening's dinner. It was a feast.

John knew he would be expected to leave a hefty tip for this kind of service and the variety of quality cuisine, in addition to the extra charge he had already paid for the private dining room. But it didn't bother him at all. He saw it as subsidizing the education of his son, Jonathan. It was time for him to learn how a gentleman entertained ladies. How to behave like a gentleman, under all conditions, would serve his son well in the coming years.

John and Felicity were seated at one end of the table and at the other end sat Jonathan with Ann on his left and Mary on his right. John watched the two young women entertain his son. They seem to be vying for his attention and John felt a little envious.

John was fond of both of the girls and thought they were very lovely and charming. He realized that Ann Ashburn's mother's family had also been a Reivers Clan. The Musgrove's did not, however, have the same black reputation as the Dacre's, but nonetheless, she came from Reiver's stock. Mary Cook on the other hand, was from a family that rivaled the Lucas and Noble Families in their antiquity and honor.

As John watched the interaction between the three young people, it seemed that Jonathan was becoming more attracted to the vivacious and outgoing Ashburn girl. He watched as she continuously reached out and touched his hand or his elbow and then drew closer to him during their conversations. She was certainly dominating the conversation. Jonathan was not ignoring Mary, but there was no doubt that Ann was more aggressive in her manner than Mary. John thought to himself, "That must be the Musgrove blood coming out in her." She was hard to ignore, for in addition to being a beauty, she ingratiated herself with interesting and humorous conversation.

Mary on the other hand, seemed to be more reserved, as one would expect from her breeding. She was certainly not shut out completely and managed to attract Jonathan's attention from time to time. Felicity Cook had been a very charming dinner partner and John had learned more about the family. All in all, the evening had gone quite well, however, it was growing late and they had to be up early the next morning.

The door opened and the innkeeper came into the room, apologizing for the interruption. John motioned for him to advance. "Pardon the interruption sir, but I have made the arrangements for your journey tomorrow and I have also done the same for the ladies. The coach leaves in the morning at dawn for Milnthorpe. You'll be traveling in a coach by the name of *The Good Intents*. The coachman on this trip is a friend of mine. His name is James Sharpe. There's been some trouble on this run in the last few months and while I don't want to alarm the ladies, I thought you should be informed about the matter. There have been a few highwaymen and footpads working this route, but with Jamie Sharp and his blunderbuss, Bess, along, I don't believe you'll have any trouble."

"My goodness, did you say highwaymen?" Asked an alarmed Felicity Cook.

"Aye, that I did ma'am, but you've no reason to worry. Jamie Sharp's a good shot with old Bess. I just thought it would be a good idea for you to knows, so that you could take precautions, just in case. We been trying to catch 'em and when we do, we's gonna hang 'em high to show what happens to footpads and highwaymen around this area."

"Hang 'em? How barbaric!" Mary had joined in the conversation. It was obvious she did not approve of hanging people.

"I think hanging's too good for them." It was Ann who chimed in with her opinion. "He should probably be drawn and quartered, don't you think, Jonathan?" Ann was not nearly as kind hearted as was her friend, Mary.

Jonathan replied to Ann, "Actually, if no one is injured, I find both punishments somewhat extreme."

Jonathan looked at Mary and smiled. She was pleased with his answer.

John turned to the innkeeper, "We appreciate all you have done for us. This was a fine meal and we certainly have enjoyed our stay so far. We'll be ready to leave first thing in the morning. It seems we have the good fortune to be traveling with these ladies for one more day and after that, they are off to Leeds and we will be going on to Manchester. We shall certainly regret the separation, but alas, all good things must come to an end."

Jonathan escorted the ladies out of the room while John settled with the innkeeper. He was generous with his tip and gave some extra shillings for the warning about the highwayman.

"How serious is this threat of highwayman and footpads around here?"

"We've had a few holdups about three months back. No one was hurt, but he did get away with some valuables. I just thought that a gentleman touring with ladies shouldn't take any chances with robbers. There's been a masked man who tried to hold up this same coach two weeks ago. He wasn't very good at it and seemed very nervous, I'm told. Old Jamie almost ran him over when he hopped out from behind the hedge and tried to stop the coach. He didn't seem to know what he was doing, but who knows if he'll try again or not. I just thought you ought to know, sir."

With that, the evening ended and they all retired to their rooms for some much needed rest.

Chapter 10

THE SECOND LEG OF THE JOURNEY WOULD take the travelers from Broughton in Furness through the village of Spark Bridge on to Haverthwaite.

They would cross the river Kent at a ford just above Levens Hall, which was the home of a famous ghost, The Grey Lady. Many people also claimed to have seen the ghost of a black dog who inhabited the stairs, along with a charming amicable lady who dressed in grey. Levens Hall also boasted a celebrated topiary garden, which was started in 1694. The journey with the three women was to end in the village of Milnthorpe.

The second coach was built much like the first one. The colors were different. The top of this coach was the same black color, but the bottom section of the coach was green, instead of red. Jamie Sharp, the new coachman, was not as entertaining as Walter Salter, so no singing or playing came from the coachman's seat.

The seating arrangement echoed the one from the previous day's journey. Jonathan found himself seated between Ann and Mary and Felicity and John sat facing them, just as a new passenger climbed inside. He wore a faded army uniform that had seen better days and he carried a large haversack strapped over his shoulder. He wore a large felt hat that was pulled down low over his eyes. He settled into the outside seat by Felicity. He was facing Mary, but offered no greeting as he entered the coach.

"Good morning, sir. How are you this fine day?" A very pleasant greeting from Mary to her fellow passenger.

"Morning, Miss," came a low, almost muffled reply, delivered without raising his head or his hat from his eyes.

Without bothering to inspect the coach, James Sharpe shouted down from the driver's seat, "Be you ready for the journey?"

The young man opposite Mary replied, "We're as ready as we will ever be."

"Aye, then, we'll be off."

There was a crack of the whip and the horses strained against the harness. The coach rocked forward, almost throwing Mary, Jonathan and Ann out of their seats, before rocking backward and thrusting them in the opposite direction. This driver was not nearly as careful of his passengers as had been Walter Salter. Unlike the previous day's beautiful weather, it was cloudy and a good bit cooler, as the green-bottomed stage rolled eastward. The Cumbrian Mountains rose to three thousand feet, just to the left of the coach.

As the journey continued, conversation with Jonathan was once again dominated by Ann. The stranger, opposite Mary, looked out of the window toward the mountains. His hat was placed at such an angle, so that it concealed his entire face from the other passengers.

Mary tried once again to engage the young man in conversation.

"And where, sir, might you be traveling this day?"

There was no reply from the man under the hat. Mary tried once again and said a little louder, "Sir, I was wondering what your journey's end might have in store for you today?"

The stranger turned slightly so that Mary could see part of his head. She realized to her horror that a large piece of the man's ear was missing. There was a large scar that reached from the ear down part of his jaw to his neck area. It was scarred over as if he had been struck with a downward thrust of a sword.

"Who knows where our journeys will end, when we start on them," he muttered. Realizing that Mary had noticed his scar by the look in her eye, he smiled faintly, and added, "Don't let that bother you, miss. This was a reward I got for serving king and country against the Frenches a few years back."

"I'm so sorry, I did not mean to stare. Please forgive me."

"Don't trouble yourself, miss. I've got more problems than a few startled stares. Now, if you'll excuse me, I'm going to try to get some more sleep, since I didn't get much last night."

"Of course. If you don't wish to be bothered with a female's idle chatter, then I will not force it upon you."

"It's not that at all, miss. I thank you for trying to pull me into conversation. I'm not used to riding on the inside of the coach with such fine folks. But the rest of the coach was full, and this was the only seat that was offered. I had to pay a little extra, but this trip is very important to me."

"I understand completely. Perhaps after you are refreshed, you can tell me some of the adventures you have obviously been through."

"Maybe so, ma'am, maybe so."

With that, the young man pulled his hat back down over his eyes and turned his head once again to gaze out the window of the coach at the distant mountains. Mary turned her attention to Jonathan and her friend, Ann. They had paused in their conversation long enough to overhear what had transpired between Mary and the cryptic stranger. They were not quite sure they had heard the young soldiers' words clearly, for he spoke in a very low voice.

John asked Felicity what she had in store for the education of her two charges. Felicity responded, "We have engaged the services of a Frenchman of distinction, who has traveled all over the world and is thought to be one of the best teachers in all of England. He has been in Leeds for two years and has been highly recommended to us by some of the finest families. He has experience at the court of the King of France and knows all of the latest waltzes from the continent. His name is Andre Duval. Perhaps you have heard of him?"

John responded, "A Monsieur Duval? I'm afraid I have not heard of him. But since we are on this journey, I can tell you an old story of another Monsieur Duval from France. This Duval was a highwayman. It will be an interesting way to pass some time, but I'll relay the story only if you're interested."

All three of the ladies and Jonathan replied in unison, "Yes, that would be fun." They were excited to hear about a highwayman, especially as they were passing through a lonely, dangerous looking country.

John began his tale. "The most gallant of the highwaymen was a French-born outlaw named Claude Duval. He was even adored by the young ladies that he held up. He was always very particular to make use of his so-called 'Gallic Charm'. His manners were always impeccable as far as his lady quarries were concerned! He once even had the audacity to dance with a beautiful young lady of high breeding after robbing her and her husband of £100. Monsieur Claude Duval was one of the most polite highwaymen to ever rob English travelers. Unfortunately for our gallant highwayman, he was soon apprehended and sentenced to hang by the neck until dead. He was put on the gallows and hanged at Tyburn on 21st January 1670. They buried the chivalrous Frenchman in Convent Garden. His grave is marked by a gravestone with the following words inscribed: "Here lies Duval, if male thou art, look to your purse, if female, to thy heart."

Mary looked as if she would swoon. Felicity reacted with the comment, "Such an ill use of a gentlemanly life."

Ann chimed in, "How exciting his short life must've been. I am certain he would be a very interesting character to have known. I wonder if our Monsieur Duval could be a descendant of this most chivalrous outlaw?"

"I certainly hope not. But I can ensure you that I will make certain of that fact as soon as we arrive in Leeds." Felicity was in no mood to take any chances after hearing the story.

"I wouldn't worry too much about the possible connection. The story that I related to you is almost one hundred years old."

"Nevertheless, it is my duty to make certain from whom these girls will be receiving lessons. And further, I had better monitor what is being taught to them by this Frenchman," Felicity said with such sincerity that they all had a good laugh. Everyone that is, except the faded soldier who continue to stare out of the window.

"Can you tell us another story about highwaymen? Who is the most famous one of them all?

John thought for a moment and said, "Let me think . . . the most famous of all highwaymen. I think that would probably be a scoundrel they hanged way back, I believe in 1739. Let's see if I can remember how it goes."

John closed his eyes and rubbed the sides of his head as he tried to remember enough of the story to entertain his traveling companions.

"I think the story goes something like this. The man's name was Dick Turpin. He is probably the most infamous highwayman of all. If you mention his name to people who know about such things, they will tell you he was a daring, dashing highwayman who operated between London and York. He rode a beautiful mare he named Black Bess. He is supposed to have ridden from London to York in less than a full day. Some say it only took him fifteen hours to make the trip. However, I'm not sure that I believe that part of his story."

"Turpin, I think, was born in Essex. His father was a man named John Turpin, who was a small farmer and a keeper of the Crown Inn. As a youth, he conducted himself in a careless and rebellious way. He tried opening a butcher's shop, but he soon began to steal sheep, lamb and cattle from his neighbors to stock his shop. They caught him and he was forced to flee to save himself. Next, he tried smuggling, but he was as inefficient at that profession as he had been as a rustler. Turpin, by this time, had assembled a gang of other crooks and cutthroats around him. They called themselves the Essex Gang. Before long, custom's men caught on to him and compelled Turpin and his cutthroats to lay low.

Forced into the woods by the law, Turpin and his gang began to target remote farms. The farms were usually occupied by old people or females, widowed and living alone. They would break into their homes at night, terrorizing and torturing

DICK TURPIN *Clearing the Old Hornsey toll bar* **GATE,**
TO THE SURPRISE OF HIS PURSUERS.

the inhabitants until they surrendered their treasures. It is said that Turpin heard of an old woman who kept a lot of money in her house. He threatened the woman with all sorts of terrible torture. The old widow was very brave and defied all of the gangs' efforts to find out where she had hidden her money."

Ann was affected by the story of the old widow woman and remarked, "Good for her. Women can be just as strong as men."

"That's true, Ann. But as it turns out her strength and courage were not enough that night. The villains hung the old widow woman over the fire in her own fireplace. It wasn't until the flames began to burn her clothing that she finally gave up the £500 pounds she had concealed."

It was Jonathan's turn to add a comment, "The villains! To treat an old woman that way is just not civilized." John nodded in agreement and continued his story.

"Raiding isolated farmsteads was what the gang did best and most often. Turpin and his companions continued to rob and torture until they had amassed quite a fortune. By 1735, Turpin and 'The Essex Gang' had become famous and were talked about and reported on in newspapers all over England. Finally the crown took action and offered a reward of £50 for their capture. Because of the reward, the authorities were able to capture two of them. Turpin decided it was getting too hot to stay around, so he headed into the East Anglian countryside and lived in the forest quietly for some time. Before long, he began partnering with a man known as 'Captain Tom King'. He was one of the most notorious highwaymen of the day. The two of them found a cave in Epping Forest that could not be seen from the road below, because of the surrounding forest, but they had a good view of the highway. From this vantage point, they could watch the road without being seen by their victims. They robbed anyone who passed close to their hiding place. By 1737, Turpin and Captain Tom King had gained such infamy that the crown put an additional bounty of £100 on their heads.

Now it was Felicity's turn to comment, "If you get the reward money high enough, that will generally result in their capture."

"Aye, it certainly got people looking for him," was John's reply. "Later that year, a gamekeeper by the name of Morris, tracked the outlaw to his hideout in the Epping Forest cave. A gun fight erupted and Turpin shot Morris dead for his trouble. Turpin dragged Morris down the hill to the road where he laid the dead man's body out on the highway for the authorities to find."

By now, all three of the ladies and Jonathan were leaning forward, hanging on every word of his tale of the outlaw and his derring-do. The soldier with half of his ear gone, had even turned slightly and was listening intently as John relayed the story of this fugitive from law and justice. John paused long enough to look around at his audience.

He smiled and continued, "Turpin's next adventure was a very strange one, indeed, and it cost him dearly in the end. It seems that late one evening, he was on the road to London when he saw an extremely handsome horse that he took a fancy to. It was being ridden by a man named Major. When they came abreast of one another, Turpin pulled his pistol and forced Major to trade his beautiful horse for the outlaw's own worn-out nag.

Major issued handbills and placed them around the pubs of London. In these handbills, he described his stolen horse, and accused Turpin of being the thief. Before long, the horse was found near the Red Lion Pub in Whitechapel. Turpin sent Captain Tom King, his partner, to retrieve Major's stolen horse from its hiding place near the pub. The magistrates were waiting and the unsuspecting King was placed under arrest. Turpin saw his friend being captured and rode toward the men holding King. He shouted to the constable, "Release my friend Tom or face the consequences." They refused his demand and replied, "Come and get him." Then, Turpin drew his pistols and fired at them in an attempt to free his partner. But his plan went awry. Instead of shooting the magistrates, the bullets hit his poor partner."

John stopped a moment to catch his breath. He knew that his tale of this highwayman was high entertainment for his young listeners. He had also noticed that even the young soldier had raised his hat from over his eyes and was listening intently as the story was beginning to build to its conclusion. John asked, "Shall I go on or are you bored with this story? "

They all answered as if with one voice, "Finish it finish it. What happened to him? We want to know."

John continued his story of the most famous English highwayman. "Just before his death, King gave the constables enough information about Turpin to force him to return to Epping Forest. Even that former haven was no longer safe for him. Turpin realized if he was to escape capture and probable hanging, he had to leave the London area. He decided to travel to Yorkshire and hide out for a while. Here he took the false name of John Palmer, rented a house in that pseudonym and started to live quietly, but well. He fell back into the life of horse stealing and cattle rustling and supplemented his income with an occasional highway robbery. He was smart enough not to commit any crimes where he lived, committing most of his foul crimes in Lincolnshire. All had gone well, until one day after returning from an unsuccessful hunt, he shot a rooster belonging to his landlord. The landlord protested to Turpin. Turpin allowed his temper to get the best of him, and threatened to kill the landlord if he didn't shut up. The landlord made a complaint to the local authorities and John Palmer was taken into custody. The local constables made queries as to how 'Mr. Palmer' earned the money he was spending so freely. Soon they found out about several outstanding complaints that had been made against 'John Palmer' for cattle and horse rustling in Lincolnshire. Turpin was held in the dungeons of York Castle while the charges were investigated. Things might have gone in another direction if he hadn't written a letter to his brother, asking him to find some person or persons from London who could give him a character reference. He thought that a good testimonial would go a long way toward an acquittal of the pending charges against him.

His brother was too cheap to pay the sixpence postage due on the letter and wasn't very fond of his brother either, so he returned it to the post office, unopened. In a most curious occurrence, Turpin's former schoolmaster, a Mr. Smith, saw the letter and thought he recognized the handwriting. The letter was taken to a local magistrate and together they opened it. Smith was able to identify the writer as the infamous Dick Turpin. The authorities sent Smith to York where he made a positive identification. Since Turpin was already in custody, they tried him very quickly.

Turpin was convicted on two charges of murder; one for the game warden named Morris and one for the shooting of his partner Captain Tom King. He was sentenced to death by hanging. His father appealed the sentence and asked to have the condemnation reduced from death to imprisonment, but his efforts fell on deaf years. It was to be the gallows for Dick Turpin.

He was allowed frequent visitors to his cell, where they drank and partied as if there was nothing amiss. Up until a few days before his execution, visitors continued to visit Turpin's cell. He was also allowed to buy new clothes and a pair of shoes with silver buckles for his execution. He hired five mourners for his funeral and paid them ten shillings each. On a cold windy April morning in 1739, Dick Turpin took his final ride through the streets of York. He stood in an open oxcart, bowing and smiling to the gaping people who had lined the streets to watch the morbid precession. To them, Dick Turpin was a hero.

They carried him to the York Racecourse, where he climbed the scaffold and waited for over half an hour while passing the time of day and joking with the guards and even his own executioner. Finally, he looked about him and after speaking a few words to a cattle topsman he spotted in the crowd who yelled that Turpin had robbed him a year before, "Hey, you, did not I take some of your cattle a few months ago?"

"Aye, that you did, but I'll not be holding a grudge against you for past deeds. God bless you and God rest your soul."

Then as cool as could be, the highwayman, Dick Turpin, stood up, placed the hangman's rope around his own neck and jumped off the ladder to his death. It took him about five minutes to die. And that's what happened to this so-called gallant outlaw. I suppose that if his life had not been brave or gallant up to that point, in death at least, he finally showed some gallantry that had evaded him during his life of crime."

There was complete silence inside the coach. Each of John's listeners was caught up in their own thoughts. The soldier let out a long sigh and turned away to look out of the window again. Jonathan and Ann both sat back and looked at each other. Felicity pulled a linen kerchief out from her sleeve and dabbed her eyes. John had done an excellent job of keeping his fellow travelers entertained with his stories of adventure. Mary was the first one to speak.

"That poor man. What an awful way to have lived and then such an awful way to end his life. Choking for five minutes on the end of a rope must have been awful. Imagine if, when he was young, someone had taken the time to show him a better way to live. If only someone had given him some guidance and occasional help, he might have accomplished many good things. He could have had a family and lived a productive life. Instead, think of the harm he caused and the misery he spread. How horrible. Even though he faced death with courage in the end, he was still being strangled to death at the end of a hangman's rope. I see nothing gallant about that."

John was concerned that he had upset Mary with his tale.

"Mary, I didn't mean to distress you, my dear, but I was asked who was the most famous highwayman of all, and this was his story."

"Oh no sir, it was most entertaining and informative. These kinds of stories should be read to all young people so they can know that even if their circumstances are not the best, choosing the way of lawlessness always leads to the grave." John replied, "You are correct in viewing these stories as you do. Although they are entertaining, each one of them contains a lesson in life. And you are right to point out that the end is always the same. It's either the hangman's noose, or if you're lucky, you're transported away from family and friends to work as a slave for a long period of time. When that sort of light is shown on that ill manner of life, I believe that even simple people would make the correct choice and elect to stay with the life they are given."

The scenery was beginning to change. The coach was rapidly drawing away from the Cumbrian Mountains and entering into the estuary plain of the Kent River. In the distance, the Irish Sea was still visible beyond the marsh. The coach turned northeast as it passed through the small village of Lindale. They headed toward the village of Leven, where they were to cross the River Kent.

When they arrived at the Kent, everyone was able to stretch their legs as the coach and passengers boarded the ferry for the short river crossing. Once again, Mary tried to engage the young soldier in conversation. He only nodded, turned away and nervously walked to the other end of the barge. They remounted the coach and soon passed close by Leven Hall, home of the famous Grey Lady ghost. They could see the stately mansion in the distance surrounded by the topiary Gardens, but they did not spy the ghost. They were once again heading south and soon reached Leasgill. This village was so small that Jamie Sharp didn't even bother to slow down or blow his horn. Chickens, pigs, goats, sheep, and people all scattered to get out of the way of the bounding coach. The young man in the faded soldier suit had been sitting up for the last half hour and had his hand in his haversack. Mary watched him as he glanced around the coach. She saw there was a tenseness in his face and bearing.

Suddenly she heard him mumble to himself, "Is he not going to slow down here?" After they passed through the village, Mary noticed that some of the tension had eased somewhat.

There was one more village between the travelers and their destination, called Heversham. The approach to Heversham was narrow and wooded. The marshes from the Kent estuary intruded to within a few hundred yards of the pathway. The road was deeply rutted and very muddy and the smell of the salt air was very strong. The horses slowed down almost to a walk at this point. Mary was trying not to stare at the young man who was obviously having some conflicted thoughts. She heard him mumble under his breath, "I can't, I can't!" Then she heard him say again to himself, "but I must- I have to- I have no choice."

He was obviously disturbed about something. Suddenly the young man opened the cover on his haversack and reached inside. When he withdrew his arm, there was a pistol in his right hand. He reached over and double cocked the weapon with his left. At the clicking sound all eyes turned to the soldier. There was an audible gasp as they realized they were facing their own footpad and this was no story. The reason for the young man's shyness and mysterious behavior was now fully revealed to his fellow passengers.

Ann was the first to recover from the shock enough to speak, "Soldier, have you lost your senses? This is not humorous. Put that gun away." She leaned toward the robber as if she was going to grab the pistol.

John reached out and blocked her with his arm and said in a very stern voice, "Be still. All of you, be still."

The one-eared soldier began to speak, but at first the words would not come. He tried again without success. Finally, after clearing his throat a third time, he was able to get out, "Your money or your life!" It was obvious they were dealing with an amateur highwayman. The hand that held the pistol was trembling as it was pointed from passenger to passenger. John was afraid that if someone made the wrong move, there would be very serious consequences.

"All of you remain very calm and do as this young man requests. I'm sure that he does not mean to harm anyone. We can all replace valuables, but we cannot replace lives."

"That's very sensible of you, but believe me, I know how to use this and I will, if I have to. Now, hand over your valuables."

He pulled the haversack off his shoulders, held it out to John and said, "Let's start with you. I've noticed that purse you carry on your belt. Please put it in the sack, along with the stick pin and the ring on your hand."

John did as he was instructed.

"Careful, not one false move. I don't want to hurt anyone, but I will do what I have to do. You ladies next. Your purses first and then your jewelry."

The women put their purses in the haversack, as instructed and began to remove their jewelry.

Mary had noticed that the robber was becoming more nervous and fearful as the robbery continued. It was also obvious that he was new at this and perhaps, not fully committed. As Mary was taking off her earrings, she looked the young man directly in the eyes and said sincerely, "You understand that with the wound to your ear and down the side of your neck, you will be very easy to describe, and therefore easily recognized and captured. You have just finished hearing about the exploits of the most famous highwaymen who have tried to solve their problems in this manner. In the beginning they are like you, driven by some necessity to start down this road. Then things don't go as planned and they turn into just plain rouges, with no thought for anyone but themselves. They all ended up in the same way, choking on the end of a rope. You look to be an intelligent fellow. What has driven you to try something like this? You must know what your end will be if you carry through with this."

The soldier's face was covered in beads of sweat. He reached up with his free hand and wiped the perspiration from his eyes. He swallowed hard and replied to Mary, "Ma'am, I served in the Army, where I got this scar. I've been back a year and a half. I have a wife and baby at home with no way to make a living. We were working salt pans over on the river and just after I returned, an extra high tide came through on a storm and washed everything away. We had no money to rebuild, so we lived on borrowed funds and there's no more to borrow. It's either this or starvation for me and my family."

"No, that is not the only thing left. If you will forgo this . . . this . . . foolish attempt that you are certainly not cut out for, then I can promise you that I, and I believe the rest of my friends here, can offer some assistance to you."

"Begging your pardon, ma'am, but the only help that the likes of me is likely to receive from the likes of you, is helping me to the gallows or to a slow death of starvation."

"That is not true. I cannot speak for other people. I can only tell you that we are all God's children and I live by the maxim 'do unto others as you would have them do unto you'. Give up this folly and I'll see there are no ill consequences."

"I wish that I could believe you ma'am and I do believe you, but there are others in this coach and they carry no such charity in their hearts."

Mary looked at Jonathan, Ann, Felicity and John.

"You have all heard what I have just told this young man. Are you in agreement with my sentiment on this?" Asked Mary.

Jonathan looked at his father who replied, "I will agree to your proposal Mary. Let me add to your proposition. I would be willing to loan this young man some reasonable funds to tide his family over. He will have to sign a note for the money to be repaid when he is able. If he can make his way to Whitehaven, I will give him employment in my tobacco warehouse."

"Mary turned back to the young man, and said, "Mister Lucas is the owner of a factory that manufactures sails. He is, additionally, an importer of tobacco from America. I believe he is also involved in the coal trade with Ireland. His is an offer not to be despised."

"Yes, but can he be trusted? How do I know that as soon as I lay down my weapon he won't turn me in to the authorities?"

"I have known Mister Lucas all of my life. I can assure you that he is a gentleman of the highest caliber. If he gives you his word, there is no better guarantee, except that the sun will surely come up tomorrow."

Felicity felt obliged to support her niece and said, "I will also see that you are treated fairly and there will be no repercussions on my part."

That left only one person who had not agreed to the arrangement. At first, Ann had taken the robbery attempt as a personal insult but she had soon realized that the young man was serious, nervous, inexperienced, and therefore, very dangerous. Her anger had turned to anxiety and fear. Mary knew her friend well and in a firm voice said, "That leaves you, Ann. I know that it is difficult for you, but before we can continue this conversation and hopefully end all this in a positive way for us all, we must have your word."

They could all see Ann struggling to come into agreement with her fellow passengers. She was a proud, passionate, young woman and did not take kindly to being wronged. She glanced at John and Felicity, swallowed hard and looked directly at the young man with the pistol. The barrel of the weapon looked as big a water barrel. She said in a firm and even tone," You have my word, as well."

The young man rubbed his face again. He looked around at his fellow passengers as tears welled up in his eyes. He glanced out of the window toward the estuary and said, "I'll be leaving you here now." He tossed the haversack to John and then uncocked his pistol.

"Miss, I just want to tell you that I think you may have saved my life tonight. I thank you and bless you for that."

He reached out to open the door and Mary caught his hand.

"Before you leave, what are you debts?"

"If I had one hundred guineas and a job, then my life would be worth living once more. I could provide for my family."

John offered, "We'll be staying at the Bird in the Hand Inn tonight. If you are serious about starting a new life, come to the inn and give us that pistol. Then I'll give you the name of my lads in Whitehaven, along with a letter from me, and then we'll see about taking care of some of your debts."

Looking at Mary, the soldier said, "You, ma'am, you must have been sent from heaven. You're a real angel. Not only have you saved my life tonight, but perhaps you've also saved my soul."

With that, the door was thrown open, and in the wink of an eye, the young man was gone. The five of them sat silently as the coach moved through the twilight. It occurred to them that without Mary's intervention, this robbery could have turned out much differently for all concerned. John was amazed at the courage she had shown and at the depth of her sincerity. She was truly concerned about the future of this troubled young man.

Although this was their last night together, none of them said very much for the rest of the evening. John arranged for another private dining room and the fare was filling, although not quite up to the standards of the food set out the night before. The young man did not show up until after they had retired to their rooms. There was a knock on the door and when John opened it, there was the young ex-soldier holding the pistol in his hand. This time the butt was pointed towards John.

"Come in, sir. Let me prepare the letter of recommendation for you. On the table is a pouch with one hundred guineas. You must give me your name and the name of the town where you live."

"My name is Alan Bercher. I come from the village of Arnside. That's where I would've been headed if . . . if . . ."

"Yes, I know. Let's not worry about that now.

I will prepare a note for you to sign for the loan and the letter of introduction to my foreman at our tobacco warehouse. His name is Barton. He'll fix you up with a position. We'll start you with loading and unloading tobacco ships. I'll also instruct him to find a place for you and your family to live that's nearby."

"Sir, I do not know how to thank you."

"Don't thank me, thank the young lady named Mary."

Chapter 11

THE NEXT MORNING, JOHN AND JONATHAN said goodbye to their three female traveling companions. The ladies were off to Leeds and the gentlemen were on to their rendezvous with William in Manchester. The remainder of their passage to Manchester was as uneventful as the first part of the journey had been eventful.

The last stop on the trip before reaching Manchester was at the fast growing town of Preston. Here, fifty years before, a famous battle had been fought between the Hanoverian government forces and the Jacobite rebel army. The war was an attempt by James Francis Edward Stuart, who was also called the Old Pretender, to regain the British throne for the exiled House of Stuart.

The battle was fought between November 9th and 14th of the year 1715. This war was often referred to as the *First Jacobite Rising*. Some of the buildings still carried the scars of that long-ago fight. John took this opportunity to teach a little history to his son. They spent their last evening together sitting by the fire at the Black Swan Inn. Jonathan was especially gripped by the stories of Rob MacGregor. MacGregor was one of the Jacobites that had fought at Preston. Customarily known by the name of *Rob Roy*, he had become a famous Scottish hero and outlaw. People in Northern England and Scotland had dubbed him the Scottish Robin Hood.

The next morning they boarded another coach for the last leg of their journey from Preston to Manchester. *The Manchester Machine*, as it was called, had seating for six people inside, as well as in the front and behind the coachman, it could carry four more. On the back of the coach, where the bags customarily were stored, was more seating within a rear platform with a raised bench. There were eight people atop with their legs and feet dangling over the sides. They were holding firmly to the brass rings. The distance between the two towns was about thirty-six miles. There were only a few fells and hills in this part of England, so the last part of the journey was covered with relative ease. The last two coaches they had taken were crowded with strangers and their conversations were very pedestrian and uninteresting. It seemed even more so as they no longer were able to be entertained by their three female companions that had taken a different road two days before.

They arrived in Manchester and soon found the residence that William had rented. The two-story corner house was close to the cotton mill project that he was designing for his clients. William was delighted at the arrival of his brother and nephew. John relayed the adventures of their travels to William over a glass of port. William was outraged as John recounted the attempted robbery by young Alan Bercher.

"Let me understand this, brother. Instead of turning this villain in to the local authorities, you have loaned him one hundred guineas and offered him a job in Whitehaven, working for you in your warehouse?"

"But uncle, you don't understand? It was Mary, who was able to persuade him to not rob us. It was really quite extraordinary. I was afraid for a moment that he was going to shoot her. And I think he would have shot Ann, for she looked as if she was about to try to take the pistol away from him all by herself. I had to help father restrain her. You should have seen Mary. She must've been divinely inspired to have had the courage and wisdom to step in and talk the soldier out of committing a travesty."

"John, is that true?"

"Yes!. Both of the young ladies showed quite a bit of spunk in the face of adversity. It was very interesting and curious. The bravery they exhibited was very different. Ann, the more passionate of the two, was ready to charge the cannon, and she would have, I believe, if we had not restrained her. And Mary Cook did not back down either. She appealed to the young man's better side and was successful in eloquently talking him out of a life of crime. It was quite an extraordinary display for one so young."

"Mary must have been passionate and persuasive, for she not only talked him out of the robbery, she talked you out of one hundred guineas!" All three of the men had a good laugh at John's expense.

"Well, I'm just glad that you two have arrived safe and sound. I'm looking forward to teaching Jonathan more about the millwright trade. There is so much change and growth going on in this area that if he becomes proficient, I believe his future will be secured."

William turned to his brother's son, and said, "Now nephew, I believe it is time for you to be off to bed. Your father and I have the final details of your apprenticeship to work out tonight."

"But uncle, it's early and I'm almost fourteen years old," Jonathan protested. His father smiled knowingly at William and explained to his son, "You must, from this moment forward, do as your uncle says. He will be your legal guardian while you are an apprentice under him."

Jonathan was not happy, but rose in compliance. Bidding them both a good night, Jonathan retired to his room.

"William, is it absolutely necessary for him to spend seven years as an apprentice so far away?"

"If he is to become a master millwright, it is what the law states. He already has a lot of the knowledge needed, so I do not believe it will take much more than four to five years for him to gain the necessary experience. But the art of being a millwright, is just that; it's an art, really. Building facilities like grist mills for grinding wheat into flour is simple enough. Your son can do that within six months. It's the newer mills that are being invented, such as this cotton mill I'm currently building, that Jonathan must learn about. The new equipment that we put in your mill just two years ago, is already in some ways, outdated. It seems like some different visionary invents a new system every year."

"Well, William, how much are you going to charge me as a premium for apprenticing my son?"

"Come now, John, he is my nephew. The only thing I would ask of you is to send him an allowance on a regular basis. He is growing up quickly and he will soon be a young man. He acts like a man even now, from all you've told me. His attraction to the ladies on your journey is evidence that Jonathan is growing in many ways. One of my main objectives is to assist him in growing into a gentleman of honor and integrity, who is known throughout England and beyond, as an extraordinary millwright. I hope that I can also help him avoid the mistakes you and I made with the ladies. I sincerely believe that Jonathan will grow into a fine gentleman whose career will flourish."

The brothers had a hearty laugh at William's statement about the young women. It had been a long time since the two of them had been out romancing the ladies together. John's marriage to the beautiful Ann Noble had put an end to his carousing. William had never married, but had become wedded to his career. As a young man he had engaged in his fair share of affairs with the young female citizens of Whitehaven. He still enjoyed women and found them interesting and attractive, but usually not as captivating as his work.

John rested for a few days before his return to Whitehaven. William took advantage of the extra time with his brother to introduce him to Richard

Arkwright, who had designed the equipment they had installed in John's mill back in Whitehaven. Arkwright invited John and William to have dinner with some of his perspective partners. The men were Jedediah Strutt, Ichabod Wright, Samuel Need and John Smalley.

Jedediah Strutt was also a millwright and had invented a machine called the Derby Rib. It produced stockings made of cotton that were quickly becoming very popular. The reason for this popularity was that cotton stockings were much cheaper than silk and considerably more comfortable than traditional English woolen hose. However, the demand for the cotton stockings was far exceeding what they were able to supply, so the gentlemen decided to meet to hopefully find a solution to the production problem.

William had been talking to the partners about the use of water power to drive their equipment. He had traveled extensively throughout England and had a thorough knowledge of many of these different types of mills. Most people thought only the grinding of grain was done efficiently by water driven machines. But, William and John knew many other industries were now powered by this natural resource.

William decided to relate the story of one of the most successful water powered manufacturing businesses in all of England.

William began. "I'm going to share a story with you that you will perhaps think I'm making up. I can assure you, that is not the case. It is a story of intrigue, success, and ultimately, punishment worthy of the gods. Good fortune has a way of bestowing her blessings on some people, while withholding her benefits to others. How many of you have heard of John Lombe?"

"Isn't he the man who built Lombe's Silk Mill in Derby? He and his half-brother, Thomas, were involved. They manufactured and marketed silk, if I recall correctly?" Queried Samuel Need.

"Yes, and the family has become very wealthy doing it," replied William. "They built a silk mill in 1722. It has always been continuously powered by the River Derwent."

"Have you seen this mill in operation?" Asked Samuel Need.

"Yes, I have. It's located on the west bank of the river and is a fine piece of workmanship by the builder. They decided to build it at this location, because it's where a fish weir had been constructed on the river. They built the mill on an island downstream on the exact site of the old fish weir. The site was ideal as three existing corn mills continue to operate on water power nearby. The silk mill is built on a series of three stone arches that allow the waters of the River

Derwent to flow through and power their waterwheel. This particular spot was a key location as the river has a strong and swift current flowing past the site. In addition to this excellent location, the London to Carlisle road crosses nearby and gives access to markets, both north and south. It also is equidistant to both London and Edinburgh.

The story of how this came to be smacks of intrigue that would do justice to the court of the king himself."

"I thought we were talking about how to power our mills? There doesn't seem to be much intrigue in that," commented an impatient Ichabod Wright.

"I think you will find the details of this epic tale as interesting as I do. As I understand it, in the last century, the English production of silk stockings produced by now antiquated framework knitting had moved out of London to the Midlands. They had the same problem you gentlemen do, as the demand for their spun silk was outstripping their ability to supply their markets."

William paused to catch his breath and to let his audience catch up on the story. He enjoyed the looks of intense interest he was receiving.

"It seems that John Lombe had obtained a position at a silk mill in Derby, built by the well-known millwright, George Sorocold, for a Mr. Thomas Cotchett of Derby. Now here's where the story gets interesting. The Italians, it seems, have been using water power to drive spinning for over a hundred years. The Italian machines had been turning out fine organzine thread which was of better quality than the English thread. As you may or may not know, organzine consists of raw silk warp threads. If you are going to weave fine silk cloth, then you must have organzine in large quantities. John Lombe at the behest of his older half-brother Thomas, decided to investigate the Italian process, so he went to work at one of the Italian mills where the silk-throwing machinery was in use. The way their machinery was water powered was a closely guarded secret as the Italians were determined to protect their processes from the outside world. John slipped into the mills during the night and meticulously sketched out their layout under dim candlelight. He returned to England in 1716 and brought with him the secret of the Italian process along with several Italian workers.

Next, he engaged the architect, Sorocold, for the second time, to design and build another larger mill based on his smuggled Italian drawings. This new mill was built on the same site as the previous one and was completed around the year 1722. It is said that the King of Sardinia heard of this new English silk mill. He knew the plans for the mill had been stolen from the Italians in Piedmont and he also knew it was John Lombe who had purloined the secrets.

The Sardinian king reacted to the emergence of English competition by placing an embargo on the export of raw silk. News of the English venture's immense success, in spite of the new restrictions, prompted the King to exact further revenge for John's audacious act. He sent a beautiful female assassin to England to seduce and eliminate the Englishman. John died just after the mill proved to be successful. He is thought to have been murdered by poisoning. It was rumored that he had a relationship with a beautiful Italian woman who appeared from time to time, shortly before his death."

John Smalley turned to comment, "I knew that his brother, Thomas Lombe, was knighted. I had no idea that his brother was murdered by the Italians. However, it does not surprise me. After all, the Borgia's and the De Medici's were Italian. Poison is a way of life with those Latins."

William continued, "Although John was dead, the mill proved to be quite a success and his brother Thomas, as you said, was knighted and also became one of the wealthiest men in England. It was all accomplished because of their ability to keep their supply of product on track with the demand by their customers. I therefore, strongly suggest that in your coming project, you use water power as well. It certainly elevated the Lombe Family."

The next morning John boarded a coach and headed back to Whitehaven. William and Jonathan accompanied him to the inn from which the coach departed. Jonathan's excitement on starting his adventure was tempered by the sight of his father's departure. It was almost as if Jonathan's carefree youth was departing on that coach. Living and working with his uncle was going to be a tremendous step to independence and manhood. His father had been demanding, but those demands mostly took the form of stringent adherence to proper behavior. Jonathan was expected to act like a gentleman. He had attended the local grammar school, where he was instructed in the usual reading, writing and arithmetic. He had excelled at arithmetic and had even become proficient in Latin. Various members of the Whitehaven gentry and some of the more wealthy merchant class also educated their sons in this manner.

John and Ann had discussed whether or not to send their son on to one of the schools of higher education such as Oxford or Cambridge. They had been dissuaded by reports of drunkenness, physical abuse, whoring, and homosexuality in those schools. These were concerns held by all parents of the time, but John and Ann decided that a practical education would be more prudent for their son, Jonathan. It gave John and Ann peace knowing he would be under the close supervision of his Uncle William through the difficult years of adolescence. So, here stood Jonathan, waving goodbye to his father, ready to start his new life as an apprentice millwright under William Lucas.

Chapter 12

ONATHAN ADAPTED WELL TO HIS NEW REGIME. He was up early with his Uncle William and accompanied him on all of his meetings with clients. He soon learned that the profession of millwright included using your muscles, as well as your mind. One of the local water driven grist mills had been damaged by a spring flood. Excess water coursing down from the mountains had broken the axle off of the water wheel. William and his nephew went out to inspect the damage. William pointed out to Jonathan which parts could be repaired and which ones would have to be replaced.

The cost of repairs were totaled along with the cost of parts that needed to be replaced. They added the labor to the number and a nice profit for themselves. Jonathan was given the task of presenting the sum total to the waiting miller. It was a very good lesson in the art of negotiating, as the miller was not pleased when he heard the total sum. The miller was also not pleased with the idea of negotiating with a "boy", as he called Jonathan.

"I may be a boy sir, but if you would like for us to repair your mill and get you back in business as quickly as possible, then this is our price."

"Taken by a boy. I suppose I have no choice. Get on with it then. Each day the mill stone doesn't turn is a day that I don't earn any money."

Jonathan was quite pleased with himself when he returned to his uncle. They were scheduled to begin the job the next morning. They arrived at the grist mill just after daylight. In addition to William and Jonathan, there were five crewmen that had worked with William on prior jobs.

"The first thing we have to do is to find a suitable replacement for that shaft. Can you tell me, Jonathan, what type of wood should we be looking for?"

"I believe you told me we should use white oak. It has the strength required for the job."

"You're right in your thinking. Now grab that axe and let's go down to those woods and see if we can find one."

The party of seven started down into the woods and after searching for thirty-five to forty minutes, Jonathan announced that he had found a white oak tree he thought would do the job. After inspecting the oak, it was agreed it was the right one to use to make the new shaft. William said to Jonathan, "It's time to get started. It shouldn't take you too long to fell that tree." He left two of the workmen to assist and turned around, leaving Jonathan with the task. Over the next eighteen months, Jonathan was introduced to most of the responsibilities that faced a millwright. He had an opportunity to work with not only the axe, but also a hammer and plane, with equal skill and precision. He learned to turn, bore and forge with the ease and dispatch of a first-rate blacksmith. One of the most important tasks he learned was how to set-out and cut-in the furrows of a millstone. After working with William on two other jobs, Jonathan was able to complete the task with an accuracy equal or superior to that of a miller, as well.

The first two years of Jonathan's apprenticeship passed rapidly. Jonathan was sixteen years old and closely approaching seventeen. His Uncle William placed him in charge of building a large grist mill just outside of Manchester. He stated his instructions to Jonathan. "This is your project and I have no doubt that you will be able to construct this mill in the proper fashion. I'm sending three of my best men with you, and I expect the job to be completed within three to four months. This will be the first project you will build from the ground up. You have worked on and are familiar with each working piece you will be installing in this mill. Take your time and listen to the fellows that I'm sending along with you. They have experience, having assisted me in building several of these grist mills over the years. If you get into a bind, remember, I am only ten miles away. You will be staying at the Green Man Inn, which is less than a mile from your project in Rochdale. I expect a good quality project, completed on time, for the monies I have allowed you to spend on this project."

"Don't worry, uncle. I will do a good job on this project. The owner will have a first-class mill when it is completed."

Jonathan shook hands with his uncle and climbed aboard the wagon that was loaded with the supplies and tools necessary for the project. There were two wagons, both loaded with saws, mallets, axes, bellows, planes, drills and other kinds of tools needed to build a grist mill. Waving goodbye to his uncle, Jonathan and the small caravan left Manchester headed toward the adjacent town of Rochdale. They arrived at their destination after a five hour journey. Rochdale is located in the valley of the River Roch. Blackstone Edge is a gritstone escarpment over fifteen hundred feet above sea level and is the prominent landscape scene viewed from the town. Saddleworth Moor and the South Pennines Mountains are close by, to the east. The mill project that Jonathan was assigned to work on was located on a tributary of the River Roch. For the first sixty days, work progressed very well. William made a surprise visit a couple of weeks into the project and seem to be well pleased with the work that had been done.

Jonathan had corresponded during the past two years with Mary Cook and her friend, Ann Ashburn. At first the letters had been very formal. Each asked the other how their education was progressing and how they were being treated by their legal guardians. Jonathan wrote with great excitement about all the different places he and his uncle had visited while working in and around Manchester. He wrote page after page about his projects and included diagrams and drawings of all types of equipment. The girls wrote of their superb French teacher, Monsieur Andre Duval, who was not only an excellent teacher, but young and handsome, as well. They wrote about learning to play the latest card games and perfecting the latest continental dances. As their education progressed these young ladies had been introduced to the society of Leeds. Aunt Felicity was one of the society matrons and invitations were extended to her and her two wards for every event that occurred socially in Leeds. Jonathan's social education was limited to interaction with workers and his uncle. As the girls' letters became more descriptive of the fun they were having, Jonathan became a little jealous at news of all the handsome young men Mary and Ann Ashburn were meeting.

Jonathan started writing about the daughters of his clients he had met and about their instant attraction to him. It must be said that his creativity when describing encounters with females even excelled his thorough descriptions of machinery. Upon receiving the letters from either Mary or Ann, Jonathan would reply that he had just met the daughter of a silk merchant or a doctor's daughter, whose company he enjoyed immensely. Most of the millers' daughters that he had the pleasure of meeting, had been sent away to private schools and were receiving almost exactly the same type of education as his two friends in Leeds. Usually, he would describe a new young lady in a way that matched the physical characteristics of Mary or Ann. It was curious that all the young women he was introduced to were brilliant, talented and extremely attractive. In fact, during the two years he had been with his uncle, Jonathan had never reported meeting anyone that was unattractive or uninteresting.

Jonathan returned to the inn one night to find two letters waiting. One was from Mary Cook and the other was from Ann Ashburn.

Jonathan opened the one from Ann Ashburn first. It read as follows:

My Dearest Jonathan,

Mary and I attended a ball last night. All of the best people in Leeds were there. I was surprised to see Hugh Dacre and his father, Thomas, as they were announced. Although I'm not very fond of Hugh, as you know, he seems to be very fond of me. It was difficult to visit with anyone else for most of the evening. He was most polite and charming, but most insistent on monopolizing my company. He had not heard of our adventures with the footpad on our journey here. It seems he has, however, met our reformed robber, Alan Bercher. He has been doing some business with your father. Hugh is to call on us again this evening and Aunt Felicity has instructed us to be receptive and charming as part of our education. Perhaps I will speak only French to him. If that does not confuse him, then I do not know what will. Our French lessons go well but it would be nice to be able to try my French out on you. Do not forget to practice your dancing. Speaking of dancing, there will be a mid-summer ball on 12 July that promises to be fabulous. It would be wonderful if you could attend. I must close now, but Jonathan, I do think of you often.

Your Affectionate Friend,

Ann

Jonathan felt twinges of jealousy rise up in his throat as he read the part about Hugh Dacre's attention to Ann. Here he was, stuck in this rotten little village, while these two beautiful girls were being courted by strangers. In Ann's case, it was worse than a stranger. It was someone that he did not like; yes, even detested. He sat for a moment and reread the letter. He sighed and laid her letter down on the table and picked up the envelope from Mary Cook.

Mary's handwriting was more delicate and refined than Ann's. Jonathan opened the letter and began to read:

My Dear Jonathan,

It seems much longer than the twenty four months since we last saw each other. I do take some solace in the correspondence we have exchanged, but I do long to hear your voice and again, enjoy your company. I have spoken to Aunt Felicity and I am not certain that we will be here much longer than the end of this year. The three of us have attended several socials at the homes of some of the families close to Aunt Felicity. Although I have enjoyed learning to navigate through society, I find myself wondering what it would be like to have you here to enjoy these parties with me. You must think me awfully forward, but I do miss seeing you on a regular basis. We had a wonderful time together growing up in Whitehaven. I must close now, but perhaps you could ask your uncle for permission to visit us here in Leeds. There is a ball scheduled for July 12 and it would be delightful if you could join us.

With affection, I am,

Mary

Jonathan missed Mary, as well. Her letter had not spoken of any attention she was receiving from the young men attending the dances and social events. But Jonathan was certain that meeting them, she was. The letters from Ann usually included the names and descriptions of the young men that were courting her and Mary. Jonathan's longing to be with one or both of the two young women was growing stronger every day as he matured. As he thought of each of the young girls, his pulse would quicken as mother nature worked her magic on the sexual awakening taking place within the young man.

Jonathan resolved that he would talk to his uncle about making the trip to Leeds for the Midsummer Ball. It was the first day of July and he was to see his uncle at the end of the week when he returned to inspect their progress. The mill was very close to completion with only about three weeks worth of work left to complete. It seemed like a reasonable request.

William arrived and was pleased with the quality of the work. He was concerned, however, that it seemed to be a little behind schedule. The miller was putting the pressure on for them to finish the project before harvest time arrived. Crops began maturing at the end of July, continuing through August and the early part of September. William and Jonathan had supper together at the inn that night. William was delighted with everything that Jonathan had been doing with his first solo project.

"Uncle William, I have been invited to Leeds at the end of this coming week to attend the Midsummer's Ball there. I would like to rent a horse and join Mary and Ann for the affair. I would only be gone a couple of days and would return promptly to complete the mill." Jonathan did not receive the reply he had hoped. William was not in the best of moods. He was wrapped up in a large cotton mill project he had been working on for two years. In addition, the miller had been vocally strident about completion of Jonathan's grist mill project. Without looking at Jonathan, he poured another glass of port. Leaning back in his chair, he raised his eyes to look at his nephew, "Jonathan, with our work schedule, I'm afraid that attending the ball is out of the question."

"But uncle, haven't I done a good job with this project you've entrusted to me so far?"

"Yes, as I told you this afternoon, I am very pleased with the quality of work you have accomplished. But you must know that we are under pressure to complete this job and if our client sees us taking time off, especially at this time of year, he will be greatly distressed. Additionally, on the way here I noticed that a good portion of the wheat crops are beginning to ripen. I have had enough trouble with our miller as it is and we must not do anything that would further antagonize the man. There will be plenty of time for you to go to socials and balls once this job is completed."

"But you don't understand," Jonathan said, not quite certain how to explain what he was feeling.

"No, it's you, young man. You are the one who does not understand. There is nothing else to be said about this. I will be glad to reward you at the successful completion of this project, but now is not the time for us to slacken in our efforts. Furthermore, whatever it is that I don't understand, is it not more important that you obey your elder and carry out my wishes?"

"But uncle, the girls who are in Leeds---"

"Girls, girls. I should've known. Jonathan, I have been your age and it felt like it was the end of the world when I wasn't allowed to attend to my own desires and wishes. In my young mind, I was devastated when I missed out on what my friends and acquaintances were doing. You will find out, as all men have, from the beginning of time, that your life will not end if you do not make the rendezvous you are obviously planning. I know this is a difficult thing for you to go through. Nonetheless, you must weather this disappointment. You will be better off for it in the end. You will stay here and you will complete this project on time and on budget. Is that clearly understood, young Master Lucas?"

Mary Cook

Jonathan turned his head away. He was choking back a feeling of disappointment and anxiety that had crept up into his throat. His uncle did not understand that Hugh Dacre was again meddling in his affairs. It was important for him not to abandon his quest for the affections of the beautiful Ann Ashburn. He felt tears of anguish, frustration and anger rising up inside, but he was able to choke out, "Yes sir. The project will be completed on time and on budget."

Satisfied with his reply, William changed the subject and began talking about the progress of the cotton mill. He also made suggestions to Jonathan about how to put the finishing touches on the grist mill. Jonathan gained control of his emotions and was able to carry on a conversation with his uncle without showing what he was really feeling inside. As William finished the bottle of port, he retired to his room, and was soon sound asleep.

Jonathan lay awake, most of the night, imagining Hugh Dacre smothering Ann with his affections. He finally drifted off to sleep, only to dream of the upcoming Midsummer's Ball. In his dream there were nameless, faceless, young men surrounding Mary Cook. In his mind he saw them as rough and grotesque. Mary was frightened and was frantically looking around and calling for help from Jonathan. He also saw a leering Hugh Dacre grabbing Ann Ashburn by the waist against her will. She was, in turn, desperately struggling to get away from the lecherous Hugh. Jonathan was trying very hard to reach the girls and come to their aid, when suddenly his dream changed. As he got nearer to the girls, their struggles and screams turned into giggles. Up close, he now saw that they were actually enjoying the attention from the men. He was horrified to find Ann actually being caressed by Hugh Dacre. She looked past Hugh's head and spied Jonathan and started laughing at him. He turned to concentrate on rescuing Mary Cook from the nameless, faceless men.

Mary didn't laugh at Jonathan, but started scolding him in French. "S'il vous plaît ne pas faire un fou De vous-même Jonathan. Ce sont mes amants français et je m'amuse." Jonathan awoke from his nightmare in a cold sweat. He got up and walked over to the wash basin and poured cold water into the bowl. He splashed the cold water on his face and thought to himself, "I can't let this happen. I know it's a just a terrible dream, but truth is sometimes revealed in dreams."

For the next few days Jonathan wrestled with his conscience. He had never disobeyed an order or instruction from either his father or his uncle. For the first time in his life he seemed to be on his own. His uncle had entrusted him with the responsibility of constructing the gristmill project using his own judgment. Perhaps it was time for Jonathan to use his judgment in other areas of his life. He was not certain whether Ann or Mary was the most important to him. Both were beautiful, but their personalities were so different and so were the feelings they aroused within him. Ann Ashburn was provocative and flirtatious in the way she looked and the things she said to him. Mary Cook, on the other hand, provoked desire in him, but it was a quieter, less volatile type of attraction. All said, both ladies caused Jonathan distress. Both of them were calling to him just like the sirens he had studied in Homer's Odyssey. His problem was that he had no mast to lash himself to, and no hand to keep him from jumping overboard and swimming to shore.

Chapter 13

THE PROPRIETOR OF THE GREEN MAN INN was only too happy to rent the young man one of his finest saddle horses. After all, he was well aware that his Uncle William, who was paying his nephew's bills, was rumored to be a very wealthy, successful individual. He was working with some of the richest merchants in Manchester, so the more money spent by Jonathan, the more profits the innkeeper would garner.

Jonathan's decision to blatantly disobey his uncle was no easy decision. His dreams, or rather his nightmares, continued and were always the same. At first the girls needed his help, but when he finally came to their rescue, he was always too late to save them. They had turned from two virtuous young virgins with a pure affection for him, into insatiable libertines with ravenous carnal appetites. In the end, his dreams and his hormones won out. Duty and obedience were summarily dismissed, so that he could answer the questions that had tormented his dreams and his waking moments.

He had become quite close with the oldest of the three workers. Henry Thomas was more like a tutor than a underling. He had worked with his Uncle William for over ten years and in truth, was as knowledgeable as William about much of the work. The difference was imagination. Henry Thomas was conservative in his approach and did not trust new ideas. He liked young Jonathan Lucas and took great pride in assisting with his education. Jonathan's plan was to leave Henry Thomas in charge to continue the work on the grist mill. He would leave for Leeds on July 11th, which was a Saturday morning. He would cover the thirty miles in one day and spend the night at an inn to rest up for the dance most of the next day, which was Sunday July 12th. The Midsummer's Ball was to begin late in the afternoon. Jonathan was anxious to surprise his two young friends. Monday the 13th, he would return to Rochdale and continue his work on the 14th. He knew the risk he was taking, but he didn't think his uncle would return until the middle of the week following, when the completion of the project was scheduled to occur. Jonathan felt sure he would be back in plenty of time to complete the mill. If somehow his uncle found out about his trip to the ball, he hoped the ensuing anger would be abated by the successful completion of the gristmill. Jonathan's three-day absence should not cause any delay, because all of the equipment was built and had been checked. All that was left to do was to complete the remaining installations and he had full confidence that Henry Thomas knew exactly what to do. They had gone over an installation schedule Jonathan had drawn up, item by item and day by day. When Jonathan was satisfied that Henry understood everything clearly, he promised to give him a bonus of two crowns if the schedule they had agreed upon was met. Henry was fine with the plan and assured Jonathan there would be no problems. Jonathan advanced one half of his bonus upfront. He knew that Henry Thomas was more than capable of handling the work in his absence. What he did not know, was that Henry Thomas was usually paid just enough to live on until the end of a job by his uncle for a very good reason. He would find out why Henry Thomas was handled in this manner in exactly three days. Reassured once again by this stalwart Welshmen, Jonathan mounted his fine looking black mare and started on the road to Leeds.

His path took him over the Blackstone Edge. It was a long climb to reach the top of the fifteen hundred foot gritstone escarpment. He stopped to examine the Aiggin Stone, a gritstone pillar. It had possibly been a way-marker, which stood beside the old packhorse route, designating the county boundary. The stone had a cross and the letters, "I and T", cut into it. Nobody knew its exact age, but it was thought to be ancient indeed. Its name was believed to be derived from the French word 'aiguille' for needle and 'aigle' for eagle. He turned and looked back across the valley where he could see the mill he was supposed to be completing. The horse was tired after the long climb, so Jonathan dismounted to let her rest a while before they continued. He found a big rock next to the Aiggin Stone and set down as he gazed over the distant valley he had just passed through. All at once a feeling of remorse swept over him. He thought about turning his horse around and forgetting the trip to Leeds. As his thoughts battled between continuing his journey or returning to his work, he reached his hand into his pocket and pulled out the two letters from the girls. He reread them both and thought to himself, "Henry Thomas is a capable man. I can trust him to do what he said he will do. I have completed every task that I have been asked to do and without complaint. If I can be trusted to complete the construction of a gristmill on my own, using my judgment, then it is time for me to be able to make some personal decisions using my judgment. I will see the project completed and I will also see this journey to visit my two friends completed." The last sentence was spoken out loud and his horse answered with a loud whinny of agreement. Jonathan smiled at his mare and took her answer as a good omen. He should have remembered it was a black horse he was riding.

The journey was a lot rougher than Jonathan had anticipated as he had to cross through the Saddleworth Moor. The moorland was a high plateau that was crisscrossed by gritstone escarpments that although large, were not as big as the Blackstone Edge. Its margins were deeply incised v-shaped valleys, or cloughs, that carried fast-flowing cold water streams. Clough was derived from the Old English word 'cloh', which means a ravine or deep valley, and there were many of those to be carefully traversed. After passing through the area, he came upon an overlying layer of peat that was cut by groughs or drainage channels. This was not as treacherous, but it was slower than the part of the moor he had just crossed. The high moorlands were very sparsely inhabited with farmsteads, mostly built of local gritstone. It was already past noon before Jonathan and his mare dropped down off of the Saddleworth Moor on to a more level and less challenging landscape.

He was able to stop in the village of Brighouse where he fed his horse, ate a meal and gained a well-needed rest. Jonathan soon remounted and crossed the River Calder. The next obstacle he came upon was the Calder and Hebble Navigation Canal. It had been started in 1757 by the engineer, John Smearton. His Uncle William had worked with the now famous Smearton on this project for a two-year period. Still friends, Smearton and William corresponded regularly. From Brighouse to Gildersome, Jonathan pushed his mount forward at a brisk pace. Both he and the mare stopped once more for a much needed rest and more food and refreshment. It was growing late, much later than Jonathan had anticipated, but thankfully, in summer, it didn't get dark in this part of England until after eleven PM.

After an hour's rest, Jonathan and the black mare pushed off for the final miles to Leeds. Both horse and rider were exhausted by the time they reached The Three Cups Inn. This was a popular spot and even though it was after midnight when they arrived, the coffee room in the inn was full of people. Jonathan secured a room or more accurately, part of a room. Since the inn was full, he was forced to share a sleeping chamber with a merchant from London. The merchant was not very pleased at being awakened and told he would be sharing his bed with a stranger. The man was in a nightgown, with a stocking nightcap on his head and the strong smell of ale on his breath. It was clear that he had had plenty to drink before retiring. Jonathan spent most of the night listening to the loud snoring coming from the large red nose of the merchant. Finally, he drifted off into a fitful sleep, probably due to total fatigue. The nightmares about his two maidens did not reoccur that evening.

The next morning Jonathan was able to sleep in. The merchant he was sharing a room with was still snoring when Jonathan finally rose and dressed. He walked downstairs and talked to the innkeeper, who was able to find a private room for Jonathan for the payment of a few extra shillings. The room was small, but adequate for his purposes. Jonathan opened his bag and pulled out his finest outfit, consisting of a long dark green jacket, brown knee britches and a shirt that matched. He had a full ruffled white scarf to wrap around his neck. His clothes were clean, but wrinkled, so he found the innkeeper's daughter and paid her to have them pressed for the evening.

Jonathan decided he would call on the ladies at midday. He pictured in his mind how the reunion would go. He felt that Ann would be the most demonstrative and surprised. He imagined her rushing to him, throwing her arms around his neck and smothering him with kisses, all the while telling him how happy she was that he had come for the ball. He knew that Mary would be much more reserved and show much less emotion than her passionate, redheaded friend. Nevertheless, she would wait her turn and greet him with an extended hand that he would kiss with passion. She would put her hand on the back of his neck and look deeply into his eyes and tell him that he had grown so much more handsome since they had last seen each other. He would be drawn toward her like a moth to a flame, but just before he placed a kiss on her lips-- out would come Aunt Felicity and chide Mary for acting unladylike. He was shaken out of his daydream by a knock on the door. The girl had brought his clothes back and she laid them out on the bed.

Jonathan dressed and went downstairs. After checking on his horse and making sure she was fed and groomed, he came upon the innkeeper who was standing just inside of the courtyard.

"Well, young man, you certainly are fancied up today."

"Yes, I'm going to call on some friends of mine and I was wondering if you could tell me where this address is?" Jonathan opened one of the letters and without revealing the contents, showed the innkeeper the address of the Cook Home. "Do you know how to get there from here?"

"Ah yes! That's the home of Felicity Cook. It's only three blocks from here and I suppose you'll be calling on those two young ladies she has staying with her. From the looks of those two, I can't say as I blame you, young man. I hope there's not a line formed at the door by the time you get there," the innkeeper said with a chuckle.

"What do you mean by that, sir?"

"Oh I'm just joking with you, lad. It seems that all the eligible young men of Leeds have been knocking on the door since those young ladies arrived."

Jonathan's eyes narrowed and his face became pinched. The innkeeper could see that perhaps his remark was not a joke this young man wanted to hear. Jonathan said, "Thank you, sir, for the directions." He quickly turned away and started to walk out of the courtyard, but he finally saw the humor in the situation. He stopped and smiling, turned back to the innkeeper, "Since I'm from out of town and should not be expected to know all of the local rules, perhaps I'll sneak in the back door and not become part of the lover's que."

The innkeeper was pleased to see that the young man had relaxed. "If we can be of any assistance to you, kind sir, please let us know. I hope you enjoy yourself at the Midsummer's Ball this evening."

Jonathan raised his arm in salute to the innkeeper and thanked his temporary landlord once more. He was off to surprise his two friends.

Jonathan found the residence of Mrs. Felicity Cook. Thankfully, there was no line of young men knocking on the door. The house was a large three-story structure standing on the corner of the street. With his adrenaline flowing, Jonathan walked up to the door and pulled the cord to ring the doorbell. A maidservant opened the door and asked, "Yes sir, how can I help you?"

"My name is Jonathan Lucas and I am here to call on Miss Mary Cook and Miss Ann Ashburn."

"Well sir, they are in the middle of their French lessons with M. Duval. I am afraid that you will have to call again, perhaps tomorrow. They are to attend the Midsummer's Ball this evening at 6 o'clock."

"Yes, I know. That is why I am here. They have both invited me to be their escort this evening."

"Whom did you say you were, sir?"

"I am Jonathan Lucas from Whitehaven," he said in a more formal tone, "I have known Mary all of my life and ..."

"Oh, now I know who you are. You're the gentleman that was with them on their journey when they were almost robbed."

"Then you have heard the story."

"Oh yes sir. I have heard it many times."

Felicity Cook appeared over her maidservant's shoulder. When she saw Jonathan, there was a look of delightful surprise. She raised her hand to her face and said, "Jonathan Lucas, you came! The girls said they had asked you, but we had heard nothing and I had no idea you would be able to join us."

The maidservant moved aside as Felicity stepped up and took Jonathan by the arm.

"The girls are going to be so surprised and happy to see you. They will not believe you are here." She led Jonathan in the direction of the parlor. He could barely hear discernible French being spoken by a male through the closed door. Felicity paused long enough to knock and then threw the door open and exclaimed, "My dears, look who has come to our door!"

The two girls had been sitting with their backs to the door, facing the instructor, who had a confused and perplexed look on his face. At first, the girls turned their heads to look over their shoulders, but stood up and turned at the same time. Then, in unison, they both shouted, "Jonathan, Jonathan," as they rushed forward. Jonathan was not prepared for this onslaught of female enthusiasm. As a matter fact, for a split second, he was startled at the intensity of their welcome. He was saved some embarrassment by Felicity as she gained control of the two charging, young women.

"Ladies, ladies, remember who you are. I know that you're both delighted and happy to see our friend once again, but remember, you are young ladies."

Mary Cook immediately slowed down and became more reserved as she continued to approach. Her countenance had changed into the epitome of propriety required of young ladies, particularly when a young man was involved. Jonathan was pleased when he saw her initial reaction and relieved that she was truly glad to see him.

Ann Ashburn, on the other hand, only gave a momentary glance to Felicity. She was not put off for a second by the attempted correction. She threw her arms around Jonathan's neck and instead of the light friendly hug and quick kiss on the cheek he had anticipated, she covered his mouth with hers in what can only be described as a brief, but sensual kiss.

Felicity reached up and took hold of her wrist. "Ann, my dear! I know you are glad to see Jonathan, but please remember--" Ann released Jonathan and turning to Felicity said, "Yes ma'am. It has just been so long since we have seen our friend, that I just could not contain myself."

She stepped back and looked at Jonathan. "My goodness," she turned to Mary and continued, "Our Jonathan is turning into quite the handsome young man. Don't you agree, Mary?"

Mary had reached the little group and just as Jonathan had visualized in his daydreams, she extended an exquisitely beautiful hand to Jonathan in greeting. And just as Jonathan had daydreamed about his reaction, he reached down and took her hand and planted a kiss. The kiss was not your ordinary polite kiss on the hand, but one that lingered perhaps a little too long for Miss Felicity's comfort. Jonathan straightened and looked into the beautiful blue eyes that were smiling at him and then looked into the brown eyes of Ann.

"It has been a long time since the three of us shared that coach ride, and all I can say to you, Miss Felicity, is that these girls and this greeting have certainly been worth the wait."

"Oh my goodness," was all that Felicity could muster. She finally replied, "And I say in reply to you, that I am thankful that I have these two girls together. One can look out for what the other is up to, for I should be concerned about leaving only two of you alone together." Smiling, Felicity turned toward the Frenchman who had been largely ignored.

"Jonathan, I would like for you to meet M. Duval. After your father's story about the other M. Duval I had this one thoroughly checked out. I am happy to say that he is not related to the highwayman of the same name."

The Frenchman approached Jonathan with an outstretched hand. "It is a great pleasure to meet you Mr. Lucas. These ladies have regaled me with your adventures on the stagecoach, until I feel that I know you very well. I was expecting a younger person, but you have obviously grown in the last few years."

Jonathan took his hand and shook it vigorously and replied somewhat relieved, "It is a pleasure to meet you too, sir. And I also had you pictured as a much younger person. The girls speak fondly of you and your efforts on their behalf. It is unfortunate that I have not been here to partake in the dance lessons and I only have knowledge of a very few words of French."

Mon. Duval said with a most pleasant grin, "Well M. Lucas, perhaps I can show you enough steps this afternoon so that you will not embarrass yourself or your hostesses at the ball this evening."

They all had a good laugh. The girl's French lessons were over for the day, that had become obvious, Andre did spend a few moments showing Jonathan some new dance steps. Afterward, Andre Duval said his goodbyes and excused himself. They spent the next couple of hours catching up on family and friends.

Ann was correct. Jonathan had turned into quite the handsome young man. He was six feet tall and the last two years of hard physical labor had added muscle to his physique. When he moved, it was with grace and purpose and both young ladies were even more attracted to him than before. Felicity could plainly see that Mary and Ann were going to be in quite a competition for the attentions of their handsome young guest.

Jonathan was a bit overwhelmed by all the fuss being made over his sudden arrival. Both of the girls had undeniably blossomed into womanhood. It was plain for anyone to see. Their two personalities were still as different as could be. Ann had lost none of her assertiveness. If anything, she seemed even more sure of what she was doing and more determined to do it. Mary was still much more subtle in her approach. She was more the counter-puncher and could conduct repartee that was sometimes biting, but always clever and funny. Ann was the type of person that always said what came to her mind. Mary on the other hand, seldom spoke without thinking about what she was about to say.

Since they were both very attractive women, Jonathan gave up trying to decide which one he was most attracted to and decided to enjoy himself while this good fortune lasted. Aunt Felicity finally was able to cajole the girls into going upstairs and getting dressed for the ball. She offered the parlor to Jonathan, so he could rest for a couple of hours. He was told to make himself completely at home and to even take a nap. Jonathan thanked her and was left alone to contemplate what would happen if something went wrong back in Rochdale.

Chapter 14

T HE BALL WAS BEING HELD AT THE NEW residence of one of Leeds' leading citizens, Edwin Lascelles, who was a very wealthy trader. Harewood House had just been completed and it was magnificent. This would be the first social event held at the stunning house and gardens. It had taken almost twelve years to complete. The mansion was designed by John Carr, who was one of the most renowned architects in England. The interior furnishings and decorations had been put together by noted interior designer, Robert Adam. The construction had taken place between 1759 and 1771.

The Lascelles Family had bought the estate soon after making their fortune in the West Indies. Their riches came from taking customs positions, slave trading, and lending money to the sugar cane planters of Barbados and other Caribbean islands within the British Empire. This was going to be a special evening in that the owners intended to show English society their remarkable wealth, power and growing influence.

As the carriage approached Harewood House, Jonathan got his first glimpse of what great wealth could produce. He had seen some of the fine homes being built in Manchester, but he had not attended any social affairs in them. However, he had been invited to several business meetings with his Uncle William and his clients, so he was not a novice when it came to interacting with people of great wealth, but this was magnificent.

As they entered the mansion, its beauty was breathtaking. Jonathan recognized the furniture made by Thomas Chippendale. He had even met Chippendale a few years earlier, when his father was shipping some of his furniture to Virginia as part of their tobacco trade.

The two younger women preceded Jonathan and Felicity as they walked through the lavish interior. After being properly announced upon their entrance, the four of them entered the ballroom. It seemed that everyone who was anyone, was in attendance that evening. It only took a few seconds after crossing the threshold before numerous male admirers surrounded the two girls. Obviously enjoying the attention, Ann and Mary were soon the center of attention from at least a dozen followers each. Jonathan was not happy with his forced exclusion. Upon seeing the expression on his face, Felicity exclaimed, "Don't worry, Jonathan, the excitement of their arrival will soon die down and they will make their way back to you. After all, you are their invitee to this soirée. I suggest that you and I enjoy these spectacular surroundings. It is truly incredible what great wealth is able to buy. Isn't your father still trading with the colonies?"

"Yes, he is. But I believe that since the loss of his partner, J.D. Younger, the trade is not as great as it once was. I am also informed that the Scottish merchants of Glasgow are continuing to compete with us for that trade."

Jonathan saw that it was hopeless to try to regain the attention of the two girls. He reluctantly decided to accompany Felicity on an inspection tour of the grand chamber in which the ball was being held. As they walked along, admiring the artwork and the furnishings, Felicity stopped after almost every step and introduced Jonathan to everyone they met. She seemed to know each person in attendance.

When he was younger, Jonathan had often attended these types of social events, back in Whitehaven, but it was never so grand. He had even attended events in Manchester with his Uncle William, but nothing prepared him for the magnificence of this place. The ballroom was crowded with people and it was difficult to move, causing them to progress at a very slow pace. The room was brightly lit by torches affixed high along the walls. Splendid crystal chandeliers hung from the ceiling, reflecting a dazzling glow of candlelight. It was very difficult to hear what anyone was saying over the murmur of hundreds of voices carrying on conversations throughout the room. It was July and there was a wave of warm air wafting through the room. The balmy breeze carried the scent of perfume and other aromas. There was a cacophony of sounds; the rustle of silk, the tapping of shoes and the opening and closing of snuff boxes. There was an orchestra situated at the far end of the hall on a raised stage. They were beginning to warm up for dancing and the music promised to be beautiful.

Jonathan was still not happy about being separated from Mary and Ann. He looked around the room and there were many pretty young ladies that took every opportunity to catch his eye and smile at this handsome stranger. Jonathan would return the smile, but did not allow his gaze to linger. He was too busy searching the room for both, or at least one, of his companions. He spied a swaggering, familiar figure. His eyes locked onto the eyes of Hugh Dacre. "So," he thought to himself, "Here is the spoiled, little rich kid, come to court Ann." He nodded in the direction of Dacre, but continued to scan the room for the girls.

Harewood House

He felt a hand on his arm and turned to look directly at Mary. "Jonathan, dear, I'm so sorry that we were separated so quickly."

"Well, as the two of you are so popular, I'm surprised you were able to work your way back," replied Jonathan with a rather cross tone.

"Do I detect a hint of jealousy? And is it for me?"

"I must admit that when we were separated, even though I was with Felicity, I would have preferred to be with my two beautiful, enchanting friends, instead of this room full of strangers."

"Do you think you can remember the dance steps that Andre showed you this afternoon?"

"Yes, I think I can."

"Well, in that instance, I have done the right thing."

"Yes and what is that?"

"I have refused all offers for the first dance tonight. My excuse is that I have a guest that I promised the first dance to this evening."

"I have danced a little in less grand homes with much smaller gatherings and far less grandiose. I hope that bit of experience coupled with the dancing lessons Monsieur Duval gave me this afternoon . . . well, I hope that I shan't embarrass you too badly this evening."

The first dance was announced just as Ann Ashburn reached them. "It looks as if I am too late to claim the first dance, Jonathan, but I am certain I can claim the second one." For a brief moment there was a challenge in the look she received from Mary.

"Nothing would please me more," said a smiling Jonathan. Just then, out of the corner of his eye, he saw his nemesis, Hugh Dacre, approach. "Why Miss Ashburn, I have been trying to attract your attention since the moment you arrived. If you have not promised the first dance to anyone else, I was hoping that you would give me the pleasure. Ann smiled slightly and turned to Jonathan and said to Dacre, "How gallant you are, Hugh. Of course you may have the first dance." She turned away from Jonathan and Mary and taking Hugh's arm, the two of them walked toward the orchestra. Jonathan watched them go without smiling. Mary gave him a quick tug and scolded him. "Don't worry, Ann has promised you the second dance," she was said in a caustic manner, which surprised Jonathan a little. Mary broke into a radiant smile that made him momentarily forget Ann and Hugh. For now, he only had eyes for Mary. The first formal dance of the evening commenced. To Jonathan, it was a dazzling, dizzying moment of sound and sights.

The soft yellow candlelight washed over the crowd, highlighting the colors of the ladies' dresses and the dapper styles worn by the men. There was every hue of the rainbow; blues, golds, creams, pastel pinks, soft reds and deep greens. The mellow candlelight seemed to soften everything and it made smiles brighter and the beautiful look even more beautiful. Everyone in that festive throng seemed, if possible, more fetching and charming.

The stringed orchestra played superbly. It was rumored they had come all the way from London. Those dancing were aware that all of the guests standing by, were watching them. It was a wonderful spectacle. Those dancing would pirouette and move in tandem to the lively music. The dancers turned on their heels, stepped to the left, stepped to the right and intermingled just before pointing toes to each other. The scene resembled a beautiful multicolored cloud passing before an exquisite sunset. The music was the oil that lubricated the movement of life throughout the grand hall.

Jonathan was nervous as he danced with Mary. He was surprised that she seemed a little nervous, as well. After a few turns, they both relaxed. Neither tripped over each other or made a false step. The rhythm of the music helped. The demure Mary kept her eyes lowered, which allowed Jonathan to watch her closely. Mary's dress was simple, but elegant. Low-cut and made of white silk, her gown was trimmed along the edge with a gold braid. Her breasts were larger than Jonathan remembered and were beautifully displayed to her advantage by the cut of the dress. Her hair was gathered up with strands of sparkling jewels and a white feather extended from the side, giving just the right touch. The gown was gathered under her breast with more golden braiding and her shoulders were bare and lovely. The sheer cloth hung loosely to the floor, but clung to the rest of her when she moved. As she danced, she showed a pair of white satin shoes displayed on small petite feet.

Her eyes were almond shaped and a beautiful blue color and her skin exuded health and youth. There was a trace of perfume, but only a trace. She suddenly looked up directly into Jonathan's gaze. "Is anything the matter?"

"No, of course not. To tell you the truth, I was staring at the most beautiful girl here tonight."

"It seems that your compliments have improved with your looks. I think you are trying to turn my head, young sir."

The more they danced, the more comfortable they became, both with the waltz and with each other. The first dance of the evening ended and Jonathan escorted Mary back toward her Aunt Felicity, who had been watching the pair with great interest. A young man Jonathan had seen rushing up to Mary upon their arrival, stepped up and said, "Excuse me sir, but I believe that this lady has promised me the second dance. So with your permission---"

Mary looked at Jonathan, "I'll be back soon."

At that moment, there was another tug on his sleeve. He had forgotten about Ann momentarily, but as he turned, the way she looked almost took his breath away. Her auburn hair was bound up in a multicolored scarf in the Oriental style. Her dress was purple silk and was tight around the waist. The way she filled the dress caused many a man to turn his head as she walked by that evening. With a dazzling smile, she enthusiastically queried, "It is my turn, is it not? Or have you forgotten so quickly?"

"Of course I haven't forgotten. You know there's no way I could forget the beautiful and vivacious Ann Ashburn."

"Why Jonathan, you had better hope that Mary and I do not compare compliments this evening," she said with a laugh that was captivating. Jonathan noticed out of the corner of his eye that Hugh Dacre was watching the two of them intently. As a servant passed, he quickly took a glass of wine from the tray and after quickly gulping it down, replaced the glass and took another before the server could move out of range.

After the second dance, Jonathan escorted Ann back to her chaperone, Aunt Felicity. In addition to enjoying the attention of their guest, it seemed that every other man was also interested in spending as much time as possible with the girls.

It took three more dances with different young men before they were reunited. The orchestra had taken a break and Jonathan suggested that he and the girls go outside and inspect the gardens.

The gardens were nothing, if not spectacular. Edwin Lascelles was evidently not content with just completing his home in grand fashion. He had brought in the famous landscape architect, Lancelot Capability Brown, to transform the grounds. Capability Brown had accomplished his task by using his famous grand, sweeping style that had made him famous throughout England. He had created an open vista of parkland starting at the rear of the mansion and it was stunning. The three young friends marveled as they walked along the pathways. They were not the only ones to admire the gardens that evening, for there were others enjoying themselves in the cool evening breeze. Brown had carefully placed trees and paths to highlight the special views. A nearby stream had been dammed, creating a large lake. The threesome turned down the walk that skirted the edge of the water. There was a full moon out and the light filtered through the overhanging trees. The pathway ended at a rose garden that was blooming in a profusion of color. They stopped to smell the roses and Jonathan pricked his finger as he reached down to pick a lovely bud and bloom.

The threesome moved to the end of the pathway where a delightful waterfall spilled over the dam and into the lake below. They passed through a rocky garden planted with primulas, astilbes, and hosta and the girls were surprised to find that Jonathan knew the names of these plants. He had gained a love of gardening from his mother and she had started educating him from a young age. He had taken every opportunity to study and learn the art of gardening from his mother and others who were willing to teach the boy.

As they crossed to the other side of the lake, they found that the rhododendron were especially lovely that evening. It had been planted copiously and was growing profusely along the lakeside walk as they turned back toward Harewood house. It had taken them forty-five minutes to an hour to make the complete circle around the shimmering lake..

As they approached the rear entrance to the mansion, they began to climb the stone stairs to reach the large outdoor terrace. They got halfway up the steps when they heard someone talking loudly and obviously affected by alcohol. As they reached the large veranda, they were greeted by the sight of an obviously inebriated Hugh Dacre with his back turned. He was taking another glass of wine from a tray and as they stepped closer, Hugh turned in their direction to see who was approaching. His glass caught Jonathan on the arm and it sloshed red wine all over Mary's dress. Without noticing what had happened, the obviously impaired Hugh fixed his gaze on Ann Ashburn.

"Ann, . . . where have you been and who have you been with? I thought you had promised me a few dances and here you are traipsing off with these . . . these . . ." and then he laughed in a loud, sarcastic voice," . . . friends. Yeah, these are your friends. Why you would be out strolling with this boy from Whitehaven, when you could be dancing with a grown man." The last of the contents of his glass splashed onto the floor and this time, onto Mary's white satin slippers.

"Hugh, you are drunk and making a spectacle of yourself," scolded Ann who had her hands on her hips. She was not pleased. At first, Jonathan had been surprised, but now he was just angry.

"You have ruined Mary's dress, you drunken fool," said Jonathan. Ann interrupted and grabbed Jonathan by the arm. "He's had way too much to drink. Let's move on. Mary, let's go so we can clean those stains. I don't think it's a total loss." The three of them turned their backs on the intoxicated Mr. Dacre. He, however, was not ready for their assemblage to end.

"Wait just one damn minute. Ann, I want you to answer my question. What are you doing walking around in the garden with this boy?"

Jonathan stopped when he heard those words. Dacre was no longer any bigger, just older and now drunker. As a matter of fact, Jonathan had him by two inches and twenty pounds. He had lost that feeling of intimidation when they were on the coach together three years before. Unfortunately for him, Hugh was not aware of that fact ... yet. A slow anger started to creep up from Jonathan's toes through the top of his head. His arms felt light as he turned to address his fellow Cumbrian. "I think that you had better take care what you say. I haven't thrashed you yet, because of two things. We are in the company of ladies and we are the guests of Harewood House. But I warn you, remember your manners or I may forget mine."

"Why you insolent little brat, YOU-thrash ME? You seem to forget who you are and who I am!" Hugh was already advancing toward Jonathan.

Hugh rushed at Jonathan and it was clear that he expected Jonathan to be intimidated as he had been growing up back in Whitehaven. As he approached, he grabbed at Jonathan's waist. Jonathan stepped aside and as he went by, Jonathan gave him a small shove in the small of his back. He went flying into the shrubbery lining the terrace, knocking over a couple of chairs and tables in the process. Jonathan looked around and was embarrassed by the scene. He looked over at Mary, who was being held around the shoulders by Ann, as they watched the repulsive spectacle unfold. Mary put her hand to her mouth as she yelled, "Look out Jonathan! He's coming again."

"You're damned right I am," Hugh's crash into the bushes had either sobered him up or gotten his adrenaline pumping, because this time he was charging without swaying. Jonathan thought to himself, "Keep your temper, but don't let this bully get away with this insult."

Hugh leapt on top of Jonathan, grabbed his arm and dropped the other down around Jonathan's leg. He was trying to lift Jonathan to toss him on his back. Jonathan twisted away and with a sharp rap of his fist, broke Hugh's grip on his arm. At the same time, he shoved him under the shoulder and rolled him over onto his back with a thud.

Hugh stood erect, slowly sizing Jonathan up. Hugh suddenly realized he was no longer an intimidating presence to this young man. He was not only drunk, he was angry that he wasn't making progress in his courtship of Ann Ashburn and he was beginning to see there was a reason for that. Could it be that she was really sweet on this kid? Hugh's eyes were red from wine and excitement, but now they narrowed with determination as he charged for the third time.

He was quicker and more determined and he was able to grab Jonathan again around the waist. Jonathan tried to turn to avoid the fall, but only succeeded in taking Hugh down with him. They both hit the stone pavers at the same time. Hugh freed himself and punched Jonathan under the right eye. Lightning bolts shot through Jonathan's head as the shock of the blow penetrated deep inside his skull. However, it produced the opposite effect on Jonathan than Hugh had intended.

Enraged, instead of intimidated, Jonathan no longer could think with a clear head. His anger had turned into a blind rage as he turned back to Hugh Dacre, spun and hit Hugh in the solar plexus. It knocked the breath out of him and he slumped backward. Like a cat pouncing on a mouse, Jonathan was on top of his adversary with his hands around his throat. The victor of the fight was no longer in doubt, but whether or not Hugh Dacre was going to live was definitely in doubt. It was now a matter of how much damage the enraged Jonathan was going to inflict. Suddenly, there were arms and hands trying to pry Jonathan's fingers from Hugh's throat. It was not until he heard a dreamlike voice saying, "Jonathan, you must let him go. Jonathan, do you hear me? Please please let him go." Mary was gently tugging at his shoulder.

Jonathan heard her words as if they had come from a faraway place. He instinctively looked over at Mary and relaxed his grip. She helped lift him up, off of Hugh. He looked around and saw a large group of people who had gathered. Most of them had a disapproving look. Who were these ruffians that were interrupting the grandest ball ever given in Leeds? Ann, Mary and Jonathan started back into the main ballroom. Felicity met them and asked, "What is the commotion about outside? Someone said two drunks were fighting." Felicity saw the disheveled look of Jonathan's clothes and the swelling under his eye. She also noticed the wine stains on Mary's dress.

"Oh no, what has happened, children?"

Hugh's voice was heard over the crowd, "You'll pay for this, Lucas! You'll pay for this, I promise you."

The foursome made their way through the crowd and called for their carriage. Felicity listened carefully to the explanation of what had transpired. Mary was the one who relayed the evening's progression to her aunt as she described the wonderful time that both she and Ann had that evening. Felicity listened intently about the delightful walk the three had taken through the magnificent gardens. She was not surprised to hear how the altercation had begun. It seems Aunt Felicity had approached Hugh several times during the girl's absence and each time he seemed a little bit more inebriated. Mary explained that it all had started with an accident. Hugh had turned around, not knowing Mary, Ann and Jonathan were behind him. He had accidentally spilled his wine on Mary's dress. They had told him it did not matter and that it could be cleaned up quickly. But then he began to make disrespectful remarks to Jonathan.

Felicity understood what had happened. Unfortunately, this breach of decorum had involved her niece and her guest. It would take time, but with an explanation to the proper people, the family name could be restored. She was sad that the girl's last outing before they returned to Whitehaven had turned out to be such a disaster. She hoped that Jonathan's injury would not be too severe. He assured her that he was fine and apologized repeatedly. Felicity replied, "There is nothing you need to apologize for, Jonathan. You had to defend yourself. I'm just sorry that this person, who caused all of this, is known to be associated with our family. In the future, Jonathan, remember the threats that he hurled at you in front of God and everyone."

Jonathan replied, "I believe that was the wine talking."

"Don't bet on it. That family has a reputation for being ruthless. I believe they had some altercations with your mother's family several generations back and that one ended in a kidnapping and murder. I do not believe that the Dacre's would go to that extreme today, but I do believe he intends to do you a bad turn. I caution you to be careful in any future dealings with that family."

Jonathan asked to be excused, as he had to be on his way back to Manchester early the next morning. He explained that he would return to his inn to try to get some much needed rest before his long journey on the morrow. He reluctantly said his goodbyes to Mary and Felicity at the front door. Strangely, Ann had already retired. Aunt Felicity thought that her early departure was perhaps due to the stress of the evening's misadventure. After all, she seemed to be the cause of Hugh's ill humor. After goodbye hugs and kisses, Jonathan, disappointed by Ann's absence, turned and started walking back to the inn. As he turned the corner he noticed a cloaked figure standing by a nearby tree. He was startled and stopped short.

"Jonathan, it's me." Ann pulled back the hood of her cape as she came forward. I only have a minute. If I'm not back in two minutes, they'll know that I'm gone. I just wanted to give you a proper send off, so you will remember me." Ann threw both her arms around Jonathan's neck and pulled him forward, kissing him fully on his mouth. This was something he had only dreamed about and he found that the reality of her warm mouth covering his, was much better than a dream."

Chapter 15

T HE RETURN TRIP TO ROCHDALE WAS A difficult one for both Jonathan and his mare. It wasn't necessarily the distance, which was only thirty-three miles, but the ruggedness of the terrain he had to recross that caused the strain. If Jonathan had been riding to win a wager, it would also have been less stressful. As it was, he was riding to cover up the first major mistake in judgment he had made in his young life. He was able to cover the necessary distance in about eight hours. The trip back, in many respects, was easier because he knew the way.

His initial plan had been to return directly to the inn in Rochdale and wait to return to his project the next morning. But his earlier than expected arrival gave him the opportunity to swing by the job, which was only a couple of miles out of his way. So it was, that late on Monday afternoon of July 13, he approached the nearly completed Beal River Mill. From a distance he was glad to see that the building was still standing. As he came closer, he noticed that there wasn't much change. The last few wheels and cogs that were supposed to be installed were still standing in the same positions they had been when he began his journey. It looked as if nothing at all had been done since he departure. He climbed down from his weary mare to have a closer inspection. As he walked inside, his fears were confirmed. There had been a small amount of work accomplished, but not much. What could have gone wrong?

The Cat Scratch Inn, where his workers were lodged, was less than a half a mile away. It was not the fanciest of accommodations but it was clean and the food was okay. Jonathan was feeling a mixture of anxiety, fear and a good deal of anger. When he walked into the inn he saw his three workers sitting at a corner table. From a distance, they seemed to be in worse condition than Hugh Dacre had been after drinking a half a keg of wine. It suddenly dawned on Jonathan that he had a major problem. It was bad enough that he had disobeyed his uncle, gotten into a common brawl in a place he was not supposed to be, but he allowed unsupervised workers to get drunk, resulting in no production for three days.

Jonathan walked up to the table as Henry Thomas looked up from a tankard of ale. "Ah, young Master Lucas, you have returned from your trip. Sit down and have a drink with us and tell us all about it."

"Well Mr. Thomas, I don't believe that I will drink with you, not now or any time in the future. I left and depended on you to finish the job and I even paid you a bonus in advance. And how do you repay me? You repay me by obviously spending the last three days drinking and accomplishing nothing. "

"Oh laddie, you seem to be a little cross with us." he grinned at his two companions. "We only followed your lead. If it were time for you to take a holiday, then we felt it must be time for our holiday, as well." This was the first time this man had addressed him in a disrespectful manner. Was it just the gin talking or was there more to it than that? Both Jonathan's father and uncle had always stressed the fact that things had to be done properly and he had felt, at times, that it was merely for form's sake. This was the first time in his life he realized there was more to it than appearances. His father had also told him that the best leaders lead by setting a good example. Choices that resulted from bad judgment always equaled problems. Jonathan realized that putting his trust in the men and even offering a bonus was not enough to assure a job completed. He clearly saw that all he really had done was to bring his workers into his deception and selfishness . . . a strategy that had failed miserably. He realized that he was trying to buy their silence on his own disobedience. Once he had shown the men that he was willing to take a risk for pleasure, they saw no reason that they should not do the same. It was a mistake that he swore he would not repeat.

"What happened to your eye? Did you fall off your horse?"

"Never mind about that," Jonathan retorted. "Do you have any of the money left that I gave you?"

"Well sir, since you asked, we've not a farthing left. Now would be a good time to advance us the balance of what you promised."

Jonathan had an idea. He turned and walked over to the innkeeper.

"Innkeeper, it's the middle of the month and we owe you for the past two weeks as well as for the two weeks coming."

"Aye sir, that's just about right."

"If you wish to collect what's owed to you, then these men cannot have another drink until I release them. Is that clear? I want to have them sober and back on the job by dawn."

"I understand and I'll be glad to have them out of my pub for a while."

"If they give you any trouble, don't hesitate to call the authorities, but also let me know."

The determined young man walked back to the table where his three helpers sat. "You will be back at work by daylight in the morning and you will be sober. There will be no further bonus and I'm a mind to dock your pay, which I advanced to you in anticipation of extra effort on your part. Instead, you repay me by getting drunk and you may have cost me my apprenticeship."

Jonathan spoke in such a stern and firm voice that Henry Thomas and his companions were left speechless. He turned on his heels and walked out the door. Although he was exhausted from all the stress, the travel and the trouble that waited for him back in Rochdale, Jonathan made a quick decision. He went to the stable and rented a fresh horse. The gelding was quickly saddled and he quickly mounted the fresh steed. Leaving the inn at a fast trot, as soon as he was clear of Rochdale, he spurred the horse into a fast gallop. He was determined to start making amends to his uncle by confessing his transgressions before they were found out. He arrived at his uncle's residence in less than an hour. He dismounted his horse filled with trepidation.

The servants all knew Jonathan, so he was admitted immediately into the home. "Your uncle is dining and I'm sure he will be glad to see you."

"I'm not so sure," Jonathan said under his breath.

The door to the dining room was already opened. William Lucas sat at the end of a long table and was just finishing his meal when he looked up to see Jonathan entering the room. Under normal circumstances he would have stood up and enthusiastically greeted his nephew. In this instance, he remained seated and with a knitted brow, poured himself another glass of port.

"Well well, to what do we owe this surprise visit?"

"Uncle, I have something to tell you." The weight upon Jonathan's conscience was overwhelming. He had never been in this position before. He felt he had made a man's mistake and therefore, had to face the consequences like a man. It was difficult, but he knew it was necessary.

"You say you have something to tell me? I hope its not bad news. There hasn't been an accident, has there?" His demeanor had taken on a very serious hue as he starred intently at his nephew.

"No Sir, there has not been an accident."

"Well, come in, sit down and tell me what has happened."

"If you don't mind, uncle, I would prefer to remain standing."

"If you wish," was William's reply.

"Uncle, I have been dishonest. I have disobeyed you."

"Let me guess, nephew. Could it be that the lure of two young ladies has led you astray?"

"How did you guess that, sir? " The surprised reply.

"It wasn't very hard to figure out. Your surprise visit and the timing of it, well, I just put two and two together."

"There's more sir."

"Besides your disobedience? "

"Yes sir. I'm afraid there are a few more things that I must tell you."

"Sit down Jonathan. You look tired and I'm sure these confessions are weighing heavily on you."

Jonathan took a deep breath and remained standing. "Thank you for your courtesy, but I'm afraid that after you hear what remains to be confessed, you may feel forced to ask me to leave."

"You haven't broken the law, have you?"

"No, things are not that bad. Before I left on Saturday, I had entrusted Henry Thomas with the task of continuing the work on the mill. I even offered him a bonus if they would work all three days and hopefully, I would return and only have to inspect their work, so that we could release the mill to the miller. I was foolish enough to advance him half of the bonus before I left. Instead of working, I am afraid they spent those three days drinking up their bonus."

For the first time William allowed a flash of anger to show on his face. "That was a foolish thing to do. Of course, it only compounded the original mistake."

"I know, I know. There's more."

William leaned forward with more intensity, "The place hasn't burned down, has it?"

"No sir. What I'm about to tell you has nothing to do with the mill."

"Get on with it," came the stern reply.

"I'm afraid I got into an altercation while at the Midsummer's Ball in Leeds."

"Is that how you got that bump under your eye?"

"Yes sir."

William forced a smile, "At least tell me that the other participant came off the worst."

"Yes sir. I was able to at least do that properly."

Jonathan related the entire story to his uncle. William listened intently for the entire hour that it took Jonathan to unburden his guilt. He had finally had the courage to take a seat at the table beside his uncle. After he had completed his narration, he looked up at his uncle and said, "I acted unwisely and against the interest of your business and my education. In doing so I have embarrassed myself and worst of all, I have damaged your reputation. I am prepared to accept whatever decision you may deem appropriate. I would not blame you if you sent me back to Whitehaven in disgrace. I certainly deserve it."

William had been impressed by the candor and sincere confession of wrongdoing he had just witnessed from his nephew.

"Let's look at this problem logically. You have transgressed, that is true. It is also true that you have certainly damaged, not only my reputation, but also your young reputation. If you make mistakes when you are young, they are much harder to overcome than a stumble once in a while in a much longer, successful career." William paused long enough to pour himself the last contents of the port sitting on the table in front of him.

"I must take some time to reflect on all that has happened before I make a decision as to your future. I want you to return to your inn this evening and see if you can round up Henry Thomas and his men tomorrow."

"I should be able to accomplish that as I left instructions to the innkeeper to cut off their supply of rum and gin. I will check on them once more, before I retire this evening, to see if that has taken place."

"I would advise against that. They will either be there or they won't. You must finish this job by the end of the week and since you have decided to make decisions independent of my judgment, you will receive no further help from me. The situation is of your making and I trust you understand how important it is, for both of our sakes, that this all ends on a positive note."

"I understand and if it can possibly be done, I will do it."

"Then I suggest, nephew, that you get started right away. I bid you good night." William stood up, bowed slightly to his nephew and walked out of the dining room. Jonathan's feeling of shame and remorse was overwhelming. Looking around the room he saw a bottle of brandy sitting on a nearby sideboard. He walked over and for the first time in his life, he took a drink of strong brandy alone. This growing up was harder to do than he had anticipated.

The next day dawned gray and wet. A storm had descended over Rochdale. Jonathan had to fight the wind and rain to reach the inn where his men were staying. When he tried to open the door to enter a gust of wind jerked it out of his hand and slammed it hard against the wall. He looked around and did not see Henry Thomas, nor any of the others. He knew where their rooms were located so he climbed the stairs, taking three at a time. As he reached the door, he rapped loudly, calling Henry's name. The door opened and inside were the three men in various stages of dress.

Accustomed as they were to Jonathan's usual casual demeanor, they were surprised to hear him yell at them. "I thought I told you to be ready at dawn."

"Yes sir. I seem to remember that you did."

"I'm surprised that you remember anything at all that I told you. You've got three minutes to be downstairs and another five minutes to have the wagons loaded and ready to go."

One of the two helpers was staring out the window and he said, "My God! It's a regular hurricane blowing outside. You don't expect us to work in this weather, do you?"

The newly authoritarian manager replied, "Yes, I do expect you to work and work hard until we finish this job. We're going to make up for the holidays that each of us had and get this project back on track. Now get dressed, get downstairs, get loaded and let's move."

The crew was downstairs and the mules were hitched to the wagon as the wind howled outside. Into the driving rain they pushed until they reached the mill project. They unloaded their equipment with difficulty and released the mules into a pasture to graze, even as the storm raged. The men were wet, hung over and miserable and were certainly not happy to be out in the storm. Luckily for them, most of the work that remained to be done was installing equipment on the interior of the mill. They soon found that Jonathan had gained a rough edge about him that was not there the week before. He no longer asked them to perform a task, but told them to do it. Where before he would ask Henry what he though should be next in their project, he now bypassed him and told them what to do and to do it quickly.

The storm finally began to abate late that evening. Jonathan did not relax his drive to get the maximum out of his workers. It was nearing midnight and they had been working by torchlight for the past few hours when finally, Henry worked up the courage to say, "It's been eight hours since we had anything to eat. If you want us to be able to work tomorrow and finish this job, then I think it's time for some rest and food." Their shame at letting Jonathan down had worn away with each passing hour. They had put up with Jonathan's iron handed manner throughout the stormy day, out of remorse, but they were tired and hungry. Jonathan started to tell them to keep working, but he realized that he was as tired and hungry as the men. He stopped, looked around and said with a softer tone of voice, "You're right, men, we were behind in this race, but we made up ground today. We should finish this job by the end of the week, Saturday to be exact, and then, we can turn it over to the miller. Let's all get some sleep and we'll start again in the morning." He paused and looked around at each of them and said, "Thanks men. We just might make it if we continue to work together."

Jonathan realized he could not drive these men much harder without taking the chance they might walk away. Their contriteness had to give way to pride of workmanship. This day, Jonathan had achieved yet another milestone in his education and personal growth. In fact, the last few days had been full of many different kinds of milestones.

By the end of the third day, everything was installed. Jonathan and Henry went over every piece of equipment to make sure it all fit together properly. They agreed to arrive early the next morning, which was Saturday, to release the water onto the waterwheel. It would be the final evaluation to see if the mill was working properly and also a test of Jonathan's determination and diligence.

The next morning, a rather large group gathered at the new Beal River Mill. William was in attendance, along with the miller and several of the surrounding farmers. Three of the farmers had come with wagons loaded with wheat, hoping to get their grain processed.

One of the workers was up at the end of the flow that diverted the Beal River to the waterwheel. During construction, the flume had been blocked with boards to keep out the water. Henry Thomas was standing on a platform underneath the building to observe what happened when water met the ten-foot diameter wheel. At a signal from Jonathan, his worker lifted the boards from the end of the flume and the water rushed toward its target. Jonathan held his breath as the water struck the wheel. It slowly began to turn and at this point, the gears had purposely not been engaged.

The group watched as the water turned the wheel round and round. The movement seemed free without any problems. After watching for about ten minutes, it was time to engage the gears. The spectators moved inside and Jonathan went over to the lever that was used to engage the gear cogs. This was going to be the important part of the process. If this went well, everyone would have cause to celebrate. If this did not go well, Jonathan could possibly be on his way back, in disgrace, to Whitehaven. The large five-foot switch handle was engaged and sure enough, everything worked as planned. The millstones turned in their counter rotating fashion. A cheer went up from the small crowd and the miller was the first to come up to Jonathan to give him a pat on the back. He shook his head and said, "I would have never guessed this day would be so successful. When your Uncle William proposed that you run this project, I can tell you, I was against it. You're so young and all, but he told me that you're going to be a great millwright and you've made a believer out of me, young man."

"Thank you sir, " replied Jonathan, "There were times when I didn't believe it myself. But, with a little help from some experienced men, I'm happy to say we were able to get your mill built."

There were several young ladies in the crowd. Most of them were farmer's daughters, but the miller's youngest daughter, who was a very pretty girl, was also in attendance. She caught Jonathan's attention with her pretty blue eyes, long blonde hair and buxom build. After what had transpired at the ball and after the trouble he had caused by disobeying his uncle, the successful completion of his first assignment lifted the weight right off of his shoulders. It seemed as if everything was beginning to look up and smooth out. The old positive confident Jonathan was back.

After the short celebration, the miller, who was anxious to start earning an income, began to unload the farmers' wagons full of grain. Jonathan, William and their crew worked with the miller to make sure everything was operating properly. When the last wagon was unloaded and the grain had been turned into flour, Jonathan approached his uncle.

"Uncle William, I know that this does not make up for my disobedience, but I hope that it will help toward proving that I am sincere in my apologies to you, for my conduct."

"Jonathan, you know that I was angry, but I have never doubted you, since the moment you walked in and voluntarily admitted your insubordination. It was good you did, because the miller had already complained to me about your absence and the lack of progress on the project."

"You mean you knew?"

"Remember, young man, I was your age once upon a time and I had all of the same desires and drives that you have developed of late. Some of us are able to control our emotions and some of us let our emotions control us. Most human beings are somewhere in the middle. We all make mistakes, but if we can learn from them, they make us stronger. I believe that you have grown in maturity and strength and I'm proud of what you have accomplished."

William offered his hand to his nephew and said, "I think it's time that you and I adjourn to the pub and have a brandy together. I believe that is your drink of choice, after your last visit to my house." Jonathan with a look of surprise, turned to his uncle and smiled, "Brandy burns as it goes down!"

Chapter 16

AN APPRENTICED MILLWRIGHT WAS BOUND by British law to remain with his master until the age of 20. Jonathan was 17 years old when he was given the job of building the Beal River Mill. For the next year, Jonathan not only worked for his Uncle William, but was also loaned out on several jobs to other prominent millwrights from time to time.

As he progressed, Jonathan was becoming an expert at finding good sites for water power. Usually these sites were found where a river narrowed down in its channel and the current picked up speed. He could now supervise the erection of foundation walls for almost any type of industrial water powered operation and could oversee the construction of the entire building. He knew about the felling of logs and also how to cut and fashion those logs into beams, boards, and shingles.

To support the water wheel shafts, he installed pillars of brick or stone underneath. He became an expert at locating white oak trees for the main water wheel shafts. The young apprentice also knew what type of wood to use for each of the mill parts. Often, he and his crew used stone or wood for bearings. Both the stone bearings and the wooden bearings were lubricated with tallow. Jonathan knew exactly where to build a dam, a millrace or a sluice, so there was sufficient water-power. He never forgot how it felt, when finally, the first Beal River Millrace was successfully set into operation.

He had also learned to keep the secrets of the millwright profession to himself and so, usually, worked in silence. Few people were lucky enough to watch him go about his work. In short, he had become a first-rate professional millwright, one of the most respected professions of the age.

During the last few years of his apprenticeship, Jonathan was allowed to return home for a month at Christmas to spend time with his family. He took this opportunity to visit two of his favorite people, Ann Ashburn and Mary Cook. They had returned to Whitehaven from Leeds shortly after their misadventure with Hugh Dacre. Jonathan's quandary over which of the girls was his favorite, only got more complicated with each meeting. He was a frequent visitor to the small village of Cleator Moor where Anns' kisses became much longer and more frequent and Mary had become much bolder, since she was no longer under the watchful eye of her Aunt Felicity. It took a lot of coaxing, but eventually Jonathan was sampling and enjoying her kisses, as well.

The social life around Whitehaven was certainly not as grand as the ball they had attended in Leeds. There were, however, plenty of parties and festivals that gave them the opportunity to gather together during the season. When Jonathan was traveling on business, the three of them kept up a constant correspondence. Since Ann and Mary no longer lived under the same roof and did not normally see each other's letters, they were becoming more intimate.

Jonathan's success and rising stature as a millwright had not gone unnoticed by the eligible young ladies around Manchester. They were not about to let this young man think solely of his two Cumbrian sweethearts. At every opportunity, they flirted with him, and before long, he was flirting back. He was also making frequent trips to see the miller's daughter, Alison Nicolas, in Rochdale.

Their first meeting occurred when he arrived at the Beal River Mill in mid-September with the excuse that he was there to make a courtesy call to assure everything was functioning as it should. Alison slipped away the moment he arrived and waited for him about a half a mile down the road behind a small wooded hill. After his perfunctory inspection, he said to the miller, "All seems to be operating well, but I'm a little concerned that I may have to replace some of the cogs in the main wheel soon. There are some small cracks beginning to form in a couple of them, but that is not unusual with new construction." He took the miller over and showed him the suspect cogs. "I suggest that you keep a close eye on these. If the cracks get worse, let me know as quickly as possible and they will be replaced. Otherwise, I shall be back after a time to make certain everything is functioning properly." With that, he excused himself and headed back in the direction of Whitehaven.

Alison stepped out from behind the trees as Jonathan started down the hill. He was not at all sure what to expect from the eye-catching seventeen-year-old miller's daughter. He slowed his horse to a walk as he approached.

"Hello Master Lucas. Did you find everything continuing to work efficiently in our mill? Or has it fallen apart due to your lack of attention?"

"Why yes, everything is fine. You are the miller's daughter, if I recall correctly?"

"Yes, that's right. I'm Alison. Why don't you get down and let's talk a while." Jonathan looked around and then dismounted. "Well Alison, it is nice to see you again. Where are you heading this morning? I noticed you when I arrived at the mill this morning, but you suddenly disappeared. I wondered where you had gone and that, perhaps, I had offended you in some way."

"On the contrary! I'm not in the least offended by you. I came out here knowing this was the way you would return and thought perhaps we could walk and talk with some privacy."

"I can't think of anything that I'd rather be doing right now, than walking and talking with you."

"Oh I bet you say that to all the girls," replied Alison with a sly grin.

"No Alison, I am required to work very hard and therefore do not have much time for social activities. In fact, I get quite lonely from time to time and it's nice to be able to talk with someone closer to my own age."

He stared down into the bold blue eyes of the beautiful young woman, who had obviously decided she wanted to get to know him. Tall, with a beautiful figure, she wore a dress that was made of white linen. Alison's breasts were pushed up by a blue corset, worn on the outside of her dress. The curving tops of her breasts peeking over the top of the corset spoke loudly of the pleasures of the flesh. She had high cheekbones, a wide mouth, and beautiful white teeth. Her eyes were set wide apart and she stared into Jonathan's eyes alluringly. Her hair was the color of ripened wheat and it hung in careless folds down below her shoulders.

"We will have to do something about your loneliness," she said to him as she reached out and took his hand. At first he didn't respond to the pressure of her fingers on his. She didn't seem to mind and after several steps, he tightened his grip. She stopped and turned to look at him. "Here, let's move off this road. There's a nice little brook just over there where you can water your horse and we can rest a while before you begin your journey back to Manchester."

She turned and darted into the woods, taking a small pathway that was barely noticeable. Jonathan hesitated. He was not convinced he should follow her. Self-assured women sometimes tended to intimidate him. She stopped, turned back and waved for him to follow. The sight of her was such a vision standing in the pathway, framed by the trees, that his resistance was short-lived.

He and his horse turned onto the pathway and followed Alison a short distance into a grassy clearing through which a brook wound its way. He reached into his saddlebags and pulled out a hobble that he placed on the front legs of his mount. Removing the bridal from the horse's head, he placed it on a log nearby. His horse, grateful to be released, started to graze on the succulent grass.

Alison was standing by the water and had taken her shoes off and was splashing one foot in the stream. Jonathan stared at this lovely creature and she returned his look, flirtatiously, over her shoulder. Although this was the first time that there had been an opportunity to speak together alone, it was plain that an overwhelming yearning for Jonathan had ignited in the miller's daughter. Jonathan stepped away from the log and walked up behind her. He placed his hands on her smooth white shoulders. She leaned back against his chest as she took his arms and wrapped them around her breasts. He could feel the warmth of her body pressing against him. Her scent was intoxicating, even though there was no hint of perfume on her.

Jonathan felt his heart pounding. He was becoming lightheaded and weak in the knees. Beside them, the brook sang its little melody as it wandered by the rocks and rushed between the banks. It was a magical moment. Even the birds were singing as if blessing the moment. She turned around to face him and reached up and put her arms around his neck, drawing him closer.

His impulse was, at first, to resist. But it was too late for that. She already had him under the age-old spell that suddenly comes upon all men. This young seventeen-year-old was no longer feeling lonely. Their lips met. The kiss was very different from the one he remembered receiving from Ann in July. Different, but It was still very nice. It was longer, deeper and unhurried. The shape of her mouth even felt different, he thought to himself. Then something unexpected happened. Alison slipped her tongue between his lips deep into his mouth. Startled, he jerked his head back away from her.

"What's the matter, don't you like that?"

"I'm not sure," Jonathan said with a hint of confusion. What he meant, but did not say, was that he was not sure if he was supposed to like it.

"It's the French way, I've been told."

"The French do have funny ways of doing things in the art of making love. At least that's what my Uncle has told me."

He decided he did like it after all and leaned down for a second try. After this encounter in the small glen, Jonathan looked forward to making this trip almost every week to make sure the mill was operating properly!

Jonathan's work and continuing apprenticeship took him to several different surrounding locations. Rarely did he stay more than six weeks in any one town. His assignments included, not only constructing all sorts of new mills, but repairing many older ones, as well. He was not able to visit Alison as often as he

would have liked, but he had seen her often enough to become addicted to their lovemaking. He had also learned one other thing. That was how to recognize when other women were interested in him. Not all of them were as pretty as the miller's daughter, but he had found a few that were even more enthusiastic than Alison in their lovemaking.

His newfound sexual awareness did nothing to diminish his affections for the two Cumbrian girls. As a matter of fact, he found himself thinking of either Ann or Mary, while he was making love to other girls. He would close his eyes and picture that the girl he had in his arms was one of the two he really wanted. If these willing maidens made him feel so passionate when he was with them, he wondered how much better it would be if he were actually making love to someone that he felt deeply about.

He and his uncle had become even closer. Jonathan was now allowed to stay after dinner and have drinks and cigars with some of his clients. Although naturally retiring in certain circumstances, when the conversation turned to a subject of interest for Jonathan, he would join in and hold his own in the discussion. In these environments, he was not only learning how to behave in adult society, but he was learning how to conduct business. William was quite the entrepreneur and had a broad range of business interests and investments. These after-dinner discussions over brandy, invariably led to a discussion of what was happening in the world.

William was an avid newspaper reader and enjoyed nothing more than having Jonathan sit and listen to his discourse on what was taking place in the world. It was very enlightening to Jonathan and although some of the subjects did not interest him as much as others, he read all of the articles from his uncle's periodicals. It seemed to Jonathan that the men running the country were not doing such a great job. There was once again trouble with the American colonies. On June 9, 1772 *The HMS Gaspee,* an armed British customs schooner ran aground off the coast of Rhode Island, chasing an American packet ship captained by a man named Thomas Lindsay.

The Americans were angered by the high British taxes and rowed out that night to *The HMS Gaspee* and seized control of the ship. According to the newspaper reports, they wounded the Scottish captain who was a certain Lieut. William Dudingston. They sent the crew and the wounded captain ashore and then set fire to the ship. British officials soon arrived in Rhode Island to investigate the incident, but they found no one willing to identify those involved. The inquiry was closed without results.

In discussions with his uncle, it was pointed out to Jonathan that if the perpetrators had been apprehended, they would not have been tried in Rhode Island, but they would have been shipped back to England for justice in a British court. This is what had angered the colonies and caused them to react the way that had.

"I'm not sure, Jonathan, if I would not have done the same thing in their place. We need good relations with the colonies. Your father has been very successful in the Virginia tobacco trade. Let's hope the trouble does not escalate, for it could be devastating to his business."

Even at home in England, he read a story about food riots. He was distressed to read an article in the Gentleman's Magazine describing what had happened:

12 April 1772

This night about eleven o clock a mob assembled at Chelmsford armed with bludgeons to the amount of about fifty and were very riotous all night. By four o'clock in the morning they increased to the number of three hundred or more when they set off for Mr. Bullen's, Mr. Morrage's, and Harrington's mills, from whence they took large quantities of flour meal, etc., and brought it in wagons under a strong guard to the market place in Chelmsford to sell at a price they approved of.

Mr. Harrington expostulated for some time with their captain or chief on the unjust and illegal methods they had taken, but to no effect for they grew exceedingly riotous and obliged Mr. Harrington to deliver them ten sacks of flour and meal, and also to promise them ten sacks more the next day. They then took his wagon and horses, loaded it and proceeded in triumph to Chelmsford.

Such is the miserable situation of people in this part of the country. They have since been at Mr. Johnson's at Baddow etc., regaling themselves at every house till they were quite riotous. They now intend paying a visit to the farmers and have this evening begun with Mr. John Ward of Bishop's Hall from which place they have taken two loads of wheat. The market place is now filled up with great quantities of wheat and flour which they have plundered.

We have sent to the war-office for troops to assist us, but none are yet arrived. The inhabitants are in great consternation; for this moment a very considerable body is marching into town with colours flying and armed with bludgeons, etc., God only knows where this will end.

Accounts are just arrived from Sudbury, Colchester, Whiteham, etc., that there is great robbing there and that the parties intend to join.

Chelmsford was almost two hundred and fifty miles away, but Jonathan was beginning to realize that even faraway events could directly affect his life and that of his family. He was beginning to view life as an adult, instead of an adolescent.

There was one event in June 1772, that caused consternation on a worldwide basis. It was a financial crisis that threatened to topple the entire economy, not only of Great Britain, but also its major trading partners. The crisis was precipitated by the failure of banks in London and Scotland. This caused crashes in the stock markets of London, Amsterdam, and Paris. Especially hard hit were stock values of the high flying East India Company. His Uncle William had been heavily invested in those shares. It was possible that his uncle could soon be facing serious financial troubles. Then in September, the mighty East India Company defaulted on its payments to the British Treasury. This seriously harmed the financial situation of the British government and British business interests everywhere.

Not only was Uncle William's personal financial state now in trouble, many of his clients were losing the ability to fund their projects. Jonathan was soon apprised of the fact that his father's tobacco import business was also in jeopardy. It was all very complicated to Jonathan, but his uncle's explanation of what was happening worldwide, both enlightened and frightened him.

William explained that the credit crisis was greatly deteriorating relations between the American Colonies and Britain. This was particularly true in the South, where his brother had his tobacco trade with Virginia. The southern colonies, which produced tobacco, rice, and indigo and exported them to Britain, were granted higher credit than the northern colonies because the north was manufacturing the same commodities as the British and were, therefore, in competition with England. The Southern colonies had borrowed millions of pounds from British banks and merchants and William explained to Jonathan that the merchants in England helped the planters sell their crops and shipped what the planters wanted to purchase from Britain. Jonathan was familiar with this process because of his father's involvement in the tobacco trade.

The planters were usually given credit for twelve months without interest. Now, because of this credit crisis, British merchants and bankers urgently needed the debts repaid. After this debacle, the American planters were facing the serious problem of finding means to pay off these debts.

Of course the planters were not prepared for large-scale debt reduction. This meant that without the benefit of dependable British credit extended to them, planters were going to be unable to continue to produce crops for export. And, even if they could manage to grow their produce during this credit crisis, they had nowhere to sell their goods.

As the end of November 1772 approached, the worrisome credit crash intensified. There were more and more worldwide bankruptcies and it became very difficult to find new projects that had financing. William decided that he would accompany Jonathan to Whitehaven to have a consultation with his brother. It looked as if Jonathan's apprenticeship was going to end a year earlier than expected. The chances of having a Merry Christmas did not look good.

Jonathan made one last inspection tour to the Beal River Mill. After the usual quick inspection, Jonathan told the miller that it would be his last regular visit for a while. He explained that conditions required him to return to his home in Whitehaven, but that if Mr. Nicholas needed any major repairs, he would be glad to return and assist.

"I'm afraid after you leave, lad, there will be a major repair to be made, but neither you nor I have the skills to repair that which will be broken," he said with a melancholy tone.

Puzzled, Jonathan replied, "Well, we can only do our best, sir. I'll say goodbye." He then shook hands with the miller and mounted his horse, troubled by the miller's last comment. As usual, Alison was waiting for him by the path to the meadow. They spent a good hour together making love. Jonathan seemed pensive and faraway. Alison noticed and asked, "What's wrong Jonathan? I can tell something is bothering you. Tell me what it is?"

"You know I'm leaving in a couple of days to return to Whitehaven."

"Yes, I know. You do that every year."

"Well, my uncle is ending my apprenticeship."

"But why, have you done something wrong?

"No it's nothing like that. He has had some financial reversals lately and we have lost some projects due to this stupid financial crisis. So it seems that I'll not be back on a regular basis, but I will write to you and I will be back as often as I can."

"Yes, do write. I can read a little, but if I'm going to be getting letters from you, I will learn to read everything. You know I'm going to miss you and I feel that you will miss me. I'm not going to burden you with tears. I know that my station as a miller's daughter means that what we have here, is all we'll ever have between us." She turned away and said in a barely audible voice, "But I will miss you." Alison stood up quickly, bent down and kissed him passionately on the mouth in the French manner and said, "Goodbye Jonathan, farewell and remember me." With this she turned and ran to the stream and blithely crossed the rocks and in a moment, disappeared from sight. Jonathan sat for a while staring into the empty woods. He knew what she had said was true. Their diverse stations in English society would not permit their relationship to become anything more. But he made her a promise as he spoke to the empty forest, "You are my first real love – I'll not soon forget you and what you taught me about life."

Chapter 17

THE CHRISTMAS SEASON OF THE YEAR 1772, although still festive, was much more subdued than in prior years. There were bankruptcies that reached even into Whitehaven, dampening the usually ebullient Christmas celebrations. Luckily for Jonathan, his father, John, was not on that unlucky list of bankrupt men.

His coal transportation business, although not glamorous, was steadily providing income. His mill that made sails continued to produce a superior product that was much sought after, not only by Whitehaven shipowners, but in ports, up and down the British seacoast. He had just landed a large contract with the British Navy that would be very profitable over the next few years. In short, after a brief turn-down in orders, the demand for the Lucas sails was outstripping the company's ability to supply them.

The tobacco business with Virginia had been barely profitable on their last two trips. It remained to be seen if that business with the American colonies would continue. All in all, John Lucas had been able to maneuver through the rough waters of the credit crisis like a true master seaman navigating a storm threatened ship.

William discussed his personal situation with his brother which directly affected his ability to continue Jonathan's apprenticeship. The hit he had taken on the East India Company stock had seriously affected his net worth. Several of the projects he was supposed to begin, had been put on hold. Due to the credit crisis, William's future prospects were uncertain.

The two brothers summoned Jonathan into his father's study. William was proud of the knowledge the young man had gained while under his tutelage. John was anxious to understand what level of expertise Jonathan had attained in the five years he had been gone. Both of the elder Lucas men questioned the young man intensely. It soon became apparent to John that his son, although only eighteen years old, was more knowledgeable by far, than his father, when it came to the profession of millwright. But more impressive was the fact that he was almost as imaginative and creative as his Uncle William. William had decided he would not relate Jonathan's disobedience to his father. The young man had turned his attitude around and had not caused any further problems. He had been zealous executing the projects given to him and instead of being an expense as an apprentice, he had become a profitable addition to William's team.

After much discussion, it was finally agreed that Jonathan would remain in Whitehaven and enter into the sail milling business with his father. For the next two years, he would remain on call for his Uncle William until the economy, perhaps, should turn around and new projects could be obtained. Jonathan had very mixed emotions about not returning with William, as he had really enjoyed his time with his uncle. The responsibility he had been given at such a young age, had given him a strong sense of self-worth and maturity. He also had pangs of regret about not seeing Alison Nicholas any longer.

On the positive side, it felt good to be home with his mother and father. But, the best part of a return to Whitehaven was the chance to spend time with Ann and Mary.

His father made the proposition that perhaps they should start to consider building a second mill or expand the existing one in order to keep up with the rising demand. It would also put Jonathan's apprenticeship knowledge to good use. He was quite pleased that his father was asking his opinion on business matters.

Jonathan had a suggestion that caught the attention of both of the brothers. He suggested they centralize their sail production in manufactories, constructing a series of simple rooms and installing a number of heavy sailcloth looms. In addition, they could add facilities for warp-winding and possibly starching. This would mean that they brought, in house, the trade of flax dressing, or preparing raw flax for spinning. Even after the installation of the equipment that William had supplied, John had continued to put a lot of the spinning and weaving out to workers' homes to enhance production. This had worked well for the first couple of years, supplementing production, but it also created a lot of quality issues with the homespun thread received. Jonathan suggested they unite both the commercial and manufacturing sides of the businesses and try to control more of the process by centralization.

"Son, that is something that we will need to think about. Of course, we will have to hire new workers and buy more equipment and that will cost money and as you know, it is very difficult to find capital nowadays."

"How are you getting along with your employees, John? There has been worker unrest in a lot of other towns lately because workers are afraid they will lose their livelihood, but I think they are wrong. They just need to learn how to operate these new machines." John was taken aback by this statement. It was unusual for William to be cautionary at the suggestion of something that would improve production.

"We have a very good worker relationship here in Whitehaven. We pay the best wages in Cumbria and try to do our best to look after the folks we hire. I think if they are reassured that no one will lose their positions, that we will actually be adding additional jobs, then such a proposal should be acceptable to our workers."

After some further discussion, John proposed that William and Jonathan come together with suggestions for implementing Jonathan's ideas. Their meeting continued well into the evening. Jonathan's excitement grew as he realized they might actually follow through on his recommendations.

The next day was Sunday. This meant going to church and hopefully, meeting Mary. Jonathan, along with his mother and father, arrived at St. James just as the morning bells were ringing. Jonathan stopped at the door and said, "Do you mind if I wait here for Mary?"

John and Ann looked at one another and smiled. "So you're still interested in Mary Cook, are you? I'm glad son. I prefer her over that Ashburn girl. It's not that I have anything against her, but our families have a long history that was not a very pleasant one."

It was the first time Jonathan's mother had alluded to the Reiver's connection of Ann's mother's family, the Musgraves.

"But mother, that was almost one hundred years ago," retorted Jonathan as he came to the defense of Ann.

"In my family, that was only yesterday. And remember, young man, it happens to be your family as well. Family characteristics have a long reach. Remember that apples don't fall off pear trees!" John and Ann turned and started into the interior of the church. Jonathan's face flushed bright red with his mother's last comment. As he watched his parents enter into the sanctuary, his thoughts about the girls were more confusing than ever. As he turned around, the sight that greeted him was Mary Cook. Arriving with her mother, the morning sun cast an ethereal haze on the two women.

Mary was in the full blossom of womanhood. Jonathan's vision narrowed, so he could see clearly this enchanting delight as she approached, smiling. It seemed at that moment to Jonathan, that Mary possessed all the allure with which Mother Nature could have blessed her. She was endowed with innocence, beauty, youth, liveliness, humility and kindness. She appeared to exude sweetness from her whole being. From her glittering eyes, there emanated a dazzling luster directed at Jonathan, who was waiting by the church door. Jonathan thought to himself, "My God, what an image of loveliness. He was stunned by the sight before him. Barely able to speak, he stammered, "Good morning, Mrs. Cook." He turned to Mary and took both of her hands in his. "I have never seen you look lovelier than you do this morning."

"There is a perfectly good reason for that, Jonathan," came a coquettish reply.

"And pray tell, what would that be?"

"I have it on good authority that you have returned to Whitehaven for a much more extended stay this year than the last five."

"It certainly looks that way."

"Then, may I presume that some of the extra time you will have, you intend to spend with me?"

"You may not only presume, you can count on it."

It was apparent that Mary's feelings towards Jonathan were the same as his were towards her. The two happy young people turned and strolled, arm in arm, into the beautiful interior of St. James as the choir began to sing. The church was even more richly adorned by this happy young girl and an equally blissful young man. They took a seat across the aisle from John and Ann. Jonathan looked slowly about him and thought to himself, "What a serenely beautiful setting. Perhaps it is time for me to settle down. I wonder if I asked her to be my wife, what she would say. My father and the rest of my family are putting their trust in me and I must not disappoint them."

Jonathan was very close to reaching a very important decision in his life. Mary was certainly a vision of loveliness that Sunday morning. She made his knees weak, but Jonathan could not quite bring himself to ask the question that was on the tip of his tongue that morning. As he walked Mary home, he realized that he was very happy with her company. He resolved that the next day he would ride over to Cleator Moor before he made a final decision.

As he was returning home from spending the afternoon with Mary, he rounded a corner and almost collided with Hugh Dacre. Before recognizing Hugh, Jonathan immediately offered an apology.

"Excuse me sir my---," realizing who he had narrowly missed, his apology trailed off into space.

"Lucas, you seem to be causing me a great deal of trouble every time we run into one another."

"Hugh, I think it's time that we forget the past and try to remain at least cordial to one another."

"I still owe you a debt that I intend to pay. But that will come in time. Until then, I see no reason for us to be unpleasant."

"Please give my congratulations to your father, Thomas, for a successful campaign for mayor here in Whitehaven," was Jonathan's reply.

"I shall do just that. That office may even come in handy one of these days. Now if you'll excuse me, I'll be on my way."

Jonathan turned and watched Dacre as he walked away. He had hoped the affair two years before, had been forgotten, but it seemed that his wish had not been granted. He had just been so happy, contemplating his future prospects, and he wasn't going to let bumping in to his old nemesis ruin his mood. His thoughts immediately turned to his trip to see Ann Ashburn the next day. Thoughts of her were almost as exhilarating as his memories of Mary from church, earlier in the morning. He needed to make the decision of which girl to seriously pursue. It really was the only thing that was causing him anxiety in his life at that moment. He could think of nothing else. He realized how very blessed he was to seemingly have the choice between these two lovely ladies.

With his father's permission, he set off just after lunch the next day heading over to Cleator Moor. Ann was ecstatic.

"Is it true that you are back in Whitehaven to stay?"

"Well, I will be moving around on different projects, but yes, I am going to be based here permanently, at least for the near future."

They went inside and sat together in the parlor. Ann was her usual beautiful, earthy, charming self. After his trysts with the miller's daughter, Jonathan had grown quite fond of things earthy. His decision was going to be even tougher than he had expected. And the job of telling one of them that he had made the choice of the other, seemed to be an impossible task.

It had always perplexed Jonathan that somehow Mary and Ann had never let his feelings toward them come between their friendship. It was a vexing problem and unfortunately, not one that he could bring to his father or his uncle, or even to a close friend. It was much too unconventional. It was not unusual for a young man to have more than one lover at a time, but you are not supposed to fall in love with two women who happen to be best friends and then have to choose one of them as your life partner. The more he thought about it, the more difficult it all became.

After Jonathan and Ann had been together for an hour, they heard the front doorbell ring.

"Are you expecting more company?"

"No, I'm not expecting anyone, but my father might be. He is in the middle of some business negotiations."

A man's muffled voice was heard through the door and there were footfalls heading down the hallway. The servant's voice rang out as he opened the door to the library where Ann's father was working. Jonathan heard clearly, "Mr. Ashburn, Mr. Hugh Dacre is here to see you."

"What the devil is he doing here?" Asked Jonathan angrily.

"It's something to do with my father's business. I think his father loaned my father some funds for us to go into a new business. With this terrible financial situation, we seem to be having some debt problems."

"If your father is indebted to that family, well, I don't have to tell you."

"I tried to tell my father, but he said that it was the only place he could find the money he needed."

About that time, the door opened and in stepped Mr. Ashburn, followed by Hugh Dacre. Jonathan and Ann stood up, still holding hands. Hugh scowled at the sight and said, "Well, it seems that we've run into each other again, Jonathan. And I see that you've wasted no time in rekindling old relationships."

Seeing the animosity flaming up between the two men, Ann released Jonathan's hand and walked over and gave Hugh a sisterly embrace and a small kiss on the cheek. Jonathan's face flushed with jealousy. Hugh had noticed and was very pleased that he had caused Jonathan some discomfort.

"Yes Hugh, Jonathan just came by and was telling me what a wonderful time he and Mary had at church yesterday."

She emphasized the name, 'Mary', to Jonathan's distress. Ann's father was obviously not happy to have found his daughter closely entwined with Jonathan. He knew that Hugh Dacre was in love with his daughter and he had encouraged her to be nice to him, because Thomas Dacre controlled their future. He had not asked her to do anything improper, but asked her only to be a little more friendly toward him because of the business relationship with his family.

Hugh, for his part, had prevailed on his father to make the loan to the Ashburn's in spite of his father's reluctance to do so. His father's generosity to Ann's family seemed, on the surface, to be working, as Ann had agreed to spend more time with Hugh.

Ann Ashburn

His courtship had not progressed much past the pleasantly formal stage, although on occasion she did seem to enjoy his company and always laughed at his jokes. She also loved the many expensive gifts he brought her each time he visited. But their relationship had not become more intimate than that. Ann only allowed him to take her hand while he opened his heart entirely to her. As he told her his inner most thoughts, she would laugh and say, "Hugh, I am sure you are not serious. There are so many girls that have much more to offer than poor me." Then, laughing, she would dance away from him and change the subject to something more mundane and less serious. But Hugh Dacre wanted this girl in the worst way and he was the type of man, who in the end, usually got what he wanted by fair means or foul.

An agitated Jonathan did not understand the pressure that Mr. Ashburn had put his daughter under. It had forced her to act in a manner that she would not have ordinarily, with Hugh. To Jonathan, there was only one reason that she behaved in this manner and it was because she had feelings for the ill mannered bully. And even if she had been under an obligation to be more pleasant to Hugh, the fact that she would acquiesce to that request was cause, in and of itself, to be concerned. Jonathan's view of this whole affair was all from his side, without much consideration for the quandary Ann's father had forced upon her. Youth certainly has its advantages, but wisdom is not usually one of them. Jonathan's anger at her behavior with his adversary made the decision for him. It may not have been fair, but it is what happened. With a coolness that was not usual from Jonathan, he turned to Mr. Ashburn and said, "If you'll excuse me, sir, I must return to Whitehaven." Mr. Ashburn replied, "We're sorry to see you leave Jonathan, won't you stay and have supper with us?"

"No Sir, I'm afraid that I have to get back. We have plans to expand our business and I am designing some new machinery to increase our production and reduce our costs." Jonathan's hurt ego was fighting back by boasting about something that would have been better kept to himself.

"It seems that young Master Lucas has very ambitious plans he has brought back from the wide, wonderful world in which he's been roaming," Hugh said with much pleasure and sarcasm.

"If you all will excuse me, I will be on my way." Jonathan nodded to Mr. Ashburn and to Hugh.

He turned to Ann and said with a chilly tone, "Good day to you, Miss Ashburn. I'm sure we will meet again sometime."

He walked out of the room. Ann raised her hand to her mouth to stifle a cry of anguish. She turned her head away from her father and Hugh, but not before both men saw the tears welling up in her eyes. Hugh turned to stare at Jonathan, who was walking down the hall without looking back. He was more determined than ever to seek revenge on this man, who had become a thorn in his side at every turn. Not only had he been insulted twice, by Jonathan in public, but it was plain that as long as he was in Ann's heart, there would be no room for him. The situation was intolerable and a solution, be it fair or foul, must be found.

Chapter 18

PLANS FOR THE EXPANSION OF THE LUCAS Sail Mill were completed by William and Jonathan in March 1773. Jonathan and his uncle had improved the design of the machinery that was already installed and the new equipment promised to be lighter and cheaper.

The next step was to rent the large warehouse formerly used in the tobacco trade. This was where they planned to centralize their operations to fabricate the new machinery and ultimately install it. They would continue to operate as they had in the past, but the new centralized facility would slowly absorb the outlying production from the old mill sites.

They signed the lease for the warehouse and before their workmen started to make changes, handbills began to appear around town, mostly in taverns. The handouts were being circulated, not only in Whitehaven, but in all of the surrounding villages.

One of the leaflets was brought to John by Alex Barton. Alex was his tobacco warehouse manager, but since the slowdown occurred, he was helping with the transformation of the rented warehouse.

"Master John, I've been see'n these around town and I thought you should know what's being said."

"Let me take a look at this, Alex?

John took the folded paper and opened the broadsheet. It was run off obviously from a cheap press. The ink was blurred and the words were unevenly spaced. John read silently to himself:

The Truth About The Coming Changes in the Lucas Sail Factory

The Lucas' are planning to bring in equipment that will put half of their employees out of work. This writer has knowledge directly from the horse's mouth that they intend to cut costs by replacing people with machines. If you value your livelihood, then you must take steps to prevent this from happening. They are not concerned with you or your family, but only the profits and money that they will gain.

Beware And Be Warned

After a moment, John put the paper down and looked at Alex. He turned to Jonathan, who was watching the scene with interest and said, "Listen to this, Jonathan, and tell me what you think."

He read the bill out loud and when he had finished, he watched his son closely for his reaction. Someone was definitely trying to stir up trouble. These were the usual rumors that occurred with any new project that involved something different or modern. John waited for the reply from his son. "I think I know where, at least part of this is coming from. Why would someone twist what, in reality, will benefit people?"

"I don't know, son, but someone is definitely attempting to inconvenience us by stirring up trouble. I wouldn't stress yourself over this. These scurrilous handbills are always being printed and circulated, stirring up unrest about something. Don't you remember last year? There was a bill that was circulated, purporting in the most lurid circumstances imaginable, that our good King George was slowly going insane. It even stated that the king's father was insane and perverted, as well. We just need to counter these arguments that are made in taverns and pubs with our sober, good workers."

Jonathan decided not to recount the conversation he had recently had with Hugh Dacre at the Ashburn Home in Cleator Moor. Ann Ashburn wasn't a popular topic of conversation with his parents and while he had his suspicions, he had no proof that Dacre was behind this obvious attack.

"I'm not sure money is the motivation behind this attack, father."

"What does that mean?"

"I'm not sure what it means, yet. But it wouldn't surprise me if Hugh Dacre was behind these bills."

"I know he was jealous of you and the Ashburn girl, but you haven't seen her since before Christmas. You seem to spend all of your time with Mary."

"I don't think you understand the disdain that he has for me. It's been there ever since we were youngsters. I thought it would have evaporated by now, but it's only gotten worse. It's just a feeling I have, but we had better be on our guard."

Jonathan had been having second thoughts about his encounter with Hugh and Ann at Cleator Moor. Although he was still angry, Ann's allure still haunted his dreams. Within a week, Jonathan made the decision to once again call on Ann. What he could not know was that Hugh was becoming more proactive in his attempts to eliminate his rival for Ann's affections. Hugh had sent one of his servants into a tavern frequented by Alex Barton. The servant bought drinks for Alex and engaged him in conversation. "Well, it looks like Master Hugh is going to be finally settling down."

"Oh, is that so?" Replied a somewhat surprised Alex.

"Oh yes. It looks as if he's going to have to, because it seems that he may become a father soon."

"Well, he's a good-looking lad with plenty of money and there's many a barmaid around that would love to bed him for the honor and the money."

"Nah, it ain't no barmaid."

"Who might it be?"

"I'm not at liberty to say. My master swore me to secrecy, but I can tell you that it's a well-to-do lady over at Cleator Moor."

"You're not telling me it's Miss Ann Ashburn?"

"I'm not telling you anything other than it's a maid from Cleator Moor."

"Well I'll be damned to hell. I never would have believed that."

Alex relayed the story to young Jonathan the next day. It was almost like taking a blow to the stomach. He replayed the scene of the week before, then he recalled the words Mary had said to him. She had told him her father had instructed her to be nice to Hugh Dacre, "for the sake of the family's future."

After this revelation, he had resolved to go forward with his courtship of Mary. However, there was something in the back of his mind that told him perhaps he was being unfair in his assessment of Miss Ashburn. But his pride took over and he vowed not to allow his past relationship with Ann to intrude on his newfound resolve. His relationship with Ann had deteriorated into despair, anger, hurt and ultimately, separation.

Work continued on the new project, but difficulties began to crop up in operations at the mill. Workers were becoming surly and negative comments were spoken with fervor when John walked through his plant. There was definitely an undercurrent of discontent about the new facility under construction. In an effort to curtail the growing fears of the workers, John decided to call a meeting to clear the air. The next day he put an advertisement in the *Cumberland Paquet* to support his arguments that would hopefully counter the grumbling with a detailed explanation of what they were trying to accomplish with the expansion. It seemed to work for a while as the grumbling settled down for the next few weeks.

However, there soon was an anonymous call for a meeting of all of the workers involved with the Lucas enterprises. There was to be a general discussion among the coworkers to consider the 'bad consequences' that would result from this proposed centralization. The organizers of the meeting were attempting to arrange opposition to the 'unacceptable ramifications' that were surely going to result from "the introduction of certain new machines" and to find support for what they called "the present mode of trade, against any proposed detrimental innovations".

No one knew for sure who was behind organizing these meetings. John tried to find out, but was unsuccessful. It seems that some of the organizers were people from out of town who had arrived mysteriously and who began buying drinks for some of the more prominent employees. Hugh Dacre's servant was also present whenever groups of grumblers gathered. The out-of-town strangers claimed to have knowledge that the proposed machines could be "operated by only one man, but could do the work of sixty". It was also rumored that the machines would "do the work in a third of the time that it normally took to produce strips of sail cloth".

As time passed and the rumors persisted, John became concerned that whoever was behind it all was determined to destroy his business. As the workers gathered to enter the mill one morning, John, with Jonathan by his side, addressed them from the front steps.

"I know there have been rumors, and that's all they are, just rumors, about all of the terrible things that are about to occur because of the improvements we are making. Let me assure you that these rumors are unfounded." There were some loud boos from the back of the crowd. "I have an offer to make to you that should alleviate some of your fears. I will agree to maintain all of your wages, as they are, for a period of at least six months. And if the orders continue to come in for our products, I will extend those wages for an additional six months, as well. I can promise you that for as long as our business continues to be strong and profitable, those of you working for us will continue to be employed here for at least the same rate you are earning today." This seemed to satisfy the crowd. Most of the employees present that morning had been working for John for several years and although, bombarded by rumors, they still trusted John Lucas.

Several weeks later, Alex Barton was ushered into the parlor, where John and Jonathan were discussing the events of the day. "Well Alex, to what do we owe your visit at this hour?"

"Well sir, I think there's trouble brewing."

"Trouble, what kind of trouble?"

"There's a crowd of those out of town troublemakers who have been rounding up all sorts of people and telling them that you lied when you told them that you're going to keep them all and pay them for six months. Mind you, most of them are not our people, but the usual troublemakers and drunkards. These outsiders are trying to organize them to attack our warehouse project."

"This sounds serious! How many of them do you suppose there are?"

"It's not a huge group, probably no more than one hundred and fifty to two hundred people. But they're trying to get the sailors and miners involved and after they're liquored up, only the good Lord knows how this thing could end."

"You're right. This could have some serious repercussions. Come with me to the mayor's home. This appears to be a job for the mayor and the magistrates. Jonathan, you stay here and bolt the door and don't let anyone in that you don't know. Stay away from the front of the house and protect your mother. We'll be back with help, as quickly as possible."

"But father, you know who the mayor is? He's Thomas Dacre."

"I'm aware of that, son, but I'm not going to see Thomas Dacre. I'm going to see the mayor and I have no doubt that he will act in the proper manner as mayor to protect private property."

The two men went to the front of the house and peered out through the window. There was a group of fifty or twenty rough looking men standing outside across the street watching the house. They closed the shutters in the front windows, bolted the door and doused the lamps.

John said, "Quick Alex, out the back door and through the garden. Jonathan, be vigilant and don't let anything happen to your mother." With that said, John and Alec disappeared out the back door through the garden and out of the garden gate. It was two blocks to the mayor's house. Keeping to the shadows, they arrived at the house of Thomas Dacre within five minutes. John rang the bell continuously but heard no one walking to the door. He then began to knock as well as ring, until finally, he heard some steps approaching. A servant opened the door and John brushed past him explaining, "I must see the mayor immediately."

"But sir, I'm afraid he's indisposed at this time."

John began to shout, "Thomas, . . . Thomas Dacre! Where are you?"

The door to his library opened and Mayor Thomas Dacre stepped out into the corridor. "What is all of the fuss about?"

"Thomas, there are rioters threatening to attack my new mill."

"Calm down, John. I haven't heard anything of rioters."

"You must be aware of the tension that has been building concerning the centralization of my business."

"Yes of course, I've heard the rumors and the mumbling, but certainly you don't think that things have gone so far as that. Do you really believe there is a real threat to your property?"

"That's exactly what I'm saying. Alex, here, has seen a group of at least two hundred men, well into their cups and they're trying to organize more, including sailors and miners. They have boasted out loud that they intend to burn my new works to the ground. And besides that, there is a group of fifteen or twenty, watching the front of my house. I need for you to call out your magistrates and protect my property."

"Well John, first we have to ascertain if there is actually a riot occurring. And as of yet, I have seen no proof that would lead me to believe there is any such credible threat imminent."

"We're heading to the warehouse and I expect you to rally your magistrates and come to help us."

Suddenly the front door to the mayor's house flew open and in ran an excited Barton Trinity, John's butler. "Master John, there's a huge crowd that's now gathered outside of the house and they're throwing bricks." John turned to the mayor, "Do you believe me now? I need all the help I can get and I need it NOW. Let's get back to the house. Quickly now, let's go!"

John and his two companions started at a dead run back toward their home. The mob had grown to about five hundred people. The three men entered through the back of the home. He found Jonathan and his wife, Ann, in the rear of the house huddled together with Ms. Trinity. The noise of the mob sounded loud, and dangerous. They could hear the impact of bricks crashing against the shuttered windows in the front of the house.

"Martin, you stay here with Jonathan and Ann. I'm picking up my pistols from the study," just then, another brick smashed through an upstairs window with a loud shattering sound. John turned and said, "on second thought, Jonathan, take your mother, Miss Trinity and Martin and go to the Cook's residence. They should be safe there. Be vigilant and stay to the shadows the entire way."

"But father, I'm going to stay here and defend this----"

"Son, I know you want to stay, but your mother's safety is the most important thing right now. Martin is too old to defend her and get her to safety, so that leaves just you. We don't have time to argue. We both have our individual jobs to do."

John softened and put his hand on his son's shoulder. "I know you're brave, but this has to be done and done this way."

"Yes sir, but when I get her to the Cook's, I'll be back to help you."

"Yes, yes, but get your mother to safety now!" This was accentuated by the sound of a brick crashing through one of the upper-level windows. John kissed his wife, shook hands with his son and exclaimed, "I would have never dreamed that something like this would ever happen here in Whitehaven."

Jonathan, Martin, Ms. Trinity and his mother exited into the garden. John went to his study and made sure that his pistols were loaded and primed. He handed one to Alex and the two of them walked to the front of the house. John unlocked the front door and stepped out to face the mob. At his appearance, the rabble grew silent except for the crackling of the bright orange-red torches circling the front of the house. John looked about slowly, but did not recognize any of the rough looking men peering up at him. He surveyed the angry faces in silence and took one step forward.

"I would like to know what you men are doing here destroying my property?"

Someone from the rear yelled out, "We're here to stop you from destroying our livelihood." This brought a roar of, "that's right" from the crowd.

John switched the pistol from his right hand to his left. He held up his hand for silence and the crowd grew quiet once more. "Who is telling you these false rumors? Our new facilities will bring more work, not less. The new machines will require more operators, not less."

Several voices from the rear chimed in, "You're lying. All you mill owners are the same. You don't care about us. Money and profits, that's what you care about. That's the only thing you care about."

The rabble grew restless once more, drowning out any sound, but the sound of rage. John again raised his hand. This time it took a little longer before the growl of the crowd diminished.

"I have been looking over your faces. I see anger. I see the effects of strong drink. But what I don't see, is any of the people that I employ. If any of my people are in the crowd, let them come forward and we will go into my home and I will sign a contract, pledging to them that their jobs are safe."

"I work for you, and I don't believe a word you're saying," a voice chimed up from the rear of the horde. John held up his hand, but this time the noise did not stop until he held up both hands.

"If you are my worker, then you are also my friend. Step forward, so that I can know who you are and so I can see if you are really one of my employees."

Another voice from a different part of the pack yelled, "You just want to know who we are, so you can get rid of us or punish us for defending what's rightfully ours."

"That is just not true! How can I make you believe there is no scheme to injure anyone of you?" Then what looked like a bat flying, hit John on the shoulder. The tone of the crowd turned ugly as another rock bounced off the wall behind Alex. Alex reached for John's arm, and said, "Are you alright, sir?"

"Yes Alex, but I'm afraid this is getting out of hand. I don't know who these people are, but they are determined to riot." At that moment, more rocks were launched in their direction. They came close to the two men. John switched his pistol back to his right hand and turned defiantly to the crowd. He shouted above the crowd noise, "I don't know who you people are. It seems that you are bound and determined to cause trouble and to wreak havoc for some purpose unknown to me. I am warning you; I will defend my property with all of the means at my disposal." Another rock was thrown. This one found its mark and hit John on his cheek under his right eye. Luckily it was a glancing blow, but it had enough force to bring John down on one knee.

He looked into the crowd and saw a large, rough bearded man step forward with a full-sized brick in his hand. The thug was preparing to hurl it in John's direction. As the man threw it, John quickly side-stepped. Bringing his pistol up, he fired at the perpetrator who was struck in the right thigh. Falling to the ground, the groans of pain could be heard in the silence that ensued after the report of the pistol. Alex, in turn, brought his pistol up to shoulder level and pointed the weapon at the crowd. "The next man who tries to throw a brick gets just the same as that man." Another voice from the back of the crowd yelled, "He's only got one shot left. He can't get us all."

"That's true, but it might be you, or you, or you," Alex said as he pointed the pistol at different individuals. Suddenly, Jonathan walked through the front door carrying two pistols. Alex glanced over his shoulder and saw him arrive with the additional weapons.

"Now we have at least three shots," shouted Alex with satisfaction and more confidence. The mob grew quiet.

John got to his feet as he spoke, "I do not know who you people are, but whatever your reason, be it hatred, be it fear, or be it for spite, I ask you to stop and think. Is it worth destroying me and my property? Think hard now! Is it really worth dying for?"

The crowd was silent. Only the groans of the wounded man could be heard. The blood was spurting in a thin, fine stream under the torchlight for the entire crowd to see. Most eyes turned toward the wounded man.

John said, "The ball has severed an artery in his leg. If you don't get this man to a doctor soon, he will bleed to death. If he is your friend, I implore you to put pressure on that wound and get him help as quickly as possible."

Several men stepped forward and gathered up the wounded man. They moved off down the street in the direction of the doctor's office and with that, the crowd began to slowly disperse. Soon all that was left were the burning torches that had been discarded by the crowd.

Chapter 19

MARY WAS SITTING IN THE CHAIR NEXT TO the window reading a book when the door opened and her friend Ann walked in. The two friends had not seen each other in over three weeks. Each of them was aware that the other was in love with the same person. After Jonathan had returned from his apprenticeship, both of them had avoided discussing anything that would bring up the potential rivalry.

The rumors that Ann was pregnant by Hugh Dacre had been well circulated. Most of the people who knew Ann did not believe the claims and put it down to malicious gossip. They were not aware that the rumor had been started by Hugh Dacre himself, in order to drive Jonathan away from Ann. His scheme had worked only too well, as two days before, Jonathan had proposed marriage to Mary Cook. She had joyfully accepted his proposal of matrimony and was looking forward to becoming Mrs. Jonathan Lucas. It was what Mary had truly wanted since they were small children going to church together.

She knew, however, that her friend, Ann, had the same desire. Mary was hoping she could be the one to break the news of the engagement to Ann. The two friends embraced.

"Where have you been for so long?" Mary began.

"So much has happened in the last three weeks, Mary. Have you heard those awful rumors circulating about me? "

"I am sorry to say that I have."

"Mary, you did not believe them, did you?"

"No, of course not! I know you better than that. Besides, unless something has happened that I don't know about, we both know what Hugh Dacre is."

"He is a lout. I believe the only reason he has loaned my father money was to force me into a relationship with him. Jonathan was there when I was impelled to be nice to the churl. And since that time, I have not seen or heard from him."

Mary blushed and turned away from her friend. She now understood the awkward moment, just after Jonathan had proposed to her, when she had innocently remarked to Jonathan, "You do know this will hurt Ann greatly?"

Jonathan had replied with a melancholy look and sighed, "That no longer matters, Mary. Ann has her own plans and it is you that I intend to spend the rest of my life with."

"But Jonathan you . . . " Jonathan had reached up and pressed two fingers against her lips. He smiled at her, gathered her in his arms and kissed her passionately. Pulling back to look at his fiancée, he said, "That should answer all of your questions, my love. I'm sure that our friend, Ann, will be fine and she will be happy for us."

"I hope so. You know that I love both of you dearly. I want her to remain my friend."

Jonathan did not reply, but began to discuss their future plans. Now, Mary had to tell Ann that she was marrying the man they both loved. Hoping to keep her most intimate friend, a friend, she turned back to Ann and said, "I have something to tell you. This will be difficult for both of us, but I hope our friendship is strong enough, deep enough and sincere enough, to withstand the strain of what I'm about to tell you."

Ann knew instinctively what was coming. She sucked in a breath quickly, as if she had been hit in the solar plexus. Her hand flew to her mouth as she uttered a small cry, "I know." Tears welled up in her eyes as she put her hand down on the arm of a chair to steady herself.

"What do you know?"

"I know that you and Jonathan are going to be married. Isn't that what you are trying to tell me?"

"Yes, but I was hoping to be the first to tell you. You must have heard this from someone else."

"No, no one has said anything to me. Not hearing from Jonathan for the last three weeks, after what happened at my house and receiving your note asking me to come today, I suspected as much. And then there was the look on your face, . . . well, I did not have to be a fortune teller to be able to feel or see what was coming. I suppose this is the way it was meant to be."

Ann straightened up and looked directly into Mary's eyes. "You know that I love you both and I wish you all the happiness in the world. You know me too well, for me to lie to you. I am disappointed that he chose you over me, but I understand why. I also wish to remain friends with the two of you. However, I am not sure that Jonathan will feel the same."

"Of course he will, my dear. I am certain he will want to retain your friendship, if you are willing to offer it."

"Perhaps, but due to my father's relationship with the Dacre Family, I think Jonathan believes these rumors to be true."

"He'll learn the truth soon enough. I shall disabuse him of those silly ideas."

"I have something else to tell you," continued Ann. "My father is being forced to take a position in one of the Dacre properties in Carlisle. It's either that or have the Dacre's foreclose on my fathers' loans. As a condition of this employment, I am to accompany my father to live with him in Carlisle."

"Oh Ann, why is this happening? It's more of Hugh Dacre's clumsy way of courting you, isn't it?"

"Yes. It's very apparent he wants me away from what he considers bad influences. I have refused and he has threatened to call in my fathers' loans and that would ruin us. The news of your impending marriage has changed my mind."

"You don't mean that you're going to----?"

"No, no, no. No matter what happens, I will not let that awful man touch me. But since I am no longer in the competition for our mutually sought after prize," she smiled for the first time since the conversation began, "I think, for now, moving to Carlisle, might be best for all concerned."

"Oh my darling, please do not let us be the reason that you make that decision. I fear for you and hate the thought of your being away from us and under the influence of that evil man." Mary was truly concerned.

Ann had regained her composure, after the shock of hearing the news she had dreaded. She again had the familiar look of confidence she usually wore. She knew that it was not the fault of either Jonathan or Mary, but evidently, was the will of providence that she should not be Jonathan's choice. She reasoned that no good could come from losing a lifelong friend because of her disappointment. After all, there were many forms of love and the love for her friend, Mary, was just as strong as her love for Jonathan. She had already forgiven them, but she had not forgiven 'providence'.

Mary's approach to the relationship was much the same. She had always admired Ann's lust for life and the way she spoke her mind, without regard for formality. Many times her friend had come to her rescue, by interceding on her behalf, in uncomfortable situations. Mary simply did not have it in her to approach the outside world, except in a conventional way. She had been brought up to act like a lady and a lady she had become. Her view of the world was seen through the proper lenses of the gentry. She was not shy, but she was reserved and maybe, that was why she was so attracted to the personality of her outspoken friend. Together they made quite a formidable pair.

"My father has already taken a house in Carlisle. We will be leaving next week. I'll send you the address so that you can keep me updated on your wedding plans, which I am sure will be beautiful."

"We haven't set a date yet, but I suppose it will be in the spring of next year. Will you come and be my maid of honor?"

"Yes, of course. I shall be there and I will participate in any way you wish. Give my love to your fiancée--- but be sure and tell him, it is only of the sisterly kind." They both broke out in big smiles as the tension between them continued to dissipate. The two women embraced for a long moment. Over jealousy and animosity, friendship had triumphed, which was an all too rare and precious occurrence in these kinds of love affairs.

John received a letter from his brother, William. Much of William's fortune had been tied up in the stock of the East India Company. The stock had still not rebounded after its fall of the past year and the East India Company was rumored to be on the brink of bankruptcy. There were nobles and high officials in the British government, who were also deeply invested in the East India Company. William's letter described what the government had done to revive the company. John read aloud to Jonathan the following:

Dear Brother,

I have just learned today that Lord North has proposed and Parliament has passed, a bill known as the Tea Act of 1773. This act is purported to grant the British East India Company a trading monopoly with the American colonies. The government intends to maintain its tax on tea, but the company will actually be able to market its tea for a price that is lower than it has ever been. As you are aware, a monopoly does not have any competition. Therefore the British East India Company will be able to lower its prices. The Americans, Lord North hopes, will be happy to buy tea at a cheaper price, even though it still contains a tax. Hopefully, this act will save the East India Company and secure acquiescence from our colonists on the tax issue. It's an excellent approach, but still there is a major flaw in this strategy. The Americans show they are not willing to pay taxes when they have no vote in the process, even if they benefit from a lower price on tea. They also know, as I do, that this lower price is not guaranteed and could be raised at any time the government feels comfortable in doing so. Let us hope that this legislation succeeds, but I have my doubts. If you still have any business with the American colonies, I advise that you be on guard.

With regards, I am,

Your Brother William

"I don't understand. Why are we having so much trouble with these colonists in America?" Jonathan asked his father.

"It is a very complex issue, son. The Americans feel they are as English as we are. They consider themselves subjects of the British crown and so they feel entitled to representation in Parliament by their own elected members. I, for one, am in agreement with them. We, here at home, have the opportunity to be represented in Parliament through our elections. If we have a grievance, then our designated members of Parliament can attempt to address those grievances. The Americans have no such option."

"But father, I've read where they send people here all the time and they are allowed to speak to Parliament on behalf of the colonies."

"That is true son, but hired lobbyists addressing Parliament does not carry the same weight as does members of Parliament. In the politics of Parliament, when one member wants something, he is willing to trade his vote on another issue to secure his objective. All a hired lobbyist can do is make arguments. He has no vote to trade and therefore, very little influence. If the current state of affairs is not soon altered, I fear for the worst."

"What do you mean, the worst?"

"I mean war, rebellion, riots. Any of these types of defiance could be the result. None of this bodes well for commerce with the Americans. As your uncle advised us, I am thinking that we should leave the American tobacco trade."

"But we still have a ship dedicated to that trade."

"I've been thinking about that. Your mother and I have made a decision, that I think you will find interesting and enjoyable, upon hearing it."

"Something that I will find interesting and enjoyable? What do you mean?"

"You know how pleased your mother and I are that you're getting married next May. We are also delighted that Mary is going to be your bride. Our ship *The Julia* will no longer be needed in the tobacco trade. We have sold *The Julia* to a Scottish shipping firm from Glasgow."

"You've sold *The Julia*?"

"Yes, and for a very good price, I might add. You know the property that has been in your mother's family for generations, just outside of Egremont, in Carlton?"

"Yes, of course, I know that property. You and I have hunted there since I was old enough to walk. We have bagged many a Christmas dinner, walking those fields and meadows. It's a truly lovely spot, overlooking the village."

"I'm glad that you like it, son, because your mother is giving it to you as a wedding present. And I am going to also give you the money from the sale of *The Julia* to build a home for you and your family. "

"I am speechless. Egremont is certainly close enough to Whitehaven, so it will not hinder my work. And when the project is completed, I can continue with my millwright duties from Egremont. How can I thank the two of you?"

"Give us many grandchildren! Several grandsons would be more than ample reward for us."

The next day Jonathan took his trap carriage over to Mary's home. He tied his horse to a hitching post and bounded up the stairs to her front door. He excitedly pulled several times on the doorbell and Mary answered the door. "My goodness, Jonathan, I thought there was a fire somewhere the way you were ringing the bell. You look excited. What is happening?"

"We are going on a short trip. Please ask your mother if we can take a ride. I have a surprise for you."

Mary nodded and darted back into the house. Soon, they climbed into the trap and Jonathan took the road to Egremont. After a five-mile trip down the Glinis Brow Road, the picturesque village of Egremont came into view. Egremont lies south of Whitehaven, on the River Ehen. The community rests at the foot of the Uldale Valley and Dent Fell. They passed through the center of the village. Jonathan was familiar with Egremont, as was Mary. They had both attended the church at St. Mary's from time to time, for weddings, funerals or festivals.

"Your family owns lands somewhere close by, as I recall?"

"It's actually in a little place called Carleton, just on the outskirts of Egremont. That's where we're going."

Mary remained quiet as the trap passed through Egremont and started climbing up a small hill. Jonathan pointed out several large fields that loomed in the distance.

"That's it, Mary. That's the place I wanted you to see."

"But why are we here?"

"You and I have something to do," replied Jonathan.

"Okay, You are certainly acting mysteriously today. What is it that we have to do? I'm no good at shearing sheep," teased Mary. Jonathan chuckled as they continued the climb.

They reached the top of the gently sloping hill and looked back on the village of Egremont. Jonathan and Mary climbed out of the trap and Jonathan hobbled his horse. Arm in arm, they walked to the center of the field. Jonathan asked, "Do you like this place?"

"It is absolutely lovely, Jonathan."

"Then, if you will, my love, our job today is to site the house we are going to build for our family."

Mary, with a squeal of delight, threw her arms around Jonathan's neck and kissed him more passionately than he had imagined she could. There were two reasons for her excitement. The first one was obvious. She was so happy they were going to have their own home. But secondly and more importantly, they were finally alone with no supervision. After they came up for air, Mary said, "How did this come about? This is like a dream come true!"

Jonathan told Mary about the letter from his Uncle William that described deteriorating conditions in the American Colonies. She knew about John's business with America and had heard that the tobacco business had been dwindling. Jonathan described the two gifts his parents were giving to them as wedding presents. He blushed when he told her what his parents wanted in return. Mary only giggled.

"I will design this house myself, with your input, of course. Our home should be under construction in two or three weeks. That means, if we are able to start construction in January, our home should be ready for us to move into about the time we become man and wife, in May."

They agreed where the house should be placed and then Jonathan pointed into the distance at a small rocky peak and said, "We're going there for a picnic."

It didn't take long to reach the foot of Dent Fell. Jonathan said to Mary, "This is one of my favorite places. I don't want you to turn around, until we reach the top." They climbed to the summit with a picnic basket. Jonathan set the basket down on a rock and said, "Now you can turn around." As Mary turned her eyes to the panorama before her, she exclaimed, "That is, truly, a beautiful sight." From this vantage point, the couple had an uninterrupted view of the Cumbrian Coast that stretched from the Ravenglass Estuary in the south, to the Soleway Firth in the north. Mary pointed northward and asked, "Is that Scotland in the distance?"

Yes, just across the Soleway Firth and if you look farther to the West, under those low hanging clouds, you'll see the Isle of Man."

"It is really a breathtaking view," exclaimed Mary. Jonathan walked a few paces to the other side of the fell, which faced to the east. Looming in the distance, were the high peaks of Pillar and Sca Fells. Jonathan would carry the memory of this amazing moment with Mary for the rest of his life.

December 1773, was cold throughout Cumberland. There were two heavy snows that blanketed the ground. Temperatures dropped, but the peoples' spirits rose in anticipation of the arrival of Christmas. Christmas, that year, was particularly joyful for Jonathan and Mary. There were several parties held to celebrate their upcoming marriage. Jonathan was truly happy. He had fallen completely in love with the beautiful Mary Cook.

At the parties, her life of propriety and grace shone clearly. She was the queen of the balls given in her honor, and never took a false step. None of the other ladies in attendance came close to rivaling her in beauty, charm, etiquette or desirability. The only person who had been able to redirect attention away from Mary, was of course, Ann. She was still, far away in Carlisle and so there was no rival for attention, especially Jonathan's.

Just after Christmas, The *Cumberland Paquet* printed a story that sent cold shivers down the spines of all the merchants of Whitehaven. The event was dubbed the Boston Tea Party. It seems that Lord North's legislation, as William had foreseen, had cured neither the problems of the East India Company nor collecting taxes without representation from the Americas. The first shipments of East India tea that reached America weren't allowed to be unloaded. In fact, not a single British East India Company's container of tea, destined for the thirteen American Colonies, was ever delivered. The Boston consignment had been dumped into the Boston Harbor.

John was thankful that he had made the decision to withdraw from the tobacco trade with Virginia. After The Boston Tea Party, trade began to drop off on both sides of the Atlantic. One good thing that did come out of it all, however, was that if war erupted, the king would be building more ships that would require more sails. As distasteful as the prospect of war was to John, it did mean that his business would continue to prosper.

Construction began on the Lucas Carleton House, as it became known, in the second week of January 1774. Jonathan oversaw the work himself and his training and expertise as a millwright served him well during the construction of his future abode. The house was completed by May 15 and fully furnished a week later. All that it lacked, was the people to enjoy living within its walls.

Jonathan Lucas and Mary Cook became man and wife on Wednesday, May 25, 1774. The wedding ceremony was held at St. Nicholas Church in Whitehaven. It was an Anglican service and contained all the pomp and circumstance peculiar to that denomination. Ann, as promised, was in attendance at the celebration. Jonathan was cordial, but distant. Mary realized there were still some deep feelings lingering between them. She decided to deal with that situation after she was safely married.

Jonathan and Mary stood side-by-side in front of the young Anglican priest conducting the ceremony. His name was Zachariah Farrington and he was just few years older than Jonathan and Mary. He had known them both as they grew to adulthood. Mary had confided her concerns about the relationship between Jonathan and Ann to him and he had reassured her that her marriage to Jonathan was the will of God and that if she was a virtuous wife, all would be well. The ceremony began.

The priests gave a welcome to everyone in attendance,

"God is love, and those who live in love, live in God and God lives in them."

After the welcome, came the preference for the marriage. It began with the words, *"In the presence of God, Father, Son and Holy Spirit, we have come together to witness the marriage of Jonathan and Mary and to pray for God's blessing on them. "*

The celebrant then asked the bride and groom to make their declarations before the congregation and God.

To Jonathan he asked, *"Jonathan will you take Mary to be your wife? Will you love her, comfort her, honor and protect her, and forsaking all others, be faithful to her as long as you both shall live?"* Jonathan looked deeply into her eyes and replied without hesitation, *"I will. "*

He then turned to Mary and asked her, *"Mary, will you take Jonathan to be your husband? Will you love him, comfort him, honor and protect him, and, forsaking all others, be faithful to him as long as you both shall live?"*

Mary replied, *"I will. "*

The minister then continued with a prayer, *"God our Father, from the beginning you have blessed creation with abundant life. Pour out your blessings upon Jonathan and Mary, that they may be joined in mutual love and companionship, in holiness and commitment to each other. We ask this through our Lord Jesus Christ, your Son, who is alive and reigns with you, in the unity of the Holy Spirit, one God, now and forever. "*

After this came readings from the Bible, a hymn and then a sermon that lasted for fifteen minutes. After the sermon was concluded, he turned to the young couple standing before him and said, *"Jonathan and Mary, "I invite you to join hands and make your vows in the presence of God and his people gathered here. "*

They turned to each other and held hands. Jonathan began,

"I, Jonathan, take you, Mary,, to be my wife, to have and to hold from this day forward, for better, for worse, for richer, for poorer, in sickness and in health, to love and to cherish, till death do us part, according to God's holy law. In the presence of God I make this vow."

It was now Mary's turn to repeat the ancient words, *"I, Mary, take you, Jonathan, to be my husband, to have and to hold from this day forward, for better, for worse, for richer, for poorer, in sickness and in health, to love and to cherish, till death do us part, according to God's holy law. In the presence of God I make this vow."*

Their ring bearers brought the rings to exchange before the priest with the appropriate ceremonial words, and the service ended with the climactic part of the ceremony called The Proclamation. The priest turned to the congregation and exclaimed,

"In the presence of God, and before this congregation, Jonathan and Mary have given their consent and made their marriage vows to each other. They have declared their marriage, by the joining of hands and by the giving and receiving of rings. I therefore proclaim that they are husband and wife." He paused and then looked around the sanctuary sternly and warned, *"Those whom God has joined together, let no man put asunder!"*

He then blessed the marriage with these final words,

"God the Father, God the Son, God the Holy Spirit, bless, preserve and keep you, the Lord mercifully grant you the riches of his grace, that you may please him both in body and soul, and, living together in faith and love, may receive the blessings of eternal life."

Thus began the life of Jonathan Lucas and his wife Mary Cook Lucas.

King George III

Chapter 20

THE BOND BETWEEN GREAT BRITAIN AND her American Colonies had frayed to the breaking point by the end of the year, 1774. In March of that year, Parliament had passed what would become known as the Coercive Acts. Lord North had convinced Parliament that the Massachusetts Colony had to be punished for their participation in the Boston Tea Party. The legislation was comprised of five different articles aimed at separating Boston and the rest of the Massachusetts Colony from the other American Colonies.

Parliament decided to close the port of Boston until the damages caused by the dumping of the East India Company tea into Boston Harbor were paid. This was called the Boston Port Act.

In addition to the Boston Port Act, the Massachusetts Government Act restricted all town meetings. It also changed the Governor's counsel from an elected assembly into one whose members were appointed by the governor. Next came the Administration of Justice Act. This act made British officials immune to criminal prosecution in Massachusetts.

They added to these prior acts, the Quartering Act. This despised legislation required the colonists to house British troops on demand, including sheltering them in their private homes.

Most of the colonists were of the protestant faith. They were greatly offended by the Quebec Act, which extended freedom of worship to Catholics in Canada. The Canadians were also granted continuation of the judicial system they had inherited from France. The Protestant Americans were not happy with the capability of Catholics to worship so close to their own borders.

The trouble that John had foreseen, was becoming closer to reality each day. In the month of September, John and Ann received good news and bad news. The good news was that Mary was pregnant. It seemed that Jonathan was making good on his end of the bargain with his father, as their first grandchild was now on the way.

The bad news came at the end of the month of November. An article in *The Cumberland Pacquet* informed the readers of Whitehaven that the American Colonies had formed their own Congress and it had convened in September. Parliament had hoped that the Coercive Acts they had passed in March, would have the effect of isolating Boston and New England from the rest of the American Colonies. They had expected the remainder of the colonies to abandon the Bostonians to harsh British martial law. Instead, it seemed that the other American Colonies had come to the aid of Boston and all the New England colonies. The colonies to the south had sent supplies and subsequently formed their own provincial Congress so they could debate what they believed was British misrule. There was serious resistance to Parliament and to the crown. This First Continental Congress, as it came to be called, passed some acts of its own.

The most important one that concerned John and all of the other merchants like him, was called the Articles of Association of 1774. It had been passed in October and stated that there was universal prohibition of almost all trade with Great Britain, with only a handful of minor exceptions. It prohibited the importation and consumption of goods from Great Britain. It also prohibited the export of any American products to the British. The articles also established citizen committees to enforce the act throughout the colonies.

Sensing trouble, John Lucas had prepared the best way he could for the coming struggle with the Americas. Once again, merchants throughout Great Britain were going to experience major difficulties by this gathering storm. Still, the sail making business was secure and John continued to profitably transport coal to Ireland.

Jonathan was kept busy repairing windmills, water mills and weaving equipment throughout the Cumberland area. Due to the uncertainty of trade in America, many new projects were put on hold, so new commissions became few and far between. This meant that Jonathan was not traveling as much as he had in the past. With more time on his hands, the farm around the Lucas Carleton House received extra attention and Jonathan was becoming quite good at farming his new estate in Egremont. In addition to his profession as a millwright, Jonathan had a penchant for gardening and was particularly fond of growing roses.

In February 1775, Jonathan's first child arrived in the midst of a heavy snowstorm. On the night of February 23rd, Mary experienced her first labor pains. At first, she was not sure this was going to be her time to deliver. She sat up in bed and held her pillow tight against her chest. She had not worried about giving birth and had been careful not to trouble Jonathan with what could be a false alarm. However, these pains seemed different. Earlier in the day, she had helped Jonathan bed his rose plants and had only decided to go in when the snow started to come down in earnest. Suddenly she had a pain so great that it caused a cry of anguish to escape, even though she tried to suppress it. Of all times to decide to arrive, this child had chosen the worst night that winter. The snow was flying about as the wind howled like a banshee.

Her cry had awakened Jonathan. Then, not hearing any sound but the wind, he started to turn over when he realized his wife was sitting up.

"Mary, what's the matter? Why are you up?

"I believe," she said, "that you need to go downstairs and asked Miss Trinity to come up."

Jonathan sat straight up and asked, "What's wrong? You don't mean to say that it's time?"

"I am beginning to have pains and they are now coming regularly, about every two or three minutes."

"How long has this been going on?"

"It started about fifteen or twenty minutes ago. At first the pain wasn't too severe, but it has gotten worse and they're coming closer together."

Jonathan threw back the covers and jumped out of bed. She heard him fumbling around at the table until he finally found his flint and steel and after a few scratches, he finally got a candle to light, however it did very little to illuminate the dark, cold room. He stepped closer, holding the candle, as another contraction hit Mary. The look on her face told him all he needed to know. Even though it was very cold in the room, beads of sweat broke out on her brow.

"I'm going to get dressed and send Miss Trinity up and then I'm going into Egremont for the doctor."

"I don't want you to go for the doctor in this awful storm. It's been snowing steadily and the wind has picked up. I believe we have a full-blown blizzard outside. It would be foolish for you to try to reach town at night in the middle of a snowstorm." She could see in her mind's eye, her husband getting lost traveling the two miles to Egremont and freezing to death. She had complete confidence in Miss Trinity. After all, she had brought her husband into this world and he was only one, among many.

"But you must have a doctor." He was half dressed and putting on his shoes.

"Jonathan," he stopped and looked up at her, "The pain has receded a little bit. Please, just get Miss Trinity. If you insist on getting the doctor, at least wait until it's daylight. If you leave this house now in this storm, I think it will do me no good, for I will be worried to death about your safety." She started to cry at the thought of her husband in such terrible weather.

He came back over to the bed. The look on her face in the midst of her pain, made him believe he had to do something quickly. He put his arms around her and gently pulled her to him and kissed her. Another contraction began and the look of fear and anxiety appeared on his face. The pain passed and she reached up and caressed his cheek. He, in turn, stared into the beautiful blue eyes of his young wife and the look that she gave him was reassuring and peaceful.

"I'll be all right, Jonathan, but I do think it's time for you to get Miss Trinity up here."

He reached down and kissed her again and started to turn away. She grabbed his arm and with a very serious expression she asked, "You do love me, don't you Jonathan?"

The question surprised him. "Of course, I love you."

He didn't anticipate the next words, as Mary spoke, "Tell me you love only me and that you do not love Ann."

What had made Mary ask such a question, especially a time as this! They had been married for over ten months and had not spoken of Ann. They never discussed how Jonathan felt about her friend. He realized she just needed reassurance and anything that would comfort her, would help her get through the coming ordeal.

"You are the only love in my life."

"She squeezed his arm and said, "Tell me that you love me, not her." Immediately another contraction contorted her body and expression.

"I don't love Ann." Jonathan wasn't sure if she heard what he said due to the sharp pain that racked her body at that moment. And he wasn't sure, deep down inside if what he told her was the truth. From time to time thoughts of Ann would creep into his mind when he was alone. He would remember the first deep passionate kiss that she had given him in Leeds. He knew this was certainly not the time or place for a discussion such as this. He saw that the pain was easing off again, so before she could ask her question again, he offered, "Mary, I love you from the depths of my heart and soul. There is no one else but you in my life. If you don't know that by now, then perhaps I have not expressed myself well enough. Since our marriage, I have never been happier and each day with you is more fulfilling than the one before. You hold on to those thoughts while I go get Miss Trinity. This is not the time for you to have any doubts. And with the imminent arrival of our child, I love you twice as much."

Miss Trinity

He kissed his wife again and lit two more candles. He took one of the candles and cupping his hand around the flame to shield it from the draft, he opened the door and went downstairs to find Miss Trinity. He came to Miss Trinity's door and knocked loudly. He could hear her climbing out of bed and stumbling over furniture as she came toward the door. The door opened and there stood a sleepy Miss Trinity.

"What is it, Master Jonathan?"

"Her pains have begun and they are getting stronger and closer together. I need to go get the doctor, but Mary is afraid for me to go out in this storm. She wants me to wait until daylight, but I'm not sure if that's the right thing to do."

"You go into the kitchen and put some water on the stove and get us a nice fire going. Let me go upstairs and see how she's doing. How do things seem to be with her?"

"She seems to be doing all right for now. She is so strong and rather peaceful, considering she's in labor."

"Well, those are good signs. Light a candle in my room and then go do what I ask. I'll be down shortly to let you know what I think."

"Here, take this one and I'll light another one in the kitchen."

Miss Trinity took the candle and disappeared up the stairwell. When she entered the room, she saw it was not a false alarm. She sat down on the side of the bed by Mary and reassured her that everything she was feeling was normal and that even though this was her first child, she had nothing to dread.

It was freezing in the house and Jonathan was glad to have a reason to do something. He built a fire in the kitchen stove and after a bit of a struggle, was finally able to get the tender to catch and soon had a good fire started. Miss Trinity came in and told Jonathan he had nothing to worry about. It would be several hours before the baby arrived and for now, Mary was doing just fine. If they ran into difficulty, she would let Jonathan know and he could risk going to get the doctor. She told him to get water boiling on the stove, keep the fire good and hot and then she turned and went back up the stairs.

Mary was glad when Miss. Trinity came back into the room. Although she was not frightened of childbirth, it was reassuring to know that someone with experience was at hand to help.

"Jonathan hasn't tried to go out in this storm to get a doctor, has he?

"No child, he's downstairs making a fire and boiling water. I told him that if you had any real difficulty, I would let him know and he could go and alert the doctor. Otherwise, you and I can handle this just fine."

Jonathan paced between the kitchen and the stairwell for at least four or five hours. He would go to the door and peep out to see if the storm was letting up and it had not. The snow was piling up against the house and the wind continued to blow at gale force. He walked into the parlor and started a fire there and then stood up and looked around. His eyes scanned the room, but took nothing in. The sound of the wind blowing was the only distraction.

The snow continued, but finally the sky began to lighten a little. He looked out the door once again and saw the dawn beginning to break. A hard gust of wind rattled the windows and the doors as Jonathan thought, "What a very wild day for his wife to be giving birth to their first child. Why couldn't this child have come a day earlier or a couple of days later? If she has any type of complications---," his thoughts were interrupted by another more powerful blast of wind buffeting the house.

As time passed and the wind died down, Jonathan thought he heard another noise. He listened closely, but could not hear anything, as the wind picked back up. He walked closer to the stairwell and heard something a second time. "That sounds like a baby's cry," he said out loud. Jonathan moved to the foot of the stairs as the gale subsided for a moment and he heard the unmistakable cry of a newborn baby.

Mary had done as good a job of giving birth. The new arrival was a healthy boy. At the next sound of the crying infant, Jonathan bounded up the stairs and was met at the door by Miss Trinity who had helped bring Jonathan into the world twenty-one years before.

"Now you just slow down, Mr. Jonathan. Your wife and your new son are doing fine."

"I have a son," Jonathan stated, rather than asked. "I have a son!" This time he shouted. He looked at Miss Trinity and in a calm, respectful manner, asked, "Can I go in?"

"Well, I think Mary is expecting you."

Jonathan opened the door and saw his wife sitting up in bed holding his son to her breast. Mary looked pale, but happy. She smiled and told her husband, "Don't just stand there with your mouth open! Come over here and meet your son." Jonathan obeyed. Mary held the child up so he could see his new baby boy.

"Why he's the most handsome little fellow I have ever seen." Jonathan apologetically looked at Mary and said, "Is everything all right with you?"

"Yes, my love. Everything is just fine with me. Would you like to hold your son?" Jonathan reached down and gingerly took the baby in his arms. He walked over to the window so he could see the baby better in the snow diffused morning light. What he saw made him proud.

"I was thinking we could name him after my Uncle William."

"Jonathan, after all the trouble that I had getting you to understand that I was the woman of your dreams, there's only one name for this child."

Jonathan was again caught off guard by Mary. He turned to his wife and asked, "What name did you have in mind?"

"Your name. He shall also be called Jonathan, after his father. It's a name I have loved and dreamed of for years. And we will call him Jonathan Lucas the 2nd after the man I am proud to call my husband."

"But don't you like the name, William? It's a grand king's name, you know."

"There's to be no more discussion. My mind's made up. Now bring young Jonathan back over here, old Father Jonathan, before he starts to cry from hunger."

Jonathan saw that further discussion about a name for their baby would be futile. Mary was a very determined woman when her mind was made up, he was learning. He returned the infant to his mother and stood there watching his wife and firstborn son. He was almost overcome with a feeling of bliss welling up inside of him. He had never felt such joy and tenderness. In that moment, he knew he had chosen the very best wife and the very best mother for his children and he thanked God above for his extraordinary blessings.

It was over a month before the snow and ice let go of its bitter grip on the land between Whitehaven and Egremont. It was the first week in April by the time the roads were fit to travel and before, John and Ann, the new grandparents, were able to reach the Lucas Carleton House. Their three girls had all given them grandchildren, whom they loved more than life, but this new arrival happened to be the first Lucas grandson. You could not tell who was the proudest, the father or the grandfather.

It had been a gloomy winter, and politically, the outlook was just as bleak. In the midst of all the bad weather and distressing news, Jonathan Lucas the 2nd had arrived. The grandparents remained at the Lucas Carleton House for almost a week and in addition to enjoying the company of their newborn grandson, John and Jonathan spent time discussing politics and business. The future was so uncertain that any potential plans would have to include several contingencies. If war broke out, they needed to put their energies in one direction. If the threat of confrontation did not materialize, but unrest continued, they would likely have to go in another direction. The best outcome of all, would be peace and harmony restored between England and her American Colonies so that industry could, once again, prosper. But they came to the conclusion that unlike seers, they did not have the power to predict the future. They would have to just wait and see what God would decree. Hopefully, at least, whatever the future held, this time, they would be prepared.

Chapter 21

IN APRIL, 1775 THE SHOOTING WAR THAT JOHN had been so afraid of, finally broke out between the colonists in America and the British Army stationed in Boston. The British Army had tried to disarm the colonial militia by a surprise march to the town of Lexington in Massachusetts, where it was suspected the rebels were storing arms. The colonists, being forewarned, were prepared for this attempt and lay in ambush. The American militia fired on the redcoats and in a running battle, drove them all the way back into Boston. They called themselves the Minutemen, because they were ready to take up arms and fight with only a minute's notice. It seemed that all-out war with the American colonies had finally arrived.

Most of the British merchants involved in trade with the American colonies, John included, still hoped that an agreement could be reached that could avoid war and restore trade. There were signs that the conflict, by arresting trade, was now going to be just as bad economically as it had been in the 1760s. It was bankrupting many on both sides of the Atlantic. Moneylenders, such as Thomas Dacre, would be in a position to benefit from this catastrophe. They generally had loaned money against the borrowers' assets at a very low loan to value ratio. The longer the conflict lasted, the more dire the consequences for people indebted in this manner. The cessation of trade meant that bankruptcies would increase with time and allow these financiers to pick up valuable properties at ludicrously low prices. In many cases, this meant acquiring properties for less than half of what they were worth.

John was of the opinion that the only way to avoid going to war, was if the king somehow intervened to settle this dispute. George III was the one individual that had the statue and the power to force the two sides into a reasonable settlement. John explained his reasoning to Jonathan, "The colonists contend, and I agree with them, that the British Parliament has never had any legitimate authority in matters concerning them, because they are not democratically represented in Parliament. They even go so far as to contend that it is their sacred duty, as Englishmen, to continue to resist these parliamentary violations of our British Constitution. If they are Englishmen, they are entitled to be represented in Parliament, just like all Englishmen."

Jonathan asked, "But how can the king help stop this insanity?"

"The Americans want the king to be an honest mediator so a solution can be found to get them out of this morass. They claim they have always been loyal to the king and that their argument is only with a Parliament that is acting illegally. I fear their hopes are misplaced, if they are looking to the king. He is close to Lord North and they are both supporters of Parliament's power, at least in these matters with the colonies. I fear that all-out war with the Americans is inevitable."

News arrived later that summer that a second confrontation had occurred. It was a pitch battle, instead of a running skirmish. Once again, the fight had taken place around Boston and it was called the Battle of Bunker Hill. The situation was going from bad to worse. John's sail making business was beginning to suffer. Trade with the colonies was almost nonexistent. That meant that hundreds of trading ships were idle, all over the British Empire. When they were not in use, their sails did not wear out and did not need to be replaced. The once steady business of making sails was now beginning to put a strain on the Lucas Familys' finances. The company was barely breaking even. If a resolution was not found soon, John would be forced to start laying off workers. It was enough to keep John up at night. The memory of the riot that threatened his life, was still vivid in his mind and he had no desire to face another mob.

Johns' doubts about the king's ability to mediate and avoid war were soon proven correct. The king's reaction to the Battle of Bunker Hill almost insured that all-out war would be the result. Instead of reconciliation, the king issued, in August, a formal declaration entitled, "A Proclamation for Suppressing Rebellion and Sedition." A copy of this proclamation was printed in *The Cumberland Pacquet*. The official response of George III of Great Britain, to the news of the Battle of Bunker Hill declared, that elements of the American colonies are in a state of 'open and avowed rebellion'. It then ordered that officials of the British Empire 'to use their utmost endeavors to withstand and suppress such a rebellion'. The Proclamation went on to encourage his subjects throughout the Empire to identify anyone engaging in 'traitorous correspondence' with the American rebels. This also included the people living in Great Britain. Those so engaged could then be 'known and punished accordingly'.

In October, the king perhaps drove the final nail in the coffin of reconciliation when he made his speech from the throne at the opening of Parliament. King

George elaborated on the earlier Proclamation by maintaining that the rebellion was being provoked by a 'desperate conspiracy' of leaders whose claims of allegiance to him were insincere. What the rebels really wanted, he stated, was the creation of an 'independent empire'. The king then revealed that he anticipated dealing with the calamity by using armed force, and that he was even contemplating accepting 'friendly offers of foreign assistance' to suppress the revolt. A small pro-American group in Parliament then warned that the king and Parliament were forcing the colonists to seek independence. This was something that many of the influential American leaders had asserted they were not in favor of doing.

There seemed to be no turning back from the brink of armed conflict. Instead of trade and prosperity, the king and Parliament had opted for war and poverty. It was clear that anyone who had been hoping the king would find a way to resolve the quarrel between the colonies and Parliament had been mistaken. It was obvious that the king was not interested in acting as a mediator, but in fact, seem to favor war. Any lingering Colonial attachment to the British Empire crumbled with the king's speech.

If John thought that things could not get much worse, he was wrong. The Parliament that convened in October 1775, bolstered the king's belligerent stance, bypassing the Prohibitory Act. Lord North and a majority in Parliament decided that more severe actions were needed to suppress the American insurrection. To accomplish this, Parliament declared a blockade against the commerce of the American Colonies.

The Prohibitory Act stated that, 'all manner of trade and commerce' would be prohibited, and any vessel trading with the colonies, 'shall be forfeited to his Majesty, as if the same were the ships and effects of open enemies'. They were trying to extinguish America's ability to continue this rebellion by prohibiting trade with Great Britain and all other trading countries. This would not only cripple America's ability to continue the war, but it would also be a catastrophe for the British merchants who had been trading with the colonies.

The Prohibitory Act was, in effect, a declaration of war by Great Britain. A blockade was considered an act of war under the laws of nations. In retaliation, Letters of Marque, which authorized individual American ship owners to seize British ships were issued by their congress. This was a practice known as privateering and it threatened to interrupt trade with other parts of the British Empire that were not part of the rebellion. With this parliamentary act, the Americans became more and more convinced that complete independence was their only redress.

Then the King stoked the fires of war, further, by declaring that his 'subjects' were out of his protection, and that he was levying war against them. He said he would do this without concerning himself with whether or not they had continued to be loyal subjects of the crown, or even if they had presented petitions for the redress of legitimate grievances, which was every Englishman's natural right.

Soon after the passing of this Prohibitory Act, the king ordered the hated Hessians into the American colonies. The king and Parliament were attempting to end the rebellion by the sacking, pillaging, and burning of the colonies. Further inflaming passions against the British, was their use of savage Indians to raid, burn and murder along the Western frontier. With these acts of aggression, it became obvious to the Americans that neither liberty, nor security, was to be had under British rule.

And so, the king and his Parliament managed to turn a mostly local quarrel with New England into a war for an independent American nation.

In March of the year 1776, Gen. George Washington forced the British to leave Boston. There were no other British forces in the thirteen colonies. The revolutionaries were now in full control of the land and it looked like they were ready to declare their independence from Great Britain.

The inevitable finally happened. In August 1776, *The Cumberland Pacquet's* headlines proclaimed,

American Colonies Declare Independence from Great Britain

Although the British army returned from Halifax, Nova Scotia and retook New York City later that summer, it was now full-scale war. John and most of the other people in England realized this war was going to be expensive. This meant that taxes had to be raised, yet again. The trade on which businessmen, like Jonathan Lucas, relied for wealth, was now severely interrupted and the increase in taxation put a severe burden on an already strained economy.

Throughout the British Empire, imports and exports suffered large declines and this triggered a deep recession. All across England, including Cumbria, stock and land prices crashed. Trade was further decimated by privateers taking thousands of British merchant ships as prizes.

By 1777, the wartime industries, such as naval suppliers and the textile industry, which made uniforms, once again started receiving orders for resupply. This revived certain sections of the economy. The Lucas Sail Mills received a large contract from the Navy, so at least for the foreseeable future, John could expect his company to continue to prosper.

Mary gave birth in 1777 to their second child, a daughter, and they named her Jane. Fortunately, Jane was not born in the middle of a snowstorm, but in late summer with a doctor in attendance. All of the world events that were causing so much trouble all around the world, barely intruded on the Lucas Carlton House.

In Carlisle, Ann Ashburn's family was not so lucky. Her father's business ventures, unlike John Lucas's, had not fared well under the pressure of the conflict with the American Colonies. He had been unable to repay his debts to the Dacres. Hugh had put extreme pressure on Ann to become his wife. He threatened to call her fathers' loans due, if she remained obstinate in her refusal to wed.

Even under this kind of cajoling, she had continued to refuse his advances. But his persistence knew no bounds. He pursued her at every opportunity and there were many opportunities, as her father had become totally dependent on the largess of the Dacre Family. Hugh expected to be repaid for that largess with his daughter.

At each rejection, Hugh's jealousy became greater, until finally, he was obsessed with anything and everything that Ann said or did. He had made her life a nightmare. His jealousy had taken him over. It had polluted his blood and turned his soul as black as coal. When he looked at her, his eyes reminded her of a snake. The more his passion grew for her, the more she was disgusted to be in his presence.

As if things could not get any worse, Ann's father became ill. His heart had never been strong, but since the failure of his business, he had become weaker and weaker. He was not a coward, but he was also not an assertive man. As Hugh's relationship with his daughter worsened, after their move to Carlisle, he realized how badly he had underestimated what Hugh was capable of, where his daughter was concerned. Hugh had accepted the fact that Ann was not in love with him and with that realization, he began to feel bitter resentment against both Ann and her father. If he could not have her, then he would see to it that no one else would have her either, especially Jonathan Lucas.

Hugh came to Ann's door early one evening in September of 1777. He had decided to make one last attempt for Ann's affection. She answered the door as there were no servants left. She wasn't happy to see Hugh, but she masked her disappointment with a smile and said, "Good evening Hugh. I didn't know father was expecting you this evening?"

"He's not expecting me and besides, it's you I came to see."

"If it's the same question Hugh, I'm afraid the answer will be the same."

"You realize that your fathers' debts are past due. I suggest that you and I go to the parlor and discuss how we handle this situation." Ann started to tell him to leave, but thought better of it, as her father was very ill. As much as it was distasteful to her, she turned and started toward the parlor. He followed close behind, thinking how lovely she was as she walked. As they passed by her father's library, the sick man called through the closed door, "Who is it?" Ann stopped and opened the door slightly. She stuck her head inside and smiled at her father. "It's Hugh, father. He's come to pay me a visit, ---again." Hugh pushed the door open just enough to look inside and said, "Good evening Mr. Ashburn. I just dropped by to say hello to Ann. I hope you're feeling better this evening."

"I feel as well as I should. I understand that we have another meeting scheduled with your barristers tomorrow."

"Yes. I hope that you will be well enough to attend."

"Don't you worry. I'll be there."

"Until tomorrow then."

Ann closed the door and Hugh followed her into the parlor. She walked over to the window and turned around and asked, "What is it you would like to discuss, Hugh?"

"Ann, you and your father are treading on thin ice financially. He has already liquidated most of his assets and the funds raised were nowhere near enough to clear the balance of his debts to us. He no longer has a business that produces an income sufficient to support the two of you. In this time of war with America, that is not unusual. Many good businessmen have been ruined. They have no choice, but to declare bankruptcy. Your father has that same option, but in this case, you have the power to save him and allow him to live out his life comfortably. All you have to do is become my wife."

"But Hugh, we have discussed this over and over again. I do not love you. As a matter of fact, I am not fond of you at all."

"In times, not long passed, people married for reasons other than love. They married for position or they married to raise themselves on a social level. Sometimes they married at the command of the king or their lord. Most marriages were arranged by parents. After the union, if it was a good union, love would often arise out of the marriage. A match with me would make you a very wealthy woman. You know my feelings for you and I would do all in my power to make you happy. I believe that, in time, you would come to love me."

"I don't doubt that you mean that sincerely Hugh, however, I decided when I was a little girl that I would not marry for those reasons. I can only wed someone that I care for as deeply as he cares for me. I wish it were different. I cannot marry you." She turned back, somewhat frightened by the look that had come into Hugh's eyes.

The spurned suitor was becoming visibly agitated. He stepped up and grabbed her by her shoulders and spun her around to him. He drew her close and bent down to kiss her. She turned her head away and cried, "No! What are you doing? Let go of me? Did you hear, let go of me."

Hugh had gone blind with passion. He dropped his left arm, wrapping it around her waist and reached behind her with his right hand and grabbed a handful of her beautiful red hair. He forced her face toward his and began kissing her, as she struggled to free herself. Lifting her off of her feet, he carried her over to the sofa and forced her onto the soft cushions. She was pinned under him, his full weight upon her. He forced his knee between her legs and reaching down with his left hand, forced her skirt up. He was mad with lust and this time he was not going to be denied. Ann managed to push hard with her leg against the corner of the couch. This threw Hugh off balance, just enough for her to slide out from under him. He grabbed at her dress and it ripped as she fell. They both tumbled to the floor with a loud crash.

"Hugh, have you lost your senses? For God's sake, stop!" But he didn't stop. She realized that the 'snake' had struck and she was in very real danger. She started to cry out for help, but her cries was muted by his frenzied kisses. His hands started to explore her body. Reaching deep down inside, she summoned all of her strength and tried to push him away. It was no use. He had the strength of a brute. Her skirt up, baring her legs, Hugh spread her legs apart with his knees. She was losing the battle.

Her strength was failing, so she did the only thing she could think of, to stop the attempted rape. She relaxed, as if she was giving in to his lust. Feeling encouraged, he kissed her once again. She bit his lower lip as hard as she could. He lifted his head and cried out in pain. His hand went from her inner thigh, to his bleeding mouth. It gave Ann the opening she needed and she yelled at the top of her lungs, "Help, please father, help me!"

The door to the parlor flew open and violently slammed into the wall. Rufus Ashburn surveyed the scene and knew exactly what was happening. He was horrified and furious. Rufus was forced into using a cane to walk and although weakened by a bad heart, he started toward Hugh, raising the cane as he advanced.

Hugh's lust had turned to anger as he felt warm blood flowing from his torn bottom lip. He looked up just in time to see the cane descending toward his face. He did not react to the threat and the cane caught him across the right side of his face. The blow came from a sick man and did not have much power behind it, rendering the blow an insult, more than an injury. Hugh rolled over, out of the way of the older man. He stood up, facing an angry Rufus Ashburn and his

Hugh Dacre

equally angry daughter. He knew there was, now, no possibility of anything, but hatred between them. Ann stood up and held her torn dress in place.

Rufus Ashburn lifted the wooden shaft and cried, "Get out! Get out, now!"

Hugh stared at them as he took his handkerchief out to hold against his lip to stop the bleeding. He stepped away from Rufus and Ann, circling behind a table, moving toward the door. He picked up his hat as he reached the entrance to the parlor. Stopping, he looked back at father and daughter. "You have both made the biggest mistake that you could possibly make. You think that you had problems before. The devil himself will not torment you as I will. And as for that married man that you still love, Jonathan Lucas..... I will bring a hurricane of troubles down on him." Then he was gone. They heard his footsteps reach the front door. Hugh opened the door and they waited to hear it close. The two of them remained motionless to reassure themselves that the fiend had actually left. After several seconds of pure silence, Rufus looked at his daughter. " I am sorry. I had no idea what a villain this man really is. I would have never dreamed that he was capable of this kind of conduct."

Before Ann could reply, her father grabbed his chest in agony and sank to the floor in a heap. "Father," she cried as she rushed over to him.

Rufus Ashburn died three days later. Ann was heartbroken and left almost penniless and without a home. The Dacres' lawyers had already foreclosed on their home back in Cumberland. She sold everything she had title to and raised enough money to bury her father. The funeral was held in Cleator Moor. The stress and strain of the past few days showed clearly on Ann's face. Mary and Jonathan attended the funeral and were shocked at the change that had taken place in this once vivacious woman. She didn't seem to really be present, acting if she barely recognized people who were lifelong acquaintances.

Mary turned to Jonathan and said, "There is something more going on with Ann, besides the loss of her father. I have known her all of my life and she is moving about as if she is going to be the next to die."

Mary finally took her friend by the arm. Ann acted as if she did not recognize Mary as she steered her toward the church. They walked inside and Ann collapsed on the first pew. She started to sob, softly at first, but Mary knew it was from deep within.

"Ann, what is it? What has happened to you? You must tell me."

Ann embraced her friend and the two women sat holding each other. Ann gave full vent to her sorrow as the tears flowed freely, soaking Mary's dress. Finally, the crying seemed to subside. Mary ventured again, "You must tell me what has happened. I know you have no family here, but Jonathan and I are your family. You must tell us what has happened to you and let us help."

Ann straightened up and took out a cloth to wipe her eyes. Suddenly, the old assertive look that Mary was used to seeing in her friend, faintly glimmered in her eyes. "I will not allow that man to ruin my life any more than he already has. Oh Mary, he is going to try to ruin yours, as well." Hugh's jealousy had become his great obsession. He was not only jealous, but demented and was a most dangerous man. He had maneuvered her and her father into his control, by forcing them to move away from their home and friends. When all of his threats to ruin her father had not succeeded in forcing her to marry him, he had let his lust take him over. If he was capable of rape, then he was capable of other, more odious crimes.

"Who is going to try to ruin my life?"

"Hugh Dacre."

"I should have guessed. He is a vile man."

"Yes Mary, he's worse than that."

Mary listened to her friend for the next hour. She let her talk and did not interrupt. She remembered the threat he had made against Jonathan on the terrace of the Harewood House in Leeds, the night of the Midsummer's Ball. That this man had become so depraved did not surprise Mary. When Ann had finally finished her story, Mary asked, "Ann, have you lost everything?"

"I have some money left from selling what I personally owned. It's not much and I shall be utterly out of funds soon enough. I have a great uncle in London. He has family and perhaps, they will take me in. I'm not certain , however. I have never met the man or any of his family."

"My God! This monster has brought you to the brink of ruin."

"Actually, I think he has pushed me past the brink of ruin." For the first time in over a week, Ann managed one of her beautiful smiles. Mary's eyes welled up with tears and she took her friend's hands in hers.

"You will come and live with us."

"Mary, you are very kind to offer. But I can't---," Mary interrupted her. "Yes you can. We have plenty of room and I need help with my two children. I can think of no one that I would rather have to help me raise and educate my family than you."

It took several more rejections of her invitation before Ann was worn down enough to give in and accept the offer of succor from Mary.

"I will come to Egremont and stay with you, at least until I have time to figure out where my life will take me next. Are you sure this will sit well with Jonathan?"

"I am absolutely sure. He will be delighted to have you stay with us." Mary smiled and winked at her friend, "I think he only chose me because of those rumors that monster circulated about you. But you, just remember, that he did choose me."

"Mary, do you think that I would repay your kindness with …"

"No, of course not! I was jesting. Maybe it was a poor one, but I was teasing, nonetheless. We need to be able to laugh, even in times like these. You have always been like a sister to me. Now it's settled. We will go directly from here to Lucas Carleton House. You will be the official nanny of the Jonathan Lucas Family and my dear sister, as well."

Later, Jonathan listened with great interest as Mary relayed Ann's life of the past few years. Upon learning of the true perfidy of Hugh Dacre, Mary watched as the anger rose in her husband. He agreed to the arrangement, without any objection, as Mary had known he would. She wondered to herself if she was making a mistake bringing Ann under the same roof with her husband, but she knew there was no alternative. She could not turn her friend out into the world with no prospects. Ann was now, a part of her family.

Chapter 22

SAIL 'MAKING REBOUNDED AFTER FRANCE joined the war against England in the American War for Independence. What had started out as a dispute between Parliament and the thirteen American Colonies over taxes, had escalated into a world war. In early February, 1778, after the Americans captured Gen. Burgoyne's army at Saratoga the previous year, France declared war on England as America's ally. The French brought as allies, Spain and The Netherlands, into the war against England. Great Britain found no nations willing to aid them in this large scale war. Britain's sea-power was tested like never before. This required sails for new ships and replacement sails for existing ones.

Hugh and his father, Thomas Dacre, had foreclosed on a sail making company in nearby Maryport which was fourteen miles up the coast from Whitehaven, toward Scotland. Hugh volunteered to take charge of the newly acquired business to the surprise of his father. He was determined to destroy Jonathan Lucas, financially and then, personally. His first move would be to wreck the Lucas Sail Mills at Whitehaven, by undercutting his pricing. Then, with his father's contacts in Parliament, he would undercut the Lucas bids on any new naval contracts.

He also planned to, once again, ferment trouble inside the Lucas's workforce. Bribery would work nicely to sabotage the quality and speed of the work. His most devastating ploy would be the use of the Dacre wealth to buy up as much flax as possible, thereby cutting off the necessary supplies to the Lucas Mills.

Jonathan had warned his father of the threats that had been made against their interests. Then John heard Dacre was now in the sail making business, in nearby Maryport. He had taken precautions by discussing the threats of rumor and sabotage with the leaders of his operation. Additionally, discussions were held with their main suppliers of flax. Some suppliers succumbed to the higher prices offered by Dacre, but a few remained loyal to Lucas. They were still vulnerable, however, to being undercut in their pricing, when attempting to obtain new business. The higher quality of their product would help them to retain business.

John had scheduled a meeting for Thursday April 23, 1778, with a naval representative to discuss a new contract to supply the navy with sails. In addition to the bribing of workers to sabotage their production, Hugh had begun to circulate rumors about the shoddy workmanship of the Lucas Mills' products. The naval representative had heard these rumors and the meeting had been scheduled to counter this malicious gossip.

Jonathan came into Whitehaven on Wednesday the 22nd, to have dinner with his father and to prepare for the meeting with the Royal Navy. He told Mary that he would be staying in Whitehaven and if the meeting went well, he would be home by Friday the 24th.

Jonathan and his father stayed up until almost midnight discussing the steps they needed to take to counter what was an obvious onslaught of mischief by Hugh Dacre. At about the same time that Jonathan was drifting off to sleep on a cold and frosty April night, an American privateer, the USS Ranger, was dropping anchor about two miles off of Whitehaven's harbor. The Captain of the privateer was none other than Johnny Paul, who was returning to the town that had given him his first job at sea. As you may recall, Whitehaven was where he had become an apprentice to John Lucas's partner, J.D. Younger, and a suitor to Jonathan's sister, Katie. Johnny's cousin, Jaden and her family had long departed Whitehaven.

It had been fourteen years since his last visit to Whitehaven. During the intervening years, many adventures and life changes had taken place in Johnny Paul. Ten years before this night, he had sailed aboard a brig coming out of the West Indies. Young Johnny Paul's career was unexpectedly advanced on that memorable return voyage.

Both the captain and the first mate came down with yellow fever. The two of them quickly died, leaving John Paul as the only experienced officer aboard ship and they were far out to sea. John was able to take command and successfully steered the brig safely to port. As a reward for this remarkable accomplishment, the appreciative Scottish owners made him the ship's new captain. By becoming captain, he was also entitled to ten percent of the voyage's profits. After two voyages to the West Indies, in this new capacity, he ran into a major problem.

In 1770, on his second voyage, John Paul savagely flogged one of his sailors. Some of the crew accused him of being 'unnecessarily cruel'. The whipped sailor died due to his injuries and Johnny Paul was arrested for the flogging and charged with murder. Although eventually he was found innocent, the episode had grievously injured his reputation.

Johnny Paul was eventually given command of a West Indiaman that mounted twenty-two guns. The ship was named *The Betsy*. All went well for about eighteen months. Captain and crew successfully engaged in profitable speculation in the Caribbean Islands of Tobago and Trinidad. Johnny Paul lost his temper, however, when part of his crew mutinied over unpaid wages. John killed a member of his crew, a mutineer named Blackton, with a sword. Johnny Paul claimed he had acted in self-defense, but he was aware that he would be tried, once again, in an Admiral's Court for murder. It would be dangerous to return to court and charged with murder for the second time, so he decided to flee. Leaving everything he had behind, he escaped to Fredericksburg, Virginia. Sadly, upon his arrival, he was forced to organize the affairs of his brother, William, who had passed away.

To aid in a successful escape from justice, Johnny Paul decided to add the surname, Jones. So he had become John Paul Jones, an American citizen. He recalled that long ago he had told Katie Lucas that he would become a Jones if he ever needed another name.

Soon after, he joined the American Navy and took to sea to fight against the British. Why he had chosen Whitehaven to raid is a matter of conjecture. It could have been because he was familiar with the harbor or it could have been that he held a grudge against the people of the town, because he felt they had destroyed his first benefactor, J.D. Younger. Perhaps it was the resentment he felt after being forced into the slave trade he detested. But, whatever the reason, he was preparing to destroy the town that had once been good to him many years before. John Paul Jones was returning to Whitehaven as captain of an enemy warship.

Two boats were let down into the water. The long boats were filled with about thirty men. Johnny Paul had armed his men with pistols and cutlasses and he personally took charge of one of the boats. His second in command was a Swedish Lieutenant, Jean Meijer. Meijer was one of the few crew members he felt he could trust. Another Swedish crew member, by the name of Shoondelin, had warned Lieutenant Meijer of an attempted mutiny two days before against Capt. Jones. A seaman by the name of Cullam, had arranged as a signal to the crew, a charge at the captain. As the attack ensued, the mutineers would take over the ship. The crew was supported by most of her officers and intended to throw John Paul Jones overboard, but being forewarned, the mutiny came to naught, as John Paul put a pistol to Master Cullam's head. John Paul's temper had not abated over the years.

Lieutenant Samuel Wallingford, a Continental Marine, commanded the other boat. His second-in-command was Midshipman, Ben Hill. Wallingford had

grumbled that, "no profit is to be gained by burning ships and property." But he had been persuaded by John Paul to participate in the raid.

"All right, lads, we've got three hours before dawn breaks. There should be about four hundred ships packed tightly together against the piers. Most of them will be loaded with coal getting ready to sail for Ireland. If this breeze holds, we should be able to start quite a blaze. Then we will do to this town what the redcoats have done to our American villages. Remember, that in America, no delicacy has been shown by the English. They take away all sorts of movable property, setting fire, not only to towns and to the homes of the rich, without distinction, but have not even spared the wretched hamlets and milch cows of the poor. Therefore, in retaliation, we'll not only set their ships ablaze, but burn the whole damned town to the ground."

The two boats began to row against the tide toward the Whitehaven Harbor. The gleaming white quays shone brightly in the light of the moon. John Paul had lost precious time and was behind schedule. He had intended to embark for the harbor just after sunset. Still mutinous, because they felt the mission was too dangerous and unprofitable, his crew was none too happy to go ashore for a raid. They were more interested in prize money, than in striking hard at the British. It took him several hours to convince his crew this needed to be done to relieve pressure for the American cause. He was intent on taking the war to the English countryside giving the British a taste of their own tactics.

The saboteurs first tried to make landing on the coast near Saltom Pit. They originally planned to run along the beach and take the Lunette Battery from land. This proved impossible as the sea was too turbulent and the beach was strewn with too many rocks. They decided to continue to row directly to the fort and soon the two boats passed silently, directly under the bastion. As light was appearing over the hills behind Whitehaven, they rowed around the end of the quay into the harbor, behind the fortifications.

"Be ready for the guardsmen. You've got to be quick and give them no time to sound the alarm."

Jones' boat came alongside the quay silently. They had shipped their oars and reached out with their hands to cushion and silence their landing.

"Quietly lads, very quietly," Jones said in barely a whisper.

Since the tide was at ebb, they were a good ten feet below the top of the battlements. "What do we do now? It's too high to reach. Let's just get the hell out of here!" The crew was still not convinced they should be on this mission.

"Lieutenant Meijer, stand tall against the stones and I'll climb up on your shoulders. I think I can reach the top from there." Jones took a knife from his belt and clenched it between his teeth as he scaled his lieutenant's back. Perched precariously on the tall Swede's shoulders, he managed to reach up with both hands and was barely able to grab hold of the walkway. He lifted himself up so that he could see the battery for the first time. They were in luck. There were no guards in sight, so he climbed up the rest of the way and motioned his men to follow him quickly.

He thought he heard a sound and ducked down behind a cannon. No one came, but neither did his men. So he crawled back to the edge and looked down into the two boats.

"Wallingford, you get around to the north side and start lighting some of those coal ships ablaze. Be sure to go into Allison's Tavern and hold everyone quietly, while we do our work. If they are awakened, they could sound the alarm. Now what's wrong with the rest of you men? There are no guards outside." The men looked at one another and still did not move.

Jones continued, "Aye, it's an awful cold morning. I would guess that the guards are in that nice warm guardhouse over there at the back of the fort, trying to keep warm. Now, come on men! You don't want to go down in history as cowards, do you? This will be an easy way to gain fame and glory. Now come on, let's get moving!"

Wallingford turned to his men and said, "Okay lads, head toward the tavern. We'll secure the tavern owner and get some dry flint 'n steel and some oil to start a nice fire to warm up this cold, gloomy, English morning. It took us so long to

John Paul Jones

get here, that we burned all the oil we had in the lanterns. Now quick lads, pull hard. Let's go." Wallingford's boat moved off toward the north end of the harbor.

The big Swede, Lieutenant Meijer, reached over and roughly grabbed one of the men closest to him and pointed upward, toward John Paul. "Up you go and be quick about it."

The reluctant men began climbing up on each other's shoulders and soon joined John Paul on top of the battlement, one by one. Within a couple of minutes, all of the men, except Lieutenant Jean Meijer, were assembled between the cannons of the fort. The lieutenant was left to guard the boat, while the rest of them completed the mission. It would not be long before full daylight arrived.

"Check your pistols, men. Be sure the prime is fresh and ready to fire. We can't afford to have wet powder and misfires." The men did as they were instructed and sure enough, about half of them had to clean their weapons of wet powder and reload. John Paul nervously whispered, "Hurry it up, men. We're not going to a church social." He turned and stepped out from the cover of the cannons "All right lads, that's the guardhouse. Let's move." They ran across the fifty yards to the back of the fort, slowing down as they approached the door. As they lined up in front of the entrance, each man cocked his pistol. John Paul gripped the doorknob and pushed open the entry. There were two guards sitting, facing the fire with their backs to the door and four more guards were sound asleep in their beds. At the sound of entry, one of the guards turned sleepily around and said, "What the . . ." His voice trailed off as he noticed fourteen pistols trained directly at him. They quickly surrounded the rest of the men, drawing them roughly out of their sleep.

Within three minutes, they were all bound to their beds and gagged. John Paul left two men to guard them and the rest headed back out to secure the fort. Sure that the garrison was now firmly under their control, John Paul turned to Joe Green, another midshipman, and said, "Joe, you come with me."

"Where we heading, Captain?"

"You see that big rock over there, about one hundred yards away?"

"Yes sir, I see it."

"Well, that rock is called Tom Hurd's rock. Just on the other side of it, is the Half-Moon Battery. Unless something has changed, there's a whole battery of thirty-two pounders located beyond the rock and they've got a range of up to a mile. If we're going to get safely away, we'll have to disable those guns." He spoke to the rest of his men, "While we're over there spiking those cannons, men, you start setting fire to the ships in this part of the harbor." Jones and Green started off at a trot. They arrived at Half-Moon Battery and began to hammer barbed steel spikes into the touch holds to disable the guns.

At just about the same time, Lieutenant Wallingford, midshipman Ben Hill and the rest of the sailors, pulled up in front of Nicolas Allison's Tavern. They forced open the front door and surprised Nicolas, who had just come down the stairs. Nicolas and his family were placed under close guard. One of the crew members, David Freeman, suggested, "Lieutenant, it's awfully cold this morning and I think we could all do with a drink."

"That's not a bad suggestion. At least we'll get a free drink out of this raid. You men, break out the rum, while I find something that will burn easily." They crowded around the bar and began to slake their thirst at Nicolas Allison's expense. Wallingford approached Nicholas and said, "Where do you keep your oil for your lamps?"

"I don't use oil! It cost too much. All I have is candles." Wallingford shook his head and turned to his second-in-command, "Ben, hand me a bottle of that rum." The midshipman did as he was bid. The alcohol worked especially well that morning on the raiding party. Whether it was from not having eaten anything for hours, or from the excitement and fatigue, the entire menagerie was soon feeling its full effects. In short, they were getting drunk, instead of obeying orders and setting ships on fire.

"Lieutenant, what are we doing here? Do you think it's right what we're trying to do?"

"I don't ever think it's right to destroy poor people's property. But orders is orders, and after we finish these bottles, we're going to have to carry our orders out. Is that understood?"

"You know if we burn the ships, the firing don't stop with just ships. This whole town is gonna go up in flames. If it was just rich men, I wouldn't care. But most of the folks in this town are coal miners, sailors, factory workers and don't forget, there's children and women here too. Are we really going to burn 'em all out?"

"Orders is orders. And I've finished this bottle. We got to do what we came here to do. Like it, or not!"

Nicholas Allison had seen an opening and spoke, "Lieutenant, you're drinkin' the worst stuff in the house. Let me get behind that bar. I've got some of the best rum from Barbados that you ever tasted. I only serve it to the richest customers."

He passed behind the bar as he spoke. Reaching down, he pulled up another bottle with a different shape. Taking a cloth from behind the bar, he wiped the dust and held it up to Wallingford. "I want you to try this and tell me if it's not the best rum you've ever drank."

"Okay, tavern keeper, but this better be good. As soon as I finish this bottle we're gonna carry out . . . " He hesitated searching for the correct words, "You know, we're going to . . . oh yeah, we're going to carry out orders." As the lieutenant turned up the new bottle, he didn't notice as his crewmen, David Freeman, slipped out the back door. As soon as Freeman was out of sight of the tavern, he broke into a run and found himself two blocks away on Marlborough Street. When he figured he was sufficiently far enough away from the earshot of his crew mates, he began pounding on doors shouting, "Fire, fire! They're trying to burn the town! They're burning the ships! They're burning the town! Wake up!" Freeman was moving from house to house, along Marlborough Street, sounding the alarm. In a flash, there were sleepy civilians milling about in the street. They gathered into a group, wondering who had sounded the alarm. When fifteen to twenty people had congregated, David Freeman returned and explained, "Captain John Paul Jones of the American Navy is in your harbor setting fire to your ships. He is also intending to burn your town down."

"How many men does he have?" asked one of the townsmen.

"He's got about thirty men and they're armed. I sure don't hold with burning poor people's property. If flames get up in the ship's rigging there will be hell to pay."

One of the group had the presence of mind to go over to the alarm and start striking the fire bell. David Freeman said, "I'll continue to wake the people. You men need to get down to the harbor to put those fires out."

"We've got fire engines and we'll get there as quickly as we can. Let's move quickly now, before the fire spreads."

The noise and commotion had awakened Jonathan. He knew the sound of the fire bell and got dressed quickly. He knew the dangers that a quick moving fire posed. He ran outside and stopped a passerby, "What's happening? What's the problem?"

"American pirates! They's setting fire to the ships in the harbor. Hurry! We need everyone at the wharf."

Jonathan turned and started running toward the waterfront, knowing the port was full of ships. Most of the Whitehaven vessels were full of coal. If it was low tide, the entire fleet would be packed close together and stuck in the mud and there would be no way to move them away from the flames. The warehouses, along the quays, were full of rum, sugar and tobacco and it would ignite and blow, as well. The warehouses were built right up against the harbor's edge to facilitate easy loading and unloading, so if the attack wasn't stopped, it could be a disaster of the first magnitude.

When Jones returned from spiking the cannons, he was disheartened not to see any ships burning. His men were all standing in a group, looking at the ships in the harbor.

"What the hell is going on? I expected to see this cold morning warmed by burning ships and a burning town."

"Captain, we have no way to start a fire. Our candles and lanterns have all burned out."

At that moment, Wallingford's group appeared, holding a burning lantern. He staggered up to his captain and said with a thick tongue, "Cap'n, it took us a little while, but we finally got some fire." He held the lantern up, showing the flame. "Wallingford, you're drunk."

"No Sir. I'm warm and after I help you set this . . . this fire, I'm going to be warmer." John Paul reached out and took the lantern out of Wallingford's hands. He turned to his men and said, "Let's move."

Quickly the saboteurs moved to the nearest ships. *The Thompson* was full of coal, bound for Dublin. Upon entering the ship, they found two boys who had been left aboard to look after *The Thompson* and the ship next to it, *The Saltham*.

Wallingford had staggered on board and was bouncing around the cabin when he stopped in front of the two lads. "How would you lads like to come to America with us?" He reached into his purse and pulled out a handful of shillings. "We could use a couple of good cabin boys like you and there's more money where this came from. What's say ye boys? How 'bout some adventure and money? That's a good combination, don't you think?" Both of the boys shook their heads, refusing Wallingford's offer. Wallingford grabbed them by the scruff of the neck and pushed them toward Ben Hill. "Gag 'em with handkerchiefs and take 'em back to the Old Quay. If they tries to run away, shoot 'em. Understood?"

The crew soon made torches by taking canvas and covering it with sulfur. They were set on fire and tossed into the cargo holds of several adjacent ships. A barrel of tar was broken open on the deck of *The Thompson* near the main mast. Just as the privateers had hoped, the fire started to take hold. As the flames began to climb higher, the Americans edged back toward their boats. The fire began in earnest in the steerage of the ship and blazed into the cabin. *The Thompson* was captained by Richard Johnson and owned by John Lucas. It was one of the biggest coal transporters in Whitehaven.

By now, the Whitehaven crowd had grown to around a hundred men. As they ran to the harbor, they glanced around and saw the fire beginning to spread on *The Thompson*. Jonathan pushed his way to the front of the crowd and saw his father's ship was in grave danger. It had just been loaded with coal the day before. He turned and shouted, "Where are those fire engine? The fire's over here! Hurry!"

The firefighters moved quickly toward the ship. The flames were licking upward on the main mast. If they didn't put it out soon, it would be too late to stop the fire from turning into a conflagration. At the sight of the crowd, the raiders gathered together, brandishing their swords and pistols. They had moved away from the ship and had stopped to assess the approaching danger from the townspeople. As Jonathan led the crowd, they suddenly saw the armed men about fifty yards away. Both groups stopped and stared at each other. Jonathan advanced toward the men. As he grew closer, the leader of the saboteurs, yelled out, "You there, stop! Don't come any closer or we'll shoot." Jonathan did as he was told. There was something familiar about that voice. He held up both of his hands. "I'm unarmed and that's my ship that you set ablaze."

John Paul stepped closer and answered, "Well pretty soon, they'll be a lot more ships burning and maybe you all will understand what your troops are doing to us in our homes. You, who are supposed to be our brothers!"

Then, like a thunderbolt, Jonathan recognized the voice. "Johnny Paul! My God it's you! You're the famous John Paul Jones!"

"And who might you be?"

"Jonathan Lucas and I've still got the tomahawk you brought back to me from America so long ago."

"Jonathan, I did not know that was your ship. But our two countries are at war, so it makes no difference. I'm sorry, but it can't be helped. "

"Well, Captain John Paul Jones, we've got half the town's menfolk here now and the rest of them will be here in a few minutes. If you're going to start shooting, you'd better get to it."

"Jonathan, I have no desire to shoot anyone. We'll be leaving now. There needs be no bloodshed unless the townspeople force us to it. Give my regards to your family. I hope they are all well. And to your sister, Katie, my special regards." With that, Captain John Paul Jones removed his hat and with a sweeping bow to Jonathan, turned away and boarded the long boats to join his crew.

"Let's go, boys, we've done all we can here. Pull hard for *The Ranger*."

Fortunately, the fire engines had arrived and were immediately deployed. Jonathan turned around and sprinted back to help extinguish the fire. With a valiant effort by all classes of people working together that cold April morning, they were successfully able to douse the flames before the fire reached the ship's rigging. The flames were extinguished before spreading to the other ships anchored close by. The sulfur coated canvas matches that had been thrown down into the other ships including, *The Saltham*, did not catch. Some soldiers were able to get a couple of cannons in working order and fired some parting shots at the marauders, without effect.

A huge disaster had been averted. The one ship that was destroyed happened to belong to the Lucas Family. This loss would put further financial strains on them along with their plight caused by the unscrupulous Dacre Clan. Fortunately, John Lucas was the type of man who never borrowed money. All of his investing was transacted with cash or it was not done at all.

Chapter 23

MASTER AND COMMANDER EDWARD Whittington had started his naval career as a sail maker. After spending five years at sea, he was given the opportunity to become a midshipman. He served four more years, before he was able to pass his examination to become a lieutenant.

After serving several years, he had attained the rank of Master and Commander and had command of his own sloop of war, *The Leopard*. He was in Whitehaven to ensure that products purchased by the Navy were of good quality. After the excitement over the raid by John Paul Jones had died down, Jonathan and his father returned to their business and met with Commander Whittington at their mill. After the usual formal introductions, the naval commander explained, "With the start of hostilities with the Americans, the British government of Lord North was slow to recognize the need for an increase in the size of the navy. After our loss at Saratoga and now the entry of the French into the war on the side of the Americans, the situation has changed dramatically."

"It's about time, is all I have to say," replied Jonathan . "When saboteurs can threaten to burn an entire English town to the ground without so much as a shot being fired by the navy, well, something must be done and done quickly"

"I can well understand your concerns, but I can assure you that we will meet this challenge from the French and the Americans. British sea power will once again be unrivaled in the world."

John said, "How does the government intend to counter these threats and how can we be of service? We have just fulfilled our last contract, and I presume that all is satisfactory to the Crown?"

"Yes, I have inspected the last shipment and your product is of very good quality, contrary to the rumors that I have been hearing. We have enacted a shipbuilding schedule that is unparalleled in history. The Royal Navy is in the process of accepting bids on contracts to build more war ships than ever before. These contracts are being distributed among shipbuilders all along the coast of England and eighteen ships of the line have been ordered. These are, in addition, to the five already under construction. As you know, it takes a minimum of three years to build one of them."

"Those are monsters and they sure take a lot of sail." John was hopefully leading the conversation in a direction that would end with more navy business. "What else are they planning to add to the fleets?"

"In addition to men of war, we, the Royal Navy, have ordered an additional fifty to fifty-five frigates and sloops. The Comptroller of the Royal Navy, Charles Middleton, is determined to restore the navy's traditional power and prestige and to protect our coastline from invasion or from raids, like the one attempted here last night."

"I take it then, commander, that you are satisfied with the product you have seen us produce and therefore, will allow us to continue to be a supplier for the Royal Navy."

Whittington replied, "My prior position of sail maker for over five years allows me to judge the quality of sails that are available to us. "In spite of the rumors, I find your product to be of exceptional quality and I look forward to continuing doing business with you in the future."

The Master and Commander rose, said goodbye and left. John turned to his son and offered, "Well, at least that's done. It doesn't mean that we will get any more contracts, but at least we're not out of the game."

Hugh Dacre learned about this turn of events when Commander Whittington toured his sail factory in Maryport. The commander was not as impressed with his operation as he had been with the Lucas Mill's output.

Since he had discovered that Ann had moved in with Jonathan and Mary, he was more determined than ever to take his revenge. He had made some progress as two of John Lucas's new employees were being paid by Hugh. Perhaps a more direct move would be successful.

There was labor unrest throughout England. Hard times had made people afraid and resentful. In the Midlands, there had been epidemics of workers vandalizing machines, attacking mills and even burning them to the ground.

Alex Barton had once again gotten word that a group of workers were planning to attack the mill. Their intent was to break in, smash the machinery and then set the mill on fire. Alex was not sure when the attack would come, but he knew the threat was real enough. John approached Thomas Dacre, the mayor, to ask for protection for his mill.

"John, we have not seen this kind of rioting for over two years. You don't seem to have any real proof, only rumors, but I will alert the lieutenant, in charge of the harbor fort. That is only a few blocks away from your mill. At the first sign of trouble, I'm sure he will be glad to send some soldiers to drive off any trouble."

"Thomas, I hope that will be enough. I have informed you and it is your duty to protect private property."

"John, you don't have to tell me how to do my job. I must have something more to go on than drunken talk emanating from a tavern. Now, if you will excuse me, I have work to do." With that, he reached down, picked up a handful of papers and began reading. John started to say something, but thought better of it and turned and walked away.

It was apparent that he was not going to get help from the mayor. When he returned home, he sent Martin Trinity to Egremont to ask his son to join him for a conference. Jonathan arrived and after discussions with his father, they agreed to take turns guarding the mill at night. For four weeks nothing happened. Then, on Saturday, February 13, 1779, John Lucas and five of his workmen were sleeping in the factory. It had been confirmed that a group of unknown men were bent upon destroying his machinery and factory. Shortly after midnight, John told his men to go to sleep. Sunday morning came around quietly and it looked as if they had been wrong about possible trouble and that maybe Sunday would eventually dawn with only the noise of ringing church bells.

At around 1:30, the dog left to guard downstairs started to bark ferociously. John leapt out of bed and began running to the room where the weapons had been stored. His men heard the alarm, as well, and all five men banded together. Suddenly, there was a loud banging noise on the main entrance door to the mill. Dressed only in their nightshirts and trousers, John and his men fanned out across the upstairs and stood with their weapons resting on the railing, facing the door below. The intruders had come prepared to do business. It seemed to John as if they were using a battering ram on his front entrance. The front door crashed open and several armed men rushed in carrying torches. John yelled, "STOP! Remove yourself from this property. We are armed and intend to do what is necessary to defend this place and ourselves." The mob halted in their tracks. The leader was a rugged looking man with a scar across one eye. He was dressed as a sailor and did not look like a worker. "Who's here and how many of you are there?" The rabble slowly began to spread out along the front wall.

"Stay where you are. One more step and we'll open fire."

The scar faced man suddenly raised his pistol in the direction of John's voice. He fired into the darkness and heard his ball thud into flesh. John had been hit in the right shoulder. The other five men on the rail with John fired simultaneously at the scar faced man. He was hit by three of the balls and fell back into the crowd, mortally wounded. Seeing their leader wounded took the starch out of the crowd. They grabbed him up and started to retreat. Another voice yelled, "Torch it!" Several torches were thrown in different directions. John had struggled to his feet and shouted down below, "Unless you want more bloodshed, I suggest you get out of here now." The thugs decided that they'd had enough. They weren't sure what they were facing, but they knew some of them would likely be wounded or killed, just like their leader. The rabble moved outside, taking their wounded companion with them. John shouted, "Get those fires put out, men." Then, he slumped to the floor and fainted. The bullet had struck him about two inches below the right shoulder and the speeding projectile severed the artery and broke several bones. John's men helped him back to his room and laid him down upon his bed. They gave him some brandy and Alex applied a bandage, but his clothes had become drenched in blood and he slipped into unconsciousness. Alex realized the seriousness of the wound and put his finger on the broken artery to staunch the flow of blood. Later, the doctor said if that had not been done, he would've been dead in ten minutes.

The mayor led an investigation of the incident, but somehow no one could ever discover who the rioters were, or what caused them to attack.

John's wound proved to be very serious, but it was not mortal. The doctor successfully removed the ball from his shoulder and he seemed to be on the road to recovery. He was experiencing severe pain, but found the inner strength to control it. John seemed to be doing well. He ate and drank and talked to visitors about the attack. He also sent Martin to Egremont to bring Jonathan to be with him, as he convalesced. The doctor was puzzled that he continued to complain about a pain in his side. Alex told the doctor that he thought he had injured it during his fall, after being shot. The doctor examined him and found nothing.

His mill workers, mostly country people, brought meager gifts of food and with eyes, full of tears, they prayed for a full recovery. John seemed to be recovering and slept well the first night. Everyone was optimistic. The doctor was vigilant, strictly limiting the number of visitors allowed to see him. Ann and her son, Jonathan, sat by his bed watching through the night, while her John slept fitfully until it was nearly dawn.

John's priest, the Rev. Zachariah Farrington, arrived the next day. He held a bedside prayer service, which deeply gratified the seriously wounded man. That evening, thinking that his father's recovery was underway, Jonathan allowed himself to sleep on the couch in the parlor.

John awoke with nausea around three in the morning. He looked around and saw his wife, still by his side, but asleep. His nausea became more acute and at the sound of his retching, Ann awoke. "What is wrong, my darling? Let me send for the doctor."

"No, I don't believe that's necessary. But I think if you will bring me a wet towel and place it on my side, it should relieve some of the pain."

Ann continued bringing him wet towels throughout the night. Soon after dawn, the doctor returned to check on his patient. John's pain was increasing. The doctor examined his patient and diagnosed pneumonia. Mary arrived in Whitehaven with her two small children as the crisis unfolded. She seemed to sense immediately that something was terribly wrong.

John sank into delirium, talking about sending *The Julia* to Virginia for tobacco once more. Then he would come back from his coma and talk to Ann and Mary and tease his two grandchildren, little Jonathan and baby Jane. He insisted to those around him that he would recover and get back to manage his mill. He was relieved to learn that the mill had been saved and no equipment had been destroyed, but John continued to decline, and eight days later, Jonathan was certain that his father could not last another day. He spoke with his mother and she agreed, weeping. Ann spoke softly, "John, I'm afraid you are too weak to recover. The doctor has told us to send for Reverend Farrington. The doctor entered and John asked, "Doctor, Ann informs me that you have told her I am to die soon, Is this true?"

The doctor answered , "Yes. I'm afraid it's true."

"Very good, very good," said John. "It is all right."

He tried to comfort his wife and son. He instructed Jonathan, "After my death, take care of and provide for your mother, who has been very kind and good to me for all of the years we've been together." Do what you think is best for the businesses and don't forget the people who work for us. Most have remained loyal and steadfast friends. Do not let this incident embitter you. Do the best that you can and take care of those who take care of you. Do not waste your time on hatred. Revenge is nothing more than a poison and it will destroy your life. Promise me."

Jonathan took his father's hand and his mother took the other. Jonathan looked at his father and took a deep breath. "I promise you, father, that I will do my best to take care of our family and our workers."

"You must also promise to not seek revenge. Spend your life building, not destroying. You must promise me."

"Yes, father, I promise you to forsake revenge and to try to spend my life building what is worthwhile."

John Lucas died at 7:32 p.m. His final words were, "Remember your promise to me, son. Build, do not destroy."

His funeral was to be held three days later. As soon as the seriousness of his condition had become known, Ann had sent for his brother, William, hoping he would arrive in time to bid farewell. The day after John died, his brother walked into their home. After greeting everyone and viewing the body, William, escorted by his nephew, Jonathan, moved into the library where the distraught young man relayed the details of the past two weeks. When Jonathan completed his narration, William stood up and thundered, "Those damned Dacres are behind this. You know it as well as I. Well, we can play that game, as well as they can."

"That's not what father wanted. He made me promise that I would not seek revenge against the instigators."

"He made you promise what?"

"He was very specific. He made me promise that I would spend the rest of my life building and not trying to destroy, out of a sense of revenge."

"Well, thank God I made no such stupid promise."

"But uncle, don't you understand? This was my father's dying request."

"He was my brother and my best friend. And now they have taken him away. He has been murdered. And I am to do nothing? We are to do nothing?"

"I don't like it anymore than you do. I know who is behind this, just as sure I know that your name is William. But, I have no proof. I will honor my father's request. However, if this continues, I will not consider my actions to be revenge. I will consider it to be self-defense."

The day of the funeral arrived. Jonathan and his mother opened their house to the mourners early that morning. John had been so popular and had done much good for almost everyone that knew him. The family served burnt wine and Savoy biscuits. They also wrapped up two biscuits, which were sealed up in wax paper, for the mourners to take home with them. Ann had engaged the firm of Henry Wilson and Company to arrange a funeral that was impressive for a man of John Lucas's position in the community.

The interior of the coffin Ann chose was made of elm and it was lined and ruffled with a fine crepe cloth and a plush mattress. John's corpse was covered with a superfine sheet and his head rested on a pillow. The outside of the lead coffin was inscribed with the words, "John Lucas, son, husband, father and grandfather." The coffin had been finished in the best manner possible, with black nails and a black drape. There were brass handles in the form of angels. They also had asked close friends to walk in front of the funeral hearse, which was drawn by four black horses with livery in black and silver. Henry Wilson and Company also printed engraved invitations in the form of a memento to be distributed to his friends, relatives and acquaintances from Whitehaven. The Anglican priest, Zachariah Farrington officiated. Saint Nicholas Church was filled, to overflowing, as the town mourned their fallen benefactor.

After the body was laid to rest in the ground, the crowd of mourners began to dissipate. William grabbed Jonathan's arm and pointed to the edge of the churchyard. There stood Thomas Dacre and his son, Hugh. "Those bastards," said William. "They're here to gloat. They think they can intimidate us by showing up here. Well, by God, they're not going to get away with it."

William started toward them. Jonathan grabbed his arm and said, "Wait! I'll go with you. Let me do the talking."

Jonathan and William strode purposefully toward Thomas and Hugh. Thomas bowed slightly and said, " Jonathan, William, my condolences and my sympathy for your loss." Hugh said nothing. Jonathan did not answer Thomas but stepped directly in front of his main adversary, Hugh. "I know you are behind this. If I could prove it, you would be headed to the gibbet. My father forgave you the night he died and he made me promise that I would not seek revenge for his death. I have made that promise and I intend to keep it. But, if this persecution continues, I tell you, now; any future actions against me, my family, my businesses or my friends, are not covered by that oath. I will call you out to answer, if this continues."

"Father, do you hear? He has made threats against me?"

"You are mistaken, Hugh. That was not a threat, that was a vow to God. And if I were you, I would ask God for his forgiveness for your horrific deeds. He may forgive you, but I never will." Jonathan turned and grabbed his uncle by the arm and they walked back to his mother, wife and family.

Chapter 24

T HE YEAR AFTER JOHN'S UNTIMELY DEATH saw an increase in production at the Lucas Sail Mill. Jonathan's talents as a millwright were also in demand, once again. At first, his Uncle William had recommended that Jonathan take on projects that he didn't have time to do. After customers saw the quality of the work that Jonathan could produce, they began to recommend his services as satisfied customers.

Over the remaining years of the war with America, Jonathan's time was divided between continuing to supervise the Whitehaven mill for his mother and constructing other projects throughout the north of England. He had become particularly adept at the construction of windmills and waterwheels as power sources. His first love was the profession of millwright. He enjoyed travel, meeting new people and the challenge of new projects. He was skillful at solving problems and designing new pieces of equipment, or modifying existing machinery.

Although he was proficient at managing the mill, it was not his first love. Alex Barton had become a very good manager under Jonathan's direction and ran the day-to-day operations of the mill. This allowed Jonathan to be away for long periods of time, working on projects for clients. There had been no more overt troubles, for the death of John Lucas had shocked even Thomas Dacre. Jonathan's stern warning to Hugh had given them both pause. In August 1779, Jonathan and Mary had their third child. It was a boy and they named him Moses. Ann had grown quite close to the family and since she did not have children of her own, she had become a second mother to Mary's brood.

One day in the fall of 1779, Mary noticed a large group of people gathering in a field between Egremont and the Lucas Carleton House. Intrigued, she walked down to find out what was taking place. It turned out that on very afternoon, the famous Anglican priest, John Wesley, would be presenting a sermon. He was well known for being the leader of the sect, called Methodist, that was prominent in Cumbria. Mary was curious as she had never heard this great man preach. She lingered, as the crowd gathered and decided to take a seat on the ground, near the front. It wasn't long before the crowd murmured, as they saw him approach.

It was said that John Wesley traveled throughout England, generally, on horseback and it wasn't unusual for him to preach two or three times each day. Mary had heard people say that he had ridden more than two hundred and fifty thousand miles on horseback and that he had given away over thirty thousand pounds to charitable causes. Wesley had also preached more than forty thousand sermons in his long career.

Mary had been brought up in the Anglican church, but had never been particularly religious. With the untimely death of John Lucas, her father-in-law, she had become more and more interested in spirituality. The crowd, that afternoon, was very excited at the prospect of hearing the inspiring words of John Wesley. They were not to be disappointed.

John Wesley rode up on horseback, dismounted and reached into his saddle bags to pull out a Bible that was worn and ragged from use. He was below medium height, was well proportioned and looked strong, despite his seventy-six years. His eyes were bright and alert, his complexion was clear and unmarked. But what struck Mary the most, was his saintly, intelligent face.

He strode to the front of the congregation that had gathered in that open field and with a kind and confident voice, began to speak.

I will be speaking to you today on the subject of God's grace. It is generally supposed, that the means of grace and the ordinances of God, are equivalent terms. We commonly mean by that expression, those that are usually termed, works of piety; that is, hearing and reading the Scripture, receiving the Lord's Supper, public and private prayer and fasting. And it is certain, these are the ordinary channels which convey the grace of God to the souls of men. But, are they the only means of grace? Are there no other ways than these, whereby God is pleased, frequently, yea, ordinarily, to convey his grace to them that either love or fear him? Surely there are works of mercy, as well as works of piety, which are the real means of grace. They are more especially such to those that perform them with a single eye. And those that neglect them, do not receive the grace, which otherwise they might. Yea, and they lose, by a continued neglect, the grace which they had received. Is it not hence, that many who were once strong in faith, are now weak and feeble-minded? And yet, they are not sensible when that weakness comes, as they neglect none of the ordinances of God. But they might see whence it comes, were they seriously to consider St. Paul's account of all true believers: "We are his workmanship, created anew in Christ Jesus unto good works, which God hath before prepared, that we might walk therein." (Eph. 2:10)

"The walking herein is essentially necessary, as to the continuance of that faith, whereby we are already saved by grace, so to the attainment of everlasting salvation. Of this we cannot doubt, if we seriously consider that these are the very words of the great Judge himself: "Come, ye blessed children of my Father, inherit the kingdom prepared for you from the foundation of the world. For I was hungry, and ye gave me meat: thirsty, and ye gave me drink: I was a stranger, and ye took me in: naked, and ye clothed me: I was sick, and ye visited me: I was in prison, and ye came unto me." (Matt. 25:34) "Verily, I say unto you, inasmuch as ye have done it to the least of these, my brethren, ye have done it unto me." If this does not convince you that the continuance in works of mercy is necessary to salvation, consider what the Judge of all says to those on the left hand: "Depart, ye cursed, into everlasting fire, prepared for the devil and his angels: For I was hungry, and ye gave me no meat: Thirsty, and ye gave me no drink: I was a stranger, and ye took me not in: Naked, and ye clothed me not: Sick and in prison, and ye visited me not. Inasmuch as ye have not done it unto one of the least of these, neither have ye done it unto me." You see, were it for this alone, they must "depart" from God "into everlasting punishment."

"Is it not strange, that this important truth should be so little understood, or, at least, should so little influence the practice of them that fear God? Suppose this representation be true, suppose the Judge of all the earth speaks right, those, and those only, that feed the hungry, give drink to the thirsty, clothe the naked, relieve the stranger, visit those that are in prison, according to their power and opportunity, shall "inherit the everlasting kingdom." And those that do not shall "depart into everlasting fire, prepared for the devil and his angels."

The sermon continued on, but the great man had already struck a chord, deep into the soul of Mary. She had taken the first part of his message to heart and then and there, decided that she must do more to help the poor that were suffering all around her. When she returned to Lucas Carlton House, Ann wanted to know, "Where have you been? I was worried about you. You have been gone some time."

"I have been listening to a man of great wisdom. There is so much suffering around us, that we have grown accustomed to it. It has become invisible to us, but it is present all the same. Starting tomorrow, I intend to begin working to help relieve our neighbors, who are in need. "There was a rapturous glow on her face that Ann had never seen before.

True to her word, Mary began to volunteer and serve. She was soon drawn deeply into the Methodist sect. She spent many hours helping to feed and clothe the poor and destitute. Class was no longer a distinction for Mary. She tended to farmers, laborers, miners, mill workers and anyone else who needed succor. She began to spend an inordinate amount of time with the sick and became quite a good nurse.

Jonathan was away a large portion of the time. His duties as a millwright were keeping him busy, in addition to his commitment to assure the sail mill remained profitable. Between his work and Mary's relief activities, Jonathan found himself spending more time with Ann Ashburn, than he did with his wife, Mary. This arrangement was becoming intolerable and their marriage had come under a tremendous strain. Jonathan had even tried to speak to his wife about curtailing her efforts, but Mary's response was, "Jonathan, you are very seldom home, anyway. Ann takes good care of our children and I am doing God's work. If you order me to discontinue what I am doing, well, you are my husband and I will obey."

Jonathan shook his head and replied, "No Mary, I will not order you, but we no longer seem to have a life together. I have been thinking, perhaps, I can convince mother, we should sell the mill. Business is good at present and it should bring a very good price. There would be enough money, so that mother will be comfortable, for as long as she lives and it would free up time for us and allow me to pursue my profession full time. "

"I have been worrying about your health, recently. No man can continue the pace that you have set without consequences," responded Mary.

Jonathan discussed the overall situation with his mother, later that week. She was a different woman since the death of her husband. Her grandchildren were her main pleasure in life. She had also worried about her son and the pace he was trying to keep. "Do you have any buyers in mind?"

"Yes, I have already spoken to John and Thomas Hartley."

"Oh yes. They are the ones that have the rope and twine manufacturing company. They have been friends of ours for many years. What makes you think they would be interested?"

"They already sell rope to the navy and this would give them another product to offer. I believe them to be fair and honorable men."

"Should we not offer the mill to the highest bidder?"

"That would open the door to the Dacres. They would not bid outright, but use surrogates. I will work myself to death, before I allow that family to have links with us."

"I quite agree. If we can come to a fair arrangement with the Hartley's, that would suit me. I will leave the negotiations in your hands, son."

The title to the mill changed hands in the year 1780. Without his extra duties at the mill, Jonathan was able to spend more time at home with his children. He was able to see his wife much more often, as well, but her absences due to her new found faith continued, so Jonathan spent even more time, alone, with Ann Ashburn. The first few years that Ann lived with them, Jonathan had been able to keep his distance and his reserve. Their relationship was one of tightly bottled-up emotions. Both of them sincerely loved Mary. Jonathan loved her as the mother of his children and as his wife. She was still a most desirable woman to him. Ann loved her as a sister and as her dearest friend. She was also thankful for Mary's willingness to take her into her home, when she had nowhere else to go. She did this, even though she knew there were still strong feelings between Ann and her husband. Ann was determined not to betray that trust, although she had to admit that deep down, she was still in love with Jonathan. Now, with Mary's absence, Jonathan and Ann both had to redouble their efforts to suppress their feelings.

The next year arrived and with it, another son to Jonathan and Mary and they named him John. This birth was the most difficult Mary had experienced. Her recovery took three times as long and although she was still beautiful, she had taken on a pale countenance and looked very delicate. The following year, yet another boy was born, named Joseph and even more, than before, it had been a particularly difficult delivery. Mary developed a fever that lasted for several days. Jonathan and Ann took turns watching over her. She was in bed for six weeks and several times, it seemed that she was on the brink of death. The fever finally broke and she slowly started to recover.

Mary had developed a persistent cough. Two years before, she had begun having coughing spells that would last a few days, but they always were soon gone and she returned to perfect health. A new physician, Anthony Alcock, had taken up residence in Egremont. Originally from Whitehaven, he had attended medical school and performed his physician's apprenticeship at the medical college in Glasgow, Scotland. Jonathan requested that he examine his wife, who was slowly recovering.

Mary had been in bed continuously for weeks. She was well aware that with each new birth the more difficult the recovery might become. But this was different and she could not understand what was taking place in her body. Little Joseph had not caused her much difficulty. She had not lost an inordinate amount of blood during the delivery, but she just could not seem to regain her strength. It flashed through her mind that some of the sick people she had been working with over the past year, showed the same symptoms she was experiencing. She thought to herself, "Their illness was caused by lack of food and poor sanitation and I have no such problems. Little Joseph must've brought me down more than I realized, and it's just taking longer to recover, because I am older." She heard a familiar knock on her door and Jonathan's voice, "Mary my dear, I have brought someone to see you."

"Come in and let me meet this mysterious person that Jonathan has spoken about." The door opened and Jonathan walked in, followed by a young man, who was very well dressed, carrying a doctor's bag. He was handsome and sported a wide, boyish smile. Jonathan stepped aside and the young physician strode purposefully to Mary's bedside.

"I'm Dr. Alcock and I understand that you've been going through quite an ordeal these last few weeks." Mary reached out a pale, delicate hand and offered it to the doctor. "I'm very happy to know you, Dr. Alcock." Her weakness was evident in her voice and delicate countenance. Anthony Alcock pulled the chair over, close to the bed. Before he could sit down, Mary began to cough again. Anthony glanced over at Jonathan and said, "Could you bring her some water?"

"Of course," came the reply as Jonathan moved to the dresser and poured a glass full of water from the pitcher. Mary held a lace handkerchief to her mouth. The coughing fit subsided as Jonathan handed her the water. She used both hands to take the glass and Jonathan put his hands to the back of her head and lifted her so that she could drink.

"How long has she been coughing like this?"

"Like this? Only since the delivery and that was about five or six weeks ago. But she seems to have had short coughing fits, on and off, for a couple of years, but those were not nearly as severe as this," replied Jonathan.

"Mary, may I see your handkerchief?" Too weak for a verbal reply, Mary nodded and handed him the handkerchief. Anthony examined the cloth closely. He stood up, walked over to his medical bag and pulled out a magnifying glass. He took the cloth and the glass over to the window and lay the cloth down on the sash. Bending closer, he peered at the cloth through the glass. What he saw confirmed his initial diagnosis. There were small drops of blood scattered throughout the fabric.

Dr. Alcott turned and walked back to the table and replaced his magnifying glass in his medical bag. He returned to sit down beside Mary.

"I understand that you have been working with the poor, especially the miners, in Whitehaven."

"Yes, that is true, Doctor. It has given me great joy to take care of my neighbor, as I was instructed, from God's word."

Anthony arose from his chair and turned to Jonathan, "Let's go downstairs. I would like to prepare some medicines for your wife." He looked back to Mary and said, "We shall return soon."

Jonathan followed the doctor as they walked down the stairs and into the parlor. "Jonathan, I don't have any easy way to tell you this. I'm afraid your wife has the white plague, better known as consumption."

There was a stunned silence. Jonathan turned away from the doctor and said, "I felt there was something else wrong. What can we do to help her?"

"It is difficult to say. We're not sure what causes the disease. It seems that each doctor has his own opinion. I have studied the work of the English physician, Benjamin Marten. He proposes that consumption is caused by amazingly small living creatures, which once they have gained a foothold in the body, generate lesions in the lungs that produce the symptoms of the disease. He believes that you can contract the disease by being in close contact with a consumptive patient, perhaps by eating and drinking with them, or by frequently conversing so near, as to draw in part of the breath the patient emits from the lungs. Consumption may be contracted by an otherwise healthy person."

"So, you believe that Mary could have contracted this disease by working with poor people who are sick with consumption?" Jonathan question was a natural one.

"As I said, no one knows for sure. Others think that a tendency to develop consumption of the lungs should be expected in people who are of a weak, delicate disposition. A person with a body that has tender, fine blood vessels such as we see in your wife, along with the slender make of her body, may cause one to be predisposed to contract this disease. She also has a long neck with a fairly flat and narrow throat. Her blood is bright red, under her thin, transparent skin. I must say that her complexion is very pale and fair and I suspect that she is very quick, intellectually. You have known her for a long time. I would hazard to say that she has had a merry, cheerful disposition from an early age. Am I correct?"

"You have described Mary exactly."

Some theorize that your wife's physiognomy almost guarantees that she would be susceptible to this illness.

"What's to be done?"

"Based on the stage of the disease, recommended treatments include regular bloodletting. We can give her expectorants and purgatives, to help clear her lungs. I think the best we can do for her, is to make certain she has a very healthy diet and regular exercise. I am afraid, however, that the disease has progressed, so the first thing to do is to make sure that she rests until she can regain some of her strength."

After a short relapse from the shock of the diagnosis of consumption, Mary was slowly beginning to recapture lost ground. It was the nature of this woman to survive. She had not allowed herself to dwell on what her future prospects might be. She reminded herself that she had to stay strong for her husband, her children and for her friend, Ann. It took several more weeks, but she was able to return to an almost normal life. She still coughed and fatigue came with the slightest physical exertion, but through her strength of will, she continued with her daily routines. Doctor Alcott had insisted that she give up her work with the poor, until he gave her permission to return. Privately, he had told Jonathan, that he doubted whether she would ever be strong enough to do much physical labor. The disease had progressed, too far, too quickly. Doctor Alcock had taken

Jonathan aside and explained to him that it was only a matter of time. Mary's health would continue to degenerate. There was no way to know how much time she had left.

For the first time in his life, Jonathan began to doubt his way forward. He had never been very religious, but he wondered about the events of the past few years. Why, he thought, had he lost his father the way that he had? Now, the love of his life was deteriorating right before his eyes. Maybe God had looked into his heart and had seen the lust that was dwelling there for Ann and he was being punished. He kept those feelings well hidden from everyone, but they say you could not hide your thoughts from God. It was a very curious situation. He was resolved to do all within his power to find a cure for his wife.

Mary realized that her remaining time on earth was growing short. Always one to think about others, she became more and more concerned about her husband, her children and Ann. Consumption brought with it a slow death. Some people even romanticized this type of passing. It was said that when you suffered from the white plague, you gained a heightened sense of spirituality. The slow progression of the disease, also allowed one to have, what was referred to, a 'good death'. This meant that the dying person had ample time to arrange their affairs. A consumptive death had become fashionable. Many upper-class women had even tried to make their skin look pale, so it would appear, as if they, too, had consumption. To some, the disease, represented purity of spirit. Mary began to dwell on the future of her family and her friend. She was adamant to see that they were well placed to deal with life after she had departed. She had known many situations where the widowed husband had remarried. Often, it resulted in the ill-treatment of the children by the first wife. Mary loved all five of her children dearly and was determined to make certain that their futures did not include an evil stepmother. These types of rivalries had plagued families since the dawn of time. She had read enough Shakespeare to know that half brothers and sisters could easily consider committing atrocities to gain advantage. A plan slowly began to take shape in Mary's mind.

Chapter 25

HE TREATY OF PARIS WAS SIGNED ON September 3, 1783. The long war with the thirteen American Colonies was finally over. It did not take long for trade with the former colonies to attain levels it had before the war. Optimism was back, as businessmen and investors, once again, were primed to make their fortunes.

Jonathan's commissions were very plentiful. For that, he was very grateful. What he was not grateful for, was the fact that most of the projects were taking him farther and farther from Egremont. Additionally, the work he was asked to perform, was more intricate and complicated, so he was absent as much as when he had been running the mill, in addition to performing his millwright duties. He was not happy to be separated from his ailing wife and his family. Mary's health continued to deteriorate on a slow, but steady pace. Instead of the elegant young woman that he had married, she had become more waif-like in her appearance.

He had been home for a week after completing a new cotton mill just outside of Lancaster. His clients paid him very well and he was frugal with his earnings. It was apparent to him, however, that for him to continue to prosper, he would have to do something more than just accept commissions to build mills for other people. He enjoyed the work, but like his Uncle William before him, he had come to understand that wealth came through ownership of property. He realized that he would have to possess some of what he was building for other people. He would have to patent some of the innovative ways he was able to modify existing methods of production. He had submitted a request for two patents, but had been turned down, because they were not found to be totally original.

It was early October and the early evening air was crisp. The chill suggested a hint of frost early the next morning. Jonathan had helped his wife, Mary, down the stairs and she was feeling and looking better, than she had in days. There was a large wood fire burning in the fireplace that kept the cold at bay.

"Jonathan, how much longer do we get to keep you here before you are off to your next construction site?"

"I'm not sure. Perhaps I can remain here at least, until next spring."

"But I thought that it was all arranged for you to go to Liverpool. You said that it was a huge mill that would employ two thousand people. I was under the impression you were going to make an exorbitant fee and that this would keep you busy for the coming year. Have they had a change of heart?"

"No, my dear, they have not had a change of heart, but I have."

"But Jonathan, I understood they had accepted your proposal and that everyone was happy with the terms. Isn't that true?"

"Yes, you are correct. The commissions are good and they have accepted my ideas on improving their power production by using the modified water wheels."

Mary persisted, "I understood that you were to start the first week in November. Has there been a delay that I do not know about?"

"No, that was the original arrangement, but I have had second thoughts."

"Second thoughts about what? If your fees are good and they have accepted your idea, this project could advance your career greatly. I'm afraid that I don't understand. Please explain what has happened."

Jonathan pulled his chair next to Mary's. He reached out and gently took both of her hands in his. He gazed at the once beautiful face, that now seemed more saint-like, than beautiful. He felt emotion welling up inside of him, as he looked into her expressive blue eyes. "Mary, I have been gone most of the time, for the past six months. My children are growing up in my absence. I do not want to waste the remaining time that you and I have together, chasing material wealth and fame. You mean more to me than all of that. I am wealthy in your love and famous as your husband. The Lucas Carlton Farm brings in a good steady income and I have done very well over the past few years as a millwright. I can afford to spend time, our remaining time here, together with you."

His eyes were brimming with tears as he felt he would explode with sorrow at the prospects of losing the woman he loved so deeply. He was expecting her to reciprocate his feelings and appreciate the sacrifice that he was making. Mary's reaction was quite different than he had anticipated.

"Jonathan Lucas, I have never taken you for a coward. I will not have you, my family, nor anyone else that I hold dear, stop living because of my illness. If it is God's will that I am to be called, before I wish to go, then I will accept that. I am not pleased by the prospect, but if it is God's will, there is nothing we can do about it. But, I can do something about the people around me. Do you think that I want to see all of your life's work fall apart over my ordeal? I expect, no, I insist, that you live your life as normally as possible. We must not let sadness and melancholy take over our lives. You will dishonor me by pitying me. Jonathan, you must not stop living. You have your life and future to think of, as well as our five children. You must show them the strength that a father should exhibit. Do not allow grief to pervade your thoughts. I know that you love me, but I need for you to be strong for my sake and the sake of our family."

Jonathan was shaken by her words. In reality, he knew she was right. Over the past week, he had allowed his grief to turn to self pity at the thought of losing his wife. Mary's comments shocked him back to reality. He had dropped his head, while she was speaking. He looked up, reached over and embraced his wife. He whispered into her ear, "May I borrow some of your strength?"

"You do not need my strength. You have just temporarily misplaced yours. In the coming months, your courage must grow stronger, for mine will surely begin to ebb away."

Jonathan remained at the Lucas Carlton House throughout the month of October. He had asked his mother to assist in the care of Mary in his absence. He knew that between the two women, Mary's' needs would be taken care of.

In November 1783, Jonathan began constructing a very large project in Liverpool. It was expected to take between nine and twelve months to complete. Mary's health stabilized and Jonathan returned home as often as he could. He was fortunate that his Uncle William had just finished a project in Manchester and so he volunteered to relieve Jonathan, so he could travel back to Egremont to spend time with his convalescing wife, as often as possible. Williams' finances had recovered, along with the value of his stock in the East India Company. He was impressed with the modifications that Jonathan was making and added some ideas of his own. Time passed quickly and the new mill was put into operation. Jonathan now thirty years old, returned to Lucas Carleton House and decided to take a well deserved rest. Mary's health remained stable and his children were growing up. His oldest son, Jonathan Lucas Junior, was almost ten years old. The two had spent a lot of time together when Jonathan was at home.

Jonathan, the younger, did not seem to be as interested in how things worked, as his father. He took after his grandfather, John, more than he did his great Uncle William and his father. Jonathan Junior was interested in the projects his father was involved in, but instead of becoming excited over the beauty of mechanical devices, that his great uncle and father had developed, it seemed that Jonathan Junior was more interested in the logistics of it all. He wanted to know how the ideas were developed and how they were able to procure the materials. He wanted to know how more powerful and efficient waterwheels or windmills, could make more money for their clients. He was more interested in the results of increased production, than in the means through which it was accomplished. Jonathan discussed with Mary and his mother whether it was time to bring in a full-time tutor for their oldest son.

Jonathan, Jr. was attending a grammar school in Egremont and he seemed to be happy with his teachers. After consultation with his mother, Mary and Ann Ashburn, they decided to delay the idea of a tutor until the boy turned twelve. The custom of placing thirteen and fourteen-year-old boys into a profession, where they became apprentices, was slowly becoming obsolete. Mary and Jonathan conversed on whether or not it would be better for him to attend a university, such as Cambridge or Oxford. But that remained a decision for the future. The rest of his children, all seem to be healthy and vibrant. The Lucas Carleton House rang with the sounds of happy children and Jonathan was intent on keeping it that way.

The project Jonathan had been working on, in Liverpool, was finally completed. He was able to return to Egremont and the Lucas Carleton House in time for the Christmas season. Mary had decided this was going to be their very best Christmas. She and Jonathan discussed plans for the holidays.

"Jonathan, you know that Christmas day is the most important time for all Christian nations. Our children are at an age where they really enjoy Christmas celebrations. I love this time of year when everyone is wishing each other a Merry Christmas and a Happy New Year. I wish to be liberal with our presents, especially this year to not only our family, but to our neighbors and to the poor.

"Of course, my dear. We want to be in a festive mood and we shall decorate the house as usual with laurels, rosemary and evergreen boughs. I always look forward to eating those Christmas pies and having some of your famous Christmas porridge. Ann doesn't care for it, but I enjoy it enormously."

"Everyone loves Christmas pies. How could they not? We make them with chopped meat, currants, beef and other tasty things. Why is it that we never eat the pies any other time besides Christmas?"

"I can't begin to tell you why. I guess it's just that we save it for Christmas, so it makes it an even more exceptional celebration." Suddenly, a thought entered into Jonathan's head. "Mary, are you feeling well, my dear? Why is there this sudden interest in Christmas celebration?"

"Oh, don't worry. I'm feeling better than I have in a while. It's just that I want to celebrate this special time of year with all of those dear to me. You have no reason to worry. I wanted you in the Christmas spirit. I will not have sadness this Christmas, only joy."

A deep snow blanketed the farm two days before Christmas. The Lucas Carlton House was situated on the cusp of a gently rising hill that overlooked the town of Egremont. On a clear, crisp, winter morning, you could see the Irish Sea two miles in the distance. Jonathan and Mary stood at the window of their second story bedroom, gazing across the white landscape, to the gray Irish Sea. Jonathan asked, "Are you warm enough, Mary?"

"Yes, I know it's very cold, but it looks like a painting today. I am warm enough. With the sea so close, I wonder why you have never taken to sailing?"

"You know, Mary, I've never thought about it that much. Everything I have done has not required that type of travel. You know it can be very dangerous. There is much to endure on the high seas. Short coastal voyages don't pose the hazards that crossing an ocean does. You can be cut off from shore for months at the time. The quarters on board ship are not much bigger than closets on land. Besides, being so closely quartered carries the risk of disease and from what I've heard, the food is atrocious. The worst thing about traveling by sea is the weather. If you're caught in a storm, the chances are very good you will not survive. No, I'll take land travel any day."

"But, it seems to me that many a fortune has been made by those brave enough to make those difficult journeys. Well, thank goodness, there will be no sea voyage today. We only have to go to St. Mary's to celebrate Christmas Eve and in this snow, that will be a difficult enough journey for me."

Later that morning, they watched as a sleigh came up the lane from Egremont.

Jonathan Junior came in the front door, all excited. "I think grandmother and Uncle William are coming up the lane." Jonathan stood up and Mary began to rise, as well. "Mary, it's too cold for you to be outside. Wait here, by the fire and Jonathan and I will get them inside." Ann Ashburn entered the room, carrying the baby, followed by the other three children. They called her Aunt Annie and she was the second mother to all five of Jonathan and Mary's children.

Ann had attempted to contact her great uncle. When she finally received a reply, it was a negative one. They had written to tell her that they had found themselves in a precarious situation, financially, and that it would be impossible for them to commit to her care. She had also been in contact with several attorneys to determine if she had any legal recourse against the Dacre's. At first, she described only what had taken place without giving them the names of her antagonists. The responses Ann then had received were all very positive and they felt that her fortune could be recouped, but when the attorneys found out who she was contemplating suing, their tone changed. The name Dacre was known far and wide. They were a family that should not be trifled with lightly.

After the revelation of who it was that Ann planned to sue, her potential attorneys had a sudden change of heart. At that point, they suddenly advised her the case was weaker than thought at first glance.

The response was generally the same from all of the law firms she contacted, "After much consideration and consultation with our partners, we have determined that your chances of successfully pursuing this action are very slim. Therefore, we feel it would be inadvisable for us to take on this case."

She did finally find a few lawyers who agreed to begin legal proceedings, but each and every one asked for an exorbitant amount of money in advance.

Jonathan would have funded her legal battle, but Ann knew that if he was involved in any way, the war between the Lucas's and the Dacre's would start anew. She therefore refused any of his offered financial assistance. The only way any of it could make sense would be for her to leave the Lucas Carleton House and find funding for her legal actions, independent of the Jonathan Lucas Family.

Several young men had become very interested in Ann during the years she was living with Jonathan and Mary. She had accepted offers for picnics and church socials and had attended several balls. Ann was never lacking for attention from the males in attendance. Mary had noticed that if Ann seemed interested in a man courting her, Jonathan would become quiet and contemplative, but Ann never let the courtships go very far. The quickest way to lose her attention was for a young man to let it be known he had fallen in love with her. When she sensed a man was becoming seriously attached, she would refuse to see him again. Jonathan would never ask about her relationships, but Mary did and she would generally do it when Jonathan was present.

"Ann, I haven't seen that young Waverly man around lately. Is there a reason for that?"

"Yes. He seemed to be getting a little too attached. We have decided it would be better not to see each other again."

At this declaration, Jonathan would come out of his melancholy mood and become lively and talkative. Ann and Mary pretended not to notice. The only one unaware, however, was Jonathan.

Jonathan walked outside and greeted his mother and his uncle. It promised to be a wonderful Christmas gathering. The children warmly greeted Grandmother Ann and, of course, she came in with an armful of presents. Uncle William brought up the rear with a second load of gifts. There was an extra large log burning in the fireplace, the traditional Yule log. About three hours before it was time for supper, they all gathered around the piano. Ann Ashburn had taken over the job of pianist, due to Mary's illness, and had become quite the expert. They started by singing Isaac Watts' most famous hymn, "Joy to the World."

It was one of the most beloved Christmas carols and everyone, children included, joined in the singing. Little Jonathan Junior insisted on singing "The Snow Lay on the Ground" and had shown quite a bit of talent for singing Christmas songs. He also entertained the rest of the family with a fine rendition of "The First Noel." Then it was Uncle William's turn and he loudly belted out his version of "God Rest You Merry Gentlemen." Ann Ashburn accompanied herself on the piano as she sang "The Holly and the Ivy."

The entire family joined in the carol, "I Saw Three Ships." The two youngest children were worn out by all of the Christmas activity, so they ended the evening with a soft version of "Lully Lullaby", often called "The Coventry Carol". This was the first Christmas that the entire family had been together since the year before John's untimely death and it would be the last Christmas gathering of the entire clan.

Chapter 26

THE WINTER OF 1784, CONTINUED COLD, windy and snowy, throughout January and February. The snow finally tapered off in March, but the wind and cold remained. Mary's health had stayed about the same throughout the winter and Jonathan was hopeful that with spring, his wife's health would improve. He had received a letter from his Uncle William, asking him to come to Manchester for a meeting to discuss their futures. The letter read:

Dear Jonathan:

I take the opportunity of writing today to request that you come to Manchester for a meeting on Tuesday, April 20th. I would like to talk with you (perhaps for a day or two), previous to my departure for London, which will probably take place on the Friday or Saturday following. If you can spare the time, I trust you will not disappoint me. The subject I wish to discuss will be, I assure you, of great importance to us both. There will be at least two other gentlemen joining us to confer on an opportunity that we should examine closely. Please let me know, by return mail, as quickly as possible if you will be able to attend. As always, with great regard and esteem,

Your Affectionate Uncle,

William

Jonathan was intrigued by this correspondence and answered in the affirmative in the following note:

Dear Uncle,

I look forward to attending your meeting on 20 April, coming. I shall arrive either on that date or one day early. It will be good to see you again, so soon after our Christmas visit. Jonathan Junior asks of you often and wishes that I send his great Uncle greetings. Until then I remain,

Your Affectionate Nephew,

Jonathan

The trip to Manchester was not overly difficult. This time he rode horseback instead of taking the coach. It was a much faster way to travel and he had become a very good horseman by now. As he passed through the same villages, he was reminded of the trip many years before when he was accompanied by his father, Miss Felicity, Mary and Ann. With those memories fresh in his mind Jonathan arrived at William's familiar home on Monday, 19th of April.

That evening they sat down to sup on a meal of roast beef, bread, potatoes and white soup made from veal stock, cream, almonds and rice. It was all topped off with dessert and more wine.

William began, "Jonathan, I'm sure you have become curious about why I have asked you here."

"I am sure that it must be important or else you would not have summoned me here."

"Quite right, quite right. Let us move to the parlor and have some Madeira. You do enjoy Madeira don't you?"

"I certainly do. It was so difficult to obtain while the war was on. You must have found a reliable source."

"Yes it is a small wine shop that I frequent often and the owner has his sources. I was able to keep a supply on hand eve during the war. As I've gotten older, I find that Brandy is not as easy to handle as it once was. You get the same benefits from the Madeira without causing the stress that Brandy does. I plan to live a long time so I thought that I should start to take better care of myself than in the past."

"You seem to be in great health. It would not surprise me to see you live to be 100 years old. I don't believe I've ever heard you complain about any aches and pains as other men your age are want to do."

"Yes, I have been blessed with a robust health so far. My eyesight is not as good as it once was, but that is to be expected in a man in his early 60's. That is why I keep these spectacles with me at all times." William patted his chest pocket as they entered the parlor and crossed over to the table were several bottles of Madeira and their large wine glasses were waiting. William poured out two tumblers of Madeira and handed one to Jonathan. "Let me propose a toast to our health and for this meeting tomorrow, let us toast to our future."

"Of course I'll drink to that uncle, and I am anxious to hear what this most mysterious opportunity is all about."

The two men turned up their glasses and drained the contents. William refilled the tumblers and motioned for Jonathan to take a seat near the fireplace. Jonathan sat down, but William remained standing by the hearth. He set his glass down on the mantelpiece. Bending down closer to the fire, he rubbed his hands together and slowly turned around facing his nephew.

"The past few years have seen a lot of changes in our lives and fortunes. You and I both have been making a comfortable living as millwrights. I believe that when we have teamed up we're as good as anyone in the nation at what we do. As a millwright, you have quite a good reputation in the north and the midlands. You are young and in the prime of your life with a growing family. Age has slowed me down somewhat and both of us are aware that this is still a young man's profession. It requires both physical and mental stamina to be successful."

He paused long enough to reach up and take his full glass from the mantelpiece. He took one swallow and replaced the glass. He then resumed, "If I am going to live to be 100, as you have suggested, then I believe that it would be prudent to take an opportunity to allow myself to live these coming years comfortably. I should like to live as a gentleman. That means living well without having to work."

"What you're saying makes sense, for I firmly believe that you will live to be 100 and it is only logical to enjoy that extra time as you say, being a gentleman. This meeting makes me think that you believe you have found a means of achieving those goals."

"How familiar are you with the sugar industry?"

"Whitehaven has always had a large trade with the West Indies. As you are aware, we even have a dock named Sugar Quay."

"Yes I know that. But are you aware of what has happened to the planters in the West Indies because of the American War?"

"I understand that they lost a lot of money and many of them went into bankruptcy."

"Do you know who Edwin Lascelles is?"

"Yes, remember I attended a ball against your wishes there sometime back."

"Oh, yes. Of course I remember that little episode all too vividly. It seems that the man did not spend his entire fortune on that mansion. Mr. Lascelles has added considerably to his already sizable fortune with his dealings in the West Indies during the war."

"Yes I understand that he lent heavily to the planters and merchants there."

"It is said that he has added more than 20 working plantations by foreclosure to his holdings in the islands. He now owns, some say, over 27,000 acres of West Indian property. Along with the land, he also acquired almost 3,000 slaves. They are worth a small fortune by themselves. All of this happened because the planters defaulted on their debts to him due to the American War."

"I was not aware that things had gotten that desperate for so many of the planters. What caused this huge problem?"

"Most of the planters were dependent on income from the sale of sugar and molasses to the American colonies. When this income stopped, because of the war, they simply did not have the ability to carry their debt burden."

"I see. But what has their sad story to do with us?"

"There are many other West Indian planters just hanging on by a thread. The men that I shall introduce you to tomorrow own property on the Island of Antigua. One of them is a distant cousin. His name is John Lucas. His partner, William Coleman, will be with him. They are merchants as well as planters and they are aware of several sugar plantations that can be purchased at a very good price and with generous terms, as well."

"That sounds interesting, but how do we figure into their plans?"

"They are looking for two things, investors with capital and someone with knowledge of windmills to repair and improve the operations there. That could be you, Jonathan."

"But uncle, that would mean a long separation from my family. You know Mary could not travel on such a voyage. Nor would I trust my children to the dangers of an ocean voyage of that magnitude."

"I thought that would be your first reaction. But you must hear what the two have to say. If things go well, our fortunes could be made. I can advance part of the necessary funding. I have also had favorable responses from investors with whom I have successfully dealt in the past. The only other part needed to make this a successful venture is you. And that's because you have the youth, knowledge and the skill to turn those plantations into the best sugar producers in the West Indies. There are also rum distilleries there, as well, that will certainly add to the potential profits. The rum market never shrinks. This venture could keep us, not just comfortable, but in addition, make us very wealthy."

"This is something that will take some time to digest. I'll have to think long and hard on this. It's late, so I'll say goodnight and begin my deliberations. I bid you a good night's sleep, uncle."

With that Jonathan climbed the stairs to his room and slowly got ready for bed. He spent his night tossing and turning and thinking. His thoughts were not stable for a moment. This proposal brought many thoughts that he had been able to suppress in his subconscious, sharply into the here and now. He had entered his marriage and known himself to be happy with his decision to choose Mary. Even with the changes that had been forced into his life by fate, he had tried to hold onto that happiness as long as he could. He was not discontented, but he felt preoccupied and often times, a restless feeling took charge of his person. His work took him to different locations, but the routines were the same. Each job relentlessly led to one that was very similar. His ability to make improvements and innovations were often times met with reluctance on the part of his clients. Many did not want to change what had been successful for them in the past.

Now here was his Uncle William tempting him with an offer that was exciting and potentially profitable. This would be an adventure that was definitely out of the ordinary for him. If it was all that William said it would be, then part of him wanted desperately to accept this challenge. The conflict arose within him when he thought of his delicate wife and his growing family. Did he dare to gamble with their futures by risking his life and the steady millwright income on this West Indian adventure. Was it an adventure or a reckless gamble? Would it not be more sensible to continue with his current humdrum life that provided a comfortable, but a dull lifestyle. He had to choose between climbing higher and reaching for the big shining apple high up on the tree or continuing to pluck the low hanging fruit from the easy to reach bottom limbs. It was not going to be an easy decision.

The next evening at 6 PM, the two West Indian merchants were introduced to Jonathan. The meeting took place in William's library. Jonathan and William sat on the right side of the fireplace and William Coleman and his partner, John Lucas, sat across facing them on the left side of the fireplace.

His uncle began the conversation, "I have outlined the basic opportunity for Jonathan's benefit. Perhaps you could fill him in on some of the details."

William Coleman nodded, "Jonathan, we have identified five sugar plantations that can be purchased at rock-bottom prices. Their owners went bankrupt several years back and the properties have been neglected over the past several years. They are still in production, but without clear ownership the profits are nonexistent at present. There are over 150 sugar plantations on the island of Antigua and over half of them have gone out of business due to the war with the Americans. The properties that we have identified can be brought back into production very quickly and profitably. We believe that improvements can be made in the sugar mills and also in the production of rum. Each of the plantations has a distillery as well as a sugar processing mill. We need someone with the expertise to make some improvements, repair existing machinery and install new equipment where necessary. Then, we need someone who can keep the whole thing operating efficiently. We would like also like for you to manage all five of the plantations. We do not expect you to manage each plantation individually. Of course, there will be an overseer in charge of each individual one. So therefore, if you choose to join this venture, you would have to find five men who could oversee production under your supervision."

Jonathan asked his first question, "This seems to be a large undertaking. Five plantations under one company. I suspect that it will also require a large amount of capital. In talking to Uncle William, it seems that he has found other investors who are willing to share the risk financially. Have you calculated the amount of capital required and if so, are you certain that the funds that have been raised by Uncle William will be sufficient to accomplish the goal of returning these plantations to production?"

"Yes, we believe that the capital raised will be sufficient. The two of us intend to be investors, as well and you, of course, will have the option to invest. But what we are really in need of is your expertise to keep the mills producing. If the prices for sugar and rum hold and we get output back up to prewar levels then it will make us all wealthy men."

"How will the ownership be divided?"

"It will be 20 percent for each of us and 20 per cent for the investors. Each party shall also be entitled to compensation for their efforts on the company's behalf. This will be the cost of doing business. It will be deducted before profits are divided between us."

"And how do you see calculating those costs?"

William Coleman turned to his partner, John Lucas and said, "I can tell he is your kinsman. He may even be more closely related than we thought." They all had a good laugh over William's remark. He continued, "If you agree to participate, you will be entitled to a fee for your services as a millwright. Additionally, you would receive compensation for managing the properties. Of course you would have your pick of the plantation houses for your lodging. Some of them are quite large and handsome. If you decide to stay and send for your family, then the property would be deeded to you at that time as a bonus."

"Gentlemen, it is a very tempting offer. When do you propose that this project begin?"

"Several of our acquisitions still require some time to be cleared up by the courts, but all the legal aspects should be completed by late fall of this year. I suspect that all should be ready and you would be sailing for Antigua in the coming spring."

"When do you require an answer from me? You understand that a move such as this will have to be discussed in detail with my family, whatever my feelings on the subject."

"John and I will be returning to Antigua soon. We have not booked passage yet, but I imagine we will be leaving no longer than 60 days from now. If we can have your answer within 30 days, that would be sufficient. Would that give you enough time to make your decision?"

"Yes, that should be adequate. I presume that Uncle William has alerted you to the fact that my wife is ill with consumption. Her health has been stable for the past couple of years and if, after consultation with the doctor, he feels that the prognosis for her is the same, then I will open discussions with her about this Antigua sugar plantation opportunity."

Later that evening after the guest left William and Jonathan sat drinking Madeira. Jonathan was staring into the fireplace seemingly lost in thought. After several minutes of silence, William cleared his throat and asked, "Well Jonathan, can you tell me what you think of their proposal? You've been awfully quiet since they left."

"I have very mixed thoughts about the proposal. First of all, I think that if sugar prices hold, and of course, the price of rum, then this could be a very profitable venture. Secondly, it seems to me that the terms offered are fair, maybe more than fair. That's on the positive side of the ledger. On the negative side, it's a long way from England to Antigua. There's also the problem I have with slavery, in general. I know that it's been around forever, but I wish there was another way. Then there's the practical side of that issue. It's a small island and if there was a significant slave rebellion that could be very dangerous. Didn't they attempt to blow up the plantation owners back in the 1730's? It was called the Antiguan Conspiracy, as I recall. All of that gives me pause. But of course, my main concern is Mary's health."

"I understand and I share your concerns, but nothing worthwhile comes without risk and sacrifice. When you are young, as you are, the future is very uncertain. I have lived most of my future already and I have seen that nothing worthwhile is accomplished without giving of yourself to the effort. Many opportunities have been presented to me. The ones that have proved to be worthwhile required reflection and choice, then action. Others that I did not choose to follow cost me no effort, but they also gave me no reward. You are young enough to recover from a mistake. When you reach my age, mistakes become more costly and it is much more difficult to recover from them. If I did not think that this was the right opportunity for you, I can promise that it would not have been brought to your attention at all. I felt it was important enough to ask you to make the journey to Manchester."

The uncle and the nephew continued their conversation for another hour as they finished one more bottle of Madeira. Later, when Jonathan was alone in his bed, he realized that there was one other reason that caused him to hesitate. He had kept his feelings for Ann as much of a secret as was humanly possible. He had not even admitted to himself, at least consciously, that he was still in love with her. At first it had not been so difficult. He had been angry over what he considered to be her betrayal with Hugh Dacre. By the time he had found out the truth, he had committed his life to Mary. Then Mary had brought Ann into their home. Jonathan had said nothing and had tried to feel nothing. He believed that he had been successful in keeping his feelings hidden and in check, but what he did not realize, was that emotions cannot be hidden from a wife or a lover. He had only succeeded in fooling himself into thinking that no one but him knew the depths of his passions. He had to admit that leaving Ann behind would be another reason not to take Uncle William up on the Antiguan adventure.

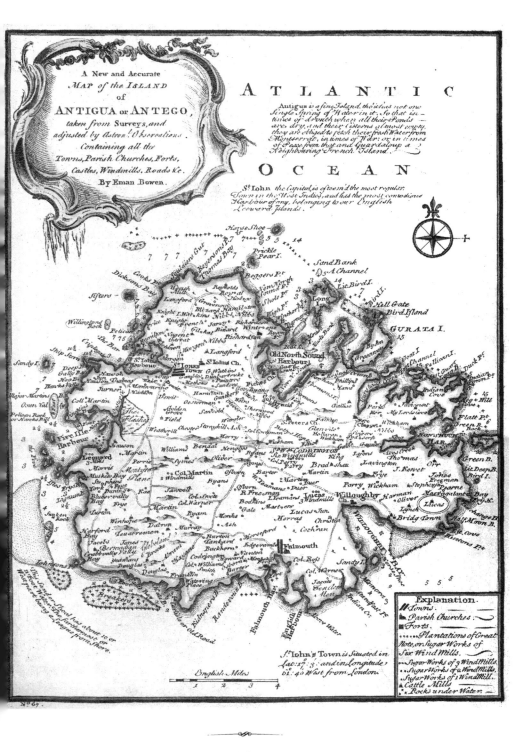

A New and Accurate
MAP of the ISLAND
of
ANTIGUA or ANTEGO,
taken from Surveys, and
adjusted by Astron.l Observations.
Containing all the
Towns, Parish Churches, Forts,
Castles, Windmills, Roads &c.
By Eman Bowen.

ATLANTIC

Antigua is a fine Island, tho' it has not one
Single Spring of Water in it; So that in
times of drought when all their Ponds
are dry, and their Cisterns almost empty,
they are obliged to fetch their fresh Water from
Montserrat, in times of War; or in times
of Peace from that and Guardalupe a
Neighbouring French Island.

OCEAN

St. Iohn the Capital, is esteem'd the most regular
Town in the West Indies, and has the most commodious
Harbour of any, belonging to our English
Leeward Islands.

GURATA I.

St. Iohn's Town is Situated in
Lat: 17.°. 3. and in Longitude
61.°. 40. West from London.

English Miles
1 2 3 4

Explanation.
Towns.
Parish Churches.
Forts.
.... Plantations of Great
Note, or Sugar Works of
Six Wind Mills.
Sugar Works of 3 Wind Mills.
Sugar Works of 2 Wind Mills.
Sugar Works of 1 Wind Mill.
Cattle Mills.
Rocks under Water.

No 67.

Chapter 27

JONATHAN ARRIVED AT THE LUCAS CARLETON House about midday, on Monday, April 26. He was greeted halfway up the lane by his son, Jonathan Junior. It was a bright clear day with a cool, north breeze blowing. Jonathan leaned down and lifted his son up into the saddle in front of him. The two of them rode the remaining half-mile toward home. Young Jonathan was full of questions for his father.

"Tell me all about your trip, father?"

"There's not much to tell, son. It was a long ride there and back, but luckily there were not any interesting adventures along the way."

"So you didn't run into any Highwayman on this trip?"

"I see that you have been talking to your mother and your Aunt Ann while I was away."

"Yes sir. I love to hear that story, as well as the others. I intend to have adventures like that one day."

"I'm not sure that's such a good idea, son. Too many of those kinds of adventures can make for a short life. There are other adventures that are a lot less dangerous and provide more fun and profit. They are no less exciting and stimulating. In fact, those are the best types of adventures to have."

"That may be true, father, but you are able to travel all over the country and have adventures and all of my adventures are with Jane and Moses and mother and Aunt Annie. When will I be old enough for you to start taking me with you, so that we can have adventures together, like you and grandpa?"

"You're ten now, son, so it will not be long before you'll be old enough. I can certainly use a helper from a smart lad like you. I should think if you're patient for another two of three years and remember to mind your mother and your aunt, then as a reward, you shall accompany me when you become thirteen."

"Do I have to wait that long?"

"I think you will find that the time will pass more quickly than you can imagine. But remember, I am counting on you to be the man of the house when I am away on business."

"You can count on me, Poppa. I can look after things until I'm ready to go with you and then we can let Brother Moses takeover. He's bossy, anyway, for a small kid. And besides, all he ever does is play with those little lead soldiers. He's always trying to get me to play army with him."

"Well Jonathan, it sounds like you have a very good plan in place. When you become my assistant and if things go well, we shall put that plan into action. That time will be here before you know it."

They reigned in the horse, just before reaching the front door. The rest of the family came out of the house as the two Jonathan's dismounted. Mary smiled at seeing the return of her husband, but before Jonathan could approach her, she started to cough into her handkerchief which she kept close at hand. She no longer had the strength to produce a racking type of cough. Recently, her attempts to clear her lungs had become a very weak, but prolonged efforts. Jonathan put his arms around her shoulders, "Here Mary, you must not be outside in this cold and damp air."

He looked down at his daughter, Jane. She had wrapped her arms around one leg and the second son, Moses, was holding on to the other. Ann had baby brother, Joseph cradled in her right arm and held little John by the hand. Jonathan turned to his son and said, "Can you manage to take care of Black Bess for me?"

"Yes sir. I'll untack her, feed her and brush her down."

"Don't forget to water her. It's been a long ride for both of us."

It had been a very pleasant homecoming for Jonathan. He had thought long and hard during his return trip, about the proposal he had received from his uncle and the two gentlemen from Antigua. He thought he had made up his mind, until he crested another hill or entered into another village. Then he would change his mind again. At first, he was resolved to go to Antigua, but it was clear to him that he must remain at home and take care of his wife.

Then his thought process circled around again and it continued unceasingly for his entire journey. When he picked up his son in the lane, was greeted by his family, and saw the ever-present, ever alluring, Ann, the desire to remain close to home won out,..........for the moment, at least. Everyone wanted to know about the trip and what the big meeting was all about. Later that evening, a grand meal was served to celebrate Jonathan's return. They had roast beef and chicken, along with a leg of mutton, which was boiled and served with caper sauce. Afterward, there was pudding, apple tarts and currant jelly.

Jonathan's report to the family was that his meeting was of no great import. It had been just another one of Uncle William's ideas about how to increase their wealth. He did tell them it was about a proposed venture in distant Antigua. "It's altogether too far away and too dangerous to be taken seriously."

Mary asked, "Then you rejected the idea?"

"No, I told them that I would think about it and discuss it with you. I must give them my answer within thirty days."

"But Jonathan, you haven't discussed it with me at all."

"After thinking it over for the past several days, I have reached the conclusion that my future lies here with you and so I will continue to practice my profession nearby."

Ann and Mary exchanged knowing glances. Tonight was not the time to press Jonathan for details. It was evident that he was fatigued and by the look on his face, perplexed as well. He had returned to a home full of love for him. They could see in his demeanor, he had a great internal battle raging.

Mary replied, "I know that you are tired, my darling. You need to get a good night's rest. We'll discuss this more, tomorrow."

"Well, I certainly can use a good night's sleep. But I'm not sure that discussion tomorrow will be of much value."

Later that evening, Jonathan assisted Mary in putting all the children to bed. It was a special time he had grown to enjoy greatly. His work had kept him away from his family for months and he was always amazed to see how much his children had grown during short absences. Jonathan Junior was growing into a young man. He seemed much older than his ten years and Jonathan had become even more fond of his oldest son.

Now it was his turn to retire for the evening and he knew instinctively that Mary was not through with her query about the meeting with Uncle William. Sure enough, as he settled into bed, Mary turned to him and in a soft voice asked, "Now that we are alone, can we discuss the proposal that was made to you? William didn't invite you all of that way for a simple project or the usual offer. If this decision affects our family's future then you know that I have a right to, at least, understand what the offer was."

Jonathan knew his wife very well. Her will had remained very strong, despite her failing health. He sat up in bed and rearranged the pillows so he could lean back against the headboard. He looked into his wife's eyes and knew that he might as well tell her everything. There would be no rest until she was certain that he had revealed all the details to her.

"The offer is a very generous one. William and the two gentlemen from the West Indies have raised enough capital to purchase and refurbish at least five sugar plantations located on the island of Antigua. If I accept the job of going to Antigua and rebuilding the sugar mills and the rum distilleries, they will play my normal millwright's fee. If I also agree to stay for at least twenty-four months and supervise the operations of the five plantations, then, additionally, I will be given a twenty per cent company ownership and lodging at one of the beautiful homes on the plantation of my choice. It is a very tempting offer."

"Jonathan, my dear, how can you even consider turning such an offer down?"

"The West Indies is a world away from the Lucas Carleton House. The sugar plantations of Antigua have a horrible reputation for their treatment of slaves."

"Yes, but they are not you. If you were to go to Antigua, there would be at least five plantations on which the slaves would be treated much more humanely. This may be God's way of helping to improve the lives of these people."

"You know the main reason I must remain here?" asked Jonathan.

"Yes, I felt as much. Jonathan, how often must we have this conversation? My illness must not stand in the way of our family living to the fullest. We shall not all die on the same day. If it be God's will, our children will be here many years after we are gone. I will not let you live your life in fear of my death. All of our lives are in the hands of God. If he presents you with opportunities to go and "increase and multiply", then you must not let his gift to you go unfulfilled. We will do fine in your absence. I do not wish my death, whenever it arrives, to come with a guilty conscience. If my illness interferes with the chance for you to fulfill your destiny, then mine will be a most unhappy death. Do you really think that you can make me happy by staying close and watching me fade away? It will accomplish the opposite. I will die a wretched death, knowing I caused you to miss out on this opportunity. Staying here just to watch me waste away will not comfort me, but knowing you are out in the world accomplishing all you can, will comfort me and bring me joy. You must accept this opportunity, Jonathan and without regret or self-reproach."

Jonathans' tears glistened in the candlelight. He could see that his wife was exhausted with the emotional effort she had put forward in her argument. He reached over and took his fragile wife into his arms and held her close. Mary whispered in his ear, "Promise me that you will accept, promise me Jonathan, promise me."

"I promise. If that is your wish, then I promise."

The next morning, Jonathan wrote the following letter to his Uncle William:

My Dear Uncle,

By this letter, I wish to inform you that I accept the offer to participate in the Antiguan venture. I trust that you will relay this acceptance to Mister Coleman and Mister Lucas. There are several matters that I must attend to before I will be free to depart for the West Indies. If it will be practicable, I would request that I be allowed to finish several projects that I have promised to undertake locally. The schedule that was laid out during our meeting in Manchester mentioned that it would take several months to complete the legal aspects of this transaction. I would therefore ask that my departure be targeted for the spring of this coming year: 1786. If this conforms with the needs of our project after discussion with the other members of the venture then I shall be ready to depart for Antigua no later than April 1786. If this meets with everyone's approval then please let me know by return post. Thank you my dear uncle for including me in this opportunity. Let us hope that God will grant us success in the New World.

Your Affectionate Nephew,

Jonathan

An affirmative answer arrived two weeks later from William. Jonathan had to travel back to Manchester to meet with Coleman and Lucas before they sailed. The legal proceedings went off without protest, but as usual, the courts were not in a hurry to conclude their involvement in these "colonial matters". William held more meetings with his investors and the year came to an end and the venture was set. Jonathan had spent a great deal of time studying the latest advances in windmills. He also kept abreast of the all the improvements in waterwheels and even traveled to Scotland to learn about distilleries. He finally felt confident he had the skills to accomplish the tasks ahead of him.

Mary's health had deteriorated as winter wore on, but that had happened each year prior and she had always gotten better with the coming of spring. This year, she knew was different. Her energy was not returning as it had before and she resolved to hide the fact from everyone and put on a brave face.

One afternoon in late March, Mary stood by the window staring out at the town of Egremont. It was a cool, windy, clear day as she listened to the sounds of her household emanating from the rooms below. The time would soon arrive when her husband would leave and they would be separated for, at least, two years. Although she always wore a brave exterior, inside there were times when her courage failed her and she wanted to cry out for him to back out of the venture and remain with her. She wanted to tell him she needed him to stay and comfort her on the last part of her life's journey. She could feel deep inside that the consumption was gaining the upper hand and her end was not going to be far distant. Mary's intuition told her she would probably not be there to greet him on his homecoming.

The fear of death was not an issue for her as she was able to take solace from her faith. The day she had heard the great John Wesley give his sermon, practically in her front yard, had truly changed her life. Her Christian beliefs had given an already strong-willed woman, the added power of purpose. No, she was not afraid to die. But, she did have an overriding fear. She knew that Jonathan would marry again. What she feared most, was the future of her children. There were many stories of husbands marrying cruel, evil women who resented the children from the previous marriage. These families wound up in terrible circumstances with their lives and futures destroyed by jealousy and greed. Jonathan was one of the most intelligent men she had ever known, but she also knew that he had a weakness when it came to women. He could be manipulated by tears, guilt and female charms. She knew this about him, because she had successfully maneuvered him many times during their marriage, using those female tactics.

Mary had thought of a solution to the worries over her children's future, just after she found out about her illness. The solution had been staring her in the face every day. Ann's tragic loss of her family and fortune had been a godsend. Mary felt that, literally. She knew that Ann's re-entry into their home was the work of God. The children adored her. She had become a second mother to them and even though he tried to conceal it from both Mary and Ann, it was clear that Jonathan had not lost his affection for the beautiful redhead. And why had Ann always stopped any man who was interested in her, from getting closer? She had been offered plenty of courtship opportunities over the years, but she showed no desire to leave to start her own home, with her own husband. Mary had even felt, at one time, that she was waiting around for her to die, but she had rejected that idea. She knew her friend too well, or at the very least, she would not allow herself to entertain such an idea.

Yes, the answer to her fears, for her family, was as plain as day. Ann and Jonathan must marry after she was gone. The only problem was that he was going to Antigua and if left to his own devices, might find someone else while there. Two to three years was a long time for a man, in the prime of life, to be without a woman's love and comfort. No, that would simply not do at all. Mary thought out loud, "Ann must go with him. He must take her as his mistress and after I am gone, they must marry." Her mind was made up. Now, all she had to do was convince Jonathan and Ann. She felt Ann would be receptive, but Jonathan would feel guilty, so he would be reluctant. She smiled and thought, "He's no match for me. I know he still loves her. He just has to be convinced that my plan is best for us all. Let's see; tears, guilt and passion. Those emotions work every time. "First things first," she thought, "I'll start my quest by convincing Ann. If the two of us unite, he doesn't stand a chance."

The following week, Mary had the opportunity she had been waiting for because Jonathan was away on business and the children were staying with their grandmother in Whitehaven. There would be no interruptions and she could command Ann's undivided attention. They were downstairs in the parlor and Ann had just brewed a pot of tea. They were sitting together as they often did, discussing anything and everything.

Mary's expression became serious and Ann noticed.

"Are you feeling all right, Mary?"

"Yes, I am fine for the moment. But I do wish to talk about something serious for a time, if that's satisfactory with you?"

"Of course it is fine with me. What concerns you?"

"You are certainly aware, that in just a short time, Jonathan will be leaving. He will be away for at least two and a half years, possibly longer."

"Yes. I understand that. And I also know that it was you that insisted he undertake this venture. I hope that you aren't having second thoughts at this late date."

"Oh, my goodness no. I am more convinced than ever that he must, for all of our sakes, take this on. No, there is something else, even more important, that I must discuss with you."

"Tell me, Mary. What is troubling you, then?"

Mary stood up, smoothed her dress with her hands and walked over to the window. The afternoon sun enveloped her, giving her an ephemeral aura, almost, as if she were an angel. She turned back to look at her friend and paused to arrange her thoughts.

"What I have to tell you will be upsetting, at first. But, if you would please give me the opportunity to lay out my case, without interruption, in the end, I believe you'll come to the same conclusion that I have. I don't have the strength to enter into a full blown discussion about what I am going to tell you. It is something that I believe has to be said and in the end, you and I, must work together to see that it is accomplished. Promise to hear me out, without interrupting. Can I have that promise?"

"Yes, of course, I promise you," responded Ann.

"Ann, I know that you still have feelings for Jonathan."

"But Mary, you can't believe that ..." Ann had interrupted her friend despite her promise. She was unable to remain quiet, after such a statement from Mary.

Mary held up her hand. Ann fell silent as Marry continued, "I need for you to remember your promise to let me speak without any kind of interruption."

"I'm sorry, but it is such a shock to hear that you would think that ..." Mary held up a hand a second time for silence. Ann halted in mid-speech and looked down at the floor. Mary waited as Ann took a breath and looked up at her friend, as if she expected to be punished.

"Thank you. Please let me finish. I know that you and Jonathan both, because you are the people you are, have not been unfaithful to me. If our lives had turned out differently, perhaps I would have different feelings about what I have said. But as fate would have it, I am happy that there are still warm sparks deep inside the two of you, for each other."

Mary started to cough and raised her handkerchief to her mouth. Ann started toward her, but Mary raised her other hand and signaled for her to stop.

"Mary, you must sit down."

Mary's coughing died down. She cleared her throat and returned to the subject at hand. "God has seen fit to warn me that he is going to call me home soon. My first thought is for my children and their future. My second thought is of my husband and his future happiness. And my third thought is of my sister and companion, who has meant so much to me, throughout my life. You have become a second mother to my children and such a comfort to me, in the past few years of this illness. It is my wish, therefore, to see that all of the people I love are taken care of after I depart. The only common sense course to take to ensure that future for everyone is to remove the normal prohibitions and allow nature to take its course between you and Jonathan . . . now."

"But Mary," Ann whispered, as her eyes glistened with tears. It was her turn to raise a handkerchief to her eyes. She was not sure of what she felt after what she had just heard. It was true, there were embers of passion for Jonathan, she had kept under control and well hidden, or so she thought. She couldn't be sure that even if she could accept Mary's offer, Jonathan would agree. After all, she was no longer twenty years old.

Mary said, "Ann, I know this is a lot to absorb in one afternoon. You must know that I love you both still, as I always have. We cannot allow Jonathan to be away from the two of us for two, perhaps three years. There is always temptation and I could never forgive myself if he brought a stranger into my home, who I could not know would take care of my family, as I know you will. So you see, my dear, I am being very selfish in proposing this to you."

It was Ann's turn to be struck with weakness. She felt her knees about to give way beneath her. Reaching out with both hands, Ann swung herself into a chair. She looked up at her friend and exclaimed, "Mary, do you realize what you are saying? Do you understand what you are asking? This is against all tradition."

"Yes, I realize exactly what I'm asking. I am asking that my family remain happy when I leave this earth. And also, I must insure that you and Jonathan become lovers and after I am gone, then you must become man and wife. Many men marry their wife's sister after their death. You are my sister. I believe the only benefit of a slow death is that I am able to pick my husband's next wife and I have chosen you. That is my dying wish. Will you grant or deny your sister's last request?"

"I cannot deny that I have repressed feelings for Jonathan. Whether or not he harbors those same feelings, I cannot know. But if he does and I agree, don't you think it would be a better idea to wait for his return?"

"No, you must accompany him on his trip to Antigua."

"But what about the children? As ill as you are, it will be very difficult to care for them without my help."

"Their grandmother has already agreed to move in with me when Jonathan departs. She does not wish to live alone in Whitehaven, particularly, with Jonathan so far away. Between Mrs. Lucas and Miss Trinity, we will be just fine here."

"You have really thought this through thoroughly, haven't you, Mary?"

"Yes, my dear. I see things quite clearly and I know this is the best course of action for all of us. I can no longer be a wife to him in my condition and I can barely be a mother to my children. I want you to be the wife that I cannot be for Jonathan, now. And when I am gone, I want you to be the mother to my children just as you are their aunt today."

"If you are positive that this is what you want, then, I am willing. But you must not believe that I have been unfaithful to you ..."

"You need not say anything more. By agreeing to do this for us, for my family and for yourself, you have given me the gift of passing peacefully. We must decide how we're going to present this to our husband, Jonathan."

Mary's health seemed to revive a little, now that she had Ann's agreement on her plan for her family. The next few days, she and Ann, discussed the best way to put this proposal forward to her husband. They knew that he would resist. But Mary, as well as Ann, knew that Jonathan could be persuaded. So it was that one week later, the children were packed off to Whitehaven for a few more days, leaving the two female conspirators alone with Jonathan. They both anticipated that Jonathan's first reaction would be negative.

"How can you propose such a thing to me? I'm not particularly religious, but it seems that men should have respect for their dying wives."

"You could show respect for me and my concerns, by accepting what we're asking. Are you so cold hearted that you would reject the last thing I ask of you?"

Ann began to sob quietly with her head in her hands, as she sat across from them on the sofa

"My God, Ann, what is wrong with you?"

"I know that I'm no longer twenty years old, but I still thought that you had, at least, some feelings left for me, even if I am turning into an old maid." Her sobs grew deeper and louder.

"By God's blood, you know that's not true. You are still beautiful and desirable." He glanced quickly up at his wife Mary, who was smiling gently at her quarry.

"Jonathan you shouldn't hurt my sister, Ann, that way." And so the conversation went. There was alternating flirting, imploring, anger and tears . . . lots of tears. Jonathan was no match for this pair of femme fatales and he finally agreed that he would take Ann with him on his journey.

Mary slept soundly that night, for the first time in a long while. Jonathan and Ann, however, did not fare as well. They were both confused by the flood of emotions that washed over them like a sudden summer thunderstorm storm. What was this relationship going to be like? They were letting passion begin to flame up again after years of barely smoldering.

Chapter 28

THE SHIP, *The GOOD FORTUNE* WAS SET TO sail for the West Indies with the tide, on April 28th, 1786 from Whitehaven. Jonathan's mother, Ann, had moved into the Lucas Carleton House with Mary and her grandchildren. She had brought along Martin and Miss Trinity. Jonathan had promised Jonathan Junior that he would send for him as soon as he turned thirteen.

He and Ann Ashburn departed April 15, for Whitehaven. It would give them almost two weeks to prepare for their voyage to Antigua. It would also give them the opportunity to be alone together for the first time in over ten years. It was rather awkward at first, to say the least. Jonathan was still feeling guilty and Ann was feeling as if she had been forced on Jonathan, by his dying wife's wishes.

For the first two days, the two of them were too self-conscious to discuss anything but the weather during their upcoming trip. Neither had ever taken a long sea voyage. Jonathan had sailed to Ireland and back on one of his father's colliers. They had both heard and read about the dangers of sea travel. On the third evening of their sojourn, awaiting departure in Whitehaven, Ann asked,

"Jonathan, I have read that during these long sea voyages, there is terrible misery on board the ships."

"That is true for some, but not all voyages."

"I have heard that the stench coming up from below is horrible as the crew and passengers, alike, become terribly seasick and many times, they suffer from all kinds of illnesses."

Jonathan replied, "I know the captain of the ship and he is a very conscientious man. I have spoken with him at length and he promises me that our ship will be very clean and only provisioned with the best food and drink available."

Still not convinced, Ann pressed on, "Well, I hear that besides the seasickness, there is the possibility of coming down with a fever, dysentery, headaches, constipation, boils, scurvy, mouth rot and that it is all caused from eating highly salted food and meat and from drinking very foul water. It is said that many people die horrible deaths on the high sea."

"It sounds like you are prepared to back out of this venture, Ann. While I am aware of the dangers, the captain will also be taking on board fresh spring water and will be bringing along a supply of live foul. I have paid for the ducks, guineas and chickens, myself, so there will be a supply of fresh eggs and fresh meat for most of the voyage. I have also secured a large cabin, adjacent to the captain's cabin. You will like the room; it has a window that lets in light and we can open it for fresh air. I will continue to do all that is within my power to make this as safe a journey as possible."

"Your preparations and precautions have certainly relieved my anxiety," replied Ann. She got up from her chair and walked over to Jonathan. She sat down beside him and reached out her hands and placed them on his forearm.

"I know it has been awkward between the two of us these last few weeks. Although we have been together under the same roof, the circumstances were much different. I also know that ten years ago, there was the passion of youth. And lastly, I realize the situation we find ourselves in today is the result of our love for Mary and her love for us. If you have lost your feelings for me, after everything that has happened......."

Jonathan interrupted, "Ann, I find you as beautiful as ever, perhaps more so. My desire for you has never died, but I have smothered it through these last years. I suppose that what confuses me most is that now, our affections for each other have been encouraged and blessed and there is nothing that prevents us from tasting love for the first time. It's quite a life's change for us all."

Ann moved closer and her eyes sparkled in the gleam of the candlelight. Jonathan reached out and ran his fingers through her luxurious red hair, cascading down onto her shoulders. He felt a tremble go through his body as if old passions were beginning to emerge. He felt like a child on Christmas morning, who had found the one thing he had always wanted, sitting under the tree.

He said in an unconvincing voice: "I think we had better take this slowly."

The narrow couch could barely hold the two of them. Ann instinctively felt this was Jonathan's last defense.

Ann clutched his arm tighter, "Jonathan, this is difficult for both of us. But this step must be taken sooner or later, if we are to be together. We must find a way to get over this awkwardness."

Jonathan reached out and patted Ann's hands. She relaxed her grip as he arose. "I agree with you that we must find a way to deal with our emotions. But I'm not sure that tonight's the night. It is late and we have much left to do. We can continue this tomorrow."

Ann watched as Jonathan turned and slowly walked to the door. He stopped before opening the door, as if he was going to turn around and say something. But with a slight shrug of his shoulders, he opened the door and walked out of the room, leaving her alone. With a look of determination, she stood up and followed him as he started up stairs.

At the sound of Ann closing the door, he stopped on the stair and turned toward her. She climbed the stairs, carrying the candelabra with her. She looked as if she was floating toward him. He took the candles from her and then, gently grasp her hand. They turned and disappeared into the dark recesses of his mother's home.

The next morning, Jonathan and Ann lay together, looking up at the bright green canopy overhead. He reached over and pulled her naked body toward him. She had not disappointed him, in any way. Their lovemaking had been all he had envisioned. They had not slept at all. It was a good thing they had several days until their ship sailed. It seemed that his desire for her had grown stronger with each caress and they spent the entire morning exploring each other's bodies. Ann was as different from Mary in her lovemaking, as she was in her personality. There was no reserve in her approach to sex and it was a grand adventure and delight. She had years of pent up desire to finally satisfy.

All too soon, the departure date arrived. Jonathan had pulled himself away from his passion just long enough to make certain all he had promised Ann would be on board. The tide turned at eleven o'clock that evening which meant the ship would sail between twelve and one o'clock that morning. Ann's heart pounded as she climbed on board *The Good Fortune*. Their possessions were already on board and properly stowed.

After inspecting the accommodations, the two of them went up on deck and watched the crew working as the ship glided out of Whitehaven Harbor, into the dark Irish Sea. The black outline of the Isle of Man loomed straight ahead in the bright moonlight. They sailed due west for about two miles and then south by southwest, heading for Saint George's Channel.

Looking back toward the English coast, Ann asked, "What's that light I see?"

Jonathan answered, "That's the lighthouse on St Bee's Head. Take a nice long look. It will be a good while before we lay eyes on it again."

As they passed the Isle of Man, Ireland came into view on the starboard side. As dawn was breaking, they could make out the point of Holyhead, jutting out as if to cut them off on their journey. Soon, they passed through Saint George's Channel and headed for the Celtic Sea.

It was a pleasant day and they had a fresh breeze following them. Their first day at sea was exciting. The seagulls were turning and twisting in the sky above. They watched as the crew climbed the rigging and worked the sails, until their necks were sore. Their first meal was taken at noon and they were pleasantly surprised at the quality of their lunch.

Now that they were at sea, the captain had a little free time and joined Ann and Jonathan for their noontime meal.

Ann asked the captain, "How long do you think this trip will be?"

The captain replied politely, "Well ma'am, that's a simple question, but I'm afraid I can't give you a simple answer. The things that determine how long it takes us to arrive, are many and varied. Some of it will depend upon the size of the ship, the size and number of sails and then the variation in the amount of cargo. The shape of the hull is also a factor. Another consideration is the time of year that we sail. If that isn't enough to consider, then the weather and the direction you're sailing, is a most important ingredient. It can take longer to sail eastbound, sometimes, than westbound. And you have to take in the techniques and methods of navigation available. And, of course, I believe one of the most important components is how much knowledge your ship's captain has."

"So we don't really have any idea how many days we're going to be aboard this boat?" Ann's question brought a curt reply from the Captain.

"Ship ma'am, this here's a ship."

"Oh yes, of course! Do we have any idea how many days we're going to be aboard this ship?"

"I can't give you a definite answer, but I can tell you that I have made it to the West Indies within twenty-eight days. Other times, it's taken me as long as forty-five. So, we will all get to know one another better before the month of May is over."

The Good Fortune made respectable progress during the first week of sailing. Reaching the Azores, the captain re-supplied the ship with fresh water and fresh meat. They only stayed long enough to load the ship and they were off on the next leg of their journey, heading to the Island of Bermuda. As the captain predicted, they got to know the crew members fairly well. The voyage ran into difficulties on the long passage between the Azores and Bermuda. The winds died and they were becalmed for ten long days. The crew took turns manning the long boats and pulling *The Good Fortune*. It was better than doing nothing.

The wind finally returned and the tired crew and anxious passengers were relieved to see the white billowing sails catch the breeze. Jonathan wondered if any of those sails had been made in his father's old Whitehaven factory. They were behind schedule, for sure, and were happy to finally spot the Island of Bermuda. Once again, they took on supplies and headed southwest toward Nassau, in the Bahamas. This leg of the trip covered a little over nine hundred miles and took anywhere from six to nine days of normal sailing. After dropping off cargo and some of the passengers in Nassau, *The Good Fortune* would turn southeast, heading toward their final destination, the Island of Antigua.

The weather was considerably warmer now. Jonathan and Ann liked to stay on the prow and watch the dolphins race with the speeding ship. They were up early one morning and off in the distance, under a tall cloud, they spied a waterspout. As the day wore on, the weather began to change.

The breeze freshened and the ship began to pick up speed. The topsails were reefed and the breeze escalated and approached gale speed. The clouds turned dark and a line of squalls approached, driving all the passengers into their cabins. There was a loud rendering crash. Ann gave Jonathan a frightened glance and he nodded, saying, "I'll find out what that was. You stay here and hold on tight."

The ship was rolling and pitching more severely than they had experienced thus far. Jonathan reached the upper deck and saw that the main sail had split. The crew was scurrying aloft and resetting another mainsail. The ship seemed to bear up again and haul upon the wind. Jonathan could tell they were in a heavy gale with seas building higher and higher around them.

Over the roar of the wind, he heard the captain shouting orders to the crew as they climbed aloft, "Furl those top-sails and lower that top-gallant yard."

Jonathan made his way to the captain, who was standing on the quarterdeck, bellowing out orders over the wind.

"This looks to be a pretty serious storm, captain."

"Aye, that it is my friend. It's pushing us off course and there's not a lot to do about it, but ride her out."

The first mate added, "Captain, I don't like the looks of that sunset. It's in the wrong place, which means we're off course and I've seen that kind'a sunset only one other time and we was lucky to live through it."

"We'll see about that later, but for now, I think we need to get that mainsail down to the deck."

"Aye Cap'n! Would be good, but in this wind, it will also be dangerous," came the reply from the first mate.

"Maybe so, but we got to get her furled or we might heave over." The Master cupped his hands and shouted the order down to his men, "Reef top-sails, reef them now!" The crew couldn't hear the exact words, but they knew what to do. Jonathan stared upward at the scene, captivated by the dance of death he was witnessing above.

The halyards and top-bow-lines were soon gone. They turned to the clue-lines and reef-tackle. The shivering sails started to descend and finally, the yards were squared up. Then as quick aloft as water cats, the crew repaired the weatherings and the ship passed to the lee. The reefs were enroll'd, and every point was made fast against the elements.

Their task above finished, they descended to the deck and sought their captain. The captain turned to Jonathan and said, "It's best if you return to your cabin and make everything fast. Try to get some rest, because before this storm is over, all aboard will need every bit of strength and energy."

Jonathan went below to their cabin. When he opened the door, he found a frightened Ann, staring up into his face. Suddenly, the ship rolled sharply on its side. Ann jumped up and threw both arms around his neck, just as the ship rolled violently in the other direction. This brought the two of them crashing down, first against the wall, which was now below them and then reeling backwards, upon the bed, as the ship righted itself.

"My God, Jonathan! The storm is growing worse." She paused before asking, "Are we going to make it?"

Jonathan held her tightly and said, "We are in God's hands now and I fear he has judged us sinners."

Ann's eyes flashed at Jonathan's words and with anger in her voice replied, "We are not the only ones on board this ship and everyone alive is a sinner. I don't want to hear that again. We will survive this somehow."

Suddenly, the first mate opened the door and said, "The master has ordered us to lighten the load. The cargo is going overboard and you must also get rid of your chest and the furniture in this cabin. Hurry, it needs be done right away."

He disappeared from their view and headed below to start unloading the cargo. They worked feverishly and soon the ship had gained a few feet of freeboard.

But the gale winds continued to increase in force. Squall after squall assaulted *The Good Fortune* as they continued to be pushed northwesterly by the storm.

It soon became impossible to remain in one place, so violent were the mounting waves. Jonathan watched helplessly as Ann was torn from his embrace and slammed into the bulkhead. He stumbled into the hallway and came back with a length of rope.

"I am going to bind you to this bed. It will keep you from crashing into the walls." When he had accomplished the task, he added, "I am going topside to see if I can help." He kissed her and went up on deck. Just as he reached the deck, the ship heeled deep on her side and it was all he could do to hold onto the doorway.

The Captain ordered, "Man the clue-garnets and you there, brail up the mizen, quick!"

A seaman yelled back, "What about the mainsails?"

The master shouted, "It's too late to worry about that now. Let the main-sheet fly!" He had not finished his sentence when the mainsail was torn to pieces in a thunderous roar that could be heard over the howling wind. Jonathan looked up at the sound and saw hundreds of strips of sail flapping loudly in the gale's whipping winds. This seemed to ease the strain for the moment and the captain said to Jonathan, "If we can stay ahead of this, we may find our way to the edge and this storm might just spit us out." He then turned his attention to the timoneer who was tightly clutching the wheel.

"You there, helmsman, bear up the helm a-weather!"

The ship labored, still under the heavy strain of the fierce winds. The timoneer responded and gained partial control of the vessel once more. They were moving swiftly before the wind, with hopes of finding the storm's edge and escaping with their lives. They were able to run in like fashion for several hours and the respite allowed for much needed rest for passengers and crew.

Jonathan was below deck, holding Ann, "I should have never brought you on this trip. It was selfish of me and I am being punished with this storm."

Ann retorted, "Do not repeat that. I am here because I want to be. If our lives end like this, then, at least I know I have been loved. Let us not regret what we cannot control. Life is this way for all men; not just us." As Ann spoke her brave words, the ship heeled over dangerously far once more. Jonathan unfastened the rope that was holding him in place and said, "Something has changed. I'll be back."

On deck, he found the Master frantically giving more commands. "What's happened?" he asked.

"The storm has passed to our leeward," he shouted. He cupped his hands and yelled to the timoneer, "Move the helm to starboard." The helmsman complied and sharply trimmed the ship to starboard. *The Good Fortune* responded and her mizzen-sails grabbed the shifted winds and she jumped ahead of the winds once more. This new direction meant more adjustments had to be made to the rigging. The crew, yet again, climbed aloft. They secured the tack that was loosened by the new direction of the wind.

Then, climbing on the other side, the seaman secured the leeward sheets and hauled the bow-line to the bowsprit-end. Next they moved back over to the bunt lines and clue lines for the top-sails. The buntlines had snapped, but by shear effort, they managed to adjust the top-sails to the change in wind direction. The main-sail was in small tatters, but they managed to secure the bow-lines, make the leeches taut and the halyards were made fast. They tied off the brail-lines to each yard-arm, along with the head-rope. Their final job was to drag the tack to the chesstree and pull aft, until the sheet was once more taut against the wind.

Once again, the vessel rode the waves like a horse galloping over hillsides. The people aboard the flying ship, felt hope for relief enter their thoughts. After several hours of daylight had passed, the oppressive seas began again to rise above them, as if they were entering into some rugged mountains. The tempest was becoming more cruel and each wave almost tipped them over.

The captain shouted, "Into the tops again, my boys! She won't stand under canvas anymore. Trim all the sails and batten down the riggun'." The captain turned to his boatswain and yelled, "Jack, see that they do a proper job. No mistakes or it could cost our lives!"

"Aye sir, I'll make sure it's tight, if I have to climb meself." The boatswain followed to insure all was done properly. He knew his crew and directed the less skilled of the seaman. The expert seaman he praised highly and gave encouragement to the fainthearted. They soon had furl'd the sails and using rolling tackle, tied them off. Their next task was to secure the lines against the wind. Three traveled up the weather-back-stays to attend to each mast-head. Others secured the parrels, lifts and clue-lines. Now the ship was topp'd and unrigged. The yard arms were secure along the booms and all of the fly'n ropes left aloft, were belayed. Jonathan watched the treacherous aerial ballet and saw that, finally, the sails were down and the rigging was clear. The crew drifted back to the master, hoping for a break in the storm, but it only got worse.

Passengers and crew felt their spirits flagging as the waves grew higher and the wind blew even stronger. Ann, for the first time since the ordeal began, was running out of optimism. They had been fighting this tempest for two and a half days. Hope of survival was becoming hard to imagine aboard *The Good Fortune*.

The sun was, now, only a faint glow as it began to fall slowly into the sea. The sunset's colors were bizarre. Jonathan, nor Ann, had ever seen the like. When finally the last of the sun's rays were swallowed up by the monstrous sea, the darkness was even more foreboding. The vessel was no longer able to hold its course.

The master and the boatswain argued over the next thing to do. The Master finally ordered the crew aloft to reef, once again. Jonathan asked him why he was considering this maneuver. His reply was, "Reefing will reduce the area of the little sail we have aloft. It should improve our stability and reduce the risk of capsizing or broaching. If we have no control, then she'll hit the bottom of a wave and go under. We've got to try." The crew took to their positions and started aloft once more. They had reached their positions and started their work when disaster struck with mortal force.

A wave that was as high as a mountain peak surged up with an enormous roll. It seemed, as if this would be the moment all was lost. For an instant, she lay half buried on her side by the dark salty brine, but the ship came back from the brink. But, it was not in time to keep three sailors from being washed out of the rigging into the jaws of the howling surf. They were torn from their hold and tried hopelessly to grab hold of something, but their muted cries for help, were soon lost to the stunned onlookers. The fear of annihilation was on every face.

The horrors of the sea and the terrors of the night had combined to rend the hearts of even the bravest of men. They were paralyzed with fear. And, if possible, circumstances worsened.

A flash of lightning revealed the onslaught of an even more monstrous mound of water. A shout from above rang down to Ann and Jonathan's cabin. "Hang on for your lives," came the warning cry as the wave tried to push the ship under completely. The cabin window burst under the blow and seawater poured in, almost filling the room with liquid death.

Jonathan lost Ann for a moment, as they were both underwater. Surfacing, Jonathan reached out and grabbed Ann by the arm. It seemed like an eternity, but *The Good Fortune* shook herself free and floated to the surface. The two of them struggled through the receding waters and climbed on the deck. Another flash of lightning revealed a scene of destruction on the deck. The life boats were gone or smashed into pieces. Gripes and lashings were torn lose. Compasses and glass was strewn all over and the most terrible of all, was that the mizzenmast had failed and crashed to the deck. It looked as if a cannon had exploded on topside. The escaping water below had opened pathways through the hull and the ship was taking on water.

"Get to the pumps, men. Hurry before we're doomed."

The captain called a council and offered up the suggestion that it was time for drastic action. One more mammoth wave or another broach and that would be the end. "We must clear away the wreckage of the mizzen mast. We'll keep her attached by lines to the ship. Let her out as far as possible and it will act as an anchor against the waves. Perhaps that will keep us from broaching. Helmsman, you must keep her straight against the ropes. Our lives depend upon it."

The night finally passed and with the dawn came a new danger. Land was near. They had no idea where they were. Had they been carried north, south, east or west? The waves were coming closer together and growing even taller. Soon they heard the unmistakable sound of crashing surf.

Ann had regained some of her strength. She held Jonathan by his waist and asked, "What happens now?"

He replied, "It depends on the coast. If it's rocky, our chances are limited, but if it's level, we may make it out alive."

Ann added," Jonathan, no matter what happens, I am not sorry."

Jonathan managed a smile and said, "Nor am I."

Just then a line of breaking waves could be seen. The water was getting shallow and the waves were converging. Suddenly a gigantic wave lifted *The Good Fortune* up and slammed her into the pounding surf. She landed, stern first. Then a second wave pushed her sideways.

Jonathan grabbed Ann around the waist and she held on to his neck with strength she didn't know she had left. The next wave rolled *The Good Fortune* over on her side, so that her remaining masts were pointed at the still, distant shore. Everyone left on board slid toward the sea as another wave lifted the crippled ship up higher and moved her closer to shore. The only thing that kept her from capsizing completely was her remaining masts. With a loud groan, the massive timbers snapped and everyone was tossed into the sea. The force of the plummet separated Jonathan and Ann. He surfaced, spitting out salt water and saw her. Out of his reach, she was being swept away with the pounding surf.

Epilogue

Jonathan Lucas did not drown when he was shipwrecked off Cape Romain on the coast of South Carolina. The young Cumbrian found safety at Peachtree Plantation, located on the South Santee River. Peachtree was a large rice plantation built by Thomas Lynch, a signer of the Declaration of Independence. While recuperating at Peachtree, his mind sowed the seeds of a future that would elevate his fortunes, as well as that of an entire society. In later years, his accomplishments would be compared to those of Eli Whitney, the inventor of the cotton gin.

He was also able to alleviate much hard work and drudgery from the lives of those unfortunate enough to be caught up in the slave system of the Old South. His life continued to be a series of adventures and hardships, combined with romance, and intrigue. Look for the continuation of "The Rice Kings" saga when the next adventure continues with his son, Jonathan Lucas II in "The Rice Kings, Book Two, America." This second novel is scheduled for release in the summer of 2015.

For more information on this series of books or on other books by this author, please visit his websites: **davidhenrylucasbooks.com and thechampionship.biz**

To contact him or comment on this or other works you can email David Henry Lucas directly at: dhlucas844@gmail.com

66673757R00154

Made in the USA
Columbia, SC
22 July 2019